REGINALD HILL

Reginald Hill was born in Co. Durham and brought up in Cumberland where he now lives quietly with his wife, Pat, and not so quietly with their labrador bitch and two Siamese cats. A full-time writer since 1980, he has written over forty books and won prizes for individual novels (including the Crime Writers' Association's prestigious Gold Dagger Award for Best Crime Novel of the Year for *Bones and Silence*) and for short stories. In 1995 he was awarded the Cartier Diamond Dagger for his lifetime contribution to crime-writing. He spent many years as a teacher in Yorkshire which provided the inspiration and setting for the novels featuring the Falstaffian figure of Andy Dalziel, Head of Mid-Yorkshire CID, and his more sensitive side-kick, Peter Pascoe, whose adventures in the detective trade have been the basis of one of the most satisfying novel sequences of the modern age. Their popularity has been carried over into the hugely successful BBC television series featuring Warren Clarke and Colin Buchanan. The same qualities of style, pace, characterization and humour are evident in the books featuring his other series character, Joe Sixsmith, the likeable redundant lathe operator turned PI from Luton. Hill says he was delighted to win the Diamond Dagger because it finally confirmed he had made the right career choice and now he can really get down to it.

REGINALD HILL

Bones and Silence

A Dalziel and Pascoe novel

We insist, it seems, on living. Then again,
indifference descends. The roar of the traffic,
the passage of undifferentiated faces, this way
and that way, drugs me into dreams; rubs
features from faces. People might walk through
me... We are only lightly covered with buttoned
cloth; and beneath these pavements are shells,
bones and silence.

VIRGINIA WOOLF, *The Waves*

HarperCollins*Publishers*

HarperCollins*Publishers*
77–85 Fulham Palace Road,
Hammersmith, London W6 8JB

This paperback edition 2000

1 3 5 7 9 8 6 4 2

Previously published in paperback by Grafton in 1991
and reprinted 4 times

First published in Great Britain by
HarperCollinsPublishers 1990

The HarperCollins website address is:
www.**fire**and**water**.com

Copyright © Reginald Hill 1990

Reginald Hill asserts the moral right to
be identified as the author of this work

ISBN 0 586 21128 4

Set in Times

Printed and bound in Great Britain by
Bookmarque Ltd, Croydon, Surrey

Part One

GOD: First when I wrought this world so wide,
Wood and wind and waters wan,
Heaven and hell was not to hide,
With herbs and grass thus I began.
In endless bliss to be and bide
And to my likeness made I man,
Lord and sire on ilka side
Of all middle earth I made him then.

A woman also with him wrought I,
All in law to lead their life,
I bade them wax and multiply,
To fulfil this world, without strife.
Sithen have men wrought so woefully
And sin is now reigning so rife,
That me repents and rues forthy
That ever I made either man or wife.

The York Cycle of Mystery Plays: 'The Building of the Ark'

Dear Mr Dalziel,

   *You don't know me. Why should you? Sometimes I think
I don't know myself. I was walking through the market
place just before Christmas when suddenly I stopped dead.
People bumped into me but it didn't matter. You see, I was
twelve again, walking across a field near Melrose Abbey,
carefully balancing a jug of milk I'd just got from the farm,
and ahead of me I could see our tent and our car and my
father shaving himself in the wing mirror and my mother
stooping over the camp stove, and I could smell bacon
frying. It was such a good smell I started thinking about the
lovely taste that went with it, and I suppose I started to walk
a bit quicker. Next thing, I caught my toe in a tussock of
grass, stumbled, and the milk went everywhere. I thought it
was the end of the world but they just laughed and made a
joke of it and gave me a huge plateful of bacon and eggs
and tomatoes and mushrooms, and in the end it almost
seemed they loved me more for spilling the milk than
fetching it safely.*

   *So there I was, standing like an idiot, blocking the
pavement, while inside I was twelve again and feeling so
loved and protected. And why?*

   *Because I was passing the Market Caff and the extractor
fan was blasting the smell of frying bacon into the cool
morning air.*

   *So how can I say I know myself when a simple smell can
shift me so far in time and space?*

   But I know you. No, how arrogant that sounds after

7

what I've just written. What I mean is I've had you pointed out to me. And I've listened to what people say about you. And a lot of it, in fact most of it, wasn't very complimentary, but this isn't an abusive letter so I won't offend you by repeating it. But even your worst detractors had to admit you were good at your job and you weren't afraid of finding out the truth. Oh, and you didn't suffer fools gladly.

Well, this is one fool you won't have to suffer much of. You see, the reason I'm writing to you is I'm going to kill myself.

I don't mean straightaway. Some time soon, though, certainly in the next twelve months. It's a sort of New Year Resolution. But in the meantime I want someone to talk to. Clearly anyone I know personally is out of the question. Also doctors, psychiatrists, all the professional helpers. You see, this isn't the famous cry for help. My mind's made up. It's just a question of fixing a date. But I've discovered in myself a strange compulsion to talk about it, to drop hints, to wink and nod. Now that's too dangerous a game to play with friends. What I think I need is a controlled outlet for all my ramblings. And you've been elected.

I'm sorry. It's a big burden to lay on anyone. But one other thing which came out of what people say about you is that my letters will be just like any other case. You might find them irritating but you won't lose any sleep over them!

I hope I've got you right. The last thing I want to do is to cause pain to a stranger – especially knowing as I do that the last thing I will do is cause pain to my friends.

Happy New Year!

Chapter 1

'I still don't see why she shot herself,' said Peter Pascoe obstinately.

'Because she was bored. Because she was trapped,' said Ellie Pascoe.

Pascoe used his stick to test the consistency of the chaise-longue over the side of which the dead woman's magnificently ruined head had dangled thirty minutes earlier. It was as hard as it looked, but his leg was aching and he sat down with a sigh of relief which he turned into a yawn as he felt his wife's sharp eyes upon him. He knew she distrusted his claims to be fit enough to go back to work tomorrow. He would have gone back today only Ellie had pointed out with some acerbity that February 15th was his birthday, and she wasn't about to give the police the chance to ruin this one as they had the last half-dozen.

So it had been another day of rest and a series of birthday treats – breakfast in bed, an early gourmet dinner, front row stalls at the Kemble Theatre's acclaimed production of *Hedda Gabler*, all rounded off with after-show drinks on the stage, provided by Eileen Chung, the Kemble's Director.

'But people *don't* do such things,' Pascoe now asserted with Yorkshire orotundity.

Ellie looked ready to argue but he went on confidentially, 'I can smell a rotting fish when I see one, lass,' and belatedly she recognized his parody of his CID boss, Andy Dalziel.

She began to smile and Pascoe smiled back.

'You two look happy,' said Eileen Chung, approaching with a new bottle of wine. 'Which is odd, considering you paid good money to be harrowed.'

'Oh, we're harrowed all right, only Peter's worst instincts tell him Hedda was murdered.'

'And how right you are, Pete, honey,' said Chung, easing her seventy-five inches of golden beauty on to the chaise-longue beside him. 'That's exactly what I wanted to get across. Let me fill your glass.'

Peter glanced round the stage. The rest of the Kemble team seemed to be taking their leave. He began to ease himself up, saying, 'I think we should be on our way . . .' but Chung drew him down again and said, 'Why the rush?'

'No rush,' he said. 'I'm not back at the rushing stage yet.'

'You've got a very distinguished limp,' she said. 'And I just love the stick.'

'He's embarrassed by the stick,' said Ellie, sitting at his other side so that he felt pleasantly squeezed. 'I suspect he feels it detracts from his macho image.'

'Pete. Baby!' said Chung, putting her hand on his knee and looking deep into his eyes. 'What's a stick but a phallic symbol? You want a bigger one maybe? I'll look in our props cupboard. And think of all the wild, wild men who've been lame. There was Oedipus, now he was a real motherfucker. And Byron. God, even his own sister wasn't safe – '

'Unhappily Peter is both an orphan and an only child,' interrupted Ellie.

'Aw shit. Pete, I'm sorry. I didn't know. But there's plenty of others without the family hang-ups. The Devil, for instance. Now he was lame.'

And Peter Pascoe, up to this moment more than content to accept this heavy-handed ribbing as a fair price for the privilege of being sandwiched between Ellie whom he loved, and Chung whom he lusted after, knew that he was betrayed.

He began to rise but Chung was already on her feet, her face alight with a let's-do-the-show-in-the-barn glow.

'The Devil,' she throbbed. 'Now there's an idea. Pete, honey, give me a profile. Fan-tastic. And with the limp, per-fection! Ellie, you know him best. Could he do it? Or could he do it?'

'He's got many diabolic qualities,' admitted Ellie.

This had gone far enough. There were some advantages to having a stick. He brought it down savagely on Hedda Gabler's coffee table, which he could do with a clear conscience as it belonged to him. Chung collected props like old Queen Mary collected antiques – she admired them into gifts. But she wasn't going to make a gift out of him.

Ellie was much to blame, but not as much as himself. He'd forgotten the golden rule – any friend of Ellie's was guilty until proven innocent, and probably longer. He'd been as suspicious as Ellie had been enthusiastic when the newly appointed Director of the Civil Theatre had clarioned her commitment to socially significant drama. But her beauty and charisma had made a rapid conquest of him. Her paymasters, the Borough Council, were less easy targets. Their stuff was brass not flesh and there was much concern lest they had taken a lefty viper to their righteous bosoms. But when her *Private Lives* (transplanted to Skegness and Huddersfield) had been a box office success surpassed only by her *Gondoliers of the Grand Union Canal*, the city fathers, realizing their clouds of doubt had brass linings, had relaxed and drifted with the cash-flow.

But it was her latest project aimed at God as well as

11

Mammon which should have set his storm warning flashing.

Chung had proposed a huge outdoor production of the Mediaeval Mysteries. It was to be an eclectic version, though with a jingoistic concentration on the York and Wakefield cycles, it would run for seven days in early summer, and all the Powers that Were looked upon the project and saw that it was good. The clergy approved because it would make religion 'relevant', the Chamber of Commerce because it would pack the town with tourists, the Community Leaders because it would revitalize cultural identity by employing vast numbers of locals as performers, and the City Council because the locals wouldn't expect to be paid. Some mutterings about idolatry and blasphemy came from a few inerrantist outposts, but these were drowned in the great surge of approval.

At first it was assumed that Chung would cast her resident company in the main speaking parts, perhaps importing a middling magnitude telly star to give some commercial clout to Jesus, but here she took everyone by surprise.

'No way,' she told Ellie. 'My gang are going to be planted deep in the crowd scenes. That's where you need the professional stiffening in this kind of caper. Stars I can create!' So the great hunt had started. Every amateur thespian in the area started sending press-cuttings to the Kemble. Aged Jack Points, stripling King Lears, Lady Macbeths of the Dales, infant prodigies, Freds 'n' Gingers, Olivier lookalikes, Gielgud soundalikes, Monroe *moue*-alikes, Streep stripalikes, the good, the bad, and the unbelievable were ready to stride and strut, fume and fret, leap and lounge, mouth and mumble, emote and expire before Chung's most seeing eye.

But for the most of them, their rehearsals were in vain. Chung saw to it that all their cuttings were returned with thanks, for she knew how precious are the records of praise, but the accompanying message was, why don't you go and get lost in the crowd scenes? For Chung had not been wasting her short time in this city. She was gregarious, went everywhere, forgot nothing. Those who met her were charmed, shocked, intrigued, revolted, amused, amazed, entranced, entramelled, but never indifferent. And though many would have loved it, few realized they had already been on Chung's casting couch. By the time she broached the Mysteries project, her mental cast list was almost complete.

Her intimates had been invited to help in snaring the more unwilling victims. Pascoe had been vastly amused when Ellie let drop some hilarious hints of Chung's remorseless quest, never for one moment suspecting that he might be himself a target!

But now his defences were fully aroused. He swung his stick at the coffee table again.

'No!' he cried. 'I won't do it!'

The women looked at each other with barely concealed amusement.

'Do what, honey?' asked Chung with solicitous innocence.

It was time to be clear beyond even the muddying powers of these practised pond-stirrers.

He said slowly, 'I am not going to be the Devil in your Mysteries. Not now. Not ever. No way.'

He examined his statement carefully. It seemed pretty limpid.

Now the women were looking at each other in amazement.

'But, Peter, of course you're not! Where did you get that idea from?' said Chung with the wide-eyed surprise of one who suspects this is no longer Kansas.

'Peter, for heaven's sake, what's got into you?'

demanded Ellie with the exasperation of a wife being shown up in front of her friends.

It was time for continued firmness. He heard himself saying, 'But you were talking about my limp . . . and the Devil being lame . . . and me fitting the part . . .'

'Just a gag, Pete. What do you take me for? Hell, with luck, by the time the show goes on you'll hardly be limping at all. I mean, you're going back to work tomorrow, aren't you? Do you think I'd take the piss out of anyone who was really disabled? Besides, you're far too nice and amiable. The man I've got in mind looks as proud and prickly as Lucifer, not your type at all!'

He had a feeling that, though not yet quite sure what the wrong was, he was sinking deeper and deeper in it. But that didn't matter. He needed to be absolutely clear that this was no set-up.

'And you definitely do not want me now, nor ever will want me, to perform an acting role in this or any of your dramatic productions?'

'Pete, I swear it, hand on heart.'

She performed the oath very solemnly, then observing the direction of his gaze, squeezed her left breast voluptuously and laughed.

'Happy now, Pete?' she asked.

'Chung, I'm sorry, it's this long convalescence all plastered up. You know, like Jimmy Stewart in *Rear Window*, you start getting paranoiac.'

'I forgive, I forgive.' Then she added in alarm, 'Hey, but you're not backing off altogether! Pete, you promised the first thing you did when you got back to work would be to get yourself seconded to my "Mysteries" committee to make sure we get full cooperation with traffic and parking and security, all that shit!'

'Of course I will,' said Pascoe expansively. 'Anything I

can do to help, short of acting – *well* short of acting – you know you've only got to ask.'

'Anything, eh?' said Chung reflectively. A tiny grin twitched Ellie's lips, like a Venetian gnat landing in your Campari soda. And it occurred to Pascoe that in *Rear Window* James Stewart hadn't been paranoiac, he'd been the one who saw things clearly.

'Anything within my . . .' he began. But it was like a trainee para opting for ground crew after he'd stepped out of the plane.

'There is one small problem you're well placed to help me with,' said Chung.

'What's that?' he asked, not because he wanted to, but because the script demanded it.

'It's nothing, really. It's just that, you know this party I'm having next Sunday, sort of combined thank-you and publicity launch for the Mystery project?'

Pascoe, who knew about it because Ellie had told him they were going, nodded.

'Well, the thing is, Pete, I sent an invite to your boss, the famous Superintendent Dalziel. It's about time the two biggest names in town got together. Only he hasn't replied.'

'He's not that keen on formal social occasions,' said Pascoe, who knew that the constable who sorted Dalziel's mail had strict instructions to file all invitations that smelled of civic tedium or arty-farty ennui in a large plastic rubbish bag.

'Well, OK, but I'd really like him to be here, Pete. Could you possibly use your influence to get him to come?'

There was something fishy here. No one could be that keen to get Dalziel to a drinks party. It was like a farmer wanting to lure a fox into his hen coop.

'Why?' said Pascoe, suspecting it might be wiser to throw a faint and get carried out rather than pursue the

15

matter further. 'Why do you want Dalziel? There's more to this than just a social gesture, isn't there?'

'You're too sharp for me, Pete,' said Chung admiringly. 'You're dead right. Thing is, I want to audition him. You see, honey, with all I've heard about him from you, and from Ellie, and from *everyone*, I think Andy Dalziel might be just about perfect for God!'

And Pascoe had to sit down again suddenly or else he might just have fainted anyway.

Chapter 2

At roughly the same time as this annunciation of his projected apotheosis, Detective-Superintendent Andrew Dalziel was being sick into a bucket.

Between retchings, his mind sought first causes. He counted, and quickly discounted, the six pints of bitter chased by six double whiskys in the Black Bull; scrutinized closely but finally acquitted the Toad-in-the-Hole and Spotted Dick washed down with a bottle of Beaujolais in the Borough Club for Professional Gentlemen; and finally indicted, examined, and condemned a glass of mineral water accepted unthinkingly when one of the pickled onions served with his cheese had gone down the wrong way.

It had probably been French. If so, that put his judgement beyond appeal. They boasted on their bottle that the stuff was untreated, this from a nation whose *treated* water could fell a healthy horse.

The retching seemed to have stopped. It occurred to him that unless he had also consumed two pairs of socks and a string vest at the Gents, the bucket had not been empty. He raised his eyes and looked around the kitchen.

He hadn't switched on the light, but even in darkness it looked in dire need of redecoration. This was the house he'd moved into when he got married and never found time or energy to move out of. On that very kitchen table he'd found his wife's last letter. It said *Your dinner is keeping warm in the oven.* He'd been mildly surprised to discover it was a ham salad. But it wasn't till next morning, when an insistent knocking roused him from the spare bed which he occupied with reluctant altruism whenever he got home later than 3.00 A.M., that he began to suspect something was wrong. Insistent knockings were a wife's responsibility. He found her bed unslept in, descended, found downstairs equally empty, opened the door and was presented with a telegram. It had been unambiguous in its statement of cause and effect, but it had been its form as much as its content which had convinced Dalziel this was the end. She'd found it easier to let strangers read these words than say them to his face!

Everyone had assumed he would sell the house and find a flat, but inertia had compounded cussedness and he'd never bothered. So now as his gaze slipped to the uncurtained window, it was a totally familiar view that he looked out upon – a small backyard which not even moonlight could beautify, bounded by a brick wall in need of pointing, containing a wooden gate in need of painting, which let into the back lane running between Dalziel's street and the rear entrances of a street of similar housing whose frequent chimneys castellated the steely night sky.

Only there was something different to look at tonight. A bedroom light went on in the house immediately behind his. A few moments later the curtains were flung aside and a naked woman stood framed in the square of golden light. Dalziel watched with interest. If this were hallucination, the Frogs might be on to something after all. Then as if to prove her reality, the woman pushed the window

17

open and leaned out into the night, taking deep breaths of wintry air which made her small but far from negligible breasts rise and subside most entertainingly.

It seemed to Dalziel that as she'd been courteous enough to remove one barrier of glass, he could hardly do less than dispose of the other.

He moved swiftly to the back door, opened it gently, and stepped out into the night. But his speed was vain. Movement had broken the spell and the gorgeous vision was fled.

'Serves me bloody right,' growled Dalziel to himself. 'Acting like a kid that's never clapped eyes on a tit before.'

He turned away to re-enter his house but something made him turn again almost immediately. Suddenly from soft porn it was all action movie on the golden screen . . . a man moving . . . something in his hand . . . another man . . . a sound as explosive as a cough too long suppressed during a *pianissimo* . . . and without conscious thought, Dalziel was off and running, cursing with increasing fervour and foulness as he crashed from one pile of household detritus to another.

His gate was unlocked. The gate of the house behind wasn't, but he went through it as though it was. He was too close now to see up into the first-floor room. It occurred to him as he charged towards the kitchen door that he might be about to meet a gunman equally anxious to get out. On the other hand there might be people inside as yet unshot, whom his approach could keep that way. Not that the debate was anything but abstract, as if an incendiary dropped on Dresden should somehow start considering the morality of tactical bombing as it fell.

The kitchen door flew open at a touch. He assumed the lay-out would be similar to his own house, which it was, saving him the bother of demolishing walls as he rushed through the entrance hall and up the stairs. There was still no sign of life, no noise, no movement. The door of the room he was heading for was ajar, spilling light on to the landing. Now at last he slowed down. If there had been sounds of violence within he would have entered violently, but there was no point in being provocative.

He tapped gently at the door and pushed it fully open.

There were three people in the room. One of them, a tall man in his thirties wearing a dark blue blazer with a brocaded badge on the pocket, was standing by the window. In his right hand was a smoking revolver. It was pointing in the general direction of a younger man in a black sweater crouched against the wall, squeezing his pallid terrified face between his hands. Also present was a naked woman sprawled across a bed. Dalziel paid these last two little attention. The young man looked to have lost the use of his legs and the woman had clearly lost the use of everything. He concentrated on the man with the gun.

'Good evening, sir,' said Dalziel genially. 'I'm a police officer. Is there somewhere we can sit down and have a little chat?'

He advanced slowly as he spoke, his face aglow with that deceptive warmth which, like a hot chestnut in your lap, can pass at first for sensuous delight. But before he got quite within scorching distance, the gun arm moved and the muzzle came round till it was pointing at Dalziel's midriff.

He was no gun expert but he had experience enough to recognize a large-calibre revolver and to know what it would do to flesh at this range.

He halted. Suddenly the debate had moved from the abstract to the actual. He turned his attention from the weapon to its wielder and to his surprise recognized him, though he had to bang shut his mental criminal files to get a name. There was a connection with the police but it wasn't professional. Not till now.

'How do, Mr Swain,' he said. 'It is Mr Swain, the builder, isn't it?'

'Yes,' said the man, his eyes focusing properly on Dalziel for the first time. 'That's right. Do I know you?'

'You may have seen me, sir,' said Dalziel genially. 'As I've seen you a couple of times. It's your firm that's extending the garages behind the police station, isn't it?'

'Yes. That's right.'

'Detective-Superintendent Dalziel.' He held out his hand, took a small step forward. Instantly the gun was thrust closer to his gut. And in the split second before launching what might have been, one way or another, a fatal attack, he realized it was not being aimed but offered.

'Thank you,' he said, taking the barrel gently between two huge fingers and wrapping the weapon in a frayed khaki handkerchief like a small gonfalon.

The transfer of the weapon released the younger man's tongue. He screamed, 'She's dead! She's dead! It's your fault, you bastard! You killed her!'

'Oh God,' said Swain. 'She was trying to kill herself . . . I had to stop her, Waterson . . . the gun went off . . . Waterson, you saw what happened . . . are you sure she's dead?'

Dalziel glanced at the man called Waterson, but cataplexy seemed to have reasserted its hold. He turned his attention to the woman. She had been shot at very close range. The gun he judged had been held under her chin. It was a powerful weapon, no doubt about that. The bullet had destroyed much of her face, removed the top of her head and still had force enough to blow a considerable hole in the ceiling. The last oozings of blood and brains dripped quietly from her long blonde hair to the carpeted floor.

'Oh yes,' said Dalziel. 'She's dead all right.'

Interestingly his stomach was feeling much calmer now. Could it be the running that had done it? Mebbe he should take up jogging. On second thoughts, it would be simpler just to avoid mineral water in future.

'What happens now, Superintendent?' asked Swain in a low voice.

Dalziel turned back to him and studied his pale narrow face. It occurred to him he didn't like the man, that on the couple of occasions he'd noticed him around the car park with his ginger-polled partner, he'd felt they were a right matching pair of Doctor Fells.

There are few things more pleasant than the coincidence of prejudice and duty.

'Impatient are we, sunshine?' he said amicably. 'What happens now is, you're nicked!'

Part Two

ADAM: Alas what have I done? For shame!
Ill counsel, woe worth thee!
Ah Eve, thou art to blame;
To this enticed thou me.

The York Cycle: 'The Fall of Man'

February 14th

Dear Mr Dalziel,

I want to say I'm sorry. I was wrong to try to involve a stranger in my problems, even someone whose job it is to track down wrongdoers. So please accept this apology and forget I ever wrote.

In case you're wondering, this doesn't mean I've changed my mind, only that next time I feel in need of an untroubled and untroubling confidant, I'll ring the Speaking Clock! That might not be such a bad idea either. Time's the great enemy. You look back and you can just about see the last time you were happy. And you look ahead and you can't even imagine the next time. You try to see the point of it all in a world so full of self-inflicted pain, and all you can see are the pointless moments piling up behind you. Perhaps counting them is the point. Perhaps the best thing I can do with time is to sit listening to the Speaking Clock, counting off the seconds till I reach the magic number where the counting finally stops.

I'm growing morbid and I don't want to leave you with a nasty taste, though I'm sure a pint of beer would wash it away. I'm writing this on St Valentine's Day, the feast of lovers. You probably won't get it till St Julianna's day. All I know about her was she specialized in being a virgin and had a long chat with the Devil! Which do you prefer? Silly question. You may be a bit different from other men but you can't be all that different! So forget Julianna. And forget me too.

Your valedictory Valentine

Chapter 1

Peter Pascoe's return to work was not the triumphal progress of his fantasies. First he found his parking spot occupied by a heap of sand. For a fraction of time too short to be measured but long enough to excoriate a nerve or two, he read a symbolic message here. But his mind had already registered that the whole of this side of the car park was rendered unusable by a scatter of breeze blocks, hard core, cement bags, and a concrete mixer.

Behind him a horn peeped impatiently. It was an old blue pick-up, squatting low on its axles. Pascoe got out of his car and viewed the scene before him. Once there had been a wall here separating the police car park from the old garden which had somehow clung on behind the neighbouring coroner's court. There'd been a tiny lawn, a tangle of shrubbery, and a weary chestnut which used to lean over the wall and drop sticky exudations on any vehicle rash enough to park beneath. Now all was gone and out of a desert of new concrete reared a range of unfinished buildings.

The pick-up's peep became a blast. Pascoe walked towards it. The window wound down and a ginger head, grizzling at the tips, emerged above a legend reading SWAIN & STRINGER Builders, Moscow Farm, Currthwaite. Tel. 33809.

'Come on,' said the ginger pate, 'some of us have got work to do.'

27

'Is that right? I'm Inspector Pascoe. It's Mr Swain, is it?'

'No, it's not,' said the man, manifestly unimpressed by Pascoe's rank. 'I'm Arnie Stringer.'

'What's going on here, Mr Stringer?'

'New inspection garages. Where've you been?' demanded the man.

'Away,' said Pascoe. 'Not the best time of year to be working outside.'

It had been unseasonably mild for a couple of weeks but there was still a nip in the air.

'If bobbies with nowt better to do don't hold us back talking, we'll mebbe get finished afore the snow comes.'

Mr Stringer was obviously a graduate of the same charm school as Dalziel.

It was nice to be back.

Retreating to the public car park, Pascoe entered via the main door like any ordinary citizen. The desk area was deserted except for a single figure who observed Pascoe's entry with nervous alarm. Pascoe sighed deeply. While he hadn't really expected the Chief Constable to greet him with the Police Medal as journalists jostled and colleagues clapped, he couldn't help feeling that three months' absence to mend a leg shattered in pursuit of duty and a murderous miner deserved a welcome livelier than this.

'Hello, Hector,' he said.

Police Constable Hector was one of Mid-Yorkshire's most reliable men. He always got it wrong. He had been everything by turns – beat bobby, community cop, schools liaison officer, collator's clerk – and nothing long. Now here he was on the desk.

'Morning, sir,' said Hector with a facial spasm possibly aimed at bright alertness, but probably a simple reaction to the taste of the felt-tipped pen which he licked as he spoke. 'How can we help you?'

Pascoe looked despairingly into that slack, purple-stained mouth and wondered once more about his pension rights. In the first few weeks of convalescence he had talked seriously about retirement, partly because at that stage he didn't believe the surgeon's prognosis of almost complete recovery, but also because it seemed to him in those long grey hospital nights that his very marriage depended on getting out of the police. He even reached the stage where he started broaching the matter to Ellie, not as a marriage-saver, of course, but as a natural consequence of his injury. She had listened with a calmness he took for approval till one day she had cut across his babble of green civilian fields with, 'I never slept with him, you know that, don't you?'

It was not a moment for looking blank and asking, 'Who?'

'I never thought you did,' he said.

'Oh. Why?' She sounded piqued.

'Because you'd have told me.'

She considered this, then replied, 'Yes, I would, wouldn't I? It's a grave disadvantage in a relationship, you know, not being trusted to lie.'

They were talking about a young miner who had been killed in the accident which crippled Pascoe and with whom Ellie had had a close and complex relationship.

'But that's not the point anyway,' said Pascoe. 'We ended up on different sides. I don't want that.'

'I don't think we did,' she said. 'On different flanks of the same side, perhaps. But not different sides.'

'That's almost worse,' he said. 'I can't even see you face to face.'

'You want me face to face, then stop whingeing about pensions and start working on that leg.'

Dalziel had come visiting shortly after.

'Ellie tells me you're thinking of retiring,' he said.

29

'Does she?'

'Don't look so bloody betrayed else they'll give you an enema! She doesn't want you to.'

'She said that to you?'

Dalziel filled his mouth with a bunch of grapes. Was this what Bacchus had really looked like? AA ought to get a picture.

'Of course she bloody didn't,' said Dalziel juicily. 'But she'd not have mentioned it else, stands to reason. Got any chocolates?'

'No. About Ellie, I thought . . .' He tailed off, not wanting a heart to heart with Dalziel. About many things, yes, but not about his marriage.

'You thought she'd be dying to get you out of the Force? Bloody right, she'd love it! But not because of her. She wants you to see the light for yourself, lad. They all do. It's not enough for them to be loved, they've got to be bloody right as well! Your mates too mean to bring you chocolates, is that it?'

'They're fattening,' said Pascoe, loyal to Ellie's embargo.

'Pity. I like chocolate. So drop this daft idea, eh? Get the years in first. And you've got that promotion coming up, they're just dragging their feet till they're sure you won't be dragging yours. Now I'd best be off and finger a few collars. Oh, I nearly forgot. Brought you a bottle of Lucozade.'

He winked as he put it on the bedside locker. The first bottle he'd left, Pascoe had taken at face value and nearly choked when a long swig had revealed pure Scotch.

This time he drank slowly, reflectively. But the only decision he reached after another grey night was that on your back was no place for making decisions.

Now here he was on his feet, thinking that on your back might not be such a bad place after all.

'Constable Hector,' he said in a low voice. 'I work here. DI Pascoe, remember?'

In Hector's memory a minute was a long time, three months an eternity.

He's going to ask for identification, thought Pascoe. But happily at that moment, Sergeant Broomfield, chief custodian of the desk, appeared.

'Mr Pascoe, good to see you back,' he said, offering his hand.

'Thanks, George,' said Pascoe with almost tearful gratitude. 'I thought I might have been forgotten.'

'No chance. Hey, have you heard about Mr Dalziel, though? Got himself a killer, single-handed, last night. He says that round here they're so certain of getting caught, they've taken to inviting CID to be present! He doesn't get any better!'

Chuckling, the sergeant retired to the nether regions while Pascoe, conscious still of Hector's baffled gaze, made his way upstairs. He had brought his stick, deciding after some debate that it was foolish to abandon it before he felt ready. But as he climbed the stairs he realized he was exaggerating its use. The reason was not far to seek. I'm reminding people I'm a wounded hero! he told himself in amazement. Because there wasn't a reception committee, and because Fat Andy has somehow contrived to upstage me, I'm flaunting my scars.

Disgusted, he shouldered the stick and tried to run lightly up the last couple of stairs, slipped and almost fell. A strong hand grasped his arm and supported him.

'I expect you'd like another three months away from here,' said Detective-Sergeant Wield. 'But there's got to be easier ways. Welcome home.'

Wield had the kind of face which must have thronged the eastern gate of Paradise after the eviction, but in those harsh features Pascoe read real concern and welcome.

'Thanks, Wieldy. I was just trying to prove how fit I am.'

'Well, if you fancy a miracle cure, come and touch God's robe. You heard about his little coup last night?'

'I got a hint from Broomfield.'

'You'll get more than a hint up here.'

Dalziel was on the phone but he waved them in expansively.

'Couldn't take the risk of hanging about, sir,' he was saying. 'He might have been away or we could've ended up with one of them hostage situations, tying up men and traffic with reporters and the SAS crawling all over the place!'

He made them both sound like rodents.

'Thank you, sir. Ten o'clock? That'll suit me fine. And I'll make sure them buggers carry on working regardless!'

He replaced the receiver.

'Good morning, sir,' said Pascoe. 'I gather congratulations are in order.'

'I believe they are,' said Dalziel complacently. 'Though Desperate Dan's got mixed feelings. Doesn't know whether to pat my back or stab it. Either way he'll need a box to stand on!'

He was referring to Dan Trimble, Chief Constable, who, though small by police standards, was not a dwarf.

'Mixed feelings? Why?'

'Being out of practice at detective work, lad, you likely didn't notice it's like a bomb site down there.' Dalziel had risen and was looking out of his window. 'That's Dan's personal project. Part of his grand modernization plan. Rumour is he set the coroner up with a rent boy to get him to part with his garden. And he probably had to flog his own ring to get those tight bastards at County Hall to allocate the money. Trouble is, if the work's not finished in March, the money is! That's why Dan was all set to give

32

me a kiss and a police medal till he heard who it was I'd nicked.'

'And who was it, sir?' asked Pascoe.

'Swain. Philip Swain. Chap whose building firm's doing the work down there. Or not as the case may be.'

He opened the window, leaned out and shouted, 'Hey! What are you buggers on? A slow motion replay? If King Cheops had had you lot, we'd be looking at the first bungalow pyramid.'

He closed the window and said, 'Got to keep 'em at it. At least till I've got my hands on Dan's congratulation Glen Morangie. He wants to see you too, Peter. Nine-thirty sharp.'

'Oh yes?' said Pascoe, hope and unease stirring simultaneously.

'That's right. By God, it's good to see you back! We've been snowed under these last few weeks. I've dumped a few things on your desk just to ease you back in again.'

Pascoe's heart sank. Dalziel's few was anyone else's avalanche.

'What exactly did happen last night,' he asked by way of diversion.

'Nowt much. I happened to see this chap, Swain, blowing his wife's head off next door, so I went in and disarmed him and brought 'em both back here . . .'

'Both? You brought the body as well?'

'Don't be daft. There were this other chap there, name of Waterson, it's his house. He were scared shitless, could hardly move or talk. The quack took one look at him, shot him full of something and got him admitted to the Infirmary. Me and Swain had a little chat, he told a lot of lies, and an hour later I was enjoying the sleep of the just. That's how neat and tidy we've been doing things since you've been away, lad, but no doubt now you're back, you'll start complicating things again.'

'I'll try not to, but I'm still a bit vague as to what precisely happened. This fellow Swain . . .'

'Nasty bit of work. Just the type to top his missus,' said Dalziel.

'You've had other dealings with him?'

'No. Only ever seen him twice before but some people you can sum up in a second,' said Dalziel solemnly. 'I gave him plenty of rope and he's just about hanged himself, I reckon. Take a look at his statement and you'll see what I mean.'

He pushed a photocopied sheet across the desk and Pascoe began to read.

I make this statement of my own free will. I have been told I need not say anything unless I wish to do so, and that whatever I say may be given in evidence. Signed: Philip Swain.

My name is Philip Keith Swain. I live at Moscow Farm, Currthwaite, Mid-Yorkshire. I am a partner in the firm of Building Contractors known as Swain and Stringer, working from the same address. I am thirty-eight years old.

A short while ago my company was engaged by Gregory Waterson of 18 Hambleton Road to convert his loft into a draughtsman's studio. During the course of this work, he visited my premises on several occasions. These visits brought him into contact with my wife, Gail. I saw that they had become very friendly but any suspicions I might have had that the relationship went further I put out of my mind for two reasons. The first was that I simply did not want to risk a confrontation with Gail. For some time she had been behaving in an increasingly irrational fashion, bouts of deep depression alternating with moods of almost manic liveliness. When she was down, she talked sometimes of killing herself, more specifically of blowing her head off. I wanted her to see a doctor but, being American by birth, she had always refused to have anything to do with English doctors whom she regarded as medieval in both equipment and attitude. She did however promise to see an American doctor as soon as she returned to the States. And this was the other reason I made no comment about Waterson. I knew Gail was going back to California in the near future.

34

Early last summer her father had died. She was very close to him and I think it was from this date that her bouts of depression set in. The news that her mother's health had gone into a rapid decline since Gail had returned to England after her father's funeral made matters worse. I think she had blamed her mother for her father's death and had not been careful to conceal her feelings, and now she was feeling guilty herself. These are necessarily amateur observations. All I knew for certain was that her mental state was far from stable, but everything pointed to nothing but good coming from her return to Los Angeles with the opportunity this would afford for sorting things out with her mother and also for consulting her family physician.

She was due to leave on Sunday February 8th. I had offered to drive her down to Heathrow, but despite the mild weather, she said she was worried about bad road conditions and she would go by train. She refused my offer to accompany her, saying she knew how much work I had on my plate, and then, when I persisted, demanding angrily if I didn't think her capable of making a simple train journey alone. At this point I desisted and in fact went to work on the Sunday morning to take advantage of the continuing good weather, and thus did not even see her out of the house. I was therefore relieved when she rang me the following day, ostensibly from Los Angeles, to say she'd arrived safely.

I heard nothing further from her but a woman rang up a couple of times and asked to speak to her. When I told her Gail was out of the country, she made a sort of disbelieving sound and rang off. Then earlier tonight she rang again. I'm certain it was the same woman, she sounded young, with a Yorkshire accent though not very strong. She asked me if I still believed Gail was in America. I said yes, of course. And she went on to say that I was wrong and if I wanted to see Gail I ought to go round to 18 Hambleton Road. Then she rang off.

I immediately rang Gail's mother in LA. I got through to the housekeeper-cum-nurse that Mrs Delgado, my mother-in-law, had taken on since her illness. She said Gail had never arrived but had sent a cable to say she was stopping off to see some friends on the East Coast and would get in touch as soon as she knew when she'd definitely arrive. No one was surprised as Gail was notoriously impulsive. I made light of the matter and advised the nurse not to mention my call to Mrs Delgado as I didn't want her to worry. But I myself was very worried and the only thing I could think of to do was go round to Hambleton Road.

I arrived at 10.30. There were lights on but Mr Waterson took a long time to answer the door. When he saw who it was, at first he looked shocked. Then he said, 'You know, don't you?' And as soon as he said that, I did.

The odd thing was I didn't get angry, perhaps because I got the feeling he was almost relieved to see me. He said, 'You'd better come in.' I said, 'Where is she?' He said, 'She's upstairs. But don't go rushing up there. She's in a very strange mood.' I asked what he meant and he said she had been drinking heavily and was talking about killing herself. I said something like, 'So she's putting you through that hoop too? Tough luck.' And he said, 'You mean you've seen her like this before? That's a relief. But that gun scared the shit out of me. Is it really loaded?'

Now this mention of a gun did really upset me. I knew Gail had guns, of course, but I thought they were safely locked up at the Mid-Yorks Gun Club where she was a member. When Waterson saw my reaction, he began to look really worried again. That was an odd thing. We should have been at each other's throats, I suppose. Instead we were, temporarily at least, united by our concern for Gail.

We went up together. Perhaps this was a mistake, for when Gail saw us, she began laughing and she gabbled something about all the useless men in her life sticking together, and the only good one she'd ever known being dead. She was drunk and naked, sitting on the bed. She had this revolver in her hands. I asked her to give it to me. She laughed again and held it with the muzzle pressed against her chin. I told her not to be silly. It wasn't the wisest thing to say, but I couldn't think of anything else. And she just laughed higher and higher and I thought I saw her finger tightening on the trigger. And that's when I jumped forward to grab at the gun.

What happened then I can't say precisely, except that the gun went off and then I was standing there holding it, and Gail was lying with her head blown to pieces across the bed, and some time after, I don't know how long, Mr Dalziel came into the room.

This dreadful accident has devastated my life. I loved my wife. I am sure that it was her dreadful feelings of guilt and unhappiness after her father's death that drove her to seek solace in infidelity. And I know that despite everything, we could have worked things out.

Signed: Philip Swain.

'Well,' said Dalziel. 'What do you reckon to that?'

'I don't know,' said Pascoe slowly. 'It's . . . odd.'

'Of course it's bloody odd. Fairy tales usually are! What he still hasn't twigged is I saw him with the gun in his hand before I heard the shot. Once we get Mr Gregory Waterson's version, it'll be two to one, and then I'll make the bugger squirm!'

This simple scenario did little to assuage Pascoe's sense of oddness. But he didn't want to seem to be muddying Dalziel's triumph so he held his peace and tried for a congratulatory smile. It lacked conviction, however, for Dalziel said, 'You've not changed, have you, lad? In fact, all them weeks lying in bed playing with yourself have likely set you back. What you need is some good solid meat to get your stomach settled. I've got just the thing. Football hooligans.'

He regarded Pascoe complacently and received in return a look of surprise. The big clubs in West and South Yorkshire had their share of maniac supporters, but City, Mid-Yorkshire's only league side, rattling around the lower divisions for years, rarely attracted serious home-grown trouble.

'I've not read about any bother,' said Pascoe. 'And anyway crowd control's uniformed's business.'

'Murder isn't,' said Dalziel grimly. 'Saturday before last, young lad vanished travelling back to Peterborough from a visit to his girlfriend in London. They found him next morning with a broken neck at the bottom of an embankment near Huntingdon.'

'Sad, but what's it to do with us?'

'Hold your horses. City were playing in North London

that day and it seems there were a lot of complaints about bevvied-up City supporters on the train the dead lad would have caught from King's Cross.'

'But you said he'd been visiting his girl, not attending a match. Why should he get picked on?'

'Colour of his eyes'd be provocation enough for some of these morons,' declared Dalziel. 'But it was more likely the colour of his scarf. Royal blue, which some bright spark in Cambridgeshire spotted was the colour of City's opponents that afternoon. Could be nowt, but there's been one or two hints lately that our local loonies are keen to get organized like the big boys, so this could be a good excuse to bang a few heads together before they get properly started, right?'

'I suppose so,' said Pascoe reluctantly. It didn't sound a very attractive assignment. He glanced at Wield in search of sympathy, but Dalziel took it as an attempt to pass the buck.

'No use trying to delegate, lad. The sergeant here's going to be busy. How's your bedside manner, Wieldy? Christ, the sight of you coming through the door would get me back on my feet pretty damn quick! Why don't you get yourself off down to the Infirmary and take this shrinking violet Waterson's statement so that I can spoil Mr lying bastard Swain's lunch? No, better still, I'll leave it till after lunch and give him indigestion. No reason why we should miss opening time at the Black Bull, is there? Not when it's celebration drinks all round!'

'You mean you're in the chair because of this collar?' asked Pascoe, trying not to sound surprised.

'Don't be daft,' said Dalziel, who was not notorious for treating his staff. 'I'll let Desperate Dan supply the booze for that. No, it's you who'll be in the chair, Peter, unless you crap on the Chief's carpet when he calls you in.'

Wield caught on before Pascoe and shook his hand,

grinning broadly and saying, 'Well done, sir!' Dalziel followed suit.

'One thing but,' he said. 'When you give Ellie the glad tidings, point out it'll be a couple of years before it makes any difference to your pension. Now sod off and start earning your Chief Inspector's pay!'

Chapter 2

Detective-Sergeant Wield parked his car in the visitors' car park and set off up the long pathway to the Infirmary. The oldest of the city's hospitals, it had been built in the days when visitors were regarded as a nuisance even greater than patients and had to prove their fitness by walking a couple of furlongs before they reached the entrance. As recompense, the old red brick glowed in the February sun and a goldheart ivy embraced it as lovingly as any stately home. Also the path ran between flowerbeds white with snowdrops. Spotting a broken stalk, Wield stopped and picked the tiny flower and carefully inserted it in his button-hole.

What a saucy fellow you're becoming! he mocked himself. You'll be advertising for friends in the *Police Gazette* next.

His lips pursed in an almost inaudible whistling as he strode along but inside he was smiling broadly and singing Bunthorne's song from *Patience*: '. . . as you walk down Piccadilly with a poppy or a lily in your mediaeval hand . . .'

His merry mood lasted along the first straight mile of corridor but by the time he reached his destined ward, the sights, sounds and smells of the place had silenced his inner carolling.

39

There was no one at the sister's desk and he went into the open ward.

'Mr Waterson? First door on your left,' said a weary nurse who looked as if she should be occupying the bed she was making.

Wield pushed open the door indicated and went in.

It occurred to him instantly that Waterson must have private medical insurance. A nurse in a ward sister's uniform was leaning over him. Their mouths were locked together and his hands were inside her starched blouse, roaming freely. No way did you get this on the National Health.

Wield coughed. The nurse reacted conventionally, doing the full guilty thing surprised bit, jumping backwards while her fingers scrabbled at her blouse buttons and blood flushed her pale and rather beautiful face like peach sauce over vanilla ice. The man, however, grinned amiably and said, 'Good morning, Doctor.'

'It is Mr Waterson, isn't it?' said Wield doubtfully.

'That's right.'

Wield produced his warrant card.

'Good lord. It's the fuzz, dear. I expect you've come for a statement? It's all ready. They wake you at sparrow fart in these places, you know, so I've had hours to compose.'

He thrust a single sheet of foolscap bearing the Local Health Authority's letter-head into Wield's hand.

The woman meanwhile had reassembled herself into the pattern of a brisk efficient ward sister.

'If you'll excuse me,' she said. 'I'll look in later.'

'Nice, isn't she?' said Waterson complacently as the nurse left.

Wield examined the man neutrally. He was approaching thirty, perhaps had even passed it. Nature had tossed youthful good looks into his cradle, and nurture in the form of an artistic hairdresser, an aesthetic dentist and possibly an expensive dermatologist, had made sure the gift wasn't wasted.

'The sister is an old friend?' he ventured. Waterson smiled. There was charm here too.

'Wash your mind out, Sergeant,' he said. 'That was no sister, that was my wife!'

Deciding this was a conundrum best postponed, Wield looked at the statement. It consisted of a single very long paragraph written in a minute but beautiful hand. It wasn't easy to read but one thing was very quickly clear. It was a lot closer to Swain's version of events than to Dalziel's!

Wield began to read it through a second time.

Gail Swain and I became lovers about a month ago. It was difficult to see as much of each other as we would have liked, so when Gail came up with a plan for us to have a longer period together I was delighted. She was going back to America on a visit to see her mother and she rearranged things so that she wouldn't need to get there till much later than she'd told her husband. I wanted to fix up a hotel somewhere but she said no, she would come to me as soon as she could and she preferred to stay with me in town. I think the idea of stopping so close to her home excited her in some way. She turned up at my house in Hambleton Road last Thursday. I know she had allegedly left for America on the Sunday but what she had been doing in the meantime she never said. She was in a rather strange mood when she arrived and though things went well enough at first, by the time the weekend was over I was seriously worried. She never left the house but stayed inside all the time, drinking heavily, watching television, playing records, and talking wildly. Sexually she made increasingly bizarre demands upon me, not I felt for her own physical satisfaction so much as my humiliation. When I suggested she ought to be thinking about leaving, she became abusive and said things like, they would need to carry her out of there for all the neighbours to see. Last night she was the worst I had seen her. When I tried to reason with her, she produced this gun and said something about this being the only thing that spoke any sense. I know nothing about guns so I had no idea if it was real or loaded or anything. She aimed it at me and said it would be nice to have some company when she went. Just then the doorbell went and when I went downstairs to answer it, I found it was Philip Swain, her husband. I was naturally taken aback but also in a strange way I was quite relieved to have someone else to share the responsibility with. It just all came spilling out how worried I was and it must have got across as genuine, for instead of throwing a jealous fit, he came upstairs to see for himself. As soon as she saw us together, she became quite hysterical. She was laughing madly and screaming abuse and waving the gun, first at us, then at herself. I went towards her to pacify her and she put the gun under her chin and said if I came any closer she would kill herself. I was still uncertain whether the gun was real or not but I could see that she was in such a state she was likely to press the trigger unawares so I made a dive at her. Next thing the gun went off and there was blood and flesh and bone everywhere. I'm afraid I just collapsed and after that everything was a blur until I awoke this morning and found myself in the Infirmary. I can see now that Gail was a highly disturbed woman and was always capable of doing damage to herself or others. But I blame myself entirely for what happened last night. If I had acted differently and called for professional help instead of trying to disarm her myself, perhaps none of this would have happened.

Signed: Gregory Waterson.

After his second reading, Wield stood in silence for a while.

'What's the matter?' said Waterson. 'Not the right format? Get it typed up any which way you like, Sergeant, and I'll sign it.'

Gathering his wits, Wield said, 'No, sir, it's fine. Will you excuse me?'

He went out. A ward sister had appeared at the desk, a stout woman with a smile of great sweetness which switched on as he approached and identified himself.

'I met Mrs Waterson a moment ago,' he said. 'Is she not on this ward?'

'No. Women's surgery. Did you want her?'

'No. At least not now. I'd like a telephone, if I could.'

'In my office, just down there.'

'Thanks. Any idea when Mr Waterson will be discharged?'

'You'll need to ask Dr Marwood. Shall I get him? He's just down the ward.'

'Yes, please.'

He went into the tiny office and dialled. He identified himself to the switchboard operator and asked to be put through to Dalziel. A moment later Pascoe answered the phone.

'That you, Wieldy? Look, the Super's in with the Chief. Anything I can do to help?'

Quickly Wield filled him in.

'Oh dear,' said Pascoe. 'No wonder you sounded relieved to get *me*.'

'It's not *quite* the same story as Swain's,' said Wield, in search of a silver lining.

'No. But it's a bloody sight closer to it than Fat Andy's version,' said Pascoe.

'You don't think he could have got it wrong?'

'Are you going to tell him that?'

'I'm only a sergeant. Chief Inspectors get the danger money,' said Wield. 'Went all right, did it, your big moment? Corks popping and such?'

'I got a cup of instant coffee. Is Waterson fit enough to come down here for a bit of close questioning?'

'He looks in rude health to me but I'm just going to check with the doctor.'

As Wield replaced the receiver, the door opened and a black man in a white coat came in. He was in his late twenties, with a hairline further back and a waistline further forward than they ought to be.

'Marwood,' he said. 'You the one wanting to know if Waterson's fit to go? The answer's yes. Sooner the better.'

43

This sounded like something more than a medical opinion.

'Thank you, Doctor,' said Wield. 'Were you on when he was admitted?'

'No, but I've seen the notes. Shock; sedation. Well, the sedation's worn off. Never lasts long with his type. Same with shock, I'd say.'

'His type?'

'Volatile,' said the doctor. 'At least that's one way of putting it.'

Wield said, 'Do you know Mr Waterson, sir? I mean, not just as a patient?'

'We've met. His wife works here.'

'And it was through her . . .?'

'Staff parties, that sort of thing. He turned up a couple of times.'

'And how did he strike you?' asked Wield.

'Did I take to him, you mean? No way! He struck me as an opinionated little shit, and crypto-racist with it. I wasn't surprised when she left him.'

'Left him?'

'You didn't know?' Marwood laughed. 'If I try to operate without knowing my patient's a haemophiliac, I get struck off. But you guys just muddle through and no one gives a damn! What's he done anyway?'

'Just helping us, sir,' said Wield, wondering how Marwood would have reacted to the scene he had interrupted minutes earlier. 'How long have they been separated?'

'Not long. She moved into a room in our nurses' annexe. Excuse me.'

A bleeper had started up in his pocket. He switched it off and picked up the phone.

'Right,' he said after a moment. Replacing the receiver, he said, 'I've got to go. Listen, medically, Waterson's fit

44

to go. But personally and off the record, I'd say the guy should be put out to pasture at the funny farm.'

He left. Wield pondered what he had heard for a while. Clearly Marwood felt about Waterson as Dalziel felt about Swain. Such strong antipathies bred bias and clouded the judgement. Wield knew all about bias, hoped he would speak out against it if necessary. But for the moment all that he was required to do was deliver Waterson safe into Dalziel's eager hands.

He went back to the small side ward.

It was empty.

Suddenly his heart felt in need of intensive care. He went out to the nurse's station. The plump sister gave him her smile.

'Where's Mr Waterson, sister?' he asked.

'Is he not in his bed?'

'No.'

'He might be in the lavvy. Or perhaps he's gone to have a shower.'

'You didn't see him? Have you been here all the time, since we talked, I mean?'

He must have sounded accusatory.

'Of course I haven't. I went off to fetch Dr Marwood to see you, didn't I?' she retorted.

'Where's the lavatory? And the shower?'

The lavatory was the nearer. It was empty. But in the shower Wield found a pair of pyjamas draped over a cubicle.

Either Waterson was wandering around naked, or . . .

He returned to the sister.

'What would happen to his clothes when he was admitted?'

'They'd be folded and put in his bedside locker,' she said.

The locker was empty.

45

'Shit,' said Wield. Only a few months earlier during the case on which Pascoe had hurt his leg, a suspect had made his escape from a hospital bed and Dalziel had rated the officer responsible a couple of points lower than PC Hector. But no reasonable person could have anticipated that a mere witness who'd volunteered a statement would do a bunk!

Then Dalziel's features flashed upon Wield's inward eye and reason slept.

'Oh shit,' he said again. Something made him glance down at his lapel. The tiny snowdrop had already wilted and died. He took it out and crushed it in his hand. Then with wandering steps and slow he made his way back to the telephone.

Chapter 3

The Reverend Eustace Horncastle was a precise man. It was through exactitude rather than excellence that he had risen to the minor eminence of minor canon, so when he said to his wife, 'The woman is pagan,' she knew the word was not lightly chosen.

Nevertheless she dared a show of opposition.

'Surely she is merely exuberant, dramatic, full of life,' she said with the wistful envy of one who knew that whatever she herself had once been full of had seeped away years since.

'Pagan,' repeated the canon with an emphasis which in a lesser man might almost have been relish.

Looking at the object of their discussion who was striding vigorously across the Market Square ahead of them, Dorothy Horncastle could not muster a second wave of disagreement. Eileen Chung's silver lurex snood

46

was a nod in the direction of religiosity, and there was perhaps something cope-like in the purple striped poncho draped round her shoulders. But devil-detection begins at the feet, and those zodiac-printed moccasins with leather thongs biting into golden calves each separately sufficient to seduce a Chosen People, were a dead giveaway. Here was essence of pagan. If you could have bottled it, the Canon's wife might have bought some.

The clerical couple were almost at a canter to keep up with those endless legs, so when Chung stopped suddenly there was a small collision.

'Whoa, Canon,' said Chung amiably.

'A canon indeed, but little woe,' said Horncastle to his wife's amazement. He rarely aimed at wit and when he did was more likely to try a Ciceronian trope than plunge into a Shakespearean pun. A suspicion formed in Dorothy's mind, to be brushed away like a naughty thought at Communion, that her husband might have invited her presence this morning not simply to represent the views of the laity (his phrase), but because he felt the need of a chaperone!

There had been one full meeting of the Mysteries committee which had been as long as an uncut *Hamlet* and not nearly as jolly. The combined verbosity of a city councillor, a union leader, a member of the Chamber of Commerce, a mediaeval historian, a journalist and Canon Horncastle, had defeated even Chung's directorial expertise and she had resolved thereafter to pick them off singly as she had picked them on singly in the first place. The diocese contained many worldlier, merrier clerics who would have given half their tithes to be religious advisers on such a project, but Chung's homework had told her Horncastle was the man. Heir apparent to the senescent Dean, he was the key figure in the Cathedral Chapter on matters relating to sacred sites and buildings, and the

Bishop was said to respect his views highly, which her interpreter assured her was Anglican for being shit-scared of him.

'I thought this might be a good site for one of the pageants,' said Chung. 'The sun will be coming round behind the Corn Market at that time of day and it'll light up the wagon like a spot.'

'If the weather is clement,' said the Canon.

'I'll rely on your good offices for that,' laughed Chung.

Dorothy Horncastle waited for her husband's expected rebuke at this meteorological blasphemy but it didn't come. Instead something horribly like a simper touched his narrow lips. The unbelievable notion rose again that perhaps he really did need protection! Not sexually, for the frost in those loins was surely proof against the most torrid touch, but there were other temptations in this pagan's armoury. She'd been mildly puzzled when at breakfast this morning Eustace had started reminiscing about his seminary triumph in the chorus line of *Samson Agonistes*. If Lucifer could fall, why not a minor canon?

It was time for a dutiful wife to come to the rescue.

She said, 'Won't the market stallholders object to their customers being turned into an audience?'

Horncastle turned his cold gaze upon her, no simper now deflecting the straight line of those lips.

'Monday is not a market day in normal circumstances, I think you'll find. When it happens also to be a Bank Holiday, it seems more than ever unlikely that there should be any commercial activity, wouldn't you say, my dear?'

The heavy sarcasm, though hardly novel, still had power to bruise. Chung, sensitive to drama, stepped in swiftly.

'Hasn't he told you that we finalized our timetable at the meeting, Mrs Horncastle? That's a man for you, thinks we're all psychic! Well, we're going for the first week in

June, which has the feast of Corpus Christi in it, that's the traditional time when these Mysteries were performed, and also this year it happens to be the week of the Spring Bank Holiday which means we can use the holiday Monday for our grand opening procession without getting snarled up with all the usual commercial traffic. So, this way everyone's happy, Church, holiday-makers, shop-keepers, historians and traffic cops!'

'It must be gratifying to make so many people happy,' said Dorothy Horncastle, smiling wanly.

She's really rather pretty, thought Chung. Ten minutes with the Leichner box, an auburn wig to match those eyes, plus a rich red gown with a fret of mourning black lace at the throat, and she'd make a perfectly presentable Olivia. Instead, unmade-up, her fine features skeletally honed by the biting wind, her hair invisible under a shapeless wool hat and her body unguessable under a shapeless tweed coat, she looked like a Village Thespians' shot at Mother Courage.

They moved on, entering the narrow skein of mediaeval streets which curled around the cathedral. Chung modified her pace so that she came between the Horncastles and modified her tone also, talking earnestly of her desire to recapture those days when the spiritual and temporal were inextricably intertwined and the Church was the one true centre of civic life. At the same time her eyes were taking in every detail of the winding cobbled ways flanked by close-crowded shops and houses whose timbered gables often threatened to meet overhead. And through her mind's eye, heavily screened so that not the slightest verbal hint should slip out to give the Canon pause, ran pictures brimming with colour and excitement of the great pageant wagons rumbling over the cobbles, heralded by music and dancers and trailing a long wash of jugglers, tumblers, fire-eaters, fools, flagellants, giants, dwarves,

49

dancing bears, merry monks, cut-price pardoners, knights on horseback, Saracens in chains, nubile Nubians . . . At about this point in his solo session, her university mediaevalist had demurred but she had silenced him with a cry of, 'Shit, man! This show's for your person-in-the-street. Ask yourself, do they want it authentic, or do they want it *fun*?' And then had won his cooperation by squeezing him well above the knee and laughing, 'OK. So maybe we'll hold the Nubians. That make you happy?' And, as she squeezed again, he could not but agree that it did.

And now they came into the cathedral close and everything changed. Little of the mediaeval had survived the 'modernization' of the eighteenth century when Wyatt the Destroyer's internal restorations had been mirrored and magnified in a ruthless external clean-up of what even antiquarians had had to admit was an ecclesiastical slum. A fourteenth-century deanery had been spared because the eighteenth-century dean had simply refused to move his large family, and a row of Jacobean almshouses had presented a similar logistical problem. Between these and a scattering of other survivals had sprung up new buildings in styles ranging from neo-classic domestic, through romantic picturesque to Victorian Gothic; and by one of those coincidences quite beyond the wit of architects and planners, the result was a delightful and harmonious meld. Nothing was here to provoke a Prince.

The close was entered through a granite gateway in a sandstone wall, and though the old wooden gates had long since vanished, there was still a sense of being admitted, of passing from the hectic and neurotic atmosphere of modern life into a balmier, more restful air.

Chung made a mental note to get the gateway measured. She wanted her procession to be fun, and she didn't want it to end in farce with a pageant firmly wedged between the pillars. She had hold of the Canon's arm now to steer him along her reconnoitred route while at the same time permitting him to imagine that it was his expertise which was showing her the best way. This was not easy as the best way could hardly be said to involve the cathedral close at all, since Charter Park, the proposed site for the daily performance of the Mystery Plays, lay as far to the west of the market place as the cathedral lay to the east. Chung had justified her diversion on ecclesiastical grounds. The grand opening procession must be seen to embrace the sacred as well as the profane.

Her real reason, however, was that she had no intention of staging her production in the Park, which was broad and flat and bounded by a main road and a canalized river, providing a choice between a static background of gloomy warehouses or a moving one of double-decker buses.

Her chosen site was much closer at hand. On the far side of the cathedral and belonging to it stretched an expanse of green and pleasant land, dotted with old trees and sinking down in a shallow valley before swelling up once more to a natural vallum whcre remnants of the city's mediaeval walls could still be seen. More substantial than these stood the ruins of St Bega's Abbey from which had come much of the impetus and, after its closure, some of the material to enlarge the small Anglo-Norman cathedral into a huge Gothic edifice which could hold its own against any in the land.

This was the setting Chung lusted after.

They had arrived at the great building itself. She paused and craned her neck to take in the soaring bulk of the lantern tower.

'It's incredible,' she said. 'How did they do all this without machines?'

'They had something better. They had God,' said the Canon.

It was a good feed. She looked at him appraisingly and

51

said, 'And that's all you need? I think I'm getting close to finding mine. Canon, would it be possible to climb the tower to get a bird's eye view of things?'

Horncastle hesitated but his wife inadvertently came to Chung's aid. Pointing across the road to a tall gabled house as narrow and forbidding as the Canon himself, she said, 'I thought as we were so near home, a cup of coffee perhaps . . .'

'Dorothy,' said the Canon testily, 'I have pledged myself to advise Miss Chung this morning. In an hour's time I have an important luncheon appointment at the Palace. I hardly feel that taking coffee in my own parlour would be a fruitful way of filling the intervening period. If you would follow me, Miss Chung.'

He headed into the cathedral. Chung smiled apologetically at his wife and said, 'Another time, huh?' before following.

It was a wearisome climb up a steep, dark, spiral staircase, but worth every ounce of sweat. The city lay stretched beneath them like an illuminated plan, and there was little to interrupt the eye's flight to the distant green and blue horizons. The only contender in terms of height was the narrow tower which had tumesced out of the old redbrick university in the expansive 'sixties, and though it flashed back the light of the cold wintry sun most defiantly, its glass and concrete hardly gave promise of another six centuries of such defiance.

Chung moved from side to side, removing her snood to let the chill wind unravel her long black hair. The Canon stood and watched her delight with proprietorial pleasure. Dorothy Horncastle emerged a few moments later from the narrow oak door and stood unnoticed.

Chung came to rest by the eastern parapet and looked down towards the dwarfed ruins of the old abbey. Horncastle came and joined her.

'It's magnificent,' she said sincerely.

'Yes. I pride myself that we have a setting and outlook dramatic enough to stand comparison with any in the country,' said the Canon complacently.

'A dramatic setting?' said Chung, eagle-eyed for an entrée. 'Yes, I see what you mean. You must be a classicist, Canon. That fold of ground there, the Greeks would have had to turn it into an amphitheatre. And the ruins, what a backcloth! No chance of transferring them to Charter Park for the Mysteries, I suppose?'

'If it were feasible, you should have them,' replied the Capon, quite happy to hypothesize the impossible in return for Chung's smile.

'Pity,' she sighed. 'That tatty park could surely do with something to match the material. But you'll be doing wonders enough if you can get us permission to route the procession through the close. I gather the Bishop is none too keen.'

'Indeed? I can assure you that whatever route we decide on today will be the route you take,' said Horncastle sharply.

'You can? That's great,' exclaimed Chung at full glow. 'But your other idea, about the ruins, that would take a real miracle, huh?'

There it was. A temptation on a tower. If he followed the best precedents, the Canon would scornfully deny ever having had any such idea about the ruins. Or he might compromise, and still take it as a joke about transferring the ruins to Charter Park. Or he might be vain enough to let himself be manipulated into accepting parenthood of a proposal to use St Bega's as the main Mysteries site, and with parenthood, responsibility.

Then she looked into his hard unblinking eyes and knew she had made a mistake. He was a bright man within his

53

limits, and she had seen only the limits and forgotten the brightness.

She smiled, acknowledging defeat, and said, 'But it's a great route. Thanks for your help.'

And submission proved the key. The Canon said, 'I think I might rise to the occasional miracle, in a purely dramatic sense, of course.'

'You mean you think you could really swing it for us to use St Bega's?'

'It would require the approval of the Chapter but that would be something of a formality once the Bishop and I showed the way. Would you like me to attempt the miracle, as you call it?'

There was the scent of a bargain here which made Chung momentarily uneasy. But clerics should know better than to do deals with pagans.

She said, 'It would be truly marvellous.'

'In that case I shall speak to his lordship at luncheon today. Now let us descend. Permit me to lead the way. The stairs are steep and there is danger here for the unvigilant.'

Oh, you're so right, baby, thought Chung as he stepped through the doorway with exaggerated care. She looked round in search of Mrs Horncastle. She was standing in the furthermost corner of the tower leaning out over the parapet. Like Chung, she had removed her headgear, revealing a tumult of chestnut hair which seemed to dance exuberantly at its release from the confines of the woollen hat. There was even some colour in the hollow cheeks now, and a brightness in the eyes as they stared into the space which divided her from the crawling dots below.

'Mrs Horncastle, we're going now. Are you all right? Mrs Horncastle!'

'What? Oh yes. Yes, of course. So sorry.'

She was like a woman waking from a dream. She looked

at the hat in her hand as if uncertain how it got there. Then she pulled it down over her rebellious hair and hurried across the roof and through the staircase door.

The darkness swallowed her.

For a moment Chung paused as if reluctant to leave this pale winter sunlight. Then, with a sigh which had nothing theatrical about it, she followed the Horncastles into the gloom.

Chapter 4

'Mr Swain, I'd like to take you over your statement again,' said Dalziel with the effulgent smile of a man who wants to sell a used Lada.

Swain glanced at his watch with the air of a man who has two minutes to spare and has started counting. Sharp-featured, deep-eyed and black-haired, he was quite striking in a Mephisthophelean kind of way. And his rather supercilious appearance was matched by the voice which said, 'I thought I'd already been as clear as I could without supplying a video, Superintendent.'

Dalziel smiled wolfishly. Pascoe guessed he was thinking: Oh, but you did, my lad! But this was no time to be seeing Swain through Dalziel's indisputably prejudiced eyes. Pascoe was more interested to find the oddities he had detected when reading the statement confirmed by his first meeting with the man. Stereotyping was of course a fascist device for perpetuating class divisions but Pascoe found himself unable to avoid a prejudice which provided your paradigmatic jobbing builder with Stringer's cloth cap, baggy trousers and vernacular speech forms, rather than Swain's Daks blazer, Cartier watch, and upper-class phonemes.

Dalziel said, 'Last night when you wrote your statement, you were naturally upset. Who wouldn't be? Man kills his wife, he's got a right to be upset. I'd just like to be sure you got things down like you really wanted. Here, take a look, tell me if there's owt you want to change.'

He pushed a photocopy of Swain's statement across the table. Swain said softly, 'A man who kills his wife? I think either I must have misheard or you must have misread, Superintendent.'

'Sorry, sir. Slip of the tongue,' said Dalziel unconvincingly. 'Though you do say as it was mebbe your efforts to get the gun off her that . . . anyroad, you just read through what you wrote and let me know if it's right.'

Swain ran his eyes down the sheets. When he finished he sighed and said, 'It's like a nightmare, all confused. I'm amazed I could have written this so clearly, but, yes, it's the most sense I can make out of the fragments. Would you like me to sign it again?'

'No need,' said the fat man. 'Signing a cheque twice won't stop it bouncing. If it's going to bounce, I mean. Anyroad, there's notes been taken, so all this is on the record.'

Wield was taking the notes. Pascoe had been invited along to observe. What the tactics were likely to be he could only guess. Dalziel's response to the news of Waterson's statement and subsequent disappearance had been stoic to the point of catalepsy, encouraging his colleagues to move in his vicinity like off-piste skiers. But his abandonment of the idea of leaving Swain to sweat till after lunch showed how seriously he was taking things.

'This wife of yours, did she make a habit of carrying guns around with her, Mr Swain?' inquired Dalziel.

'Of course not. At least, not to my knowledge.'

'Not to your knowledge, eh? And I dare say you

56

would've noticed if she'd started slipping three pounds of Colt Python down her cleavage, wouldn't you?'

'Of what?'

'Colt Python, weighs forty-four ounces unloaded, overall length eleven and a quarter inches, fires the .357 Magnum cartridge,' said Dalziel quoting the lab's preliminary weapon report.

'Was that what it was?' said Swain. 'I've no interest in guns .'

'So you'd never seen this one before?'

'Never.'

'Is that so? You did know she was a member of a gun club, didn't you?' said Dalziel.

'Of course I did .'

'And you never noticed any of her weapons about the house? They have to be kept under lock and key, Mr Swain, in a proper cabinet. You mean to tell me that a pro builder like you never noticed this interesting extension to your wife's wardrobe?'

Dalziel's sneers were as subtle as birdshit down a windscreen. Swain said wearily, 'The guns weren't kept in the house, except on the odd occasion she'd been shooting in some competition at another club and needed to store one overnight. That's the only reason we had the secure cabinet put in. Otherwise they were kept in the club armoury.'

Dalziel looked nonplussed for a moment.

'When was the last time she had a gun at home, then?' he asked.

'A couple of years ago, I'd say,' said Swain. 'She gave up competition shooting, you see, so there was never any reason to remove them from the club.'

'And you aren't a member of this club?'

'No. I told you. I hate guns, ever since . . . well, I've always hated them. And I was right, wasn't I?'

His voice rose to something not far short of a shout. Dalziel regarded him speculatively for a while, then he turned on a sympathetic smile, his face lighting up like the Ministry of Love.

'I'm glad you feel like that about guns, Mr Swain. My sentiments entirely. I gather there's a very different attitude to gun-ownership in the States.'

He made the States sound like somewhere beyond Alpha Centauri.

'I believe so,' said Swain. He put his hand to his brow as if to massage a headache. Then he asked in a low voice, 'Has my mother-in-law, Mrs Delgado, been told?'

'I expect so,' said Dalziel negligently. 'Leastways we told the Los Angeles police. She's sick, you say?'

'Yes. She's pretty well bedridden now. The most optimistic prognosis is a year, perhaps eighteen months.'

'So your missus would be planning a long trip mebbe.'

'It was open-ended. Naturally, if the end looked imminent, Gail would have stayed.'

'So that's why she took most of her clothes?'

'What? Oh yes, of course. You've been poking around the house.'

'Not me personally. One of my officers. Routine. But he did say it looked like there'd been a good clear-out.'

'If you'd ever seen what Gail packed for a weekend in the country, you'd not be surprised at that, Superintendent,' said Swain sadly.

'Oh aye, I know what you mean,' said Dalziel with a rueful shake of his head to express male solidarity. 'How long do you reckon she'd have stayed in Hambleton Road, Mr Swain?'

'How the hell should I know? You'd better ask Waterson that.'

'I shall. Make a note to ask Mr Waterson when you see him, Sergeant Wield,' said Dalziel.

Pascoe felt Wield wince beneath his totem-pole impassivity. The Sergeant had set all the systems at top pressure to track down Waterson, but so far there'd been no trace. Wield had spoken briefly to the wife before leaving the hospital. She had denied any knowledge of her husband's intentions or whereabouts, and agreed to make herself available for a longer interview at the end of her shift.

Dalziel leaned forward and said, 'Talking of Waterson, what do you reckon to him, Mr Swain? Setting aside the fact he were knocking off your wife.'

Swain looked at him in amazement and Pascoe tensed his muscles to intervene. Then Swain shook his head and said, 'I'd heard about you, Dalziel, but no one got close to the reality.'

Dalziel looked modestly pleased and said, 'Well, like they say, only God can make a tree. So? Waterson?'

'I don't know. He seemed all right. Lively. Pretty bright. Not a good payer, but who is these days?'

'I hope you'll not have any bother when you finish our car park and garages,' said Dalziel righteously. 'Had to twist his arm a bit, did you?'

'I had to bill him a few times and give him a couple of phone calls.'

'No solicitor's letters delivered by a pair of brickies with a German Shepherd?'

'You've been attending too many trials,' said Swain. 'If anything, I went more than usually easy with Waterson. I felt some sympathy with him. He was like me a couple of years back, trying to set up by himself after he'd been made redundant, and I know how careful you've got to be with the money then. Also I gather his wife left him. There's ironic for you! I felt sorry for the bastard because his wife had left him and she probably did it because she found he was screwing around with mine!'

'Mebbe so. You met her, did you?'

'Mrs Waterson? Only once. The day the job started. I got the distinct impression that was the first she knew of it. I never saw her again but I'm not around all the time. Arnie Stringer, my partner, usually takes care of on-site supervision.'

'Does he now? Now that is good news, Mr Swain.'

'What do you mean?'

'Nowt, except it's a comfort to know your men will be able to get on with our garages while we've got you banged up in here,' said Dalziel cheerfully.

It was not the worst of his provocations but it was the one that hit the button. Swain shot to his feet and shouted, 'You great lump of blubber, I've had enough of this. I don't have to sit here listening to your loutish maunderings. Can't you get it into your thick skull, she was my wife, and she's dead, and I blame myself . . . she's dead, and I blame . . .'

As rapidly as he had risen, he slumped in his chair again, pressed his face into his hands and his whole body went into a spasm of almost silent sobbing.

Dalziel viewed the scene with the detachment of a first-night critic, belched, stood up and said, 'I don't know about you lot, but my belly feels like me throat's been slit. Lunch.'

Outside he said, 'He's good. Best free show since Crippen broke down at his wife's funeral.'

'That's a bit hard,' protested Pascoe. 'He's got good cause to be upset.'

'You mean, because I'm on to his nasty game?' growled Dalziel.

Pascoe grimaced and said, 'Look, sir, with this statement of Waterson's in the files . . . I know there's a bit of difference, but with two of them on more or less the same lines . . .'

'Aye, it is odd, that,' said Dalziel deliberately misunderstanding. 'Wieldy, you've had the rare privilege of seeing both these buggers while they're *compos mentis*. How do you read it? Any chance of 'em being a pair of poofs cooking up this Irish Stew between 'em?'

Was the question more or less offensive for being addressed to a gay? And did it make any difference that Wield had received a measure of protection from Dalziel when others were ready to ladle on the persecution with generous hand?

Wield said, 'I'd say no, they're not gay. Though they're not always easy to spot, are they? Incidentally, I ran them both through the computer just in case no one else heard your instructions last night, sir.'

Is he being cheeky? wondered Dalziel, who was notorious for his distrust of any form of intelligence that couldn't sup ale. 'Man who lets a key witness go missing should think twice before he's cheeky. All right, lad, what did the Mighty Wurlitzer say?'

'Nothing known about Swain,' said Wield. 'But Waterson lost his driving licence last week.'

'Oh, great,' mocked Dalziel. 'That changes everything, that does.'

'What did he do, Wieldy?' asked Pascoe defensively.

'Nowt really. He'd totted up penalty points pretty regularly for motor offences, but a couple of weeks back he got flashed because one of his rear lights was on the blink and he took off like a jet. They picked him up later all apologetic, thought he'd probably be drunk, but he was well inside the limit. So they did him for speeding and that put him over the top.'

'For crying out loud!' said Dalziel in exasperation. 'Can't either of you contribute owt useful? Peter, what do you reckon to these two?'

'I've not met Waterson,' Pascoe pointed out. 'But he sounds . . . wayward.'

'Wayward, eh?' said Dalziel. 'I'll make a note. And Swain? Does he sound wayward too?'

'No, but he *sounds* a very odd kind of small-time builder.'

'What? Too educated, you mean? You'd best not let yourself be heard talking like that at home else you'll be washing your mouth out with carbolic. But I know what you mean. He's a very odd kind of fellow all round. Has to be if he thinks he can get the better of me! But we're wasting good drinking time. We'll have to postpone your celebration, but . . .'

'There's still an hour,' said Pascoe.

'Aye, but Wieldy here won't be with us, will you, Sergeant? He's got another hospital appointment, if he doesn't manage to lose this one too. You and me though, Peter, we'll have a jar and go over these two statements with a fine-tooth comb.'

'Three statements,' said Pascoe, crossing his fingers and trying to cross his toes.

'Three? What do you mean – three?'

Wield took a small step towards the window as if contemplating hurling himself through it when hostilities broke out.

'There's Swain's,' Dalziel went on. 'And there's Waterson's. What other bugger's made a statement that needs looking at?'

Pascoe wondered if the window were wide enough for a double defenestration.

He took a deep breath and thought that no matter what they paid chief inspectors, it wasn't enough.

'Yours,' he said. 'Sir.'

Chapter 5

The nurses' annexe at the Infirmary was a nineteen-sixties purpose-built block situated about a furlong from the main building and linked to it by what had once been a pleasant tree-lined walk. Pleasant, that is, in summer and daylight. A series of late-night assaults a decade before had made protection more important than pleasance, and now the pathway was flanked by more lamp standards than trees and corridored in high tensile steel link-fencing.

Wield found Pamela Waterson's room on the third floor. When she opened the door she regarded him blankly for a second, then said, 'Oh, it's you,' and turned away.

He followed her into the room where she flopped wearily into a chair. Her long blonde hair was loose now, its bright tresses about her face accentuating the dark shadows under her eyes.

'I'm sorry,' he said, 'I can see you're very tired.'

'You don't have to be a detective to work that out,' she answered bitterly. 'I was tired when I came off my last shift two hours late because my relief had a car accident. Then I only managed an hour's sleep before I was due on again – '

'Why was that?' interrupted Wield.

'Nothing special,' she said, lighting her third cigarette since his arrival. 'Life goes on, all the ordinary tedious things that take a few minutes when you're on top of them. Shopping, paying bills, washing, ironing – '

'Do you have a family, Mrs Waterson?' he interrupted again.

'Do I look like I have a family?' she said, gesturing around.

Presumably she simply meant that a bedsitter in a nurses' block was not a place to bring up a family, but Wield seized the opportunity for an open examination of the room.

There was little to be learned from the mainly institutional furniture. On the wall above the bed there was a little wooden crucifix; on another wall above a small bookcase hung a charcoal sketch of a female head whose laughing vitality delayed identification with the weary woman before him. He let his gaze fall to the books. Pascoe laid great store on books as revealers of personality. Mrs Waterson's choice ran mainly to biography and her taste was wide. There were a couple of Royals, Charles and Earl Mountbatten; several showbiz, including Monroe, Garland, the Beatles and Olivier; one political, Lloyd George; and a scattering of literary, ranging from Byron and Shelley through Emily Brontë and Oscar Wilde to Sylvia Plath and Simone de Beauvoir.

Looking for the meaning of her own life in other people's patterns was the way Pascoe would probably see it. Dalziel on the other hand would say, 'Sod the books! Poke about behind them, see what she's hiding!'

Wield knew all about hiding, knew also that we hide far less than we think. For years he had hidden his true sexual identity behind the dustjacket of a straight, middle-of-the-road, unemotional cop. But when he finally decided to come out, no delicate glowing butterfly emerged. He was still the same old lumpy green caterpillar nibbling systematically at the leaf till the holes joined up and he could see clear to the other side.

He returned now to his nibbling and pointed at the crucifix.

'You're a Catholic, are you, Mrs Waterson?'

'What? Oh, I see. And that means I should be producing every year like a brood mare?'

'I didn't say that. But there could be kids who stayed with their dad or went to gran when the bust-up happened.'

'Well, there weren't. And what do you know about my bust-up? Who've you been talking to? Some tittle-tattle at the hospital? God, if they worked as hard as I do, they'd have no time to gossip!'

She spoke with a fervour which brought colour to her wan cheeks. Wield, who had been trying to apportion the turmoil he discerned here between concern for her work and other causes possibly linked to his investigation, pushed a large emotional counter towards the job.

'Do you like being a nurse?' he asked with deliberate fatuity.

'Like? You mean, is it a vocation? Or, do I go around the wards singing?'

'Bit of both, I suppose. I mean, you must be good at it. How old are you, twenty-six, twenty-seven? And you're a ward sister already.'

She laughed and lit another cigarette.

'I'm twenty-four, Sergeant, and when I came here three years ago, they said I looked sixteen. And as for being a sister, I'm that because these days nurses are coming in in dribs and leaving in droves. Me, I reckon I didn't have half the experience necessary for it, and sometimes when I'm alone on the ward in the middle of the night and it's all quiet except for the odd groan and fart, and I can hardly keep my eyes open, I get to thinking that if something happens, some life or death emergency, I'm the one who'll be making the decisions till they rouse some poor bloody doctor who can probably hardly keep his eyes open either. Then I start shaking, partly with fear and partly with anger, at the sheer unfairness of expecting me to do the job at all.'

How relevant was all this? wondered Wield. It might

have something to do with the case in terms of the break-up of the Waterson marriage. Or it might be a deliberate tactic of diversion. But this he doubted. There was too much genuine passion not to mention desperation for this outburst to be tactical.

It was time to get back to the point.

'So,' he said, 'when you came on shift today you were told your husband had been admitted.'

'Not straight away,' she said. 'Not for a couple of hours. It was Dr Marwood who told me.'

'What was your reaction?'

'Well, I wanted to know if he was all right, naturally. And when Ellison . . . Dr Marwood said it was just some kind of nervous tension and he'd been sedated but seemed fine this morning, I got worried in case it had something to do with me.'

'Would that have surprised you?'

She thought about this, then said, 'Yes, it would. He could get very emotional, Greg, you know, fly off the handle, have a fit of what they'd call hysterics in a woman. But it was always at something specific. Often it was completely illogical, but there had to be something, not just sitting at home brooding about things that had happened. And in any case, I doubt if he did much brooding about what had happened to us.'

'What had happened to you, Mrs Waterson?' asked Wield.

'I don't see that that has anything to do with you,' she retorted. 'Look, what you're here for is to find if I can help you track down Greg, right? Well, I can't. I walked out on him three weeks ago and till this morning I'd not seen him since.'

'Mrs Waterson, when I arrived this morning, you didn't look like, well, like a woman separated from her husband.'

'Because I was letting him kiss me and feel me up?'

'That's right.'

She smiled and drew on her cigarette, both with visible effort.

'Sergeant, I went to see him in my break. I was exhausted. You can't imagine what a relief it was to talk to someone who wasn't talking to me professionally. And when he got hold of me, well, at least he wasn't grabbing at me to complain about a pain or ask for a bedpan. It was nice and soothing when he started stroking me, like a massage. Oh yes, when you arrived I probably looked as if I was ready to get into bed with him, and I was. But not to make love, just to sleep . . . sleep . . . sleep . . .'

She leaned back and closed her eyes. Wield felt very sorry for her but not so sorry that he was going to return to Dalziel with questions unasked.

He said, 'What did you and your husband talk about this morning?'

She opened her eyes with difficulty and looked at him blankly.

'What did he say about the reasons for him being there?' he pressed.

'What makes you think he said anything?' she evaded.

'Well, so far you've not asked me a single question about it, luv,' he said. 'And that sounds like a lack of curiosity which could be a record.'

'You're not daft,' she said wearily. 'All right. He told me everything. He'd written it all down. Did he not show it to you? Why'd that fat bobby, Dalziel, not come himself?'

That fat bobby. Wield liked it. But Waterson hadn't mentioned Dalziel in his written statement. Significant?

'Do you know Mr Dalziel?' he asked.

'I've seen him, naturally. He doesn't bother much with curtains. And everyone roundabout talks about him. He's what you call a character, I suppose.'

'I suppose he is,' said Wield. 'Did you believe your husband's statement, Mrs Waterson?'

'Of course, no problem. Things fall apart around him, always have done. Give him a pencil and he'll draw you a near-on perfect circle. But I've known him cut his finger spreading butter and he can break a cup just stirring his tea. Put him and a gun in the same room and someone's almost bound to get hurt. Story of his life.'

She yawned widely. He wasn't going to be able to keep this interview going much longer. There were more ways of escape than decamping.

'Did you know he was having an affair with Mrs Swain?' he asked.

'Not specifically,' she said, standing up and moving slowly towards the narrow bed which occupied one corner of the room. 'But I know all about her, all that matters, I mean.'

'What does that mean?'

'It means she'd be slim, with long legs, good figure, blonde hair. Names don't matter. I sometimes doubt if Greg knows their names. He's like a little boy in a sweet shop. He just points at the lemon popsicles, and because he's such a charming little boy, he usually gets what he's pointing at.'

As she spoke, she loosened her skirt, stepped out of it, and began to unbutton her blouse. There was nothing seductive or suggestive in the action even if Wield had been seducible or suggestible in that direction. She was on automatic pilot, preparing for crashdown. Wield did notice, however, that she fitted her husband's blueprint very well.

'Was it because of the women you left him?' he asked.

'No,' she replied. 'Not just the women.'

'What, then?' he asked, wondering if sleep or her answer would break the tape first. It was a close run thing.

'. . . it was like . . . going home . . . to another shift
. . . and it was always . . . Saturday night . . . on casualty
. . .' she said. Then she slipped on to the bed with one
arm still in her blouse and was instantly asleep.

Wield stood looking at her for a while. His two exem-
plars came into his mind. First he did what Pascoe would
have done, eased her arm out of the blouse sleeve and
folded the duvet gently over her body.

Then he did what Dalziel would have done and started
to search the room.

Chapter 6

Down at the Black Bull, Dalziel was trying to change the
subject.

'Did you have a look at them letters?' he interrupted.

'Which letters?' said Pascoe.

'From that barmy woman. I put 'em on your desk.
Surely you've had time to read a couple of letters?'

Pascoe sighed, recalling the small alp of files which had
reared out of his in-tray that morning. In fact he had read
the letters, if only for their relative lack of bulk.

'Yes, I saw them. Very interesting. Now about your
statement . . .'

Having grasped the nettle, and also having paid for the
first two rounds despite the official postponement of his
celebration, Pascoe was determined not to let go.

'I just said what I saw, lad.'

'Which was Swain holding the gun. Then Waterson
making a grab for him. Then the gun went off?'

'I heard the gun going off, didn't see it,' corrected
Dalziel. 'Now, about them letters, I'd like your opinion,
you being such a clever sod.'

'Yes, sir. You're sure about the sequence?'

'Of course I'm bloody sure!'

'Then Waterson must be covering up for Swain?'

'See? I was right. You are a clever sod,' said Dalziel, finishing his second pint. 'All we've got to do is find the bugger, kick some sense into him, and I get to stay flavour of the month. Now, these letters . . .'

Pascoe gave up. For the time being.

'What's your interest, sir?' he asked. 'She says she'll not be writing again.'

'She'll write again, never fear,' growled Dalziel. 'Then she'll top herself, and I don't want any bugger saying we did bugger-all. So get something down on paper, pass the buck to social services, the Samaritans, anyone so long as we look squeaky clean to the coroner. Here come our hot pies. I'll have another pint to wash the taste away when you're ready.'

'I thought it was a rise in salary I was getting,' said Pascoe, nursing his half full glass. 'I didn't realize it was an entertainment allowance.'

Dalziel thought this so funny he choked on his pie and, his own glass being empty, he finished Pascoe's.

'That's better,' he gasped. 'And I see you're ready now, so how about them drinks?'

It's pinpricks not principles that engender treason. As Pascoe put the foaming pint before his chief he said casually, 'Talking of free booze, there'll be some going on Sunday evening if you're interested. A little reception at the Kemble in connection with these Mystery Plays they're putting on in the summer. Ellie's a mate of Eileen Chung's and she said they're keen to have some police liaison. These theatricals pour the plonk like there's no tomorrow and I don't see why those blighters in traffic should enjoy all the freebies, so I've fixed for us to get invited.'

'Good thinking, lad. They can come in later and do the

work! Chung, eh? I've seen her and I've heard a lot about her but we've never actually met. I'd like that. I think the arts deserve every thinking citizen's support.'

He squinted over his glass to catch Pascoe's reaction, then he added, 'And I've always been partial to a bit of dusky chuff,' and laughed so much he started coughing again.

Back at the station the laughter stopped when Dalziel found the full post-mortem report on Gail Swain on his desk. It confirmed the cause of death as massive brain damage from the .357 Magnum cartridge which had been recovered from Waterson's converted attic after bursting its way through from the bedroom below. Blood alcohol was present at the level of 155 milligrams per 100 millilitres, which meant, as Dalziel observed, that she was well pissed. Remains of what the pathologist designated as an exotic meal, probably Chinese or Indian, were found in her stomach. She was a heavy smoker, had had her appendix removed, had sustained a fracture of her left tibia not less than three years before, had had no children, and had had sex a couple of hours before her death.

She was also a heroin user.

Dalziel threw back his head and bellowed, 'Seymour!'

Thirty seconds later a broad-shouldered redhead peered anxiously through the door. Detective-Constable Dennis Seymour's ear was not refined enough to distinguish *furioso* from simple *fortissimo* so he always anticipated the worst.

'Had a good poke around Swain's house, did you?' said Dalziel.

'Yes, sir. Report's on your desk, sir.'

'I've read it. It's not a bad report far as it goes. But I couldn't see owt in it about drugs.'

'Drugs?' Seymour's good-looking face went rigid with alarm. 'I wasn't told to look for drugs, sir.'

'You weren't told to look for Barbary apes either, but I dare say if you'd found a pair fornicating on the kitchen floor, you might have mentioned them!'

'What I meant, sir, was I saw no sign of drugs.'

'Oh aye? Checked every bottle in the bathroom cabinet, did we? Stuck your finger in every tin and jar in the kitchen and had a lick?'

Seymour shook his head. He looked so contrite that Dalziel, who was not above admitting an injustice once it had served its turn, said, 'Not your fault, lad. You weren't told. Though the way to get on is to do things you're not told, as long as they're not things you've been told not to, except if you know for sure they need doing. Ask Mr Pascoe to step in here a moment, will you?'

With the mingled relief and bafflement of a supplicant leaving the sibyl's cave, Seymour departed. Dalziel picked up the phone and spoke to Sergeant Broomfield on the desk below.

'Get the quack along here, will you, George? I want him to give Swain a going-over for drug abuse.'

'Yes, sir. What if he don't want to be gone over, sir?'

'Tell him it's routine. A pre-release examination just so he can't come back with accusations about brutality. He *hasn't* fallen off a chair or accidentally banged his head against someone's boot, has he?'

'No, sir. Very well behaved. One thing, though: he's asked to contact his solicitor.'

'Taken his time, hasn't he? He got the chance last night, it's in the record. Which crook acts for him?'

'Mr Eden Thackeray.'

'Old Eden? Shit. Get the quack quick as you can, George.'

He put the phone down and looked up at Pascoe who'd just come in.

'What's this about drugs, sir?'

'Seymour been blubbing? I had high hopes of him once, but I reckon he's not been the same since he started screwing that Irish waitress. Sap your strength, the Irish do. I'd pump bromide into their potatoes. Take a look at this.'

He tossed the PM report over the desk.

'Take Seymour back to Swain's house and see what you can find. I doubt it'll be much, though. He didn't look to me like a user. A night in the cells and it'd have started to show. Also he'd have been a lot keener to contact his brief to get him out. As for her, if she set out to screw her way back to LA, she's not likely to have left a cache of scag under the floorboards. But there may be traces. And if he knew, then maybe he can point us at the pusher.'

'Right, sir,' said Pascoe. 'By the way, these letters you were so concerned about. I thought I'd – '

'Sod the bloody letters,' said Dalziel irritably. 'We're here to sort out crooks, not piss around with hysterics! I'm surprised at you for wanting to waste my time!'

Half an hour later Pascoe drove into Currthwaite, a village in danger of being annexed into a suburb, albeit a pretty plush suburb. On the town side the invasion was practically complete with the old rolling parkland now dotted with a range of well fortified high-class executive dwellings. Even when he entered the village proper between a Norman church in mellow York stone and a blockhouse chapel in angry brick, the High Street cottages were signalling their surrender with window-boxes without and Sanderson curtains within, and everywhere he looked he saw the greenwellied conquerors marching their labradors in a non-stop victory parade.

Moscow Farm at the far end of the village showed signs of having fallen to the same attack. Snowcemed, window-boxed, double-glazed, burglar-alarmed, sauna'd, showered, and centrally heated, it bore as much relation to an old working farmhouse as Washington Heights to Wuthering Heights. But when he looked out of the french window at the rear, Pascoe saw there had been an active resistance movement, for the old farmyard after being prettied into a patio had regressed into a builder's yard.

'I bet the rest of the village don't much like it,' said Seymour. 'Not with the kind of prices they're asking round here.'

'You're into the property market, are you?' asked Pascoe.

'Want to be. I got engaged.'

'Congratulations. To Bernadette, I take it?'

Bernadette McCrystal was the Irish waitress whose debilitating influence Dalziel so deplored. Pascoe had met and liked her, though he doubted if marrying her was going to herald halcyon weather in Seymour's voyage through life.

'Of course,' said Seymour a touch indignantly.

'I'll buy you a drink. Now let's get on.'

Ninety minutes later to Seymour's undisguised relief they had found nothing.

'I didn't fancy going back to the Super with a barrow-load of coke.'

'Still time,' observed Pascoe. 'Out there is where they'll keep the barrows. I'll take a look. I'd like a word with his secretary anyway. You take one more look round here.'

He went out into the yard. It was enclosed on two sides by wings of old agricultural buildings, stables, barns and byres, which, red-tiled and white-painted, had something of an almost Mediterranean look in the thin February

74

sunlight. It was a delusion soon shattered as he stepped out into the chilly air.

The firm's business office was in what must once have been a hayloft above the byre which was now used as a garage. It was reached by a flight of external stairs which Pascoe would not have fancied in icy weather.

He knocked at the door and went in. Behind a desk reading a paperback whose cover promised a bodice-ripper but whose title claimed *Jane Eyre*, sat a young woman he knew to be Swain's secretary. She had emerged briefly on their arrival, but on spotting Seymour whom she'd met on his first visit, she had retreated to Mr Rochester.

'Hello,' said Pascoe. 'Busy?'

She rested her book against the typewriter on her desk and said, 'Can I help you?'

She was rather square-featured and plumply built, had straight brown hair, almost shoulder length, wore no discernible make-up and spoke in a husky contralto voice with a strong local accent.

Pascoe picked up the book and examined the illustration which showed a terrified young woman whose bodice was undoubtedly ripped fleeing from a burning house in whose doorway stood a Munster-like figure.

'I don't remember that bit,' he said.

'Makes you want to read the book,' she explained. 'More than them bloody teachers ever did.'

It was a point, perhaps two.

He put the book down on the typewriter and looked around. He found he was shivering slightly. The house had been warm and he'd taken off his topcoat, but here, despite a double-barred electric wall heater, the atmosphere was still dank and chilly. The woman at the desk on second inspection proved to be less plump than he'd thought. She had insulated herself with at least two sweaters and a cardigan.

'It's a bit nippy in here,' he said, touching the white-washed wall. The stones were probably three feet thick and colder on the inside than on the out. 'With all that room in the house, you'd have thought Mr Swain would have had his office in there rather than out here.'

'Mrs Swain wouldn't have it,' said the woman.

'Did he tell you that?'

She considered.

'No,' she said.

'How do you know, then?'

She considered once more, then said indifferently, 'Don't know, but I know.'

Pascoe sorted this out. Surprisingly it made sense.

'How long have you been working here, Miss . . . I'm sorry . . .?'

'Shirley Appleyard. And it's Mrs.'

'Sorry. You look so young,' he said with full flarch. It was like shining a torch into a black hole.

'I'm nineteen,' she said. 'I've been here two years.'

'Do you like it?'

She shrugged and said, 'It's a job. Better than nowt, these days.'

'Yes, they're hard to come by,' said Pascoe, switching to the sympathetic concerned approach. 'You did well, there was probably a lot of competition.'

'No,' she said. 'I got it because me dad's Mr Swain's partner.'

'Mr Stringer, you mean? That's handy,' said Pascoe.

'You mean I should give thanks to God for being so lucky? Don't worry, I get told that at least twice a day and three times on Sundays.'

She spoke with a dull indifference worse than resentment. Pascoe, as always curious beyond professional need, said, 'I met your father this morning. He seemed a little out of sorts . . .'

'You mean he didn't strike you as being full of Christian charity?' she said with an ironic grimace. 'He's not that kind of Christian. Didn't you notice the chapel over from the church as you came through the village? Red brick. That's Dad. All the way through.'

Pascoe smiled and said, 'You live in the village still? With your parents?'

'Aye. Holly Cottage. That's it you can see at the corner of the field.'

Pascoe looked out of the window. Visible through the open end of the yard was a small cottage about fifty yards away.

'You've not far to come,' he said. 'Your husband lives there too, does he?'

'He's away working, if it's any of your business,' she retorted with sudden anger. 'And what's all this to do with Mrs Swain getting shot?'

'Shot? Now where did you hear that?' wondered Pascoe. The media so far hadn't got past the general story of a shooting in Hambleton Road, and he was reluctant to think that Seymour had been indiscreet on his earlier visit.

'Dad rang up this morning to say there'd been some bother, something about Mrs Swain and a shooting, he didn't seem very clear, but he was just ringing to tell me to say nowt if anyone got on to me at work and started asking questions about the Swains.'

'Excluding the police, of course,' smiled Pascoe.

'He didn't say that,' she answered without returning his smile. 'So she *has* been shot, then? Dead?'

Pascoe said carefully, 'There *has* been a shooting, yes. And yes, I'm afraid Mrs Swain is dead. And I hope, despite your father, you'll feel able to answer a couple of questions, Mrs Appleyard.'

'Such as?'

'Such as, what did you reckon to Mrs Swain?' said Pascoe.

'She were all right,' said Shirley Appleyard. 'Bit stuck up, but always polite enough when we met.'

'She seemed a nice-looking woman from her photos,' said Pascoe. He was thinking of the wedding album they'd found in the house, and trying not to think of the bloody ruin on the official police pictures.

'Not bad,' said the girl. 'And she knew how to make the best of herself. Clothes and jewels and make-up, I mean. Nothing flashy, but you could tell just by looking it cost an arm and a leg.'

The labels in the clothes brought from Hambleton Road confirmed this. And there'd been an engagement ring and a matching pendant which, if the stones were real, must have cost a few thousand at the least.

'When did you last see her?' he asked.

'Week last Friday. I bumped into her in the yard. She said ta-ra.'

'Just that?'

'She didn't actually say ta-ra,' said the girl impatiently. 'It were something like, we'd likely not see each other before she went off that weekend, so goodbye.'

'I thought she was just going on a trip. Didn't that sound a bit final to you, as if she didn't think she'd be coming back?'

'Mebbe,' said Shirley Appleyard. 'Or mebbe she just didn't expect to find me here when she came back.'

'Oh? Why's that?'

'Business weren't good. Once this job for you lot's done, there's nowt else on the books. So it could be she reckoned the whole thing would have folded by then.'

'But she had money, didn't she?' prompted Pascoe.

'Oh aye, but not to pour into this sort of thing.' She

gestured at the yard. 'She were generous enough by all accounts with things like art and music, wildlife and restoration funds, you know, all the posh sort of things where you meet the top people. I don't think she'd have been sorry to stop being a builder's wife.'

'Well, she's managed that,' said Pascoe. 'Did she strike you as a moody kind of person: you know, on top of the world sometimes, then down in the dumps a bit later?'

His effort to put the question casually failed completely.

'Drugs, you mean,' said the girl. 'Is that what you're looking for?'

Pascoe thought of reading the Riot Act, of lying through his teeth, then decided that neither of these courses was going to get him anywhere.

'Would it surprise you?' he asked.

'Why should it?' she asked. 'People'll do owt for a bit of pleasure these days. But Mrs Swain, I'd not have said she was more up and down than most, though with her money, she'd be able to afford a steady enough supply for it not to show, wouldn't she?'

It was a reasonable answer. The more he talked to this girl, the more he felt the need for a sharp mental reprimand. On first sight he'd been ready to categorize her as being as lumpy mentally as she looked physically. Now he realized he'd been very wrong on both counts.

He said, 'From what you say, Mrs Swain wouldn't have much to do with the day-to-day running of the business?'

'Nowt at all.'

He went on, 'Might she bump into any of your customers, though?'

'Not in a big room she wouldn't. There were never that many.'

Pascoe laughed out loud and this natural response was far more effective than his earlier hackneyed attempt at charm, for the girl gave him her first smile.

'A Mr Gregory Waterson, for instance?' he went on. 'Do you know if she ever met him?'

'Him who had the studio conversion? Oh yes, she met him.'

'You saw them together?'

'He came here a couple of times about the job. Once neither Mr Swain nor Dad were around, but he met Mrs Swain in the yard and went into the house with her.'

'Oh?'

'Not what you're thinking,' she said. 'Not that I reckon he didn't try his hand.'

'What makes you say that?'

'I'd been roughing out some figures for him and I went to the house myself to give him them and I got the impression he'd been coming on strong and Mrs Swain had told him where to get off.'

'I see. Did you get the impression he'd persist?'

'Oh aye. Thought he were God's gift.'

'But you didn't agree with his estimate?'

She shrugged. 'Funny kind of gift for God to make, I'd say.'

'But a matter of taste perhaps? Would Mrs Swain perhaps be more interested than she let herself show at first?'

'How should I know that?' she asked scornfully.

'Sorry,' repeated Pascoe. 'But as an observer, how would you say things were generally between the Swains?'

Again she shrugged.

'It was a marriage,' she said. 'Anything's possible.'

Pascoe laughed and said, 'That's a touch cynical, isn't it? If you don't believe in the power of true love, I think you've got the wrong book.'

She picked up her discarded *Jane Eyre*.

'You mean it ends happy?' she said. She sounded disappointed.

'Afraid so. You'll need to try men for unhappy endings,' said Pascoe with gentle mockery. 'Try *Tess of the d'Urbervilles*. Or *Anna Karenina*. Now they're really miserable!'

He grinned as he spoke and was rewarded with a second faint smile.

'What's the rest of this building used for?' he asked.

'Down below, you mean? That was the old byre and stables, I think. Now it's used for garages and to store stuff they don't like to leave out in the wet.'

'Is it open? I'd like to take a look.'

'It'll be locked. Dad doesn't trust anybody.'

She picked up a bunch of keys, rose and led the way down the outside stair. She was right. All the doors were padlocked. She stood and watched as Pascoe poked around in a desultory fashion. He had little hope that he was going to find a barrowful of dope out here, and if it were hidden by the thimbleful, it would take a trained dog to sniff it out.

Finished, he walked out into the yard again.

'Same kind of stuff over there?' he asked, looking at the barn on the far side.

'No. That's empty.'

'Better have a glance all the same.'

Again she was right. The stone floor was swept clean. He looked up into the rafters, screwing his eyes up against the darkness. He thought he saw a movement. There were certainly patches of darker darkness against the dull grey of the slates.

'Bats,' said the girl.

'What?'

'Bats. Pipistrelles, I think they call them.'

He took an involuntary step backwards. Dark places he'd never cared much for, even less since his experience down the mine. And the creatures of darkness, in particular bats, made him shudder. Ellie, in whom he detected a definite green shift in recent months, had become a member of a local Bat Preservation Group. Had she opted for whales or wild orchids, he could have gone along with her in passion, perhaps even in person; but while intellectually one hundred per cent in favour of the rights of bats, the thought of actually touching them filled him with horror.

'It's all right. They're hibernating,' said Shirley Appleyard.

Ashamed of being detected in this unmanly behaviour, Pascoe said brusquely, 'Why's this place not used for anything?'

'Don't know. There was some talk of Mrs Swain turning it into an indoor shooting gallery.'

'And what happened?'

'Came to nowt. Mebbe because of the bats. You can't disturb them, you know. Or mebbe Mr Swain didn't like the idea because of his brother.'

'His brother?'

'The one who used to own this place. Tom Swain.'

It rang a faint bell.

'Didn't he . . .?'

'Shot himself a few years back. In here,' said the girl, deadpan.

'In here? Not very lucky with guns, the Swains, are they?'

The girl didn't reply. Pascoe looked around the barn. Bats and a ghost. He couldn't blame Swain for objecting to his wife's proposal.

He said, 'It looks as if someone's got some plan for it now.'

'Because it's been cleared out?' The girl shrugged. 'There was nothing but a load of rusty old farm stuff here. Mr Swain got rid of it a couple of weeks back.'

'So he is planning to use it?'

'Mebbe. I think he were more interested in the money he got for the scrap.'

'Really?' said Pascoe, alert to this hint of financial problems. 'Money a bit short, is it?'

'You'd need to ask Mr Swain or my dad about that,' said the girl.

'Sorry. I'm not going behind their backs, but you did mention the scrap,' he said conciliatorily.

'Yes, I did,' she admitted. 'It were just that it amused me at the time.'

She looked the kind of person who might well treasure up anything which proved a source of amusement.

'What was funny about it?' he asked.

'Just the name of the dealer, that was all. They called him Swindles.'

'Joe Swindles?' said Pascoe.

'That's right. You know him? That figures.'

It was true that the police and Joe Swindles were long acquainted, but the old boy had gone for some years now without overstepping the mark, and in fairness Pascoe said, 'Just socially. There's nothing against him.'

'Too clever, is he?'

Pascoe laughed, then stopped as he was sure he heard a respondent squeaking from up in the rafters.

He said, 'Well, that'll do, I think,' and stepped out into the sunlight.

The girl took this as her dismissal and went back up the stairway to her office without saying anything more.

He watched her, frowning, then went back into the house.

Seymour was on his knees in the kitchen with his head in the electric oven.

'If you're trying to kill yourself,' said Pascoe, 'I'd opt for gas. If not, then pack up. I'll just ring in, then we're on our way to the gun club.'

He dialled the station and got through to Wield.

'Is he in?' he asked.

'Eden Thackeray's turned up to see Swain,' said the Sergeant. 'The Super's taken him upstairs for a chat and a drink.'

'Will he be long?'

'Depends,' said Wield. 'You know he fixed up for Swain to be checked out for drugs? Well, the doctor's been held up on some emergency and the Super won't be wanting to let old Eden at his client before he's been given the once over. Is it anything important?'

'Just a negative on drugs at Moscow,' said Pascoe. 'But the business doesn't look too healthy financially. Send him a note in, will you? How'd you get on?'

Wield gave him a brief account of his interview with Mrs Waterson. As he listened Pascoe flicked through the pages of the wedding album which he'd laid on the table by the phone. Shirley Appleyard had been a little ungenerous. Certainly at the time she was married, Gail Swain had been rather more than all right. He paused at an all-female group photograph by the side of a palm-fringed swimming pool. Even among those tanned and cosseted women she stood out, slim, radiant, her fair hair glowing like a candle flame.

But as he drove away from Moscow Farm a few moments later it was an image of a stocky, unkempt, pale-faced woman reading *Jane Eyre* that he took with him.

Chapter 7

'Philip Swain is an interesting, not to say complex character,' said Eden Thackeray. 'I'm surprised you were not
previously acquainted, Andrew.'

'We were. He's the jobbing builder mucking up our car
park,' said Dalziel.

'I mean socially. As twin luminaries in our great social
galaxy, I would have expected your orbits to cross before
now.'

Dalziel grinned. He enjoyed Thackeray's gentle piss-
taking in much the same way as the solicitor enjoyed his
more gamesome assaults. Superficially everything about
the two men was different, but it was mainly a difference
of style. Beneath his bland exterior, the senior partner of
Messrs Thackeray, Amberson, Mellor and Thackeray was
as sharp, ruthless, and even anarchic as Dalziel himself.

'They've crossed now,' said the fat man. 'And they used
to build gibbets at crossroads. So why's he interesting,
apart from having shot his missus?'

'Andrew, please. A slip of the tongue, I realize, but you
really should be more careful.'

'I'm the most careful bugger you'll meet in a summer
day at Scarborough Fair,' said Dalziel. But he smiled as
he spoke. Information came before provocation. He had
said nothing yet about the content of his own witness
statement. On the other hand, to balance matters, he
hadn't mentioned Waterson's either, nor the latter's
defection.

'Mrs Swain's suicide is part of a long tragic history for
that family,' resumed Thackeray. 'He's a Swain of
Currthwaite, you knew that, of course?'

'I know he lives out there. I thought he'd be just another townie with a daft American wife playing at country living.'

'Not entirely unjust,' admitted Thackeray, holding his glass to the light to admire the crystal facets and also, apparently fortuitously, to point its emptiness. Dalziel groaned satirically and refilled it with the twelve-year-old Islay he'd dug out of his desk on the lawyer's arrival.

'How kind. Yes, Swain is by education and, I suspect, inclination, a townie. But there have been Swains at Currthwaite since Elizabeth's day. Minor country gentry rather than good yeoman stock, I'd say. Indeed, they have usually appeared if not reluctant, certainly rather feckless farmers. But with a great sense of loyalty to the place. They were forever getting into debt, and on many occasions even lost the farm, but somehow they always contrived to get it back. Their saving grace has been that, despite the fact that few of them have shown any talent for safe investment and humdrum business, there is a consistently recurring strain of ingenuity and opportunism which has hitherto pulled them back from the brink of complete disaster.'

'Good con-men, that's what you mean?' said Dalziel.

Thackeray sighed and said, 'What I mean is what I say, Andrew. To continue, Philip is the product of the family's last period of prosperity in the post-war years.'

'Spiv time,' grunted Dalziel. 'Sorry. Go on.'

'His elder brother, Tom, was naturally in line for the farm, and Philip was packed off to college to read business studies. It was a superstitious rather than a sensible choice. Philip's bent was entirely practical and something like engineering would have made much more sense, but I think his father hoped that by laying him on the altar of commerce, he might at last appease Mammon and usher in a long period of prosperity for the Swains.'

'You don't half talk pretty,' said Dalziel, topping up their glasses. 'Is that how you get to charge so much?'

'It helps. Where was I? Oh yes. Philip did all right, nothing spectacular, but family influence helped him to a job locally with Atlas Tayler who you may recall were successfully making the transition from old electrics to new electronics in the 'seventies. He was still playing his promising young executive role there five years later when they got taken over by the American company, Delgado International, who were keen to establish a European base.'

'Delgado. Hey, he called his mother-in-law Mrs Delgado.'

'Perhaps because that's her name, Andrew,' said Thackeray kindly. 'Yes, he married into the family, albeit a cadet branch. He and Gail met when the Americans ferried a group of their new staff out to head office in Los Angeles on a re-orientation course. They fell in love. No doubt the family looked him over, decided there was no harm in adding a bit of family loyalty to the financial ties binding Atlas Tayler to them, and gave their approval. So it was back here after the honeymoon and onward and upward in his executive career. Meanwhile, back at Moscow Farm, his father had died and brother Tom was making a real pig's ear of running things. It was hard to lose money when the EEC were practically paying farmers to grow less, but Tom was the worst kind of Swain.'

'I doubt it,' growled Dalziel.

'For heaven's sake, Andrew, I'm telling you all this so you will understand what a decent and reliable citizen my client is,' snapped Thackeray.

'Oh aye? I thought you were just spinning things out till the bottle was empty,' said Dalziel. 'Also, it doesn't say much for the family lawyer letting all these Swains get so deep in trouble.'

'I'm very conscious of that. But there's a secretive streak about them when it comes to money matters,' said the lawyer, frowning. 'I doubt if even Philip knew just how bad things were with the farm, though I know he'd been putting what funds he could afford at Tom's disposal for some time. But finally it all got too much for the poor man and one day he went into the barn and blew his brains out. That's why even you should realize what a devastating effect this new tragedy will have had upon my client.'

'Aye, it must be a bit rough,' said Dalziel with spurious sympathy. 'So that's how Phil got his hands on Moscow, was it?'

'Yes, but it was an inheritance more troublesome than covetable. Everything that could be mortgaged was, and all the buildings had fallen into a sad state of disrepair. There was no way that Philip's salary could take care of things, but happily his wife had a not inconsiderable *dot* and was sufficiently taken by the notion of family roots to pour out dollars with a liberal hand till Moscow Farm became a place fit for a Californian to live in. I suspect that was the happiest time of their marriage. She got a real kick out of interior decorating, by plastic card of course, while he enjoyed himself even more by planning and helping with the restructuring.'

'What about farming?'

'His practical bent didn't extend to things that mooed or needed planting. But he hung on to the land. A wise move, when you see what has happened since between the village and the town. To this government, a Green Belt is a martial arts qualification needed for survival in the Cabinet. Once the land to the east is all gone, there'll be planning permission for the asking on Moscow's acres to the west, and prices will rocket.'

'Right,' said Dalziel. 'So we've got Philip Swain with a good job, his family home all refurbished, and lots of valuable development land in the foreseeable future. How come he ends up as a small builder with cash-flow problems?'

Thackeray sipped his whisky and wondered why Dalziel was being so blatant. The phone rang on the fat man's desk. He picked it up, listened, said, 'You're sure? Shit. All right, stick him in two. I'll be down shortly.'

'Bad news?'

'Depends how you look at it. So what happened when Delgado decided to back out of Britain?' Dalziel asked.

'You recall that?'

'Aye. Five hundred lost jobs was still making headlines two years ago,' growled Dalziel. 'And wasn't there a lot of flak about a Yankee con-trick?'

'Indeed. Delgado's certainly played their cards very close to the chest. Right up to the announcement of closure, everyone thought they were in fact planning to expand their UK investment instead of relocating it in the cheaper pastures of Spain. There were rumours of a takeover bid for a company in Milton Keynes. Of course it could never be proved that Delgado's started them deliberately, but certainly they were up and away before the unions knew what had hit them.'

'But not Swain?'

'No. Philip took his redundancy money like the rest of them. He had the usual Swain longing to be master of Moscow *and* his own life. Like a good Thatcherite, he decided to create his own small business. He chose building, partly because he believed he'd discovered a constructive talent in himself while putting the farm to rights. And partly because of Arnold Stringer.'

'That's the big gingery chap who's Swain's foreman?'

'Swain's partner,' corrected Thackeray. 'Also his childhood playmate. There have been Stringers in Currthwaite as long as Swains, peasant stock as opposed to gentlemen

89

farmers, of course, and chapel rather than church, but such divisions were never urged upon the young. Indeed, according to local folklore, a Swain cuckoo has from time to time slipped into the Stringer nest. Whatever the truth, the two boys went happily to the village school together. Later of course their paths diverged. Stringer was a farm worker at Moscow at fifteen, decided there was no future in it when he got married at eighteen, took a job on a building site, and eventually set up on his own in a small way. And that's how he stayed. It's clear he wasn't cut out to be one of Mrs T's success stories. He still lives in one of the few Moscow farm cottages still standing and it was natural that when Philip took over he should push the basic re-building work his way. It was equally natural that when Philip started looking for an entrée into the construction business, he should opt for energizing his old schoolmate's firm. Stringer's trade expertise, Swain's social contacts, it was potentially a winning combination.'

'You approved?' said Dalziel.

'I felt there were worse ways for him to invest his lump sum,' said Thackeray carefully. 'He is a Swain, after all, and I was fearful he might just pour his redundancy pay-off down some empty gold mine.'

'And since then?' said Dalziel refilling their glasses.

'Since then, what?'

'Well, this winning combination hasn't exactly been bothering Wimpey's, has it? As far as I can make out, doing our car park and garages is the biggest job they've ever had. And like I say, my lad, Pascoe, reckons there's not a lot of money in the bank. Though likely things'll be different now his missus has been sent off?'

'Andrew,' said the lawyer warningly.

'Just thinking aloud,' said Dalziel. 'Another thing strikes me. Situated like he was, married into the family and all, he must have been a right useless wanker for Delgado's to turn him off like a factory hand.'

'That is where you're wrong,' said Thackeray. 'I happen to know that Swain was offered a top executive post with an excellent salary at head office in Los Angeles.'

'But he couldn't bear to leave sunny Currthwaite, is that it?'

'Partly, yes,' said the lawyer seriously. 'But there was something else which may help you understand the quality of the man. Because they did not trust his native loyalties, Philip was not made privy to Delgado's plans. When news of the closure came out, he was enraged.'

'Was he now? Aye, he struck me as a good actor too.'

'This was no act, believe me,' urged Thackeray. 'You ask the unions involved. There's not one of them will hear a bad word against Swain.'

'So you're telling me Swain jacked in his sinecure with Delgado's as an act of solidarity with his downtrodden comrades?' said Dalziel.

'Andrew, I'm not telling you anything,' said Thackeray, suddenly aware how far he'd let himself be led in discussing his client's background. 'I'm merely passing the time of day till whatever obstacle lies in the way of my immediate interview with my client is removed. With another kind of officer I might by now have grown suspicious. But if one member of the Gentlemen's Club cannot trust another, what is the world coming to? Incidentally, talking of the Gents, I gather you have not yet taken up your allocation of Ball tickets, so I have brought them along. They are in great demand so any you do not want for your own guests will be easily disposable. It's twenty-five pounds the double ticket, so that will be two hundred and fifty pounds.'

'Christ,' said Dalziel. 'When we were lads, you could go

to a good hop, with a guaranteed jump after, if it weren't raining, all for one and six. *And* she paid for her own.'

'That was a long time ago, long enough for the present good cause to seem not unattractive, perhaps. Think of it as an investment.'

Dalziel glared at him balefully as he wrote a cheque. The Gents were sponsoring the Mayor's Spring Charity Ball which this year was in aid of the local Hospice Appeal fund. He tossed the cheque over the table and said, 'I'll just go and see what's holding things up.'

'Take your time,' said Thackeray, reaching for the Islay.

Dalziel went down to No. 2 interview room feeling irritated. Things weren't going smoothly. First of all the police doctor's late arrival had necessitated keeping Thackeray occupied, a tactic which had so far cost him two hundred and fifty pounds and a deal of malt. Then had come Pascoe's message that Moscow Farm was clean. And finally he'd just been told on the phone that the doctor could find no signs of addiction, physical or psychological, on Swain.

The builder was looking weary but still in control. Dalziel, aware of Thackeray's imminence, came straight to the point.

'How long had your wife been a drug addict, Mr Swain?'

Swain made no effort at shock or indignation but shook his head and said, 'So this is what this has all been about?'

'You knew about her habit, then?'

'She was my wife, for God's sake. How couldn't I know? All right, she had a problem but she'd kicked it.'

'That's not what the pathologist says.'

'You mean she was snorting again? No, I didn't know.'

'Snorting? No, lad, not snorting. She'd got more perforations than a sheet of stamps,' exaggerated Dalziel.

His reaction was startling. He stared at Dalziel incredulously and cried, 'You what? Injecting, you mean? Oh Christ! The bastard!'

And as he spoke these words he smashed his left fist hard into his right palm, you could see the knuckle prints. This was genuine beyond histrionics. But who was he thumping? wondered Dalziel.

'This bastard, who is he?' he asked gently. 'Do you mean Waterson?'

'What? No. Of course not. He's not the type. There's no way it could be him.' He didn't sound very convincing.

'Supplying the drugs, you mean?'

'Yes. That's the bastard I want.'

'Oh aye? Bit late for revenge, isn't it? I mean, she's snuffed it now, with a bit of help from her friends.'

Swain looked at him with real hatred.

'Where's my lawyer?' he demanded. 'Why haven't I seen my lawyer?'

'Because last night you didn't want to disturb his beauty sleep,' said Dalziel. 'Who was your wife's doctor, Mr Swain? Perhaps he knows more about her problems than you seem to.'

Swain didn't rise to this bait but said, 'Dr Herbert, same as me. But she never went near him. He'd have said. Nothing unprofessional, but we've known each other a long time.'

'Nod and a wink, eh?' said Dalziel, nodding and winking most grotesquely. 'But she must have seen someone when she broke her leg.'

'Sorry. Can't help you,' said Swain.

'You mean your wife breaks her leg and you don't know who's treating her? Christ, it's a wonder she didn't blow your head off!'

Swain took a deep breath.

'I don't have to stand this, Dalziel,' he said quietly. 'I realize if you get me to take a swing at you, then you'd really have something to hit me with. Well, I won't give you that satisfaction. I want to see my lawyer. Now!'

Dalziel said, 'Your wife's dead, Mr Swain. Why should I need owt else to hit you with? I'll get Mr Thackeray now. I reckon you need him.'

At the door he paused and said, 'You never did finish telling me about that doctor . . .'

Swain sighed and said, 'She had a skiing accident in Vermont. I wasn't there. But I'm sure, being Americans, there'll be records. If it's important.'

'Important?' said Dalziel. 'Can't imagine where you got that idea.'

He went back to his room. Thackeray rose as he entered.

'He's all yours,' said Dalziel. 'Might be a bit upset. We've just been talking about his wife's drug habit.'

If he'd expected any shock/horror response from the lawyer, he was disappointed.

Thackeray sighed and said, 'Andrew, I know how much your job means to you, but I hope you will not let it obscure your basic humanitarianism. No one expects you to wear kid gloves, but it would help us all if during the course of your investigation you remembered that my client has suffered a deep and grievous loss.'

Dalziel scratched his thigh, picked up the malt whisky bottle, held it up to the light.

'Looks like he's not the only one,' he said.

Chapter 8

The Rangemaster at the Mid-Yorks Gun Club was properly macho, his shag of curly black hair echoed in designer stubble along the jaw and in designer thatch at the open neck of his lumberjack's shirt. Below, he tapered to narrow hips and a pair of faded jeans so unambiguously tight, it was clear he was carrying no concealed weapons. He affected a mid-Atlantic baritone which occasionally let him down, or rather up, into a Geordie squeak. His name was Mitchell but he invited them to join everyone in calling him Mitch.

'Tell me, Mr Mitchell,' said Pascoe, 'is Rangemaster a usual title for someone in your position?'

'Don't know that it is,' he answered. 'Sounds good though, don't it?'

'Do it? Perhaps you could give us a job description?'

His fears that he might have got hold of some fantasizing handyman were allayed as Mitchell gave him an outline of the club's set-up and his role in it. He was in fact the resident steward, coach and adviser on all matters pertaining to arms, qualified by a five-year stint in the Army (nudges and winks towards the SAS) followed by a one-year poly management course. He had a half share in the club, the other half belonging to a local businessman who was a shooting enthusiast. By the time he'd finished talking, it was clear that perhaps eighty per cent of his self-presentation was a sales ploy, which left twenty per cent as self-image.

But image and accent vanished together when told of Gail Swain's death.

'Oh no. Man, that's really terrible,' he said, sitting down. 'She were a real canny lass. Gail dead! I canna believe it.'

'It's true, I'm afraid,' said Pascoe.

'How'd it happen? What was it? An accident?'

'It seems possible,' he said carefully. 'What I'm here about is her guns. She kept them here, I believe.'

'Oh yes. All the time. Well, nearly. There might have been an odd time when she took one home, if she'd been away at a competition, say. But why're you interested . . . it wasn't a shooting accident, was it?'

'I'm afraid a gun *was* involved,' said Pascoe. 'What weapons did she own?'

'She had a Beretta .25, a Hammerli match target pistol, a Colt Python and a Harrington and Richardson Sidekick,' he replied without hesitation.

'Quite an armoury. And where would these be kept?'

For answer Mitchell took them through into another room and pointed at a metal door.

'You won't find anything like that outside a bank,' he said proudly. 'No one gets in here, I tell you.'

He unlocked the door to reveal a range of padlocked gun cabinets.

'I'm glad to hear it,' said Pascoe, who privately saw no reason why gun enthusiasts shouldn't try out both their accuracy and their fantasies with spring-loaded weapons that fired ping-pong balls. 'And how do the members get hold of their weapons?'

'They tell me what they want and I fetch them out,' said Mitchell.

'How often did Mrs Swain use the club?'

'She used to be a real regular but not so much lately.'

'And Mr Swain?'

'He wasn't a member, but he sometimes came to functions with his wife. He knew a lot of people, of course. The Swains are an old local family.'

'That matters?'

'We're very democratic, but the old country families who've been used to guns from early on are our founder members, so to speak. I'd say it mattered to Gail, being a Swain.'

'Did she have any special friends?'

'Not in the club. She was a bit of a loner, really. I know she liked to do the right things for someone in her position, sit on committees, that sort of thing, but maybe she didn't feel certain enough how things worked to risk getting too

96

close to anyone. It can't be easy being a rich Yank round here.'

There was no trace of irony in his voice.

'But her husband didn't feel it incumbent on him to join?'

'Oh no. He's one on his own too. But there have been Swains in the club, I mean real Swains. His brother Tom . . . but you'll know about him.'

Pascoe nodded with the air of a man who knows everything. Seymour, he noted approvingly, had vanished. His amiable smile beneath a shock of unruly red hair was a delicate picklock of confidences, especially female. If there was tittle to be tattled, Seymour was your man.

He said, 'And which of Mrs Swain's weapons are still here?'

Mitchell said, 'None. She took them all away last time I saw her.'

'And you let her?' said Pascoe. 'You didn't express surprise? You said yourself the only time she ever took a weapon home was when she was shooting away in a competition. How often would that be?'

'Didn't apply any longer in Gail's case,' said Mitchell. 'She hadn't done any competition shooting in nearly two years. But obviously she wanted them this time because she was going home. Her mother's ill.'

'She must have made other visits to the States. Long visits. Last year, for instance,' said Pascoe, recollecting Swain's statement. 'Didn't her father die?'

'Yes. She was away for a couple of months.'

'And did she take any of her guns then?'

'No. Perhaps this time she wanted to do some shooting over there. Not much opportunity at a funeral, is there? OK, she could easily get replacements in the States. It's like buying bars of chocolate over there. But you get into a special relationship with your own pieces. And of course the Hammerli was specially tailored to her hand.'

Pascoe had a feeling that Mitchell could have told him more, but whether it would have been pertinent, whether indeed it would have been factual or merely idle gossip, he couldn't guess. At the moment a too aggressive interrogation would merely serve to feed that gossip.

'One more question,' said Pascoe. 'If Mrs Swain wanted to carry one of her weapons around with her – because she felt in need of personal protection, say – which would she be most likely to have chosen?'

'The Beretta probably, or the Sidekick,' Mitchell answered promptly.

'Why?'

'Well, she wouldn't choose the Python, not unless she was planning to blow somebody away. It's big and it's heavy and it takes the .357 Magnum cartridge which is a danger to people in the next room if you happen to miss. The Hammerli on the other hand is a specialized weapon, OK for punching holes in a target but not much else. It takes one .22 rimfire cartridge at a time and it's got a hair trigger, not the kind of thing you carry in your pocket. Why do you ask?'

'The curiosity of an idle mind,' smiled Pascoe.

He took a last look at the array of dully gleaming guns in their padlocked cabinets.

'See anything you fancy?' inquired Mitchell. 'We've always room for law officers at the MYGC.'

'I was just wondering how many rifles make a good ploughshare,' said Pascoe. And went in search of Seymour.

He found the redhead in conclave with a wizened woman of indeterminate years. The wide amiable smile had vanished but not before it had been all too effective if

Pascoe read truly the desperate grimace which greeted his appearance.

With difficulty breaking free from a grip like the mummy's hand, Seymour stood up, took a brief farewell, and followed his chief out to the car park.

'Bernadette would not like it,' said Pascoe judiciously.

'Bernadette wouldn't believe it,' said Seymour. 'I'm not sure I do.'

'What did she say to you?'

'I said, why was the place so empty. I expected to hear people banging away all over the shop. And she said they didn't open till evenings on a Tuesday, but as for banging away, we could soon alter that if I liked . . .'

'Seymour, you'll die of an over-active double entendre one of these days,' sighed Pascoe. 'But I'm not interested in your foreplay. I meant, what did she say that might interest us?'

'Her name's Mrs Martin. Babs to her friends. She's in charge of the kitchen,' said Seymour. 'There's a hatch from the kitchen into the members' lounge. I doubt if there's much said in there that she doesn't hear.'

They got into Pascoe's car. He started the engine and pointed it back towards the centre of town.

'And?' he said.

'Mrs Swain was always around till about eighteen months ago. Since then she's dropped out of all team and social events and when she did come, it was purely to fire off a few rounds and usually at the quietest time of the day.'

'Damn. Mitchell said she'd dropped out of the competition team and I forgot to ask him why,' said Pascoe, annoyed.

'No need to ask Mitchell when you've got Babs,' said Seymour. 'It seems that after Swain started his own building firm, he was so keen to make a go of it, he wasn't averse to canvassing old chums for jobs. Meaning anything from grouting a gazebo to getting them to use their influence to swing a small council contract his way. Babs says from what she overheard it was the general opinion that Gail Swain was highly embarrassed by this. Before, she'd come across as the high-powered Californian jet-setter injecting a bit of glam into a staid old Yorkshire family. Now she was just the wife of a small builder pestering his mates for hand-outs.'

'And did his mates mind?'

'From what Babs says, they rather admired Swain for his cheek. As for his wife, they were mainly amused to see her taken down a peg. Evidently she was a better shot than most of them and didn't mind letting them know.'

'So she decided to duck out rather than brazen it out? Well, well. I think we should offer your friend Babs a job in CID!'

They drove on in silence for a while.

'Sir,' said Seymour. 'Does any of this really matter? I mean, we know what happened, more or less. And we know how it happened, more or less.'

'The little more, and how much it is,' said Pascoe. 'The little less, and what worlds away.'

'Pardon?' said Seymour, thinking he sometimes preferred Dalziel's brutal directness to Pascoe's gentle obliquities. And when they had the Super's preferred guilty candidate banged up in the cells, that was quite enough to satisfy an ambitious young constable who could see no promotion points in proving Dalziel wrong.

But all that changed when they reached the station.

As they pulled into the car park, a metallic blue BMW pulled out. Both cars halted to give the other right of way and in the front seat of the BMW Pascoe recognized Eden Thackeray driving and by his side Philip Swain.

Thackeray waved, both in recognition and thanks, then drove on.

'Christ,' said Seymour, twisting in his seat. 'That was Swain. He's getting away!'

'Aided and abetted by one of the town's leading lawyers?' said Pascoe. 'Or do you think Swain has a gun made out of moulded bread dough and stained with boot blacking pressed into his side? In which case, Dennis, which would you prefer – to undertake the high speed car chase or to rush inside and untie Mr Dalziel?'

'My mother used to say something sarcastic about sarcasm,' muttered Seymour.

'Mine too,' laughed Pascoe. 'So let's both go in and untie the Super, shall we?'

Part Three

GOD: Of all the mights I have made most next after me,
        I make thee as master and mirror of my might;
        I bield thee here bainly, in bliss for to be,
        I name thee for Lucifer, as bearer of light.

The York Cycle: 'The Creation'

Dear Mr Dalziel,

So I've changed my mind again! There's so much in the world I'd like to change but my mind's the only bit I can get at. I mean I've changed my mind about writing to you, not about killing myself. That's the only sure thing in my life. If I didn't have that to look forward to, I think I'd just curl up and die. (Joke.)

You must be thinking I'm really unstable, chopping and changing like this. The trouble is things have been happening fast, things to stretch me out, and I got to thinking: I don't need to put up with this; why not do it now? I came very close, believe me. But I want it to be something properly planned, a choice, not a whim.

Afterwards, though, I found myself desperate to talk to someone. I came close several times. A friendly word, a sympathetic smile, and I was ready to confide all! But in my mind, I kept on hearing your voice calling my name, which of course you don't know, and I knew I had to get back to you. You see, others would want to stop me, but all you'll be interested in is whether I'm proposing to commit a crime. Well, I'm not. It used to be a crime, but not any more. So you've got no reason to waste public money in using your famous expertise to find me. With you I'm quite safe. It's like having my personal confessor. Except I don't want absolution, just an unshockable ear! Incidentally, as far as I know, no saint has bagged this day so I dedicate it to you, though you may need to pull off a miracle to satisfy the powers that be that you've earned it!

Here endeth today's confession.

Chapter 1

'Peter, for God's sake!' gasped Ellie Pascoe as they ran their third amber. 'Are you trying to kill us?'

'We're late,' said Pascoe.

'For picking up Fat Andy? What's to hurry? And I don't see why you said you'd pick him up anyway.'

'Three reasons. One: we promised Chung we'd get him there and this guarantees it.'

'Why are you so concerned about pleasing Chung when it's Andy who's your chum?' she inquired with one of those elenctic U-turns that so often left Pascoe facing the wrong way.

'Come on! You were in on the arm-twisting!' he accused.

'That was before I knew it was going to cost us fifty quid,' said Ellie. 'Let the sod get a taxi with his rake-off!'

Pascoe, uncomfortable in his role of Judas goat leading Dalziel towards Godhead, had been easy meat when the Fat Man had started touting his tickets to the Mayor's Ball. 'It's for a good cause,' he'd protested to Ellie. 'It's conspicuous charity,' she'd retorted. 'If all those fascist ego-trippers *just* gave the ticket money to the Hospice Fund, plus what they'll probably spend on new outfits, booze, getting there, etc., we could all have two beds to die in!'

'Second reason,' said Pascoe. 'You've never actually penetrated the monster's lair. Now's your chance!'

When Dalziel returned hospitality, he took you to a pub

or a restaurant. Ellie could not deny her often expressed curiosity about his unimaginable home life.

'All right,' she said. 'That's two. So let's hear the third.'

'If two are good enough, that's a majority,' he said evasively.

'Don't be smart, Peter. It doesn't sit right on a Chief Inspector. What's three?'

'In a minute. We're almost there.'

Suddenly he gave a loud double blast on his horn, causing Ellie to jump.

'What was that for?' she demanded.

'Thought I saw a cat,' he said vaguely, turning left, then left again almost immediately.

'Are we lost?'

'No. Here it is.' He pulled up and got out, looking at his watch.

'We've plenty of time,' said Ellie. 'Is this really it? I was expecting something a little more gothic.'

'You really ought to watch more old movies. When he's abroad, all he needs is a coffin full of earth from his native Transylvania.'

Dalziel flung open the door at the first ring of the bell. He was immaculate in white shirt, red and green striped tie, and a suit of superb cut in a high quality charcoal grey worsted. For an unhappy moment Pascoe thought that he was ready for an immediate departure, then he noticed he was barefooted.

'Ellie, what fettle?' he said heartily. 'It's been a long time.'

'Hello, Andy,' she replied. 'You're looking very smart.'

'The suit, you mean? Man with a good suit can go anywhere, isn't that what they say? Come away in. Take your coat off, Ellie, so you'll feel the benefit. By God, you don't look so bad yourself. Just wait till I get you up at the Mayor's Ball. We'll show these young 'uns a thing or two!'

Pascoe blew his nose violently in a vain effort to smother his snort of laughter at this coetaneous assumption. Ellie glared at him and Dalziel said, 'Help yourselves to booze. I'll not be long.'

The room they were left in was small and square and contained a three-piece suite in uncut moquette; a fourteen-inch television; a glass-fronted cabinet with a Queen Anne style tea service; a Victorian commode; a marble fireplace polished to look like plastic; a mantel bearing a stopped carriage clock, two brass candlesticks, three brass monkeys, and a chipped ashtray inscribed *A Present from Bridlington*; above the fireplace hung a round mirror in need of resilvering which interrupted the flight of three china ducks across a sky-blue wallpaper trellissed with pink dog-roses.

'It's like a BBC set for a 'fifties play,' said Ellie, running a finger delicately along the mantel. It came up dustless.

'He probably has a woman who comes in and does,' said Pascoe.

'Just like you, eh? Where's this booze he told us to help ourselves to?'

Pascoe opened the commode. It was packed full of glasses and bottles, all whisky, some single malts, some blended. He poured from one picked at random and handed a glass to Ellie. Then he glanced at his watch again.

'Peter, settle down. It's an informal do, it doesn't matter what time we get there within reason.'

'Lad getting impatient, is he?' said Dalziel, coming into the room. 'He's quite right, though. When the booze is free, don't be backward about coming forward.'

'All right if you're not driving,' said Pascoe. 'In fact, start as I mean to go on, could you put a spot of water in this, sir?'

He handed his glass to Dalziel, who wore the expression

of a priest asked by a communicant for a little salt on his wafer. Then, shaking his head sadly, he left the room.

'Dilution does not affect blood alcohol level,' Ellie began to lecture, but her audience was in the process of following his host out of the room.

'Come to make sure I drown it?' growled Dalziel at the kitchen sink.

'Just a drop,' said Pascoe placatingly. 'So this is where you were that night?'

'What? Oh aye.'

'And you were in the dark?' Pascoe flicked the light switch up and down a couple of times, leaving it off.

'That's right.'

'You never said what you were doing. I mean, do you spend a lot of time just standing here in the dark?'

'I do what I bloody well like in my own house.'

'Yes, of course. My God. What's that?' exclaimed Pascoe.

In the first floor of the house immediately behind a light had come on in a room with the curtains open. A man stood before the open window, brandishing something in his right hand.

'Bloody hell!' said Dalziel. 'What the fuck's going on?'

Pascoe opened the kitchen door and both men pressed out into the yard. A second man appeared. There seemed to be a brief struggle and he was pushed away.

'Come on,' said Dalziel, setting off down the yard. Distantly Pascoe heard a muffled bang and he went after the fat man, cursing as he hit obstacles that Dalziel seemed able to plough through.

Out of the gate, across the alley, into the garden of the house on Hambleton Road; the back door was unlocked; through the kitchen, up the stairs; Pascoe's leg was aching badly and it was all he could do to keep up, but he was close behind as the Super burst into the bedroom.

A man in a dark blue blazer with a starting pistol in his hand stood by the window. Another man in a black roll-neck sweater crouched by the wall. And on the bed, imperturbable as ever, sat Sergeant Wield.

Dalziel spun round to face Pascoe.

'What's this, lad?' he said softly. 'Games evening, is it?'

Pascoe smiled wanly. In the five days since Swain's release, nothing had happened. Dalziel was unrelenting in his belief that Swain was involved in his wife's death far beyond the admission of moral responsibility made in his statement. While not denying a strong intuitive antipathy for the man, he claimed his conviction was based firmly on the evidence of his own eyes. The fact that Waterson's statement in so far as it differed from Swain's tended to place even less blame at his door didn't impress Dalziel in the least. Give him ten minutes with Waterson, he said, and he'd soon alter that. But, perhaps fortunately, Waterson had managed to disappear without trace, and the daily sight of Swain supervising the car park extension was clearly such an irritant that Pascoe had begun to fear his superior might say or do something more than normally outrageous.

Thus it had seemed a good idea to see if he could provoke bit of self-doubt in the fat man by staging this 'reconstruction'.

Now all at once it didn't seem like such a good idea after all.

'Just a bit of reconstruction, sir, to get timings right,' he said brightly.

'Reconstruction? Then you ought to do it properly. I didn't see any tart flashing her tits in the moonlight.'

'No. Sorry, sir. Short on tarts. But in other respects, how was it?'

Dalziel looked at him with speculation edging anger out

111

of his eyes. Then he let his gaze drift from the man with the gun to the man by the wall.

'You want me to say that Constable Clark there with the gun was the man I saw first, don't you? But I don't think he was. I think it was the other way round, it was Billings I saw first and they've switched the gun. Right?'

'Sorry, sir. But no, it was Clark.'

'But it was me you saw with him, not Billings,' said Wield.

Dalziel stared at the sergeant, who was wearing a dark grey leather bomber jacket.

'And it wasn't a gun Clark was carrying but this.'

Pascoe picked up a pipe from the bed.

'Clever,' said Dalziel. 'But neither Swain nor Waterson smoke pipes, do they? And I still heard the gun go off *after* I saw Swain holding it.'

Pascoe thought: This is one step forward, two back! He said, 'Like tonight?'

'Aye, the same sequence.'

'Yes, sir. Only they fired the starting pistol *before* Clark appeared at the window. The bang we heard afterwards was Dennis Seymour with a paper bag in the garden shed.'

There was a long and dreadful silence.

'All right, you buggers,' said Dalziel finally. 'So you reckon you've proved I'm as unreliable as any other witness, eh? Well, prove away, but I know what I know. This was your idea, was it, Peter? I always had you down as clever but I never had you down as unkind. No need to make a fool of people when all you've got to do is ask.'

Oh Christ, thought Pascoe. Vicious anger he'd been prepared for but not pained reproach.

He said, 'I'm sorry, sir, but I thought the element of surprise . . .'

'Oh, it's a surprise right enough, Peter. I'll remember

you like surprises. And I'll tell you another thing you got wrong.'

He swung to face Wield.

'That tart on the bed even with her face shot off was a bloody sight prettier than *him*!'

He left, banging the door behind him.

Wield looked at Pascoe, then began to smile.

'Thought we'd really upset him there,' he said.

'Me, too,' said Pascoe. 'But I'll tell you what. I'm not going to stand near the edge of any station platforms for a bit!'

By the time they got to the Kemble, Dalziel's good humour was almost completely restored by Ellie's sympathetic hearing of 'the daft tricks that clever bugger she'd married had been up to'. But the truce was rudely shattered when they entered the theatre foyer and the first person they saw was Philip Swain.

'What's this? Have you got me here for more games, Peter?' snarled Dalziel, stopping dead.

Pascoe, with cause enough for guilt at entrapping the fat man, could only stutter a most unconvincing denial which Dalziel brushed aside as he advanced towards Swain and demanded, 'What the hell are you doing here?'

Swain, who had paused at the cloakroom to remove an elegant overcoat, lost none of his composure.

'Superintendent, good evening,' he said. 'What am I doing here? My wife was something of a patron of the drama and I feel I owe it to her memory to keep up that support. More to the point, what are *you* doing here? I shouldn't have thought it was your scene.'

He let his gaze drift across a poster advertising *Hedda Gabler*, which had just finished, to one advertising a post-London one-woman show based on Virginia Woolf which was opening next day, then back to Dalziel.

'Oh, I like a bit of good acting as well as the next man,' said Dalziel.

'What on earth is all this about?' Ellie whispered in Pascoe's ear.

'That's this guy Swain Dalziel's so het up about.'

'Oh, Peter, you *didn't* arrange for him to be here, did you?' she said in a tone of indignation which, considering the conspiracy she and Chung had embroiled him in, took Pascoe's breath away.

Swain moved away up the stairs to the bar area where the party was being held and the Pascoes joined Dalziel to hand their topcoats in. He glowered at Pascoe and said, 'Is that it for the evening, lad? Or is Desperate Dan waiting up there to tell me I've been busted back to the beat?'

'Ha-ha,' laughed Pascoe inanely. Ellie dug her elbow in his ribs and led Dalziel forward to where at the head of the stairway Chung was receiving her guests.

'Ellie, darling, glad you could come. And Pete, honey, you too. And who is this? Is this he, the one, the only? O brave new world that has such creatures in it!'

'How do, missus,' said Dalziel. 'By God, you're a big 'un!'

'I love him already,' said Chung. 'Andy, may I call you Andy? You haven't got a drink. There's plonk for the herd, but you don't look like a plonk man. Won't you join me at the bar?'

'Depends on the price of admission,' said Dalziel, heavily jocular.

'Only your soul,' she said. 'But you get to drink Highland Park. Incidentally they've got spirit glasses like eggcups here. Can you make do with a half-pint tumbler?'

'I can mebbe force myself,' said Dalziel.

'Putty in her hands,' said Ellie as Dalziel was led away.

'She'll need big hands, that's a lot of putty,' said Pascoe.

'She seems to have been well briefed, though. I wonder who her mole can be?'

Ellie said defensively, 'It's common knowledge he likes his Highland Park.'

'Try telling that to the judge! I notice it doesn't seem to be common knowledge that I too would not object to a spot of the Highland Park.'

'Better stick to the Highland Spring,' Ellie advised. 'Remember, it's your turn to drive home. That fellow Swain certainly seems to know everybody.'

Pascoe followed her gaze. Swain was talking very much at home with a group among whom Pascoe recognized the President of the Chamber of Commerce, the Council Leader, and their wives.

'Old family,' he said, echoing the awful Mitch.

'Do *you* think he killed his wife?' asked Ellie.

'There's no hard evidence,' said Pascoe. 'In fact no evidence at all except what Andy says he saw.'

'Which you were trying to explode earlier? Well, I'd say he looks to me the type who might well have killed his wife, but he's quite dishy in a dangerous kind of way. Poor chap, I feel quite sorry for him.'

Pascoe sighed and said mildly, 'I should have thought you might have targeted your sorrow on the wife.'

'Oh, her. I think I remember her vaguely now I come to think of it. She must have been the one who came to a couple of Arts Committees. American. Pushy. Capitalist. Neurotic. Always bound for a bad end.'

The Resistance always saved its most unremitting hate for collaborators, Pascoe reminded himself.

He said, 'I still don't see why you feel sorry for him.'

'Well, whether he killed her or not, he's here not because he wants to be, but to brazen it out, isn't he? Perhaps he even got word Fat Andy might be here. Either way, he's jumping from a great height on all the nasty rumours that must be running around. But he can't be enjoying it.'

The trouble with Ellie was that there was always a mad logic behind her apparently most irrational assertions.

Pascoe spent the next half-hour mingling, but finally his leg began to ache and he made the fatal error of seeking support and respite in a corner. Within two minutes he found himself trapped there by two of the most boring men he'd ever met. One was Professor Unstone, an opinionated mediaevalist who used his bloated belly to ram home arguments; the other was Canon Horncastle, pale, bespectacled, his flesh honed almost to the bone by sanctity, but no less assertive in debate. Pascoe, feeling he could contribute little to their discussion of the social significance of the Mysteries, twice attempted exodus and was thwarted first by the mediaeval belly then by the clerical elbow. Their only point of accord seemed to occur whenever they glanced towards the bar where the granite of Dalziel's and the gold of Chung's foreheads still formed an excluding arch over the Highland Park. Then, quite clearly across the disputants' features he saw written in letters of fire and letters of ice the same emotion – resentment.

'I thought Chung would be making a speech,' he managed to slip into one of these pregnant pauses.

'I dare say she will, once her attention ceases to be so rudely monopolized,' said the Canon sharply.

'Who is that creature she's talking to, anyway?' asked the Professor. 'I didn't know they featured Sumo wrestling at the Kemble.'

This was a bit rich coming from the only man in the room who could have offered Dalziel the best of three falls.

'That,' said Pascoe, 'is Superintendent Andrew Dalziel,

my boss, who will be glad to know that academic objectivity and Christian charity are still alive and well in the world. Excuse me.'

The belly and the elbows parted like the Red Sea and he moved away to join Ellie who was deep in conversation with a middle-aged, somewhat drab-looking woman in a tweed suit and sensible shoes.

'Hello,' said Ellie. 'Enjoying yourself?'

'I've just been squeezed between the two dullest men imaginable,' he said. 'And I'm much in need of light relief.'

'Yes, we noticed you in the corner,' said Ellie rather too brightly. 'Dorothy, this is my husband, Peter. Peter, this is Dorothy Horncastle.'

'Hello,' said Pascoe, not registering for a second. But Ellie left no doubt.

'Canon Horncastle's wife,' she said. 'Excuse me. I really must have a word with Councillor Wood about the coffee machine at the Unemployed Centre.'

It may have been intended as a tactful removal of her witness to Pascoe's embarrassment but all he felt was deserted.

'What I meant was not being into the mediaeval period myself. I couldn't really follow the ins and outs of a highly specialized discussion though I've no doubt that of itself . . .'

He stuttered to a stop under Dorothy Horncastle's gaze. It wasn't, he thought, a sophisticated coolness underpinned by amusement at his embarrassment, but a genuine disinterest in his slighting of her husband.

'You're a policeman, I gather,' she said.

'Yes. CID.'

'One of Mr Dalziel's men?'

'That's right. You know the Superintendent?'

'Only by reputation,' she said. 'Is he an old friend of Miss Chung's?'

'No, though you'd think so, wouldn't you?' smiled Pascoe, looking to where the tête-à-tête was just being broken up by the irrepressible assault of the Press in the form of Sammy Ruddlesdin of the *Evening Post*.

'He has the reputation of being a man of surprising insight,' said Dorothy Horncastle.

'Does he? I mean, yes, I suppose he does. Would you like to meet him?'

She considered, then smiled as if at some inner joke.

'Perhaps later,' she said.

Chung had left Dalziel to Ruddlesdin and was making her way towards them. She didn't stop, however, but said in passing, 'Hi, Dorothy. Pete,' and gave him a long-lashed wink and an almost imperceptible thumbs-up, before joining the mediaeval disputants. Unstone became a quivering jelly of delight, bowing over her hand to plant a reechy kiss. Even the gelid Canon, though making no attempt at a physical salute, thawed visibly in the solar energy of Chung's presence. Pascoe realized that Mrs Horncastle was watching the scene with great intensity. She could hardly be experiencing jealousy, could she?

He said, 'Well, Chung seems to have stopped them arguing, which is more than I could.'

'He thinks he's God,' she said.

'I'm sorry?'

'My husband thinks he's God.'

Pascoe re-examined the man in the light of this suggestion. He had to admit that, though on short acquaintance he had characterized the Canon as prissy, pratty, and priggish, he had stopped well short of paranoid.

'Is there any particular way in which he puts this belief to the test?' he inquired. 'I mean, miracles, levitation, that sort of thing?'

118

'What?' Suddenly the woman smiled away a decade. 'Oh no. I don't mean he is mentally deluded, Mr Pascoe. He simply believes that Miss Chung is going to ask him to be God in the Mysteries.'

'That's a relief,' said Pascoe, returning her smile. 'Though I fear he may prove to be deluded after all.'

It was a slip of the tongue he couldn't even blame on booze and she was on to it in a trice.

'Why do you say that? Has she got someone else for the part?'

'I don't know,' hedged Pascoe. 'I just heard a rumour she had someone else in mind.'

'Who?'

Certainly no word passed Pascoe's lips and he would have sworn that his face remained a blank, but somehow this surprisingly acute lady read his secret there, for suddenly she said, 'Mr Dalziel? You mean Mr Dalziel, don't you? Why, he's just perfect!' And let out a peal of such joyous laughter that her husband turned to glower at her as though she'd started singing a drunken ditty.

Chung seized the moment to detach herself from the sacred and profane pair and head back to the bar, on to which willing hands hoisted her when she requested quite unnecessary assistance.

She didn't need to call for quiet. Her seventy-five inches of perfectly proportioned beauty would have stopped people looking at the Boy David.

'No long speech,' she said. 'I've got myself a team of doers, not debaters, and because of your efforts, every obstacle has been overcome, and now it's all systems go and I can promise you that in just over three months' time, this city is going to see the greatest dramatic event mounted here for nigh on four centuries!'

Everyone applauded enthusiastically. Pascoe guessed that a large majority of those present had done even less than himself to further the project. But Chung had the power to make everyone feel good.

'The main casting is practically complete,' she went on. 'But I'm not going to publish this just yet. These aren't professional actors but private people with their own lives to pursue. I want to work with them individually for a while before introducing them to the media. As well as their lines, perhaps I can teach them a few survival techniques!

'One thing that has changed is the performance site. The Council generously offered us Charter Park for the duration, but I didn't feel good about taking over the city's largest and most popular green space, particularly during a holiday week. Then I got an offer I couldn't refuse because it was a suggestion of sheer genius. The man who made it won't thank me for revealing his name. In his line of work, doing good by stealth is considered the virtue, but I'm afraid he's going to find, now he's got mixed up with show business folk, that it's hiding your light that's considered the sin. So put your hands together for the man who not only spotted that the best site for our performances dramatically, historically, and atmospherically, was the ruins of St Bega's Abbey in the lee of our great cathedral, but also got us permission to use it. Canon Eustace Horncastle!'

The Canon looked genuinely distressed as his fellow guests began to applaud. Pascoe noticed his wife did not join in but her defection seemed more than compensated for by a sudden swell of noise from the entrance to the bar. It took a second or two to register that this after all was not a spontaneous overflow of applause. A man and two women had entered the bar. One of the women was hidden behind a placard on which was printed THOU SHALT NOT TAKE THE NAME OF THE LORD THY GOD IN VAIN. The other two intruders were chanting,

'Anti-Christ! Sabbath-breakers!' more or less in unison, with a curious mixture of religious fervour and English embarrassment at creating a scene.

Slowly the clapping faded away till only the chanting remained. The woman, middle-aged with an anxious, washed-out face, soon gave up under the puzzled scrutiny of the assembled guests but the man kept the burden going with harsh insistence. Dark-suited, white-shirted, black-tied, he looked familiar. Then it came to Pascoe – this was Arnie Stringer, Swain's building partner, hitherto only seen in a cloth cap and overalls.

'Shouldn't you intervene?' wondered Mrs Horncastle.

'Senior officer on the scene makes the decisions,' said Pascoe smugly.

And sure enough, there was Dalziel, glass in hand, beginning to move from the bar. Whether his purpose was honeyed diplomacy or cracking of heads was not to be revealed, for Chung leaned forward, rested her hand on his shoulder and jumped lightly to the ground.

She walked forward to the intruders and stood smiling at them till even Stringer's voice faded.

'Hello,' she said. 'I'm Eileen Chung. This is my party. You're very welcome.'

For a second they looked nonplussed, then the woman said with nervous force, 'Remember the sabbath day and keep it holy! *Exodus* 20, verse 8.'

'I hope there's nothing unholy going on here,' said Chung. 'And wasn't the sabbath made for man, not man for the sabbath, *Mark* 2, verse 27?'

The woman looked ready to collapse under this unexpected counterblow, but suddenly Arnie Stringer intervened.

'It's not what's going off here that's the trouble,' he said. 'It's these plays.'

'You don't like the plays?' said Chung.

'I'll not object to a good play in its rightful place but that's here, in a theatre, not out in the street and on consecrated ground,' he said. 'Especially not when there's going to be papish processions and men pretending to be God and Jesus. I find that offensive, missus. And there's a lot more like me.'

'We tried to consult every aspect of local opinion,' said Chung.

'Oh aye? You consulted him – ' a finger stabbed at the Canon – 'whose bosses want to sell out to Rome. And him – ' the President of the Chamber of Commerce – 'who'd sell his own grannie if he could get a good price. And him – ' the Head of the Community Project Group – 'who reckons charity begins in the Indian Ocean and equality's about being black. And him – ' the local NUM boss – 'who's spent so long acting as a worker, no wonder he feels at home in a place like this. And him – ' Dalziel – 'who sups so much of that stuff, he probably thinks he's still in the Middle Ages anyway. Oh aye, you asked all them, missus, knowing the answer you'd get. But you didn't ask me what I thought. Nor a lot like me either.'

It was a statement not without force and dignity, and Pascoe could see Chung was professionally impressed. Poor sod, he thought. He'll end up as St Peter if he's not careful!

'I'm sorry,' said Chung. 'Let's remedy that. Not now though, as I've my guests to look after. Why not stay and join us in some refreshment. Plenty of soft drinks going, I prefer them myself. No? OK, some other time. Hey, I love the banner. Who did the lettering?'

The banner-bearer lowered it and to Pascoe's surprise revealed herself as Shirley Appleyard. She hadn't struck him as being much in tune with her father's religious beliefs.

'I did,' she said.

The two women examined each other with undisguised curiosity.

'It's really very striking,' said Chung. 'Such strength, such directness.'

'She were always good at art,' declared the older woman with a pride that could only derive from parenthood.

'We've not come here to chit-chat about art,' growled Stringer.

'Of course not,' said Chung. 'Look, I'd really love to talk, I mean it. I'll be here tomorrow lunch-time, why not come then? I'm sure there's nothing separating us that a frank and free exchange of views won't clear.'

As she spoke Chung was drawing the protesters with her towards the stairway. They passed quite close to Swain, who raised his glass with what might have been an ironic smile to Stringer as he passed. Then the little group vanished down the stairs and behind them the silence was swept away by a wave of excited speculation.

'Isn't she marvellous?' said Pascoe, and when Mrs Horncastle didn't at once reply, he added with a votary's vigour, 'Don't you agree?'

'I'm sorry. Of course I agree. I was just detecting in myself a disturbing strain of envy! Yes, of course she's marvellous, and how marvellous it must feel to be so complete, so at one with yourself.'

Chung returned, cutting off congratulation by resuming her speech, though this time she kept her feet on the ground. She said pretty thank-you's to a lot more people and by the time she had finished, the interruption was almost forgotten.

Half an hour later the party was breaking up. Swain had left immediately Chung had finished. Pascoe, who had been keeping a professional eye on him, had noticed that when not actively engaged in talking or, more often, listening, he looked haggard and weary. How else should he look in the circumstances, no matter which set of circumstances applied?

Ellie came up to him and said, 'Message from the Almighty. He won't be needing his chariot of fire again tonight. I think he's got himself a date with a bottle of Highland Park.'

'Well, well. First round to Chung. Can she pull it off?'

Ellie shuddered and said, 'I don't think she'd go that far.'

'I don't know. She certainly let the bloat Unstone paddle her palm and chew his way up her ulna.'

'Peter!'

'There goes your dirty mind again. I still reckon she's boxing outside her weight. She'll find him a lot harder to sort out than a bunch of Prod militants.'

Ellie smiled, then said, 'She's got me helping too, you know.'

'What as? Double agent?'

The gibe came out sharper than he intended but she ignored it and said, 'No. Sort of PR, liaising with the Press, that sort of thing.'

'That's great,' said Pascoe with compensatory enthusiasm. 'She's got herself a bargain.'

'I'll say. She's not paying anything.'

'At twenty thou per annum, she'd still have a bargain,' said Pascoe firmly and Ellie smiled her pleasure.

'Let's go home,' she said.

'Good thinking. But not empty-handed. This is the way to the props room, isn't it? Well, I've delivered Dalziel and I'm not leaving here without my reward. I don't mind Hedda Gabler blowing her brains out over my coffee table but I draw the line at Virginia bloody Woolf!'

'I think you'll find she drowned herself,' laughed Ellie.

'Then I thank God we don't have a goldfish pond. But

let's grab the table anyway before Chung gets ideas about a rustic bridge!'

They went out together arm in arm. Dalziel and Chung watched them go.

'Nice people,' said Chung.

'I'll drink to that,' said Dalziel.

'Will they make it, do you think?'

'It'll take a miracle,' said Dalziel.

'Why do you say that?' she asked almost angrily.

'Because young Peter there can make it all the way to the top. But she won't want him there because her let-out at the moment is she can still blame all the police fuck-ups on the scum-bags running things. So if he gets there, she won't stay. And if he doesn't get there, he'll know who to blame.'

'That's pretty damn cynical,' she protested.

'Realistic. And I did say it'd take a miracle. What's a nice lass like you doing with these Mysteries if you don't believe in the God of miracles?'

'Now it's funny you should say that, Andy,' said Eileen Chung.

Chapter 2

On the Friday after Chung's party, Pascoe went to the police lab to collect a report on Dalziel's letters. The arrival of a third as forecast by the fat man had spurred him to action. The originals had come here and copies had gone to Dr Pottle at the Central Hospital Psychiatric Unit.

The Head of the Forensic Examination Unit was called Gentry. A small parchment-faced man who looked as if he might have recently been excavated from the Valley of the Kings, he was nicknamed with constabulary subtlety

Dr Death. But he ran a tight tomb, and though the report was short, Pascoe did not doubt that it was comprehensive.

The letters had been typed on a Tippa portable, made in Holland by the Adler company. There was an alignment problem with the capital P. The typist was competent and probably trained, certainly not merely two-fingered. The paper used was Size A5, pale blue, of a brand available in any stationery shop. It had been rubbed clear of all fingerprints. The stamps had been moistened with water, not spittle, and the envelopes were self-sealing. The letters had all been posted in town but at different times of day.

Next stop was the Central Hospital. Pascoe knocked at a door marked Dr Pottle, and a voice shouted, 'In!' like a short-tempered owner addressing a recalcitrant dog.

Pascoe entered. A small man with an Einstein moustache and his head wreathed in tobacco smoke regarded him over an untidy desk.

'It's you,' he said ungraciously. 'Are you always so prompt?'

'That depends what it tells you about me,' said Pascoe, who had grown used to Pottle's little ways at the same time as he'd come to respect his insights on the occasions he acted as police consultant.

Pottle pulled at his cigarette and said smokily, 'It tells me you've got nothing better to do or else you'd have no compunction about keeping me waiting. Let's see. Your letters are here somewhere if they haven't been stolen. I get some very strange people in this room and I don't mean patients. No. Here they are.'

He unearthed the photocopies Pascoe had supplied him with, shook some ash off them and began to scan them as if for the first time. Pascoe was not deceived. Pottle offered a sense of disorder, a feeling that things around him were in such a constant state of flux that you could safely toss anything you liked into the maelstrom. 'A psychiatrist must be either God or the Devil, Lord of Hosts or King of Chaos. God doesn't need forty fags a day, so that limits my options,' he'd once confided. But even his confidences were lead-ons, as Pascoe had realized fifteen minutes later when he found himself talking about his ambivalent attitudes to the police.

'You've got trouble here,' Pottle said after a moment. 'What do you want – close reasoning or quick conclusions? Or need I ask?'

'I look forward to following your close reasoning in your written report,' said Pascoe. 'But to be going on with . . .'

'Right.' He lit a cigarette from the one he was smoking and stubbed the butt out in a huge but overflowing ashtray. His raggedy moustache was dyed yellow with nicotine. Pascoe hoped he didn't drink a lot of soup.

'Gender,' he began. 'Six to four on it's a woman so I'll refer to she but without prejudice. As with Shakespeare's Dark Lady, ours may turn out to be a fellow, though I doubt it. Age is equally indefinite. Upper cut-off, fiftyish; lower cut-off, fifteenish. OK so far, Mr Pascoe?'

'Er, yes, thank you,' said Pascoe.

'Why do you say *yes, thanks* when you're looking *yes, but*? I bet you'd got this one pegged as a middle-aged woman straight off, am I right?'

Pascoe grinned sheepishly and nodded.

'Stereotyping may help catch petty criminals,' said Pottle, 'but it's no use here. Assuming our Dark Lady is a lady, I can find no evidence of a menopausal syndrome, nor any of a mind which thinks itself old. The lower age limit is merely that of potential maturation. Now can I go on?'

'Please do,' said Pascoe, trying to set his face into a Wield-like mask.

'OK. Our Dark Lady is intelligent and literate, these things are self-evident. But you should rid yourself of any prejudice that this means she is highly educated and middle-class. This may well be true but it does not follow from anything I can see in these letters. Nor does her evident acquaintance with hagiology necessarily predicate religiosity, though I would guess there might be a Catholic or High Anglican background. Or even a reaction against a hard-line Nonconformist upbringing. I can't go much further forward as far as what we might call the external profile is concerned. Nothing on job, marital status, politics, preferred soap powder, et cetera. Not much help for an identification parade, is it?'

'It'd stretch a long way,' agreed Pascoe. 'But the internal profile . . .?'

'Have you had much to do with suicides, Mr Pascoe?' asked Pottle.

'As a young cop, I picked up the pieces a couple of times, once almost literally. A chap stepped in front of a train . . . And a lot of car accidents seemed to me inexplicable without some degree of intent. Since I've been in CID, there've been at least two suicides I can think of in connection with cases I've been working on.'

'So you've had more practical experience than most. What about the theory? You did social studies at university, didn't you?'

'I had a nodding acquaintance with Durkheim, but more in terms of methodology than subject.'

'Durkheim,' said Pottle dismissively. 'I thought even sociologists found him pretty irrelevant other than historically nowadays.'

'I did read some more modern stuff,' said Pascoe defensively.

'Since you joined the police?' asked Pottle. 'No? Too busy picking up the pieces to be bothered with the theories, I suppose.'

'The reason I'm here is that in this case I don't want

there to be any pieces to pick up,' declared Pascoe angrily. And then he grew angrier with himself for letting Pottle get under his skin.

'So you want me to tell you if our not impossible she is serious about killing herself? And if I say she is, what then? As she herself says, it's not a crime. Hardly a police problem.'

Pascoe was well aware of how Dalziel would probably react if he found out the hours and resources that were being spent on the letters. Yet it had been Dalziel who drew his attention to the problem in the first place, Dalziel who'd been so certain the third letter would come.

He said, 'It would be a crime not to do anything, I think.'

Pottle suddenly grinned.

'You're quite right. So let us proceed. My reading is that yes, she's undoubtedly serious. It's a commonplace of prospective suicides that they send out strong hints of their intention. Partly these are simply the spontaneous overflow of naturally strong emotion as the moment of this most final of acts approaches. Partly they are a warning, an appeal for interference. And partly they are a solacing game, or even a responsibility-shifting gamble. From her own admission, our Dark Lady is bright enough to understand much of this and to have chosen a single channel for all these urges to self-betrayal.'

'But why pick Mr Dalziel as that channel?'

'Several reasons. She states some of them. Your beloved leader has a reputation as a hard man. She doesn't want to pick on a bleeding heart, she doesn't want to give pain. Above all, she wishes to be in control of her situation, and I'm sure she believes that she's writing to Dalziel to maintain this control.'

'You say *she believes*,' said Pascoe, frowning. 'You mean there's something else?'

'Very sharp,' applauded Pottle. 'Look at it this way: even the most random human choice usually has its reasons that reason does not perceive; in this case the obvious reason for writing to Mr Dalziel *is* the obvious reason! He is a detective, a chief of detectives. His job is to find things out, to track down fugitives, to rip the mask off those who would remain hidden and unidentified. See how frequently she refers to his function, his expertise. She is at the same time appealing for discovery and offering him a challenge, inviting him to play her game. Or perhaps take part in her gamble. You see, by invoking the law of chance she distances the act of personal decision.'

He paused. Pascoe said, 'So how do we take up this challenge?'

Pottle replied. 'That's your business, I'm afraid. Sorry, I don't mean to be rude. All I mean is that, while I hope I've been of some help, I suspect that in the end because of their addressee, any clues these letters contain will be such as your own professional expertise can best decipher.'

'Thanks for telling me to do my job,' smiled Pascoe.

'And now perhaps you'll leave me to do mine, unless there's anything else?'

'Now you mention it,' said Pascoe. 'And while we're talking about suicide . . .'

As succinctly as he could, he gave the facts of the Gail Swain case. Pottle listened without interrupting for the space of two cigarettes.

'Right,' he said when Pascoe finished. 'Let's start at the heart of the matter. Question: could Gail Swain have chosen to kill herself in this way on this occasion? Answer: why not? She would, of course, have had to be contemplating suicide for some time. You say she had no close friends in whom she might have confided. But rich Californians are conditioned to turn to poor psychiatrists in times of trouble, are they not? Cherchez le shrink. She vanished for a few days before turning up at Hambleton Road, you say. Perhaps she spent them on some Harley Street couch and then decided if she was going to be lying on her back she might as well get some pleasure out of it. But she likes to have with her at all times the means of opting out. With some people this means a bottle of pills. With her, a gun-freak, it would naturally mean guns. But why *that* gun when she had other, less cumbersome weapons? I'd have been surprised if in these circumstances she hadn't gone for the biggest, the heaviest, the deadliest. For self-defence, you go for speed and ease of use. For self-destruction you want to be sure. As for the particular occasion, if in her depressed condition she believed the men in her life were the root of all evil, then the sudden appearance of both of them side by side could have provided an irresistible audience. Or it could even be that she herself contrived that audience. You say that the husband turned up as the result of an anonymous call from a woman? For some people disguising the voice is not difficult, especially with British Telecom's special distorting devices.'

Pascoe, who had been jotting down notes, smiled and said, 'What about the drug element?'

'An effect as much as a cause from the sound of it,' said Pottle. 'It can only lend strength to the suicide scenario. But from what you say, you have difficulty in that the Witch-Finder General Dalziel sees things very differently. I could easily supply you with a sketch of the paranoid personality which would explain all, but I don't want to upset your sense of loyalty. So let's ask, could he be right? In which case Swain and Waterson would have to be in cahoots, or one of them have such a grip over the other that he was forced to obey. You ask me why Waterson should vanish. I can think of so many reasons, from amnesia to insolvency, that speculation without more information is useless. More interesting is why Swain should choose to kill his wife in this way. A conspiracy removes mere sexual jealousy as a motive. It also suggests he knew in advance that she wasn't going straight to America. But it's all too complicated. If he wants rid of her merely to inherit her money, say, there are any number of domestic accidents which are relatively easy to contrive. Why take the risk of involving a third party at all? No, all the evidence suggests, particularly in the light of your own interesting little experiment, that Mr Dalziel is absolutely and comprehensively wrong. But I don't envy you the task of so persuading him!'

Pascoe laughed and said, 'Me neither. Thanks a lot.'

He stood up and winced. His leg tended to stiffen up if he forgot to keep it moving.

Pottle said, 'How is it, being back in harness?'

Pascoe had been treated at the Central and Pottle had visited his sick-bed on a couple of occasions.

'I'm not sure yet. Sometimes it's like I've never been away. Then the leg creaks. Or the mind.'

'You came close to death,' said Pottle. 'You shouldn't forget it.'

'I doubt if I'll do that,' said Pascoe wryly.

'I mean, don't try to forget it. For your own sake. Also, it could help you helping others. This Dark Lady of yours, for instance. You may know more about her kind of darkness than you imagine.'

Pascoe frowned at this uncomfortable thought.

He said, 'I do wonder, have we got a right to interfere?'

'Perhaps not,' said Pottle. 'But when someone challenges you to a game, you've got a right to play. And if you've got a right to play, you've got a right to win!'

Chapter 3

There is a pleasure in keeping a secret, and an equal if opposite pleasure in passing one on. But there are few things more annoying than to find that the secret you have nursed in your bosom beyond reach of nudge or wink is common currency.

As Pascoe left the station that evening, George Broomfield fell into step beside him and said, 'Is it right then he's going to do it?'

He rolled his eyes expressively upwards. The mime was ambiguous but there was a quality or perhaps quantity of *he* which identified the man beyond reasonable doubt.

'A desk job, you mean? They'd have to nail him to it!' laughed Pascoe.

'No. I mean God. Haven't you heard the rumour? They say he's to be God in these Mysteries!'

Broomfield spoke with the hopeful incredulity of a curate who's just heard his bishop's been nicked in a brothel.

'Where'd you hear that?' asked Pascoe in amazement. It was only the previous Sunday that he'd lured Dalziel within Lorelei distance of Chung.

'It's all over. I got it from this lass who works in Mr Trimble's office. I was sure you'd have heard, being so close.'

'Sorry, George. Can't help you. Excuse me, there's someone over there I want a word with.'

He walked away, annoyed at what he'd heard and annoyed also that his abruptness might have fuelled the rumour. There was no real reason why he should speak with the young woman who'd just come out of the road leading to the still unusable official car park, but he had to go through the motions in case Broomfield was watching.

'Hello, Mrs Appleyard,' he said. 'How did Jane Eyre end up?'

'Like a guide dog, fetching and carrying for master. I thought you said it had a happy ending!'

'It's been a long time since I read it,' evaded Pascoe. 'I saw you at the Kemble the other night.'

'You were there? That figures. What do they say? Where there's booze there's bobbies.'

This slur provoked Pascoe to an untypical discourtesy.

'I hadn't got you down as a Bible-puncher,' he said.

'No? You know a lot about me, do you?'

'Only what you've volunteered. And I understood you to hint that you weren't in sympathy with your father's fundamentalism.'

'Is that what I said?' She paused as if examining the justice of his claim, then nodded and went on, 'Well, likely I did, cos I'm not.'

'Then why . . .?'

'Because I couldn't let Mam go along alone. She believes the same as him. Leastways, she's long since given up trying to think any other way. But she's not built to go shouting the odds in public, she'd much rather sit quiet at home and be a bother to no one. I can't stop her going when he gives the command, but I can go along with her to make sure he doesn't push her too far.'

'I see. And the banner?'

'Oh, that. Mam was right, I were always good at that sort of thing. Could have gone to art school if . . . well, anyroad, I knew if I didn't do something half decent, Dad would likely turn up with a raggedy bit of hardboard with STUFF THE POPE scrawled on it in whitewash!'

Pascoe laughed, then asked, 'Did your father accept Chung's invitation?'

'Yes, he did. I went too. He'd have dragged Mam along else.'

This time her claim to the protection motive didn't ring quite true.

'And what happened?'

'She were great,' said the girl with simple admiration. 'She sat him down and just talked about these Mysteries, how there was nothing papish about them, how in fact they were the way ordinary folk took religion away from the priests and put it in their own language. She talked really straight, she didn't try to make him look ignorant or owt like that, and when he spoke, she really listened like what he said was important. She were really great.'

Pascoe smiled inwardly. No need to tell him what tunes the enchantress played.

'And did she have anything to say to you?' he asked.

'A bit. Dad had to get back here, and we chatted on a while longer. She asked if I'd like to do a poster for the Mysteries. I said I might.'

'Would your father approve?' he asked provocatively.

'What's that got to do with it? Anyroad, he went off happy enough,' she said with the scorn one convert often feels for another. 'And I'd best be off now. I just came to deliver the lads' wages and I've got a lot of shopping to do while Dad dishes them out.'

Pascoe frowned. 'Do they get paid in cash?'

'When they're not being paid in promises. What's it to you anyway?' she added aggressively as if compensating for her indiscretion.

'Young women picking up wage money from a bank make easy targets,' said Pascoe. 'What did you mean, promise?'

'Nowt. There was a cash-flow problem, but it's been sorted.'

Pascoe decided it was time for a little blunt poking, Dalziel-fashion.

'Because of Mrs Swain's death, you mean? But it'll be a while yet before her will can be proved.'

'Mebbe so. But the bank must reckon it's going to be OK.'

'And what do you reckon, Mrs Appleyard?' he asked.

'Nowt to do with me,' she said indifferently. 'But he's walking around loose, isn't he, so it doesn't seem like you're going to charge him with anything serious.'

She was looking over his shoulder as she spoke and all her previous animation had left her face. Pascoe turned and saw that Stringer and Swain had come together out of the car park and were standing deep in conversation. Swain patted Stringer apparently reassuringly on the arm and walked away. Stringer watched him go, then turned to re-enter the car park. Only now did he spot his daughter.

He came towards them.

''Evening, Mr Stringer,' said Pascoe.

He got a nod in reply, then the man said to the girl, 'You ready, then? Let's be off. Can't expect your mam to take care of the boy all night too.'

So there was a child. And the husband?

She said, 'I told you. I've got some shopping to do.'

'Have you not done it yet? God, it must be grand being able to waste your life chatting at street corners.'

His hard blue-eyed stare left no doubt he included Pascoe in this censure.

His daughter said, 'I'll not be a minute,' and set off along the pavement.

'I gather I'll soon be able to have my parking spot back,' said Pascoe pleasantly.

'What? Oh aye. We're near on done.'

136

'And after that? Got anything lined up while the weather lasts?'

For some reason this seemed to irritate Stringer.

'I'm not a bloody brickie on the lump!' he said. 'I'm a partner.'

'Even so, you still need work to make profits.'

'We'll get by. What's it to do wi' you, anyroad?'

'Just polite sympathetic interest, Mr Stringer.'

'Police nosiness, you mean. And you can stuff your sympathy. I've always taken care of me own without any help.'

'I'm sure. You must be proud of your grandson. How old is he now?'

'Near on two,' said Stringer. 'He's a fair enough kiddie.'

Pascoe guessed this was as near a boast as the man could get.

'Takes after his grandad, does he?' he said, hoping to encourage the thaw. He certainly got instant heat.

'He'd better not take after his dad, that's for sure!'

'I'm sorry? His father . . . is he . . .?'

'Is he what?' demanded Stringer.

'I don't know. Dead perhaps?'

'Dead? What the hell makes you say that?' said Stringer angrily.

'Mr Stringer,' said Pascoe acidly. 'Clearly you feel there is something undesirable about your son-in-law. If you care to explain what, perhaps I will be able to avoid giving you offence.'

Rather to his surprise, his appeal got a positive response, even if it was rather oblique.

'It's a sick world we live in,' said Stringer with the intonation of authority rather than opinion.

'It's certainly a curate's egg-shaped world,' agreed Pascoe. 'But in what particular respect do you detect this sickness?'

'Everything! If it wasn't so sick, why should God have sent things like Aids and drugs to punish the wicked?'

Pascoe groaned inwardly. He'd forgotten Stringer was something of a religious nut, and religious nuttiness was his one conversational no-go area.

'As punishments, they seem to get doled out pretty indiscriminately,' he suggested. 'But I suppose we all have our work to do, even God. I certainly have. Good night, Mr Stringer.'

But he was not to escape so easily. The builder grabbed his arm and said, 'You asked about my son-in-law, mister. Do you not want an answer?'

'No, really, I'm sorry. It's none of my business . . .'

'Aye, you're right there. But I'll tell you anyway,' said Stringer. 'And it'll mebbe stop you bothering other folk with nosey questions. This Tony Appleyard, he put my lass in the club three years back. I'd never heard of him till then. She were still at school, a really bright lass, she could have made something of herself, then this nasty little sod. . . Well, it had to be sorted. He wanted her to have an abortion, but that's murder in my book. And in hers too, I'm glad to say. So I had a quiet word with him. I gave him the benefit of the doubt. You come from a country family like me, you know that there's plenty of marriages start with getting caught, not getting wed, and most on 'em turn out all right in the end. They didn't want to get wed, mark you. Said it didn't matter these days, but I said it mattered to me and it mattered to God. And it'll matter to the kiddie when it gets older. So they got wed.'

He paused. Pascoe said, 'And did it work out?'

'Don't make me laugh!' instructed the man unnecessarily. 'That feckless bugger? A fitter he called himself. Fit for sod-all, that's what he were! He worked at Atlas Tayler's but he got laid off when the Yanks pulled out. I could have fixed him up with a labouring job in the firm, but oh no, he wanted his trade, he said. And in the end he set off south looking for work. Well, he found something, by all reports, making good money, at least good enough for him to live the life of Riley by himself with no thought of sending owt back for his wife and kiddie.'

'You mean he's not come back to see them?' said Pascoe.

'Come back? Why should a useless bastard like that come back unless it were to bring more trouble with him?' exclaimed Stringer. 'I even went looking for him not long back, but he must have got wind of it, for he'd moved on without any forwarding address. Well, I tell you, he'll not have moved far enough for me!'

'And what about Shirley?' asked Pascoe, taken aback by the force of the man's emotion. 'What does she feel about all this? How's it affected her?'

'If you'd known her a few years back, you'd not need to ask that,' said Stringer. 'Here, take a look.'

From his wallet he took a colour snapshot. It was a picture of Stringer and a girl of twelve or thirteen, sitting together at a small folding table under a striped canvas awning. They were both smiling widely at the camera. The girl wasn't beautiful, but she was fresh-faced, vital, carefree, and it took a long hard stare to discern in this child the lineaments of Shirley Appleyard.

Her father was much more recognizable, but the passing of those years had stamped a mark of pain and anger and bafflement on his features too.

'Lovely girl,' said Pascoe.

He didn't mean it to sound past tense, but that's how Stringer heard it.

'Yes, she were,' he said, half to himself. 'Lovely girl. Everyone said so. And she reckoned there was no one like her dad. Went everywhere with me, told me everything. Then it all started to change. Like milk going sour.

139

Gradual at first, everything looks the same . . . but in the end, it's not to be hid! You got any kids, mister?'

'One. A girl.'

'Then you'll likely understand.'

Understand what? wondered Pascoe as he drove home. Stringer did not strike him as a man for whom a trouble shared was a trouble halved. But as he read Rosie her bedtime story, he found himself speculating how he would feel about anyone who mucked up his daughter's life, and he did not find much comfort in the speculation.

He went downstairs to find Ellie at the dining-room table surrounded by the files and papers she'd started gathering as a result of her election as Chung's unpaid PRO. They exchanged smiles, then he wandered into the lounge and poured himself a drink. He knew there was a chat show on the television he usually liked to watch but he couldn't be bothered to switch it on tonight. Suddenly Ellie slipped on to the arm of his chair and rested her elbow on his shoulder.

'You look glum,' she said. 'Something bothering you?'

'No. Just life.'

'In that case, stop worrying. In the end it cures itself, they tell me.'

'That's on the National Health,' he said. 'Some people go private and jump the queue.'

'I'm sorry? What's this? My mystery for tonight?'

'No. There's this woman, Gail Swain, blew her head off. At least that's how it looks to me. And there's this other woman who's been writing to Dalziel saying she's going to kill herself.'

'Good lord. You never mentioned this before.'

'No. Well, she stopped and it seemed to be all over, then she just started again,' he said lamely.

'I see. Why Dalziel? And if Dalziel, how you?'

'In extremis even atheists say their prayers. And it is a leader's privilege to delegate.'

Ellie laughed, then said, 'These letters, any chance of taking a peek?'

Pascoe hesitated before replying, 'I don't have them with me. I left them at work.'

It was true, but it was not the true reason for the hesitation and he guessed that Ellie sensed it. Prior to the case which left him with his still painful leg, he had confided without inhibition or censorship in Ellie. If asked then, he would have said he did it out of complete love, complete trust. But in the grey hospital hours he had found himself wondering if he hadn't simply been testing that trust and that love to destruction. Finally had come a time when they found themselves in public and private opposition and, retrospectively, he found himself identifying a certain perverse satisfaction in having reached a boundary. As he emerged from the greyness, so that identification had become far less positive. But it added an extra and sufficient weight to the pressures keeping partially closed what had once been totally open.

Ellie rose and yawned. 'No bother,' she said lightly. 'I've got enough on my plate without solving your cases for you.'

He followed her back into the dining-room, eager to minimize damage.

'How's the unpaid job?' he asked.

'Could be fun. But time-consuming. I'll never be nasty about PR men again.'

'Like to bet?' smiled Pascoe. 'Incidentally, you might like to do a bit of PR liaising with Chung on my behalf: Somehow word's got out that she's keen to cast Dalziel as God. Could you assure her my lips have been sealed? I don't want to end up in some oriental death-lock.'

'You could have fooled me,' said Ellie. 'But I shouldn't

worry. Leaks from the Kemble are like leaks from the Cabinet. She-who-must-be-obeyed drills the holes.'

'Chung? But why?'

'It's called pressure, dear. What's the best way of getting Dalziel to do something?'

'I don't know. Bribery? Corruption? Telling him not to do it . . .'

'Well done! I've no doubt Chung will be trying all the other techniques and some we haven't thought of besides. But for him to be told *not* to do it, the people who tell him have got to know he's been asked, right?'

'This is all too clever for me. And how come Chung knew what buttons to press so quickly anyway . . . Oh no! Ellie, you haven't got yourself involved as psychological adviser as well as PR person, have you?'

She blushed beautifully. Normally he was a great admirer of his wife's blushes but admiration and trepidation were poor partners. If Dalziel were even to begin to suspect the collective guilt of the Pascoe household . . . The phone rang before he could launch into remonstrance. He picked it up nervously, certain it was going to be Dalziel. Instead he heard Wield's voice.

'Sorry to bother you, only there's been some trouble at the Rose and Crown in Bradgate. You know there's a floodlit match tonight? Well, some visitors got into a barney with some of City's supporters. Landlord tried to intervene and he's ended up in hospital. Thought you should know.'

It was a kindness. Normally the Sergeant wouldn't have bothered Pascoe with a pub brawl, but Dalziel had been making ever more abrasive noises about the lack of visible progress on the football hooligan front, and it would be well to be word-perfect on this incident.

'I'll wander down there,' said Pascoe. 'Super around, is he?'

'No. I gather Mr Trimble asked him to drop in for a chat earlier and he came out with a face like fat. Pulled the handle off the door when he shut it behind him, I hear tell. Any idea what's upset him?'

'I hope not, Wieldy,' said Pascoe fervently. 'I sincerely hope not!'

By the time Dalziel reached the Kemble, he was cooling down. Retaliation was after all the better part of rage. A wild swing could move a lot of air, but it took a carefully planted boot in the balls to bring tears to the eyes.

Nor was it simply a matter of personal esteem and self-satisfaction. Dan Trimble wasn't a bad sort of fellow, friendly, bright, and not ungenerous with his Glen Morangie. Mid-Yorkshire could have done a lot worse. But a Chief Constable had to understand that while he might indeed among constables be a chief, when it came to detective-superintendents, he was at best second among equals.

The man's first error had been to tell him bluntly that it was time he tied up the Swain case. He was being pressurized by Eden Thackeray, by the coroner's office, by the Press, and even by the Delgado Corporation's American lawyers who were concerned (a) to have the body released for interment in the family vault and (b) to have the circumstances of death cleared up so that the process of dealing with Gail Swain's will could be commenced, particularly as this involved a substantial block of Delgado shares recently inherited from her father.

'I'll be blunt, Andy,' said Trimble. 'I've given you plenty of rope, but it doesn't look as if you can hang Swain with it, does it? We have his statement and Waterson's statement which concur on the main issues – '

'Once I get my hands on Waterson, I'll change all that!' interrupted Dalziel.

Trimble looked at him doubtfully, then said, 'How close are you to finding him?'

'Very close,' lied Dalziel.

'I hope you're not bullshitting me, Andy,' said Trimble quietly. 'I like to back my men, but I'm getting bad vibrations here. Everything points to a verdict of suicide. The way I see it, the most serious charge on offer will be harassment against you if you don't wrap this thing up quickly. So be warned!'

That had been bad enough but worse had followed. Clearly relieved at having got the professional unpleasantness out of the way, and perhaps already congratulating himself on how easily he'd got his famous Yorkshire bear to do the Cornish Floral Dance, Trimble poured the whisky and said with a smile, 'Changing the subject, I had to laugh at lunch today. Someone said he'd heard that one of my officers was to play God in these Mysteries. I told him there was room for only one God in the Mid-Yorkshire Force, and like cleanliness, he was next to it! He assured me he'd had this on good authority, and I assured him on even better authority that if any of my officers proposed to bring the Force into disrepute by letting himself be wheeled round town on a carnival float in his nightgown, I'd be the first to know!'

Dalziel regarded him blankly, but behind the cold granite slab of his forehead bubbled a thermal spring of thought. He'd met Chung's invitation to be God with the great guffaw of derision it deserved, but she hadn't been put out, merely smiling and making a joke, and pouring more whisky with such a generous hand that he'd left her with the promise that he'd think about it.

Well, he'd thought, and guffawed again, and was seeing her this evening to drink more of her Scotch; and assure her firmly but suggestively that his ambitions were earthy rather than divine.

But now all of a sudden he was feeling there was something going off here that he didn't quite grasp.

He said, 'What you mean, sir, is, if someone wanted to do summat like that, you reckon you could ban him?'

'I'd hope it would never come to that, but oh yes, Andrew, never doubt it. I could and I would!'

So there he was, professionally and personally put in his place. He'd almost crushed his tumbler into a crystal ball and shown Trimble his future in it. But a wise man does bad by stealth, and so he had fled the field, leaving the Cornish pixie to his suppositious triumph.

A tumblerful of Chung's Highland Park took the last of the heat from his head, and when the sinuous Eurasian said, 'You seem a bit down, Andy. Anything bothering you?' he was able to laugh and reply, 'Nowt I can't sort out.'

A few moments later, however, rather to his surprise, he found himself telling her all about Trimble's interference in the Swain case, though he was careful to avoid any mention of names. It was a futile discretion, however, for after only a few sentences, Chung interrupted with, 'Hey, this is Phil Swain you're talking about, right? But I thought he must be right in the clear. I mean, he was at my party! I must say I was surprised to see him after what happened to his poor wife, she was on our Arts Committee.'

'You knew her well?' asked Dalziel, alert for new information.

'No, hardly at all. This great interest she's supposed to have had didn't show in practice. She only attended every second meeting. I reckon her membership was cosmetic, but fair do's, she was always ready to lead the way when we were touting for cash.'

'That must have pleased her husband,' sneered Dalziel. 'Did you ever hear her talk about him?'

'No. I saw them together a few times and they seemed

145

all right. To tell the truth, it was him I felt sorry for. She always struck me as a bit of an up-and-down lady who expected people to dance to her moods.'

Dalziel frowned at this further witness to Gail Swain's volatility.

Chung said, 'You don't like Phil Swain much, do you?'

'I wouldn't say I don't like him,' said Dalziel. 'I hate the bastard's guts!'

'But he is in the clear, right?'

'Not while I'm breathing! What's your interest, luv?'

She hesitated, then said, 'Hell, look, I'd better come clean, Andy. I want you for God, no, don't say anything yet. I chose you because you've got a kind of special aura. Well, Phil Swain's got an aura too, not for God I hasten to say, but I had put out some feelers, then this awful business about his wife happened and I thought that was that. But when he turned up at the party last Sunday, I got to wondering if he might like something to take his mind off things, you know, sort of occupational therapy . . . but it's you I really want, Andy, and if Phil taking part would really be an obstacle, seeing how you feel about him, well, I'll definitely cross him off my list, if only you'll say yes.'

She spoke hesitantly, uncertainly, but why did he get a feeling that every one of these words had been as carefully thought into place as the notes on a musical score? He had a sense for the second time this night of being none too gently manipulated, but there was a world of difference between Trimble's Cornish wrestling and this oriental massage.

'What was it you wanted the bugger for anyway?' he asked, accepting his cue.

'That's the thing that would make it so difficult, Andy,' said Chung, golden cat's eyes suddenly moon-orbed. 'I

146

wanted him for Lucifer. He'd have to appear with you in the opening pageant so you could cast him down into hell.'

Dalziel began to laugh. At last oriental subtlety and CID technique were on the same wavelength. The end of all interrogation was to make the poor sod want to say what you wanted him to say!

'You know what, luv?' he said. 'You remind me of me!'

And Chung leaned forward so close that he couldn't get his glass to his lips, and murmured, 'I think I have finally found my God.'

Part Four

MAK: Now were time for a man that lacks what he would;
To stalk privily unto a fold,
And nimbly to work then, and be not too bold,
For he might abuy the bargain, if it were told
At the ending.
Now were the time to reel;
But he needs good counsel
That fain would fare well,
And has but little spending.

The Towneley Cycle: 'The Second Shepherds' Pageant'

Dear Mr Dalziel,

Still here. Still resolved. I envy you your job. You may not be winning, but at least you spend your time doing something positive about human unhappiness. I look at my life and wonder how I got where I am. Is it in the stars? The genes? Or is there one decision which, changed, would have changed everything? Well, there's no way to test that, is there? What you see is what you've got. What the world sees is another matter. Perhaps I'm seeing you all wrong, as the world probably sees me all wrong. Perhaps beneath it all, you too are uncertain, confused, unhappy.

No! I can't, I won't believe it! Not Detective-Superintendent Dalziel! I'm not saying that you don't find it horrible that so many people get so brutally killed in this beautiful world of ours, but I'm pretty certain you feel it a blessing that you don't care for most of them! You would probably have thought Alnoth, whose feast day it is, was a nut to live as a hermit in the forest, but you'd have uprooted trees to track down the robbers who murdered him!

Well, that was a long time ago. Looking back, the easiest way to trace the progress of the human race is to follow the blood. Looking forward . . . is there anything to look forward to? Yes, of course; there's the Mayor's Ball, dedicated this year to Death with Dignity. How fitting. Can I make it? Let me check my diary. Yes, I should still be around. What about you? I do hope you go. Who knows? Perhaps we could even dance the last waltz together!

Chapter 1

March came in like a lamb though the forecasters, looking down at their print-outs and up at their rooks' nests, predicted its tail would wag with unprecedented ferocity.

Sergeant Wield, landed with the late shift, wasn't much bothered by the weather without, as long as he got a quiet night within, but at 10.30 his phone rang and a vaguely familiar voice said, 'You want Waterson, try the Sally.'

The line went dead. Wield got the station exchange.

'That call, was it for me by name or just for CID?'

'He asked for you, Sarge.'

Wield stood up and pulled his coat on. Weather had become a consideration. There was a mild and muggy night rubbing against his window-pane, but a trail that started in a nice warm pub could lead anywhere. Or nowhere.

The Pilgrim's Salvation stood against the old city wall in a quarter where decay had halted just short of disintegration, and desperate efforts were being made to revivify the mainly Victorian housing stock.

The Sally went back far beyond the nineteenth century, however. Sacred legend claimed that a famous sinner on pilgrimage to the cathedral had died here before he could claim forgiveness by reaching the holy shrine. Miraculously his abandoned staff had taken root beneath the city wall in testimony of God's unlimited mercy. A more profane provenance merely pointed out that this was the first inn the northern heathens reached on entering the city after their long and thirsty journey.

Five hundred years later it was still the haunt of sinners in search of all kinds of succour, but also, increasingly, of staider citizens in search of atmosphere. Which category Waterson might fall into was not yet Wield's concern. He had wasted far too much time on anonymous tips to lose more in idle speculation.

But tonight his time was not being wasted. As he approached the Sally its door opened, spilling light, music, and a quartet of pilgrims on to the pavement. Among them in the moment before the closing door cut off the light, he glimpsed his man. He had only seen him once before but Dalziel's heavy rebukes had stamped those features on to his soul.

Wield had halted and now he remained in the shadows. He hoped he wouldn't have to pluck Waterson from the bosom of his companions. Even if the acquaintance were casual, pub loyalties could be alcoholically strong. But if the man got into the blue Peugeot estate they were all standing round, he would have to take the chance.

He was going to be lucky. Two of the others got into the car, the third remained on the pavement a little longer talking to Waterson before getting into the driver's seat. Wield paused long enough to take the car's number as it passed him, then set out after Waterson who was walking briskly away in the opposite direction. He could simply have called out the man's name. There was after all no criminal charge involved here, so no reason for Waterson to run. But he'd kept his head down so successfully for almost two weeks that he clearly wasn't keen to renew acquaintance with the police, and if his vanity kept him as fit as it kept him fashionable, Wield didn't fancy a race. Time enough to close the gap when they reached busier streets.

Unfortunately Waterson's route was taking them away from the city centre through an old residential area, fairly upmarket sixty years ago but since declined to bedsit commerce within and sexual commerce without. A recent purge had temporarily frightened off the kerb crawlers and driven the pros centrewards, so tonight was quiet. Directly ahead was a small park called Kipling Gardens. Once this had been a well-known pick-up point for gays, but AIDS had cut down traffic here without the need of a police purge. Waterson walked briskly past the main gate. Ahead, the road turned down the further side of the park and Wield prepared to accelerate and make up a bit of ground once his quarry was out of sight. But just as he reached the corner, Waterson halted as if sensing a follower, and swung round. Fortunately Wield was just passing the park entrance and he sidestepped smartly into the shadow of the tall brick gateposts. Here he stood completely still, straining his ears for a renewal of Waterson's footsteps and wondering if he'd been spotted.

'Looking for someone, friend,' said a soft voice behind him.

Startled, he turned. A young man in a brass-studded leather jerkin was smiling at him out of the darkness. He didn't look much more than sixteen or seventeen. Wield smiled back and said, 'Some other time, son. I'm meeting a friend.'

It was a gentle dismissal, partly because he didn't want to risk attracting Waterson's attention but mainly because he had no desire to hassle this kid. But he paid dearly for it.

'Here, we've got ourselves one,' said the youth.

And suddenly the darkness behind him was crowded with figures, four, five, six, Wield didn't have time to count, for they were on him, swinging lengths of wood, branches they seemed to be, fresh ripped off trees in the

155

park, less lethal than clubs or metal piping perhaps, but still heavy enough to rip and cut when wielded with such ferocity.

'Dirty fucking queer passing your fucking AIDS round decent people,' gasped the first youth between blows. This was a crazy irony. Wield's care and control had kept him clear of such situations all his life. Now he was being beaten up by mistake. So he thought later, but not now, for now all his thinking was concentrated on keeping on his feet. Once on the ground, the boots would start coming in and God knows what damage might be done.

He'd got his back to the gatepost and his arms were raised to shield his head. A vehicle went by, its headlights sliding over him like a searchlight in a prison camp. He heard it slow to a halt and thought for a moment rescue was coming. His attackers thought so too and hesitated. Then the engine revved noisily and the vehicle accelerated away.

Now the assault resumed with increased fury. His forehead was gashed and blood was streaming down his face. A concerted attack must drive him on to his knees, but fortunately they were coming at him in individual bursts, then springing back, like dogs attacking a badger, which though its situation is hopeless, still has the power to inflict a valedictory wound.

But what wound do they fear from me? Wield asked himself. No weapon, strength failing, covered in blood . . . then it came to him. The AIDS propaganda hadn't done much to still their stupid fears or increase their negligible tolerance, but it had driven home one lesson. The main danger of non-sexual infection came from blood. Hence their keenness to keep their distance as they destroyed him.

Throwing back his head he let out a scream of such ferocity that it momentarily stilled the assault, and into that fraction of silence he bellowed. 'You're right! I've got it! And this time tomorrow you'll all have it too!' And putting his hand to his gashed brow, he started to flick blood into their faces like a priest with an aspergillum.

For a moment it seemed as if their terror would be transformed into even greater violence, but as the first bough was raised to recommence the assault, Wield gasped, 'Sixty seconds you've got to wash it off. Don't you listen to the telly?'

His spurious statistic worked. One of the gang turned and ran into the park. There was a drinking fountain at its centre. The others realized where he was going and with one accord hurled their branches before Wield like palm leaves, and next moment he was alone.

He didn't wait for them to return from their laving, but staggered out of the gateway and across the street. There was no sign of Waterson. Not that Wield could have done much if the man had been standing next to him. It took all his strength to carry him to a house with a light on. Not even his warrant card could persuade the householder to undo the door chain but at least he rang the police, who came prepared to sort out a drunken brawler rather than succour a colleague in distress.

They drove him to the Infirmary where they jumped the long casualty queue with indifferent ease. A pretty Pakistani nurse had started cleaning him up when the cubicle curtain was drawn aside and a voice said, 'Oh my. What happened to you, Sergeant?'

Wield swivelled his eyes to look at Ellison Marwood.

'I got beat up,' he said.

'Anyone I know?' said Marwood, beginning to examine him.

'I doubt it,' said Wield, wincing as the West Indian's fingers probed. 'Are you the only doctor they've got here?'

'You want someone else, man?'

'No. I didn't mean that,' said Wield. 'All I meant . . .'

'Relax. If I really thought it was a racist crack, I would just have left you lying on this trolley for a couple of hours. No, you're just unlucky. If you'd got beaten up half an hour earlier, you'd have missed me. I've just come on. You're my first of the night, so at least I've got both eyes open.'

It took another hour to get Wield X-rayed and stitched. By the time it was done he felt rather worse than when he'd arrived, but Marwood assured him there were no fractures and that a day in bed with a good analgesic would see him fit for work.

'It would be easy to swing you a week in bed if you wanted, but you strike me as one of these grit-your-teeth and do-your-duty types.'

'Man who works twenty-four-hour shifts shouldn't mock dedication, Doctor,' said Wield. 'How's Mrs Waterson keeping?'

'Why do you ask?' said Marwood aggressively.

'Last time we talked, she seemed a bit tense.'

'Do you blame her?' demanded Marwood. 'Once you find Waterson and put him out of the way, she'll be all right, believe me.'

It was the verbal echo that did it . . . once you find Waterson . . . want to find Waterson . . .

'Why'd you ring me earlier tonight, Dr Marwood?' asked Wield casually.

'Ring you? What are you talking about?' said the doctor, but without a great deal of force or surprise.

'All incoming CID calls are taped,' lied Wield. 'It'd be easy to run a check.'

Marwood made no further denial. It was almost as if he were glad to drop the need for pretence. 'OK, it's a fair cop,' he said. 'I'm sorry I did it anonymously but that's the way you fellows work, isn't it? You don't care where the tip-off comes from as long as it's good.'

'This one was good,' agreed Wield. 'Trouble is, it didn't work out.'

'You let him get away, you mean? He didn't do this to you, did he? Not that little weed?'

'He looked pretty fit to me.'

'Physically maybe. But he'd not have the bottle to beat you up, not even if he threw one of his fits.'

'Fits?'

'He can get very aggressive at times. You'd think he was going to pull off one of your arms and start beating you over the head with it. But if you yell Boo! he goes running. He's all mouth, that one.'

'How did you know he was going to be in the Sally?' Wield asked.

'Information received,' said Marwood. 'An anonymous tip. Which I don't have on tape.'

He grinned as he spoke. Wield didn't grin back. It would have been painful and also people generally didn't notice.

He said, 'Mrs Waterson, I suppose.'

'Mrs Waterson's nothing to do with this.'

Marwood had stopped grinning.

'And I suppose she'd got nowt to do with it when Waterson threw his fit and you had to say boo to him.'

'Maybe she did, but so what?' Marwood visibly forced himself to relax. 'Look, man, it was no big deal. It was a hospital party. I danced with her a couple of times. I like her, she's a lovely dancer. He'd had a couple of drinks and he followed me to the gents and started in at me like he'd caught us screwing or something. I was really worried for a moment till he said something about niggers which got me so mad I started yelling back, then suddenly he was retreating so fast I don't think I'd have caught him on

159

a bicycle. When I mentioned it to Pam, to Mrs Waterson, she said it happened all the time.'

'With people he got jealous of?'

'Oh no. He was usually too busy playing his own away games to get jealous. But these explosions could happen any place, any time. That's what lost him his job. He flew off the handle over something and yelled at his boss. It had happened before and he'd got away with it. He was good at his work and they made allowances for artistic temperament. But this time he went too far. So he blew up again, told them he'd go into business on his own account and walked out.'

'You must know Mrs Waterson pretty well for her to tell you all this.'

'Pretty well, but not as well as you're thinking, Sergeant. We're not lovers. She needs someone to talk to, someone to trust. And the only reason I'm telling you this is so you'll have no need to go bothering her with questions. She's going through a hard time and it wouldn't take much more pressure to make her crack.'

Wield sighed. Why did people imagine that vulnerability was a defence against police questioning, especially when a woman was dead and both the men involved in her death were roving free?

'You do know it's a violent death we're investigating?' he said.

'I thought it was some kind of accident. Or was it more than that? Is that why you want to talk to the bastard?'

'He's a witness, that's all,' said Wield, who saw no reason to make Marwood privy to all the other complications in the case. 'Now perhaps you'll tell me how you knew Waterson would be in that pub.'

Marwood shrugged and said, 'All right. It *was* Pam. I bumped into her as she was coming into the hospital earlier. She was upset, needed someone to spill it out to, and I was handy. She probably regrets it now.'

'Yes, she probably does,' said Wield ironically. 'So what did she say?'

'She told me that Waterson had rung her earlier and asked her to meet him in the Sally. He said he needed money and could she bring some. He turned up late so they didn't have much time to talk. In any case when she handed over what cash she could get together, he said it wasn't enough and looked set for one of his explosions so she got out quick.'

'Leaving Waterson inside?'

'Yes. And I thought things might be resolved by getting you round there to pick him up. All right, if you wanted to bang him up for a while, that wouldn't bother me either. But I seem to have underestimated your capacity to cock things up.'

'Yes, sir,' said Wield. 'Thanks for your call anyway.'

'Any time.' The doctor hesitated, then said, 'Look, I'd prefer Mrs Waterson didn't know it was me . . .'

Wield grimaced. For his part he felt the doctor deserved the promise of confidentiality, but there was no way of getting Dalziel to rubber stamp humanitarian gestures.

'We'll try to be discreet, sir,' he said. 'But she will have to be interviewed, you understand that?'

'I suppose so,' said Marwood unhappily. 'But it'll be you doing the questioning, will it? You'll keep her out of that fat bastard Dalziel's clutches?'

'No, sorry, can't guarantee that,' said Wield, shaking his head. The resulting pain was like an affirmation of his wisdom at not making that kind of promise. And affirmation even stronger was unsuspectedly close at hand.

The door opened and the pretty Pakistani looked in.

'Sorry, but there's someone out here . . .'

She was gently but irresistibly eased aside and over the

161

threshold tripped the fat bastard himself. He looked from the nurse to Marwood and back again. Then, advancing on Wield, he said, 'Dr Livingstone, I presume? What in Christ's name have the natives been doing to you?'

Chapter 2

From each according to his ability: to each according to his need.

Dalziel had once stated this as the basis of his allocation of CID duties during an investigation. Pascoe had not cared to inquire if its source was a conscious or unconscious irony. But the morning after Waterson's second vanishing act and Wield's first gay assault, he had to admit the Fat Man seemed to have got it just about right.

He, Dalziel, had undertaken to grill the landlord of the Pilgrim's Salvation, and it was a universally acknowledged fact that grilling was hot and thirsty work. Seymour had been despatched to see if his boyish charm could get more out of Pamela Waterson than the Superintendent had managed the previous night during an interview inhibited by the pressure of her duties and the presence of Ellison Marwood.

And he, Peter Pascoe, husband of a woman who was constantly urging upon him the need for more pulses and bran in his carnivorous diet, found himself in a health food shop.

The clue which had drawn him here was the car number Wield had noted. A computer check revealed the owner of the blue Peugeot Estate to be a Mr Harold Park of 27a String Lane. This was an off-city-centre street whose buildings were listed as being of architectural interest, though it was hard to imagine to whom. There was no visible 27a but 27 was a single-fronted, grimy-windowed shop called Food For Thought, sole prop. Gordon Govan. Pascoe entered and found himself at the end of a short queue of three monks being served by a shadowy figure with an accent like Billy Connolly with a bad cold. Finally the brown-robed figures left, lugging several hundred-weight of assorted seeds and grasses. Pascoe could only hope they bred budgies. He stepped up to the counter and the accent was joined by a pair of bright blue eyes and a tangle of gingery beard.

'Mr Govan, is it?' said Pascoe. 'Excuse me, but I'm looking for 27a.'

'Is that so?' mused the Scot, rolling non-existent r's.

'It is indeed. A Mr Harold Park.'

'You don't say?'

Pascoe sighed and produced his warrant card.

'The polis, is it? You should have said. I get some really weird characters in here.'

'Like monks?'

'Och, the wee brownies, you mean? Aye, we do a lot of business with the religious communities. They say it's in the Bible, but I reckon that stuff damps the libido, and that'd be a kind of advantage in their situation, I'm thinking. You know, a bit of roughage is cheaper than a bit of rough. Paul's Epistle to the Aberdonians.'

This threw an entirely new light on Ellie's leguminous evangelism. Pascoe switched it off and said, 'Mr Park? Can you help?'

'Aye. 27a's a wee flat above the shop. You reach it up the entry round the side. But he's no' there just now. He's a traveller, you see. Sometimes a whole week or more goes by without sight nor sound of him.'

'What's his line?'

'Veterinary products, I'm thinking. Pills for poodles, that kind of thing. Can I take a message?'

'You can ask him to contact me when he gets back. Here's my card. But I'll probably call back again anyway.'

'Aye, you'd be wise to do that,' said Govan, accompanying him to the door. 'Some people don't rush to help the polis, know what I mean? Me, I like to keep a good relationship going. Never know when we might need each other, eh? Man, I hope you've not far to your car. It looks like coming on rain. Or worse.'

It was indeed a cold snarling sort of day and in the east beyond the just visible cathedral tower a swelling bank of cloud threatened the snow this mild winter had so far spared them.

Pascoe turned up his collar and said, 'I'm almost parked in the close. Nearest I could get, the Lane's so narrow.'

'Och, man, you should have come round the back. There's loading yards behind all these shops, did you not know that?'

Of course he knew. He'd been a cop too long in this town not to know its ins and outs. He just hadn't thought, that was all. Or rather he'd thought like a citizen instead of a policeman. Perhaps it wasn't just his leg that had needed a repair job.

He was scurrying along the pavement, head down in anticipation of the oncoming storm, and once again it was ordinary citizen Pascoe in charge, not DI Pascoe, for he was totally unaware of the pursuer at his heels till the attack was launched.

He felt his arm seized from behind. He began to turn, defensive reflexes lumbering into life, but it was too late. A hand caught at the nape of his neck, his head was dragged back, and the main assault was launched at his unprotected face. He felt a soft warm moistness against his mouth, and just as he registered what was happening and started to enjoy it, contact was broken and Chung said, 'Now that's for being a good boy, Pete, honey.'

164

'What do I get for being a bad boy?' gasped Pascoe.

'We'll have to debate that with Ellie,' laughed Chung. 'But not in the street where we may frighten the natives.'

Several of the natives were already looking at them with undisguised interest. Pascoe couldn't blame them. It wasn't often that you saw a defenceless policeman being sexually assaulted in Mid-Yorkshire.

He said, 'OK, what have I done?'

'We got him, Pete! He's said he'll do it. Hallelujah! I've found my God!'

'He's really said he'll do it?' said Pascoe incredulously.

'I had to work on him a bit,' she grinned. 'But yes, I've hooked the big one. And I just wanted to say thank you, Pete. Without you, I couldn't even have got started.'

'Oh no,' said Pascoe emphatically. 'It was nothing to do with me!'

'Don't be modest, sweetie.'

Chung sank a little in Pascoe's admiration. A director of the top rank ought to be able to tell the difference between modesty and blind terror.

'Walk with me a ways,' said Chung, her grip on his arm brooking no denial. 'I'm on my way to the close to break the news to the Canon. Seems he may have got some silly notion he was up for the part and we don't want him sulking, do we?'

After a few paces her need to use her arms when talking gave him his release but he didn't try to escape. There was in her company such an overflow of vitality that a man would need to be a very dull clod to want to evade that warm aureole.

She was talking about her plans for the Mysteries and after a while Pascoe managed to distance himself sufficiently from her infectious enthusiasm to say, 'Chung, what I don't really get is why you're so keen on these plays. I should have thought they embodied just about every ism that ever got up your nose. I can see how you can direct Shakespeare to get your own ideas across, but surely this stuff is pretty intractable?'

She punched him. It may have been intended as a playful blow but the ribs that received it felt like they could now fit into a thirty-six jacket instead of his normal forty-two.

'So that's how you see me, huh? A preachy polemicist? Well, maybe, but that's not where I start, Pete. The play's the thing, the conscience-catching comes a long way second. This is where it all began, these are the roots, the modern European theatre starts here – '

'I thought the Greeks – ' interrupted Pascoe foolishly.

'Same sort of thing, but it died and had to start all over again, this time with *our* society, *our* psychology, our meteorology, *our* gods; and we can tune in at a stage far earlier in evolutionary terms than Greek classical drama.'

'You sound very . . . Euro-minded,' said Pascoe cautiously.

'What dat you say, my man?' mocked Chung. 'Don't let the slanty eyes fool you, my boy. My daddy brought my mummy back from Malaya with him and this little girl was brought up in would you believe Birmingham?'

She laughed joyously at the idea. Why it should seem so incongruous Pascoe wasn't sure, but he found himself laughing too.

By now they had passed his car park and were at the entrance to the close. Pascoe halted and said firmly, 'I am not going any further. You can spike your Canon without my moral support.'

'Hey, if I need a policeman, I'll blow my whistle,' said Chung. 'But don't go. Come into the cathedral with me, let me show you something.'

Once more he was whirled along, this time out of the chill winter air into the chiller aseasonal atmosphere of the great church. It was empty except for a couple of shadowy figures, which Pascoe hoped were human, gliding along a side aisle. His agnosticism was not proof against the humbling power of these vibrant spaces but Chung's flame burnt bright enough to meet whatever occupied them on level terms. She led him to the choir and made him stoop to look at the woodcarvings beneath the misericords. They consisted of figures, some individual, some in small groups, but all finely differentiated, of men at their trades and at their play. Here were tanners, tinkers, herds and hunters; here were men playing pipes and tabors, shawms and citoles; here were dancers, dicers, tumblers and mummers.

'The guy who carved these knew those people, he'd seen them, he knew they were as important and everlasting as anything else in this place. I'm not doing any prissy historical reconstruction, Pete. I'm plugging into the continuum. Come on, there's some more in the Pliny Chapel.'

But when they reached the chapel they found it was occupied. Named after Sir William de Pliny, whose tomb stood here, topped by a full-size brass effigy of himself and his wife, with a small dog at their feet, this tiny chapel was set aside for private prayer. Standing at the foot of the tomb with her head bowed was a woman. Pascoe paused on the threshold but Chung went straight in. For a second he thought this was crass insensitivity, then she spoke and he realized it was quite the opposite.

'Mrs Horncastle, are you all right?'

He didn't recognize the woman till she looked up. But in the brief moment before she re-organized her features to a social smile, he recognized Chung was right to be concerned.

'Miss Chung. How are you?' she said.

'I'm fine. Like I say, how are *you*?'

'Oh, don't worry about me. Really I'm fine too.'

'You looked upset,' said Chung bluntly.

'Did I? Perhaps I did. It's silly. Don't laugh, but it's the dog.'

'The dog?'

'Yes.' She set her hand on the little brass dog's head and stroked it.

'I used to have a dog very like this, a little terrier, Sandy, I called him. He got on Eustace's nerves. Well, he could be naughty, I suppose. And whenever he wanted a walk, he used to jump up and lick my face, then run to the door and leap up at the handle as if he were trying to open it. Sometimes he scratched the paint and Eustace became really furious. But it was only paint, wasn't it?'

'I'd say so,' said Chung gravely. 'What happened to Sandy?'

'He died. He somehow got out by himself and wandered out of the close into the main road and got knocked over. People said I should get another, but Eustace said I would be foolish to risk getting so upset again over a dumb beast so I never did. I'd often noticed how like Sandy the Pliny dog was – at least I thought so, though Eustace said I was imagining the resemblance. But they were alike.'

Suddenly she laughed and said, 'Do you have dreams, Miss Chung?'

'You mean, like ambitions?'

'Oh no. I gave those up long ago. I mean dreams, while you're asleep. I expect you do. Who doesn't? They mean nothing. Well, I had a dream, only I've had it two or three times and repetition suggests significance, doesn't it? I dreamt I woke up but couldn't move and after a while I realized that I was made of brass, like Lady de Pliny here, lying on top of our tomb with a brass Eustace by my side. And even though I was brass, it was so cold, so bitterly cold, I could feel my whole being contracting with the chill of it, and I wanted to scream out in agony, only I couldn't, being brass. Then I felt a movement against my legs, and on and on, higher and higher, till suddenly there was the touch of something warm and moist on my face and I realized the little dog at my feet was licking me. Gradually the warmth of his tongue began to spread through my body till finally I was able to move. What pain those first movements cost me! I was like an old arthritic woman, tottery, weak, uncertain. I looked around and my little strength failed again. I wasn't just on a tomb, I was *in* a tomb, surrounded by solid walls running with damp and unbroken except by a huge metal door. It had a handle, but even when I crawled across to the door and pulled myself up by the handle, putting my full weight on it, I couldn't feel the slightest movement. Full of despair, all I could think of was to stagger back to my plinth and lie down again alongside Eustace, this time for ever. But when I set off back, the dog rushed by me and began leaping up at the handle, just like Sandy used to when he wanted to go for a walk. Of course, at home he could never reach it and even if he could, he could never have turned it. There I stood by my brass husband, watching the poor little beast leaping higher and higher, but always in vain, and do you know, I felt sorrier for him than I did for myself. So I determined to stagger back to the door and have one more try, when suddenly he gave a mighty bound and his teeth caught around the handle and for a moment he hung there, feet scrabbling at the door, and he looked so pathetic I could have wept. Then slowly the handle began to move. I couldn't believe it. Lower and lower he pulled it, lower and lower. Then there was a loud grating noise and the door swung slowly open, and through it I could see a sunlit lawn and hear birds singing. And Sandy let go and dropped to the ground and stood outside in the sunlight, barking at me to join him.

'Now wasn't that a silly dream, Miss Chung? A silly woman's dream?'

She tried for the bright tone of one who is amused at her own absurdity but Chung did not respond in kind.

'Oh no, Mrs Horncastle,' she said. 'I don't see anything silly in it. Nothing at all.'

She put her arm round the woman's shoulders as she spoke and Pascoe, who had been edging further and further back as the story progressed, turned and hurried from the gloomy cathedral alone and felt a quite illogical relief to find himself out in the chill winter daylight once again.

In fact it wasn't just the contrast which made the day seem brighter. Winter had threatened to deceive once more, and a pallid sun was giving the storm clouds a pewter lining. Dan Trimble would be pleased. A couple more days of decent weather should see the car park and garage complex completed well within its funding schedule. And it would be nice to be able to park near the rear door again instead of across the street.

The builders were hard at it erecting the small gatehouse modern security concerns made almost obligatory. It would be annoying to be checked in and out of your own backyard, but better than the risk of some madman driving in at will with a truckload of Semtex. He glimpsed Arnie Stringer but there was no sign of Swain though he'd noticed him on arrival that morning. Perhaps now his financial problems were likely to be over, he didn't feel the need to soil his own hands for more than a couple of hours each day.

As he passed the desk, Sergeant Broomfield looked up and said, 'Any luck?'

'Not yet. Any word on the yobboes who did Wieldy?'

'Nothing. But talking of yobboes, the *Post* has been at us about that barney in the Rose and Crown. They're doing a feature evidently. You can guess the sort of thing. The football might be lousy, but City supporters are after promotion to the hooligans' first division.'

'Shit. That's just putting ideas into their tiny minds,' groaned Pascoe. The landlord of the Rose and Crown was still in hospital with a serious eye injury. The eyes of all the potential witnesses seemed to have been damaged also for no two of them gave corresponding descriptions of any of the brawlers.

'Seymour back yet?' he asked.

'Don't be silly. It's only ten-fifteen. Send young Dennis into a nurses' home and you can't really expect him to surface for at least twenty-four hours! The Super's back though.'

'How'd he look?'

'Not happy. I asked him if he'd had any luck at the Sally and he said the landlord was as helpful as a knitted noddy, and his ale was lousy too.'

'Bad as that! I'll let him alone for a bit, I think.'

'He's got company anyway,' said Broomfield.

'Oh? Who?'

The sergeant shrugged and said, 'Who knows? *He* was on the desk when they turned up.'

He nodded towards the inner office where PC Hector sat, his head bowed over a typewriter with the rapt concentration of a chimpanzee wondering how best to start *Hamlet*.

Pascoe sighed and went on his way.

He was mildly curious as to the identity of Dalziel's visitors, though it wasn't an itch that required immediate scratching. But as he reached the CID floor he heard the cry of a wounded mastodon. His expert ear identified its root emotion as rage. Normal procedure was to lock yourself in a cupboard until you knew its object, but for once feeling safe, he indulged his curiosity by tapping at the Superintendent's door, sticking his head inside and asking, 'Did you call, sir?'

The mystery of the visitors was solved. They were Philip Swain and Eden Thackeray. The solicitor smiled at him. Swain, who looked pale and haggard, ignored him. And Dalziel snarled, 'No, I bloody didn't, but now you're here, you'd best come in. I'd like a witness if, as seems bloody likely, I'm about to be slandered!'

'Please, please,' said Thackeray suavely. 'There can be no slander because there are no accusations. To clear the air, let me say at the outset that we do not dispute that my client gave his statement voluntarily, there was no question of coercion, and everything was done according to the rules.'

'Thank you very much,' growled Dalziel.

'Now all he wants to do, voluntarily, without coercion, and strictly following the rules, is modify that statement slightly,' continued the solicitor.

'Is that all?' said Dalziel with heavy sarcasm.

'I have here copies of his revised statement. Perhaps I should read it to you so that any problems of comprehension or interpretation may be ironed out.'

The solicitor put on a pair of hornrimmed spectacles and coughed drily behind his hand. It was clear to Pascoe that besides serving his client's needs, he was really enjoying himself.

He began to speak.

'I should stress in preamble that the statement is exactly as Mr Swain dictated it, free from my own or anyone else's emendation or intervention.'

He coughed once more and began reading.

'"When Superintendent Dalziel brought me to the station on the night Gail died, I think I was in a state of shock. Everything felt so unreal, distant, unimportant. Everything except Gail's death, that is. This state of shock

172

continued for some time after that night but it wasn't till I went to see my doctor on Mr Thackeray's advice that it was diagnosed.

'"I shall always feel I bear some guilt for Gail's death. Somehow I must have failed her. And perhaps if I hadn't rushed round to Waterson's house that night, things could have been worked out. Whatever the truth of the matter, I now see that in my first statement these feelings warped my judgement and my memory to the point where I wanted to assume total guilt, even stretching beyond the moral and psychological to the physical, and claim that my hand was actually on the gun when it went off. Now I can recollect and more importantly admit what really happened.

'"When Gail started waving the gun around, it was Waterson not me who made a grab at it. Perhaps he felt threatened, perhaps his sole concern was to prevent her from doing herself harm. I don't know. All I know is that the gun went off and Waterson seemed to go to pieces. He staggered away from Gail with the gun in his hand. I took it from him for fear he might inadvertently fire it again and cause further harm. He collapsed against the wall and I remained where I was, clearly in a state of shock, till Mr Dalziel arrived.

'"I am not attempting to evade responsibility by modifying my original statement, merely to record the exact truth, for I now see this must be the first step in my attempt to come to terms with my loss, my grief, my guilt."

Thackeray stopped reading and said, 'That is my client's revised and movingly frank statement, which I am sure you will accept in the spirit in which it is offered.'

Dalziel, who had listened like a country squire at a Lenten sermon, yawned widely and said, 'Aye, I think I can promise that much.'

'Thank you,' said Thackeray. 'No doubt the other witness, Mr Waterson, will confirm this version of events in his statement when it becomes available.'

Oh, you cunning old devil! Pascoe thought admiringly. Somehow you've got wind of Waterson's statement, or perhaps you've simply made an inspired guess. Here was an adversary truly worthy of Dalziel!

'We're still trying to locate Mr Waterson,' said Dalziel evasively.

'Strange what heavy weather you're making of it,' said Thackeray. 'And I fail to see why Mr Waterson's absence, however motivated, should further delay an early settlement of this matter. Common humanity cries out for the inquest to be resumed and the remains to be released to next-of-kin. My client has suffered too much already.'

'Not at our hands,' said Dalziel. 'You said yourself, everything were by the book.'

'Indeed it was,' agreed the solicitor. 'Nothing was missed. Except perhaps a few opportunities. For instance, when you called in your doctor to look at Mr Waterson on the night of the *accident*, you didn't ask him to examine Mr Swain too.'

'No need. Waterson were a nervous wreck. Mr Swain here were fine. He looked a sight better than he does now, if you don't mind me saying.'

Swain, who hadn't opened his mouth since Pascoe arrived, glared angrily at Dalziel but Thackeray patted his arm soothingly and said, 'Yes, I recall you mention in your own statement how calm and collected Mr Swain appeared to be. And you stressed this again the following day when we first discussed the case. I got the impression then that you were drawing inferences from your observation which were not to my client's advantage.'

'I just state the facts as I see 'em, nowt more.'

'Of course. What you didn't see was the possibility that

174

this apparent control of my client's emotions might in fact be symptomatic of the shock which has since been diagnosed and whose delayed and more obvious physical manifestations are, as you have just observed, only now becoming visible. What a pity with a doctor on the spot that night that you didn't . . .'

'He were examined the next day,' interrupted Dalziel.

'Indeed,' said Thackeray. 'But we must ask ourselves, Superintendent, what were the instructions you gave the examining doctor on that occasion. Incidentally, my acceptance that things were done according to the rules on Tuesday night does not of course extend to include that examination on Wednesday afternoon. Where consent is obtained by deception, there is no legality.'

Dalziel was slumped low in his chair, a posture which pushed his embonpoint into corrugations along whose valley bottoms beneath his shirt his fingers scraped glacially. He was beginning to look defeated. It was not an edifying sight.

'If you want to tell the world I had Mr Swain examined because his missus were a junkie, go ahead,' he snapped. 'Seems to me all this fine talk amounts to is instead of one statement from your client, we've got two. More the merrier, say I.'

It was an untypically feeble counter, underlined by Thackeray's formally polite appreciative chuckle.

'That's it,' he said. 'Let's think of them as rough draft and fair copy. It's so easy to get things wrong the first time, isn't it? You of all people should understand that, Mr Dalziel.'

'Eh?'

'Your own statement, I mean. Don't look so alarmed. I haven't been burgling your office. I was talking to Mr Trimble about another matter, and I happened to mention my concern at these delays, and in particular at the distress

175

it must be causing Mrs Delgado who is too ill to travel and who is naturally impatient for her child's body to be released to the States for burial. And Mr Trimble, though sympathetic, told me that where witnesses clashed, and one of them was a senior police officer, he must obviously place a strong reliance on that man's version of things.'

'That was nice of him,' said Dalziel savagely.

'Indeed. I drew the assumption that it must be yourself he was referring to, and I wonder now whether you might not care to take a long look at the detail of your own statement. No one is perfect. I'm sure your own vast experience contains many instances of a highly trained observer proving to have been deceived.'

Dalziel shot Pascoe a glance of promissory malice. Surely he can't think I've been talking to Eden about my little experiment!

Thackeray had risen and stood with his hand on Swain's shoulder as he spoke. Now he exerted a gentle pressure and the man rose.

'That's good,' said Dalziel. 'You can hardly see the strings!'

'I'm sorry?' said Thackeray with dangerous mildness.

Pascoe tried to telepath a warning to his chief. This was a lost battle. Nothing to do but keep your head down and regroup. Pointless to stand up in the trenches and hurl clods at the triumphant tanks.

But Dalziel wanted a medal more than his supper.

'I just meant, funny thing, this shock. Takes away the power of speech, does it, unless someone else writes the lines?'

Swain looked ready to retort angrily, but Thackeray was swift with a palliative misunderstanding.

'If you're referring to my client's decision to take part in the forthcoming production of the Mystery Plays, certainly this has been recommended as a useful therapy.

Role-playing has an honourable history in psychological rehabilitation and what better way of coming to terms with guilt than exploring the greatest guilt of all?'

Pascoe was agog at the implication of this. Could Swain really have a part in Chung's production? And if so . . . but Thackeray hadn't finished.

'I hear you too are planning to tread the boards, Superintendent?' he said pleasantly.

'That's right.'

'As God, I gather? I hope you also might find the experience therapeutic. But I hope even more that your evident willingness to share a stage with Mr Swain signals an end to harassment and an early wrapping up of this tragic affair. Good day.'

He left. Swain followed, but paused at the door and said, with no expression on his face or in his voice to hint whether he was being mocking or conciliatory, 'See you at rehearsal.' Then he too was gone.

Dalziel opened a drawer in his desk, took out a bottle and a glass, poured an unhealthy measure and drank long and deep.

'Well, come on,' he said. 'When you look like that, you've either got piles or you're chewing on a serious thought. Spit it out!'

'No, it's nothing,' said Pascoe. 'Except that, well, it's an odd business, this . . .'

'You've noticed that, have you? Well, thank God we promoted you. Man as sharp as that deserves to go right to the top!'

The unfairness of Dalziel's picking on an easy target after his recent mauling by Thackeray did not surprise Pascoe, but it stung him.

'But there's no reason why it should be seen as a sinister oddness,' he continued briskly. 'In fact, it's all far too daft for planning. Couldn't it be that what we've got here is

177

quite simply what both Swain and Waterson say – and what with very little adjustment you partially witnessed – a suicide, or at worst a tragic accident?'

'You think I'm getting obsessed, is that it?'

'No,' lied Pascoe. 'In fact, very likely you're thinking on these lines already. Like Mr Thackeray said, you wouldn't have agreed to taking part in Chung's Mysteries with Swain if you'd still been after him. Would you?'

'Mebbe not,' said Dalziel. 'I'm not sure, lad, and that's the truth of it. Every bugger seems to know more than me and be two or three steps ahead of me just now. Almost like we've got a mole.'

Oh God, thought Pascoe, thinking of his part and Ellie's part in feeding Dalziel to Chung. But more worrying even than this was the sight of his notoriously invulnerable chief in doubt and disarray.

As if sensing Pascoe's concern, Dalziel tried for a confident smile and said, 'But not to worry, eh? I'm to be God Allbloodymighty, and by God, one way or another I'll send Swain down to hell and make old Eden jump out of his dusty briefs before I'm done with him.'

It wasn't bad as a cry of defiance, but it seemed to Pascoe that he'd got his lines wrong. It wasn't God but the fallen angels who went in for cries of defiance which might rise to, but could never disturb, the real Allbloodymighty sitting on his crystal throne.

Chapter 3

Perhaps the great secret of Dennis Seymour's likeability was that he didn't work at it. He was Juan rather than Giovanni, his charm was intuitive not calculated, and its rewards came more as surprises than triumphs.

Having committed himself to his beautiful Bernadette, he was genuinely reluctant to put himself in the way of other offers. Not that he ever sought them, but it was incredible what a sympathetic interrogation could lead to. Recently a 'friend' in the Force had hinted to Bernadette that her fiancé was CID's sexual stormtrooper and this hadn't gone down too well, so Seymour adopted his coldest, most official manner when he called on Pamela Waterson.

To start with she replied in kind, indeed was almost hostile; Seymour wouldn't have minded if she'd stayed this way, but he couldn't help being genuinely sympathetic when she told him she was too tired to put up with much questioning, and *she* couldn't help responding to his genuine sympathy. After fifteen minutes they were sitting on a sofa, drinking coffee and capping each other's awful-job anecdotes.

'What really gets up my nose is being me,' she said finally after a long recital of plaints.

'Sorry?'

'What I mean is, I don't have to put up with all this crap. Overworked, understaffed, poorly paid, lousy facilities, being told I'm a selfless angel when I do my job, and a selfish shit when I moan about it; I could walk away from all this, you know. Head for the private sector tomorrow, get everything I want. Or go abroad and get twice as much as I need. Only, because I'm *me*, I won't do it, I can't do it. It's crazy, isn't it? Like sitting in a prison cell with only two ways out, a door to comfortable freedom or a window with a thousand-foot drop to bare rock, and knowing you can never take the door.'

'You're sure about that?' said Seymour.

'Of course I'm sure! I've just said it, haven't I?' she said angrily.

'No, what I mean is, there's usually more than two ways out of things.'

'Is that so? Name me another two,' she challenged.

'All right,' grinned Seymour. 'What would happen if you threw a bedpan at the Chief Health Officer?'

'I'd get sacked.'

'That's one. And what would happen if you got pregnant?'

'At the moment I think they'd call the poor little blighter Jesus,' she said sadly.

'It'd make two whatever they called him. Do you fancy a family, luv?'

'I took it for granted when I got married,' she said. 'I'm a Catholic, you see. Not good, but still Catholic. He had other ideas. I took the easy line and went along. No, that's not fair. I went along because that's what I wanted then. Now I wish . . . but it's too late . . .'

'It's definitely over between you then? You'll get divorced?'

She shook her head. 'No divorce,' she said. 'I'm still that much of a Catholic. But yes, it's definitely over. Oh, I still fancy him, I suppose. That funny-looking fellow who came the first time likely told you he caught us cuddling. Not that it meant anything. There's nothing so comfortable as a cuddle when you're tired and depressed.'

She glanced at Seymour thoughtfully as she spoke and he took a long draught of air from his empty coffee cup.

'You see,' she resumed, 'I didn't leave him because I found out he was different after we married. Rather, it was because he was more like himself than I realized.'

'Eh?' said Seymour.

She smiled and said, 'Does sound daft, doesn't it? What I mean is, before we married, I knew he talked big but got easily scared; I knew he was crazy about natural blondes with long legs. But none of it mattered. Knowing how frightened he got just seemed to make us closer, and I believed I could steer him clear of situations which might make him blow up. As for blondes with long legs, well, I was one, wasn't I? So what happened? Nothing, except that I found that to prove how unscared he was, he could get himself involved in stupid things. And I couldn't be around all the time to stop him blowing up. And his love of willowy blondes didn't stop with me. Like I say, I can't put the blame on not knowing what he was like!'

'What kind of stupid things did he get himself involved in?' wondered Seymour.

'Things like trying to set up on his own. I mean, you're mad to be self-employed when no one in his right senses would work for you in the first place!'

'But you still like him? So when he rang and asked you to meet him, you went?'

'Of course. Why not?' she demanded.

'You knew the police wanted him to help in a serious inquiry,' said Seymour as sternly as he could manage.

'Oh, *that*,' she said dismissively. 'You'll find him in the end. This business is just a silly tragic accident, right? It'd probably all be cleared up by now if he hadn't run off.'

'Very probably. So why'd he run?'

'I don't know. Because it made him feel important, likely.'

'Is that what he told you when you met?' said Seymour.

'No. I asked him about it, naturally, but he just got all mysterious, and that was one of the games I stopped playing with him very early on.'

'So what else did you talk about?'

'I can't remember all of it. Just the bad bits when he started getting excited. That's the trouble with Greg, the good bits are lovely, he can be charming, amusing, marvellous to be with ninety per cent of the time, but once you've had a taste of the other ten per cent, that's what you remember.'

'So tell me about the bad bits at the Sally,' said Seymour.

'Well, there were two. When I gave him Mr Swain's message – '

'Mr Swain?'

'Yes. He rang me a few days ago and asked if Greg had been in touch. When I said no, he said if I did hear from him, would I let him know?'

'So you told Mr Swain Greg had made contact?'

'Yes, and he said would I ask Greg to get in touch with him?'

'And what did Greg say when you told him this?'

'That was when he started getting excited, and it wasn't till I convinced him I'd not let on to Mr Swain where we were meeting that he calmed down. He said to tell Mr Swain not to worry, he'd definitely be hearing from him.'

'And has Swain rung you since last night?'

'Not that I know of.'

'Fine. Now what else upset your husband? You said there were two.'

'Yes. That was when he asked me for money. He said he was hard up and couldn't get to a bank. I gave him what I'd brought with me. About forty pounds, it was all I could manage. He told me it wasn't enough, he needed a lot more than that, and began to get very excited. God, he was trying to keep out of sight and he still couldn't control himself!'

She shook her head in exasperation, but there was still affection there too. There had to be something very attractive about this lunatic!

'So what happened?'

'I did the only thing possible to defuse things. I left.'

'And your husband?'

'When I looked back he was heading for the bar with my money.'

'And would this explosion transfer itself to somebody else?'

'Oh no. If he was by himself he might sit in a corner muttering for a while. But in a pub, he'd be all charm and good cheer in a couple of moments once I was away. That's always been the unfair thing about Greg. He comes out of these bouts fine; it's those around him who are fond of him that have things mucked up for them.'

She was close to tears. Seymour squeezed her hand, then hastily let it go. He tried to make his next question unambiguously official.

'Mrs Waterson,' he said. 'It's in everyone's interest for us to find Greg. Did he give any hint where he was staying? Until we talk with him, we can't wrap this thing up, you see. Has he got any close friends who might be putting him up?'

'If he has, they'll have blonde hair and long legs,' she said. 'Do I sound bitter? Well, perhaps I am, but not jealous bitter. Just that, well, it's sometimes a hell of a job making sense out of life, and this kind of stuff doesn't help. Are you married?'

'Me? No,' said Seymour uneasily. 'Heavily engaged, though.'

It felt a good time to retreat. He began to rise.

'One-way traffic, is it?' she said. 'Sorry. Look, sit down. Relax. Have some more coffee.'

'I can't,' said Seymour. 'I've got work to do.'

'Isn't that what you're doing here? Look, I'm enjoying talking to you. All right, so you're a cop, but it makes a change from nurses and doctors, believe me. And you're not like the others I've met. The ugly one, he was all right but I couldn't feel easy with him. And Mr Dalziel, he gave the impression he'd just keep going till he got everything

183

sorted out the way he wanted. That must be a great way to feel. Anyway, with him looking after the shop, what's your hurry?'

If she'd smiled seductively at him, Seymour would have been off at the double. But she just regarded him very seriously, very calmly, and though he had been aware from the start of her long legs and lissom figure, he now saw for the first time how truly beautiful she was, and simultaneously glimpsed the real depth of unhappiness beneath the revealed discontent.

Reluctantly, telling himself it was duty's call he was answering, he began to sit down again when the flat bell rang.

'I'll get it,' he said. There was an outside chance it might be Waterson, and he didn't want to give him a start.

But the face which glowered hostilely at him was black.

'Dr Marwood,' said Pamela Waterson behind him.

'I just thought I'd look in to see you were all right,' said the doctor. 'Don't let these fellows wear you out.'

'I'd say it's the hospital that wears her out,' retorted Seymour.

'Would you now? Who are you?'

'Detective-Constable Seymour.'

'Constable? It's been sergeants and superintendents up till now. Does a constable mean we're getting near the bottom of the barrel?'

A rude riposte flared in Seymour's mind but he damped it down.

'I'm just doing my job, sir,' he said woodenly. 'And for the time being I've finished it. Thank you for answering my questions, Mrs Waterson, and for the coffee. Excuse me, sir.'

He pushed past Marwood. Behind him as he descended the stairs he heard a brief exchange, then the door closing. But to his surprise, Marwood wasn't on the inside of it.

Footsteps came slapping down the concrete stair behind him and as he reached the vestibule of the nurses' home, Marwood's voice called, 'Constable. Mr Seymour. Hang on a minute.'

He stopped and turned.

'Yes, sir,' he said.

'Look, I was rude up there. I'm sorry.'

'Were you, sir? I didn't notice.'

'Balls. You almost gave me a mouthful. What stopped you? Me being a doctor or me being a black?'

The question was asked in as casually non-aggressive a fashion as it could be, but Seymour spotted its have-you-stopped-beating-your-wife quality and responded deftly, 'Me being a policeman, sir.'

Marwood laughed and said, 'I see you all come from the same mould in Mid-Yorkshire. You may look completely different, but inside you're all pretty sharp.'

Compliments now. The apology might have been due, but this meant he was after something. Giving or taking? wondered Seymour.

'I get worried about Mrs Waterson,' said the doctor as they strolled towards the car park together. 'She's been under a lot of pressure lately.'

Seymour unlocked the door of his car without answering. If Marwood had more to say, he'd say it.

He got in the car, closed the door, wound down the window and waited.

After a moment, the doctor said, 'Seems to me you people are making a real meal out of getting hold of that man of hers.'

'Doing our best, sir. The Super doesn't like getting the dogs out for a low-key inquiry.'

This was the merest zephyr of a provocation but Marwood felt it.

185

'Low-key? That woman back there's a nervous wreck and you call it low-key!'

'I'm sorry for Mrs Waterson's domestic problems, sir, but honestly I don't see that they're anything to do with us. We just want to talk to her husband to sort a few things out, then hopefully we can turn him loose to get his marriage straight. I get the impression they're still genuinely fond of each other.'

And this was provocation at gale force.

'Hey, listen, man, there's no way that marriage can ever be straight. He's unbalanced. More, he's a crook. Is that what it takes to get you people off your arses and going full pelt? He's a crook!'

'And what kind of crook is he, sir?' asked Seymour with what he hoped was just enough incredulity to push Marwood over the starting line. For now he guessed that the doctor's dilemma was not being able to get what he wanted unless he gave what he did not want to give.

Probably what he wanted was for Waterson to be put right out of the picture. But for some reason he felt this would put him out of the picture too.

And at last the explanation came.

'He's the kind of crook who asks his wife to steal drugs for him from the hospital!' grated Marwood. 'Now I haven't told you that. If you tell anyone I've told you that, especially Mrs Waterson, I'll deny it. But it's the truth. Now will you get the dogs out and put the useless shit behind bars where he belongs?'

Chapter 4

Initially, Seymour's report did little to rouse Dalziel's spirits.

'Drugs again,' he said. 'Shit. And did she do it?'

'Dr Marwood says not. I don't think he'd have told me about it if she had. It's Waterson he wants to get at, not her.'

'Sounds to me very like it's her he wants to get at,' said Dalziel salaciously. 'And what does she say?'

'I didn't ask her, sir,' said Seymour. 'I thought it best to get back here. Also if I'd gone straight back to her room, she'd have known it was the doctor who told me.'

'Give me strength,' said Dalziel. 'Did your mummy tell you always follow doctor's orders, or what? Listen, son, we're not a caring profession, we're a catching profession. It's crime you should worry about, not some black bugger's sensibilities.'

'I don't think his colour is terribly relevant,' interposed Pascoe.

'No? What if he's a yardie boss out to grab the Yorkie bar concession? What are you grinning at, Seymour? Why don't you browse through your Moriarty and see how many offences he's committed? For starters, the sod knew a crime had been attempted, but he kept it to himself. And why did she tell him, anyway? Could be she wanted to oblige hubby and the easiest way to get at the real happy stuff was to screw a doctor. Mebbe Marwood's running scared with all this police interest in the Infirmary so he's trying to get his retaliation in first. Mebbe Waterson's the Mid-Yorks drug king and Mrs Swain was

187

his customer as well as his tart. Didn't any of this cross your mind?'

Seymour, wilting under the assault, said bravely, 'I don't believe that about Marwood and Mrs Waterson. She's really unhappy, I think, and he's genuinely worried about her because he, well, because he's in love with her.'

'Oh aye?' said Dalziel in disgust. 'Forget Moriarty. Bugger off back to your Mills and Boon.'

Seymour, uncertain whether this was his dismissal, looked to Pascoe who jerked his head towards the door. As he went out, the Chief Inspector caught his eye and drooped his lid in the suspicion of a wink.

'You were a bit hard on the boy,' said Pascoe after the door had shut.

'You reckon? You rate him, don't you? Needs stiffening up if you ask me.'

'You make him a bit nervous, that's all,' said Pascoe.

'Me?' said Dalziel in amazement. 'Bloody hell. Now I've heard everything. Only thing that's making Seymour nervous is getting used to the rhythm method likely. Young Bernadette's clean, by the way.'

'Clean?' said Pascoe, scandalized. 'What do you mean? AIDS? And how . . .?'

'Don't be daft. No, you weren't around, were you? When he got himself engaged and it dawned on me this thing wasn't going to burn itself out, I passed Miss McCrystal's details on to Special Branch. Well, it wouldn't help his career if it turned out his in-laws were card-carrying Provos, would it? But it was OK. They looked at the family up, down and sideways, and though they'll sing "The Wearing o' the Green" with the worst of them, it's Guinness talk not gun talk.'

'I'm sure Seymour will be delighted to have Special Branch's approval,' said Pascoe stonily.

'Oh, they don't approve. In their eyes, any Irish connection's a bad connection, but I told 'em to sod off and get back to scratching John McCormack records. So, what do you make of this stuff your protégé's brought back?'

'I don't know. I haven't met Mrs Waterson or this doctor. Seymour obviously thought they were straight. What did you make of them?'

'I only saw 'em briefly, I was more concerned with checking Wieldy was all right. This Marwood, that's twice he's tried to drop Waterson in it. Twice he's double-crossed the woman by breaking her confidence.'

'All's fair in love and war.'

'Aye, but which is this?'

'You weren't serious about him being a drug-pusher, were you?' said Pascoe.

'Because he's a doctor, you mean? So were Pritchard and Palmer and Crippen and Cream! You have a look at him, Peter. And do a bit of straight talking with the woman. You should have gone yourself in the first place. Seymour's too susceptible. One thing in his report makes sense, though. Here where the woman said if Waterson was staying with a friend, she'd have long legs and blonde hair. She could be right. Let's try to get a line on his love-life before Mrs Swain, shall we?'

'He's beginning to look a lot better bet as the pusher, isn't he?' said Pascoe.

'You reckon? Why?'

Pascoe started ticking off arguments on his fingers.

'One, Mrs Swain was a user and Swain seems in the clear on that. Two, he tried to get his wife to supply hospital dope. Three, it would explain his reluctance to put himself under a spotlight by answering questions about the shooting, even though it was . . . looks like an accident.'

He stood before Dalziel with his three fingers raised like

a primary teacher's visual aid. The fat man reached out and took hold of his forefinger.

'Nice,' he said, 'except that, one, he volunteered a statement when he could have kept stumm and pleaded shock which in his case seemed a lot more likely than with Swain. Two, his up and down behaviour makes him sound more like a user than a pusher, though I know the two aren't exclusive. And three, he was touching his wife for a few quid last night, and I've not come across many poor pushers.'

With each argument he forced one of Pascoe's fingers back into his palm, leaving him with a clenched fist and wondering where he could best use it.

Then Dalziel laughed and said, 'But you may well be right, Peter. One thing, accident or not, we've got plenty of reason now to go full pelt after Mr Gregory bloody Waterson!'

'Yes, sir,' said Pascoe, glad to see that the dullness which had descended on his chief as a result of Eden Thackeray's visit seemed to be lightening. 'One other thing, though, about those letters . . .'

'Not those bloody letters again! I wish I'd just burnt the things. You mustn't let yourself be distracted from the real work, lad. I want you back down at the Infirmary really leaning on Mrs Waterson, and I don't mean feeling her up like young Seymour! So don't hang about. It's not long to opening time and we've done bugger-all yet. Thank God Wieldy will be back tomorrow. Have you seen him yet? Sixteen stitches he had on his face last night, and I tell you, you could hardly notice the difference. If anything, it was a slight improvement!'

His laughter followed Pascoe down the corridor. Perhaps after all there were worse things than the dullness of defeat.

* * *

Pamela Waterson was not pleased to be disturbed by her second policeman that morning, but when she heard what Pascoe had to say, her resentment turned to something more guarded, less readable.

'Who told you this?' she asked quietly.

Pascoe shrugged and watched her trying to work out either the informer or her response to the information.

'Yes, it's true,' she said finally. 'A few weeks back, before our final split, he asked me if I could steal some drugs. I said no. End of story.'

'You didn't mention this to my colleagues.'

'Why should I? There wasn't any crime, was there?'

'Come on, Mrs Waterson. He wasn't asking you for aspirin for his headache, was he? Did he specify?'

'No. He didn't get the chance. It was the last straw for me. One of the last straws. I choked him off, told him we were through and left.'

She hadn't asked Pascoe to sit down. People often thought that keeping a cop standing got rid of him quicker. It didn't. He leaned against the back of a chair and studied the woman. She looked calm and controlled, the kind of face you would want to see from your vulnerable hospital bed. But he could sense something beneath it – what was it Seymour had said? – she was very unhappy; yes, that was it, but more too; last straws were still being loaded on her, he suspected. He knew from experience that physical suffering makes you selfish, but there were kinds of mental and spiritual suffering in which the woes of others beat on you like hammer blows, and in that state a nurse might easily feel each death, each decline, in her ward as a personal defeat.

He said, 'Is your husband an addict, Mrs Waterson?'

She said, 'He doesn't inject, didn't, anyway, I'd have known when we were together. Hash, yes. Who doesn't? Amphetamines sometimes, and I don't doubt if there's coke to be sniffed, he'll sniff it. But I'd not have called him an addict.'

She sounded defensive. Both Wield and Seymour had felt that her feelings for her estranged husband were ambivalent. Being a Catholic provided acceptable reasons for avoiding a divorce. Even God was sometimes usable.

'When he asked you to steal the drugs, did you understand they were for his personal use?'

'Yes, of course. What else? Oh hell, you're not wondering if he's a dealer, are you? For God's sake, he can't organize his own life, let alone a drug ring! If you gave him an hour glass, it'd lose time. If he was pushing the stuff himself, he'd have it on tap and he wouldn't be hard up, would he?'

She was echoing Dalziel's logic. Pascoe smiled ruefully at finding himself on the receiving end of the same put-down twice in an hour.

Then, resuming his most serious expression, he said, 'Your husband's hard up, you say? Didn't he get any severance pay when he left his job?'

'As a matter of fact he did. He wasn't entitled as he walked out of his own accord, but they gave him a generous ex gratia payment, I suppose because they liked him. Couldn't stick him, but they liked him.' She laughed humourlessly. 'Like me.'

'So where's that gone?'

'God knows. That studio conversion he had done in the attic must have cost. He couldn't work in the spare room, not Greg. Always the grandiose ideas. Had to have his own studio . . .'

Her voice tailed off. Pascoe followed her train of thought . . . if Greg hadn't got Swain to build his studio, he'd not have met Gail Swain and she wouldn't be dead and Greg wouldn't be . . .

What the hell *was* Waterson doing?

He said, 'All right, so you can't see your husband as a pusher. But try this. If someone your husband wanted to impress found themselves short of whatever turned them on, wouldn't he like to project himself as Jack the Lad, Mr Fixit, the man with the best connections?'

She explored her hollowed cheeks with her fingertips, deep blue eyes directed at without being focused on his face. Then she gave a parody of a smile and said softly, 'I thought you said you didn't know my husband.'

'You think I'm right, then?'

'That's the way he is. Especially with the blondes.'

Whatever she said, in the Irish stew of reasons for leaving her husband, sexual jealousy was the red meat. It made the next question easier.

He said, very brisk and businesslike, 'We'd like to talk with anyone who may have had a relationship with your husband. Discreetly as we can, of course. We wouldn't want other families getting hurt.'

He felt a pang of shame at his slyness in offering her at the same time a conscience-salver and an incentive. Which weighed the stronger he couldn't guess, but she replied without hesitation, 'Christine Coombes. Beverley King.'

'Only two?' he said, recognizing his Dalzielesque crassness even as he spoke.

'Two I'm certain of,' she said without apparent resentment. 'Lots of strong suspicions but I'm not turning you loose on suspicions.'

So that was her conscience taken care of. He asked, 'This certainty . . .?'

'Mrs Coombes I found letters from. Miss King, I caught him in the stirrups.'

'Good lord. I mean, I'm sorry. Is there anything else you can tell me? Addresses, say?'

'No idea. King works at Greg's old firm and Chris Coombes is married to Peter Coombes, the personnel

193

director, so you can see he didn't mind doing it on his own doorstep, almost literally in King's case.'

She had been standing stiff and erect during all this interview. Now her leg muscles seemed to lose their strength, she staggered slightly and sat down.

Pascoe said, 'Are you all right, Mrs Waterson?'

'Fine. Look, why don't you sit down, I've been very rude . . .'

He looked at her uneasily. He preferred her strength.

'No, thanks, I really have to be on my way and I think I've taken up enough of your time anyway. Thanks for your help. I hope this all works out for you somehow. Don't get up. I'll let myself out.'

He left guiltily. On the stairs he met a nurse coming up. He stopped her and said, 'You know Mrs Waterson? She looks a bit under the weather to me. If you could just look in casually in a couple of minutes, see she's all right . . . thank you.'

He went on his way feeling slightly better, but not much.

Chapter 5

Andrew Dalziel, despite what his friends said, was no paranoiac. He did not believe himself to be infallibly perfect or unjustly persecuted. His great strength was that he walked away from his mistakes like a horse from its droppings, and as he himself once remarked, if you leave crap on people's carpets, you've got to expect a bit of persecution.

But when he believed himself right, he did not readily accept evidence that he might be wrong, not while there was any stone left unturned.

Gail Swain was, of course, the keystone, but there wasn't much future in turning a corpse. Philip Swain was for the moment safely bastioned by the formidable Eden Thackeray and it would take a pickaxe to turn him. Gregory Waterson sounded as if he could be turned by a strong ant, but they had to find the useless bugger first. Which left very few candidates for up-ending.

After Pascoe's departure, he took another look at a memo he had received that morning. If Pascoe could have seen it, he would have realized just how desperate Dalziel was getting for this was from the Central Police Computer which he usually regarded with all the enthusiasm of Ned Ludd for a stocking-frame. It read: SAS PERSONNEL RECORDS NOT ACCESSIBLE WITHOUT MOD, AUTHORIZATION BUT SEARCH OF ARMY RECORDS REVEALS CPL MITCHELL, GARY, BORN CONSETT NORTHUMBERLAND 8.6.59 ENLISTED CATERING CORPS 1977, DISCHARGED 1983, NO CRIMINAL RECORD.

Beggars couldn't be choosers, he told himself. And with a bovine belch which reminded him how close it was to lunch-time, he rose and went to do a bit of stone-twisting at the Mid-Yorkshire Gun Club.

The club clearly did good midday business as anxious executives got rid of their morning tensions. A distant fusillade from some indoor range punctured the air as he waited in a small and militarily tidy office. After a few minutes a tall athletic-looking man came in. He had earmuffs round his neck, an irritated expression on his face, and a broken revolver in his hand which he laid carefully on top of a filing cabinet.

'I'm Mitchell,' he said, sitting on a swivel chair, crossing his legs on his desk and scratching his designer stubble. 'Hope this won't take too long. I said everything I had to say to your errand boy couple of weeks back.'

Dalziel said solicitously, 'Nasty thing, that acne. Still,

they say you get rid of it when you grow up. Was that why you gave up the cooking?'

The fingers stopped scratching, thought of becoming a fist, decided against it.

'What do you want, Superintendent is it?'

'Detective-Superintendent Dalziel. But *sir* will do, Corporal. All I want's some facts. You were screwing Mrs Swain, right?'

'No!'

'But you tried your hand?'

'I asked her to have a drink with me a couple of times. She said yes, but she made it clear that was as far as it went. She was that kind of chick, you know, all up front.'

'Pardon?' said Dalziel, inserting a huge little finger into his ear and wagging it around. 'Didn't quite get that.'

Mitchell ignored the provocation and said, 'All we ever did was talk, nothing more.'

'What did you talk about?'

'Guns. Shooting,' said Mitchell vaguely.

'Piss off, noddy,' said Dalziel. 'Don't tell me you didn't talk about your fascinating life and hard times.'

'Why should I?'

'Because a corny would-be stud like you would imagine that was the way to turn her on. Get her rabbiting on about *her* troubles and next thing you could be doing some real rabbiting under the table. Isn't that how it works? So tell me about it.'

'About my life and hard times?' said Mitchell, trying hard to eyeball Dalziel in this battle of words.

'I'd rather read a ketchup bottle,' said Dalziel. 'What did *she* say to *you*?'

'Listen, you fat slob, I've had enough of this. There's some very important people use this club . . .'

Mitchell was now pure Geordie. Dalziel leaned forward and grasped his knee in a crocodile grip.

'Aye,' he said softly. 'And how will these important people like it when their club's closed down 'cos its corporal cook rangemaster doesn't have the sense to observe regulations? I've spotted at least three you're in breach of already, and that's without looking. Once I really start poking about I doubt if you'd get a licence to run a fairground stall.'

'You're bluffing,' said Mitchell. 'This place is run by the book.'

'Aye, but it's me shouting the odds,' grinned Dalziel. 'What's up anyway, lad? She's dead, remember. She's not going to sue for breach of confidence!'

Mitchell hesitated. He's wondering how far I'll really go if he doesn't give me something, thought Dalziel. He wandered across to the cabinet and picked up the revolver. There were a couple of rounds in the cylinder. He closed it, cocked it, squeezed the trigger. There was a loud explosion and the ceiling light shattered. Mitchell moved with tremendous speed. The athletic part of his image at least was no fraud, and glass shards were still pattering to the floor as he grabbed the gun from Dalziel's hand.

'Jesus! Are you crazy?' he demanded, whitefaced.

'Me?' said Dalziel indignantly. 'Leaving loaded weapons lying around in public, that's crazy!'

Mitchell went back to his desk, unlocked a drawer, dropped the gun inside, and relocked it. He regarded Dalziel with undisguised amazement.

'I can't believe in you,' he said. 'Who do you think you are? Wyatt Earp?'

'It's not me who goes poncing round like a Yankee film star,' said Dalziel comfortably. 'Now, you were telling me about Mrs Swain.'

It was little enough to shoot up a man's ceiling for. At most, it confirmed what Dalziel knew or had deduced from other sources.

Gail Swain had grown confidential over drinks a couple of times. Dalziel guessed that after Mitchell had made his sexual play and been put pretty firmly in his place, Gail had been happy to keep him dangling as a devotee cum confidant. She didn't seem to get on well enough with other women to have made any close friends in England, so perhaps she needed a Mitchell in her life. After Atlas Tayler closed, she'd complained with more incomprehension than bitterness about Swain's refusal to take the post Delgado's offered in the States at three times his British salary. But real resentment had started creeping in when Swain's building business hadn't got off the ground and he started canvassing auld acquaintance for new jobs.

'She didn't like that, and I think Swain tried to cut it down to a minimum because of this, but when she came back from her father's funeral, everything changed.'

'Why?'

'Two reasons,' said Mitchell. 'First she came back with an even better job offer for her husband. I don't think she could believe that he would refuse again.'

'And the second reason?'

'She was rotten rich! I don't know how much, millions maybe. She'd not been short before, but now it was dropping off her and Swain could see no reason why she shouldn't invest in his building company in a big way. She didn't see it like that and told him not a penny would he see till he was settled in LA. That's when he started up badgering his old mates again. He knew this really got up her nose and reckoned he could bounce her into coughing up the cash rather than suffer the embarrassment of being married to a notorious cadger. To tell the truth she was a hell of a snob, and he knew it.'

'But it didn't work?'

'Hell, no. Snob she might be, but she had true grit,' said Mitchell, who having decided that Dalziel was not to be denied was now relaxing into his role. 'The trouble as I saw it, was that those two were just on completely different wavelengths. She couldn't see why he wasn't jumping at the chance to go and live in sunny California. But he'd obviously really got the hump with Delgado's for closing down Atlas Tayler like they did. Also I don't think she could really grasp that he actually *preferred* being his own boss here in Yorkshire!'

'She told you this?'

'Most of it. She got really pissed one night, she was so upset. I don't know what Swain was playing at. I'd have gone like a shot.'

'But you never got invited,' observed Dalziel.

'No. She was a one-man woman, till the divorce courts got to work anyway. Even though her one man was a full-time loser!'

Dalziel smiled grimly. This wanker really did think he was the bee's knees. If a lass didn't fancy a bit on the side with him she didn't fancy it with anyone!

'You don't like Philip Swain?' he said.

'Missing a chance like that, he has to be a real asshole!' said Mitchell. 'Not that I knew him all that well personally. Like I told the other cop, he was never a member. But I remember his brother, he *was* a member, and no, I didn't much care for him either. Christ, the way he talked you'd have thought that Moscow Farm was a palace and the Swains were royalty!'

'Tom Swain, would that be? The one who shot himself?'

'That's right. Look, Superintendent, if that's all, I really should get back to my members. You'll keep my name out of things, won't you? I don't want the ladies round here to get the idea I'm the kind who kisses and tells!'

His macho image was back on full beam.

Dalziel said negligently, 'Don't see why not. After all, you've told me next to nowt I didn't know already.'

When they've coughed, give 'em a hard slap between the shoulder-blades, telling 'em it's all useless crap, and you never know what last little gobbet they'll spit out.

'Oh? Then you'll know that Tom Swain tried to touch Gail for money to save the farm.'

'Gail? Surely it would be his brother he turned to?'

'Philip didn't have money. Only his salary and that wasn't enough to keep his wife in Gucci knickers. No, Tom went to the source and she turned him down flat.'

'She told you this?'

'Indirectly. Also I heard him trying to put the bite on her one night here at the club. She didn't like that and really choked him off. Next day, bang! No wonder she felt guilty. That's why she helped Philip get Moscow Farm back into shape, of course. Guilt. He could have milked it for ever if the silly twit hadn't decided he'd rather be poor in this hole than rolling in it in LA.'

'But why should she feel so guilty?' wondered Dalziel. 'I mean, Tom Swain must have tried to borrow money from everyone. Why should *her* refusal be seen as the one that pushed him over?'

'Well, he pointed a pretty steady finger, I'd say. All right, so they said he probably picked it because it was the one most certain to do the job, but it was clear as a farewell note to me.'

'What the hell are you talking about, laddie?' demanded Dalziel. 'Picked what?'

Mitchell looked at him for a moment, then let out a bellow of triumphant laughter.

'You don't know, do you? I know it wasn't made anything of at the inquest, but you'd think you blighters would keep full notes somewhere. Let me lighten your darkness, Mr Dalziel. The gun Tom Swain used to blow his head off was his sister-in-law's Colt Python!'

Chapter 6

Peter Coombes was thin and dark with an ascetic mien more suited to a Jesuit mission than a modern personnel office, and an intense, unblinking gaze which made Pascoe feel uneasily that his thoughts were showing. It didn't help to find that when he broke the eye contact, over the other's shoulder he was looking at a framed photograph of a beautiful blonde woman lying on a lawn with a collie and two young children.

Coombes glanced round, as though indeed catching something of Pascoe's thought, and said proudly, 'My family. And I don't exclude the dog. Do you have children, Mr Pascoe?'

'One. A girl. No dog,' said Pascoe.

'Yes. I suppose in your line of work,' said Coombes, mysteriously incomplete, leaving Pascoe to work out whether policing unfitted you for dog-ownership or more than one act of procreation.

'It's about your Mr Waterson,' said Pascoe, accepting Coombes's gestured invitation to sit in an easy chair by a coffee table. Presumably the hard chair in front of Coombes's desk was reserved for another class of interviewee.

'Not *our* Mr Waterson, not any more,' corrected Coombes. 'Is there any chance of being told what this is all about?'

'I'm sorry. All I can say is, this has nothing to do with your firm, except in so far as Mr Waterson was once employed here. You have a Miss King on your staff, I believe? Beverley King?'

It had seemed good thinking to kill two birds with one

stone. Coombes was the obvious man to consult about personnel, and it gave Pascoe a chance to assess how things were in the Coombes household. If Christine Coombes were still living in the family house with her husband, two children and a dog, it didn't seem likely she'd have Waterson concealed in the potting-shed.

'Wrong again, I'm afraid,' said Coombes. 'Yes, we did have a Miss King working for us. No, we don't any more.'

'Really? When did she leave?' asked Pascoe, alert.

To his disappointment, the reply was, 'A few weeks ago. I can easily check. Would I be right in guessing your interest in Miss King is connected with your inquiries about Mr Waterson?'

He was obviously as careful as the priest he resembled.

Pascoe said bluntly, 'You knew she and Mr Waterson were having an affair?'

'Indeed,' he said gravely.

'How did you know?'

'I caught them in a compromising situation in the office one lunch-time.'

'What did you do?'

'I invited them to see me later that day.'

'Together?' said Pascoe, surprised.

'Of course not. Greg – Mr Waterson – and I had a friendly chat. I assured him I was not sitting in moral judgement but had to insist for the sake of the firm's reputation and the smooth running of office life, he carried on his love-life outside the premises.'

'And what was his reaction?'

'He seemed amused,' said Coombes. 'In fact he laughed out loud. He said he'd do his best, but I couldn't understand why he found it all so entertaining.'

He fixed his eyes earnestly on Pascoe and Pascoe willed himself not to let his own slip past the man once more to the photograph of his wife lying on the lawn.

'Did you take the same line with Miss King?' he asked.

'Hardly.'

'Oh? Why not?'

'Miss King had only been with us a couple of months. She had not made a good impression.'

'What exactly was her job?' interrupted Pascoe.

'We took her on as a typist. She had word-processing and computing skills and we had hopes we might be able to use her in these fields as vacancies occurred, but to be quite frank, her timekeeping, attention to detail and general attitude were such as to have made this most unlikely.'

'How come she applied for a typist's job with these qualifications?'

'She didn't so much apply as present herself,' said Coombes. 'She'd worked in London for Chester Belcourt, our parent company. A note from one of their directors said she'd had some personal problems which might be eased by a return to Yorkshire and if there was anything we could do to help her with employment it would be a kindness to her and a favour to him.'

'Return, you say? She's local, then?'

'Monksley. Do you know it?'

Monksley was a small village on the northern moors, rather isolated without the compensation of being picturesque.

'Vaguely,' said Pascoe. 'Is that where she's living?'

'We did have an address there to start with, I believe, but after she joined us, she moved into town in a manner of speaking.'

'What manner was that?' inquired Pascoe.

'She rented a boat, called *Bluebell*, would you believe? One of those tubs moored along Bulmer's Wharf,' he said with distaste. 'I'm sure you know *them*.'

Pascoe smiled. The old warehouses once serviced by

Bulmer's Wharf had been demolished and a small estate of maisonettes erected on the site. The contractors, eager to maximize their return, had also rented out moorings along the wharf. It may not have been their intention that people should set up in more or less permanent residence there, but this was what had happened and eventually, inevitably, tensions had developed between the property-owning land-lubbers and the generally more raffish boat-people. A few months earlier these had exploded into accusations that one or more of the boats had been used as a bawdy house. Investigation had revealed little more than a penchant for uninhibited parties on the part of a couple of girl tenants, but there had passed permanently into middle-class mythology this fantasy of a fleet of floating brothels, each richly appointed as Cleopatra's barge, where lovers kept stroke to the tune of flutes.

'I don't know them personally,' said Pascoe. 'But I see you do. What happened at your interview with Miss King, Mr Coombes?'

'Nothing pleasant, I assure you. I tried to speak to her rationally but she entered full of defiance and moved very rapidly through insolence to abuse. To cut a long story short, she resigned.'

'Walked out, you mean.'

'Indeed. This led to another unpleasant scene, this time with Mr Waterson who accused me of sacking her. I urged him to check his facts, but he walked out too.'

'Was this the occasion of his leaving the firm permanently?'

'Not immediately. We had become fairly inured to Gregory Waterson's explosions here. They were regarded by some as outbursts of temperament. But a few days later he really went over the top at a meeting with our managing director when there was a client present. All this business of Miss King came out once more and I gather he was personally abusive towards me and eventually to our managing director, *and* the client. Enough's enough. He seemed really amazed when he was told that this was the end. The directors were generous, more generous than they needed to have been in view of the circumstances. I doubt if there's an industrial tribunal in the land that would have awarded him a penny.'

It struck Pascoe that Coombes was in sympathy with this hardness rather than his directors' generosity and he wondered what hints of Waterson's liaison with his wife had reached the man's ears. No doubt Waterson's final outburst had left no stone unthrown. But he couldn't feel too much sympathy for a man whose reaction to an office affair was to pontificate at the girl and have a friendly chat with the man.

He stood up and said, 'If I could have Miss King's address. In Monksley as well as Bulmer's Wharf. And I'd also like the name of the director of Chester Belcourt who recommended her to you.'

There was no real need for this. He asked merely as a sign of his distaste and he saw that Coombes took the message. Pascoe guessed that next time he came to this office, if there was a next time, it would be the hard seat in front of the desk for him.

Bulmer's Wharf proved a double disappointment, being more like an aquatic Wimpey Estate than a floating Street of a Thousand Pleasures. Also, where *Bluebell* should have been was a gap. A middle-aged woman nursing a sullen baby on the boat next door confirmed that Beverley King had lived there till three maybe four weeks ago when *Bluebell* had moved off without warning or explanation. She thought she recognized Waterson as a frequent visitor from Pascoe's description but could offer no further help, except her expert nautical opinion that *Bluebell*'s only remaining ambitions were submarine and any voyage of more than a few miles would probably see them realized.

Frustrated, Pascoe left. His route back to the station took him along String Lane. He'd forgotten about Harold Park, but as he approached Food For Thought, he noticed a grimy Peugeot estate parked outside with Govan, the bearded Scot, talking to someone through its window. Pascoe couldn't see the number, but it was worth checking.

As he drew near, the Peugeot's indicator started winking as it tried to force its way back into the stream of traffic. Pascoe halted alongside and leaned across to open his window. The Peugeot driver did the same. He had a round red farmer's face which looked fertile ground for rustic jollity but was presently tared with indignation.

'What's your problem, mate?' he demanded.

'Mr Park?'

'Who's asking?'

Taking this as affirmative, Pascoe introduced himself.

'I called earlier. I wonder if we could have a word. It won't take long,' said Pascoe with a reassuring smile. Behind him someone tooted impatiently. He went forward another twenty yards and found a spot to park illegally. Then he got out and walked back to where Park was now standing on the pavement talking to Govan, the shopkeeper. Jollity had resumed its rightful place and the man greeted him effusively, 'Sorry about that, Mr Pascoe. Thought you were some half-baked twit wanted to leave his car there while he popped in to Mr Govan's for a bag of ginseng. As a matter of fact I was just on my way to look you up. Mr Govan said you'd called and as I'm a bird of rare passage so to speak, I thought I'd better check it out.'

It wasn't a local nor any kind of northern accent. Pascoe

thought he detected a West Country burr overlaid with something closer to London.

'That was very good citizenly of you, Mr Park,' he replied.

'Self-interest. I don't want to have a heart attack because you decide to flag me down on the motorway,' he said with a hearty laugh. 'Step inside out of the weather.'

Pascoe found himself ushered into a narrow and smelly passage alongside the shop and through a flaking door. Here Park paused to empty a box stuffed full of what looked like junk mail before leading the way up a flight of creaking and uncarpeted stairs and through another door which decoratively was the twin of that below.

After all this squalor, the flat was a pleasant surprise. A single large living-room, with kitchenette and shower-room off, it was freshly decorated and comfortably appointed.

'This is nice,' said Pascoe.

'Isn't it,' said Park proudly. 'I like to leave it scruffy outside. I'm away such a lot, the less attractive it looks to the criminal fraternity the better. Am I right or am I right, Mr Pascoe?'

'Very wise. I gather you're a traveller, Mr Park.'

'That's right. Veterinary products. It's pretty specialized so a small patch is no use to me. When I've got something good to sell, I've got to push it as wide as I can if I'm to live as well as I like, so draw a line south of the Wash and north of Carlisle, that's my area. Can I get you a cup of tea?'

He went into the kitchenette without waiting for an answer. Pascoe picked up an ornately carved rosewood box from the table, opened it and studied its contents. Two safety-pins, a button and a china thimble. After a moment he sensed he was being studied in his turn.

Looking up, he saw Park smiling at him from the kitchenette.

'Sorry,' he said closing the box. 'Habit.'

'That's all right. You look at whatever you like, my son. I've got some nice stuff. Morocco, that's where that box came from. I always like to bring something nice back from abroad. Poke around the cupboards. God knows what you'll find.'

Pascoe didn't accept the invitation but he did walk around the room peering at some rather pleasant water-colours of local scenery. There was only one window and it overlooked the back yards and loading areas of the String Lane shops. Immediately below he spotted Mr Govan's ginger mop. The Scot was closing the rear door of a small blue van. He then walked round to the driver's door, halted, looked down, and swung his foot at the front wheel. It was impossible to hear what he was saying, but the mime was so perfect that Pascoe had no difficulty in imagining the rich Scots oaths that greeted his discovery of the flat tyre.

'Sugar?'

'No, thanks,' he said turning. He sat down in a comfortable white leather chair and sipped the excellent tea which Park offered him.

'Now what can I do for the police?' said the traveller.

'Last night I believe you were drinking at the Pilgrim's Salvation,' said Pascoe.

'That's right. But not too much,' said Park defensively.

'I'm pleased to hear it. Do you use the Sally a lot, Mr Park?'

'Occasionally. No more than three or four other pubs.'

'And was there any special reason you chose it last night?'

'No. I just fancied a drink and the Sally popped into my mind.'

'So you weren't meeting anyone there?'

'No. What's this all about, Mr Pascoe? You're getting me worried.'

'No need,' smiled Pascoe. 'The two men who got into your car with you when you left, who were they?'

Park looked at him in amazement, with a pink edge of indignation.

'What is this?' he demanded. 'Am I being watched or something?'

'Nothing like that,' said Pascoe. 'The men?'

'I don't know, do I? I was leaving and I said, anyone want a lift towards the centre? and these two chaps said thanks very much.'

'You always offer complete strangers lifts?'

'I didn't say they were complete strangers, did I? We'd got talking, half a dozen of us, chewing the fat the way you do in a pub. These two, one was called Bob and the other Geoff. I dropped 'em off together at the corner of the market place. You're not telling me they were wrong 'uns, are you? I can't believe it!'

Pascoe shook his head slightly and said, 'There was another man with you outside the pub. He didn't get in the car but walked off by himself.'

'Oh, him. What was his name? Glen, I think. He joined in the chat and left the same time I did. I offered him a lift but he said no, he was going in the other direction. Is it him you're interested in?'

'Possibly. When he left you outside, you didn't get any hint of where precisely he might be heading?'

Park thought a while then shook his head.

'No, sorry. Who is he anyway? What's he done?'

'Nothing, except prove rather elusive,' said Pascoe, rising. 'Thanks very much for your time, Mr Park.'

Down on the pavement a pasty-faced girl with lank brown hair was rattling the handle of the shop door.

Govan had shut up early, it seemed. Pity. The girl looked much in need of health food.

He started his car and edged out into String Lane. He should at least have felt some satisfaction at removing one more query from his list, but his mind was ill at ease. Park had a powerful personality. It was easy to see he'd make a good salesman. But the further you got away from him, the more his jollity, his amiability, his plausibility, began to seem a surface. His uncollected mail showed he hadn't been up to his flat, so he must have just arrived back in String Lane when Pascoe spotted him. Govan, like a good citizen, had told him instantly that the police wanted to talk to him, and Park, like an even better citizen, had set off for the police station without even getting out of his car . . . were ever two such good citizens gathered before in one place? Then up the stairs, the easy chit-chat, the making of tea, the invitation to poke around his cupboards . . . while down below, Govan had shut up shop in the middle of market day and was loading something into his van . . .

He was at the end of String Lane. He turned left and left again into a narrow, almost tunnel-like entry which if his geometry was right ought to open up into the service area behind the shops. It did. And there was the blue van, jacked up with a wheel leaning against its side. The rear doors were open and Govan stood there, in his hands a cardboard box which he was handing to Harold Park.

Pascoe got out of his car, stooping to pick up his walking stick which lay alongside the front seat. He used it as little as possible, but there were still occasions when it came in useful.

The two men looked at him as if he were a pantomime demon, popped up from a trap. Park was the first to recover.

'Hello, again,' he said, beaming. 'Forget something?

Me too. I'd asked Mr Govan to store these samples for me and I'd almost gone off without 'em.'

He held out the box for inspection. The black lettering on it read *Romany Rye Veterinary Products 24 x 500 grams Flea Powder*.

'How interesting. I'll try some of that on my pussy,' said Pascoe, reaching for the box. He saw the age-old debate argued out on Park's face: fight or run. Saw the ballots cast. And as the salesman with a nimbleness which belied his bulk turned and headed for the open rear door, Pascoe used his own casting vote by hooking his walking stick around the man's left ankle.

He hit the rough ground with a crash which made Pascoe wince with empathized pain. Behind him he heard movement and turned to ward off any proposed attack. But Govan too had voted for flight. Pascoe watched with interest as he leapt into his van and started the engine. It would have been a splendid racing start, rear tyres screaming as they burnt rubber in search of traction. As it was, the jack collapsed, the front bumper ploughed into the ground, and the only screaming that was to be heard was the Scot's as his face collided with the windscreen.

Pascoe sighed, returned to his car and unhooked his radio mike.

'Assistance, please,' he said. 'Rear of Food For Thought, the health food store on String Lane. One car will be enough. But we'd better have an ambulance.'

Chapter 7

It was Andrew Dalziel's proud boast that he could go anywhere and receive the same welcome. Only the words sometimes varied.

'What the hell do you want?' demanded Philip Swain. 'Haven't we seen enough of each other for one day?'

'I thought you were keen to start rehearsing the Mysteries,' said Dalziel, smiling like a turnip lantern. 'Can I come in?'

'You can wait there till I ring Thackeray,' growled Swain. He turned and retreated to a wall phone.

Dalziel stood obediently on the doorstep, still smiling. Two things he'd done between his pint and pie at the Black Bull and coming out to Currthwaite. First he'd rung Messrs Thackeray, etc. and ascertained that old Eden was out at a client conference in Harrogate. Secondly he had checked the inquest record on Tom Swain.

Mitchell was right. The gun had indeed been his sister-in-law's Python which he had borrowed from the club armoury, allegedly to test its power on the range. It had been Philip Swain who discovered his brother's body out in the barn, a site selected, according to Tom's farewell letter, because he did not wish to taint any room in the farmhouse with distressing memories. This letter had seemed to be the most businesslike document the elder Swain had prepared during his disastrous tutelage of the farm. In it he carefully catalogued his debts, separating them into prospective, imminent, immediate, overdue and *sub judice*. Perhaps his intention was a definitive assessment of the situation before opting for this most final of solutions. If so, his plan had been incontrovertibly confirmed. The grand total was vast. Most of it was still to pay off after Philip Swain inherited, and Dalziel had come to sympathize with Gail Swain. She must have had to dig deep even before the physical refurbishment of the place began. No wonder she broke the pitcher when her husband came back to the well after his building firm ran into trouble.

Swain hung the phone up angrily. Dalziel continued to smile. Now it was decision time for the builder: follow Thackeray's advice and refuse to talk until the lawyer was available, or show how little he had to fear by letting the policeman in?

A firm believer in his own maxim, never offer a choice unless you don't mind which choice is made, Dalziel said with lively interest, 'Why's it called Moscow Farm, Mr Swain? I mean, a place this old must go back before us ignorant buggers up here in Yorkshire had ever heard of Moscow. How old is it, anyway?'

It was hard not to answer two questions on a subject so dear to Swain's heart.

He said, 'Seventeenth-century, most of the present building. But there's bits of the mediaeval walls still in situ, and records show there was a settlement here before Domesday.'

'And Moscow?'

'The name's changed a couple of times, usually after it passed out of the family's hands for a while. Beginning of the last century we lost it and one of my ancestors went off to do a bit of soldiering in Europe. A mercenary. Five years later he turned up rich enough to buy it back. He changed the name to Moscow. The story was that he somehow made his cash during Napoleon's retreat, though it was never clear whose side he was officially on.'

'How the hell do you make money out of something like that?' wondered Dalziel, genuinely curious now.

'Looting the poor bastards who froze to death, I expect,' said Swain. 'As you may have heard, it's an old family tradition that anything's permissible when it comes to the farm.'

He spoke sardonically, clearly intending to let Dalziel see he knew what the fat man was up to, but the gibe faded into surprise as he became aware of his surroundings. Somehow as they talked he and Dalziel had moved from the doorstep to the sitting-room and the fat man was now sitting at his ease in a broad old-fashioned wing chair.

'What the devil is it you want?' exploded Swain.

Dalziel's expression became earnest.

'First I want to say I'm sorry we seem to have got off on the wrong foot, Mr Swain. Now I've got a clear picture of what really happened, I'd like to start over again, so that, like Mr Thackeray said, we can get this all cleared up and you can enjoy your sorrow in private.'

'I'll drink to that,' said Swain, regaining some of his equilibrium.

'Now that's a grand idea. Scotch'll be lovely.'

Swain looked a little put out to be taken so literally, but he fetched Dalziel a reasonably large Scotch with a reasonably good grace.

'That's better,' said Dalziel. 'Nippy out. Looks like we're getting the real winter at last. You'll have been glad it kept off so long.'

'Will I?'

'Because of the car park job, I mean. Can't be much fun laying bricks in a blizzard. But no work, no pay, eh?'

'Dan Trimble wanted it done as soon as possible,' said Swain, inserting the familiarity casually. 'And the long term weather forecast was good.'

'But not the short term financial forecast? Still, no

214

worries now, not once all them lovely dollars drop into your account.'

'What's that supposed to mean?' demanded Swain, angry again, but this time in control of his anger.

'Whoah!' exclaimed Dalziel. 'Don't get mad. I thought that was all behind us. I'm not meaning to be offensive, Mr Swain. You'll get your wife's brass, that's only right, that's the way she wanted it, else why make your wills the way you did?'

'What do you know about our wills?' asked Swain.

In fact Dalziel knew very little except what he'd guessed, but he saw no reason not to sow a little discord between Swain and his lawyer.

'You mustn't blame anyone,' he said. 'There's nowt confidential about a will. Question some people might ask though is, if your missus had managed to get back to the States, would she have changed it?'

'Changed it? Why?'

'In my experience, wives aren't bothered much about benefiting their husbands after giving them the old heave-ho!' sneered Dalziel.

But Swain was out of reach of his provocation now.

'Who says Gail was leaving me?' he asked quietly.

'Come on, Mr Swain. Stands to reason, doesn't it? She wanted you to take up a post with the family firm in California, you wanted her to pump money into your business here. She gives you an ultimatum, then shacks up with her boyfriend. Any chance of a drop more of this? It's a Glenlivet, isn't it?'

It was the need of thinking space rather than hospitality which took Swain back to the drinks cupboard, but Dalziel didn't mind. His gratitude was all to God for making some men clever enough to squeeze whisky out of barleycorn, and himself clever enough to squeeze it out of a stone.

215

'You seem to have been very busy sticking your nose into my affairs, Dalziel,' said the builder grimly.

'Your *wife's* affairs. Sorry, I didn't mean . . . but now you've brought the subject up, did she have a lot of affairs, Mr Swain, or was Waterson a one-off?'

'I don't know! How the hell should I know? Waterson was the first that I knew of and it came as a great shock to me!'

'Aye, so you said. But you didn't live in each other's pockets, did you? You had your interests, she had hers. Like this Arts Committee. And the Gun Club. Must've spent a lot of time there, made some close friends, especially when she were on the team.'

Swain's grimness dissolved into a harsh laugh.

'Mitchell, you mean? For heaven's sake, man, Gail grew up surrounded by real Hollywood studs. You don't think she was going to find that pathetic imitation anything but amusing, do you?'

'There's all kinds of amusement,' probed Dalziel.

Swain took a long pull at his whisky. To drown a resurgence of rage? If so, the Scotch proved a good palliative, for his response was measured and reasonable.

'OK, look, I don't know. I was deceived once, so why not a dozen times?'

He should have let his anger speak. It would have rung truer than this rueful acceptance of possible cuckoldry, thought Dalziel. Or was he, as Pascoe clearly thought, letting prejudice colour all his responses to Swain? He felt a sudden uncharacteristic flood of self-doubt. OK, so the man had plenty of motive for killing his wife, but most men did, and vice versa. Might it not after all have been simply a happy accident that just when he must have thought all was lost, Gail had turned out not to be in Los Angeles changing her will, but in Hambleton Road, killing herself?

216

He looked at Swain and thought, No! Swains don't have that sort of luck! In fact from what he'd learned of the family, they seemed to suffer from congenital bad luck. What they did have, some of them, was a certain capacity for grabbing at straws, for plucking their own salvation out of other people's disaster.

Sod all the contradictions and contra-evidence! Sod pious Pascoe and his clever little experiments! In Dalziel's book of certainties Swain had killed his wife, and Dalziel had as good as seen him do it! The flood of self-doubt had parted and he was safely through it, but there was still a long trek to the Promised Land.

He said, 'A man needs to be busy himself to be deceived, Mr Swain.'

'My work did keep me occupied, yes.'

'I mean . . . you know . . . *busy*.'

Dalziel made a pumping motion with his forearm and said, 'Sauce for the goose, eh? Of course, it's different for a man.'

He gave his vilest leer. He had little hope of coaxing a confidence from the man but he might bludgeon a brag. If (and why not?) Swain were having a bit on the side, that would strengthen his motivation, and it might be worth giving this not improbable *she* a good shaking to see what came out of her. Between the sheets was the non-Catholic's confessional.

'Is it? How the hell would you know?'

Swain was answering his words not his thoughts, but it was just as offensive. Oh, I shall have you, my lad, promised Dalziel.

He changed tack and said, very serious, 'All I'm saying, sir, is, if there is a lady, better to tell us now rather than risk us stumbling on her unawares and mebbe causing embarrassment. I can promise maximum discretion. We'd just want to see her for purposes of elimination. Like you wanted to see Mrs Swain at Hambleton Road. For purposes of elimination.'

He spoke with the sweet reasonableness of a hard left politician proposing revolution, and vastly enjoyed the millisec in which Swain reacted to tone before registering content.

For another longer moment he thought he had triggered the expected explosion but from somewhere deep down in himself Swain drew up reserves of control.

'Thackeray warned me about you,' he said. 'But he didn't tell me the half. Well, I'll tell you what, Mr Dalziel. You provoke away all you like. I've got nothing to hide. The only games I'll play with you will be on Eileen Chung's stage. I suppose that was your clever little idea too? Well, I'm calling your bluff, Dalziel. It may please your ego to play God to my Lucifer, but wrap you up though Chung might, it'll be plain to everyone you're still a fat slob!'

There it was. The anger burning through.

'And you, Mr Swain?' said Dalziel softly. 'What'll people see in you?'

Swain laughed, back in charge.

'*All the mirth that is made is marked in me!*' he said. 'You see, I've started learning my lines already. I hope you can keep up, Superintendent. Now, good day.'

'Good day to you too,' said Dalziel pleasantly. 'And thanks for your time.'

He left the room, closing the door firmly behind him. He had noticed an extension phone on a table in the sitting-room. He went to the wall phone in the hall and gently lifted the receiver. Swain was dialling. The number was ringing. He waited.

A woman's voice spoke and for a second he felt a frisson of self-congratulatory delight. Then the words registered.

'Thackeray, Amberson, Mellor and Thackeray, can I help you?'

'Shit,' said Dalziel, replacing the receiver. Like so many things, it worked more often on the television screen than it did in life.

He left but not by the front door. Pascoe had reported something about a secretary who had an office out back. Who knows? Perhaps Swain was conventional enough to be banging his secretary. Or perhaps she was nosey enough to listen in to his telephone calls.

Outside he ran nimbly up the steps leading to the office, paused to get his breath, then entered with a suddenness intended to be impressive.

The girl behind the desk glanced up from her book but gave little sign of being impressed. Her silence forced him to speak.

'Mrs Appleyard?' he said. 'Detective-Superintendent Dalziel.'

'Yes?'

'You don't seem surprised.'

'You've told me who I am and who you are, both of which I knew. What's to be surprised over?'

Dalziel examined this and found it pleasingly pragmatic.

'Mind if I ask you a few questions?' he said.

She returned her attention to her book without replying.

Dalziel scratched his armpit and wondered how best to proceed.

'Mr Swain a good boss, is he?' he essayed.

'He's all right,' she said without looking up.

'How'd he get on with his missus?'

She put her book down and examined him in a way which made him feel on sale. She was a plain, ordinary-looking girl but her cool brown eyes had a disconcerting steadiness.

'You want me to help you. Why?'

'Well, it's everyone's duty to help the police, isn't it? I mean, how else can we fight crime?'

Even to his own ears his platitudes lacked conviction.

She said, 'That's not what I meant. Why should *I* help *you*?'

The pronouns were emphasized. He considered his answer carefully. He had the feeling there were several wrong answers but only one right one.

He said, 'Because mebbe I could help you.'

This seemed to amuse her momentarily, then she became serious again.

'You reckon? All right, I want to find my husband.'

Straight down to bargaining, thought Dalziel admiringly. With him not even knowing whether she had owt to bargain with!

He said, 'Lost him, have you?'

She explained briefly, clearly, like Wield making a report.

'His name's Tony Appleyard. We got married three years back when we found I were pregnant. Then he got made redundant and after a while he got so fed up, he went down south to look for work. He were a fitter by trade but he ended up in London, Brent it were, labouring on the lump till he got something better. He wrote and sent money when he could, at first anyway. He was livmg in this place with a lot of other men, lodging-house he called it but it sounded like a doss house. I used to write regular, but his answers got less and less frequent. Christmas I thought he might come back but there was only a card for the kiddie. I got so I was thinking of going down there to see for myself, but Dad said he'd go. He went in the middle ofJanuary. At the house they told him Tony had moved out a week before and not left a forwarding address. I've been in touch with the police down there and up here, the uniformed lot, I mean. They all said it was nowt to do with them. What a grown man did was up to him as long as it wasn't a crime and leaving your wife and kid evidently isn't. But I reckon they could find him if they wanted. If you wanted.'

Dalziel said gently, 'Why do you want to find him, love? Court order for maintenance won't do much good unless he's got a regular job.'

'Mebbe that's why he's moved on,' said the woman. 'Mebbe he's shacking up with someone else. Don't worry, I've thought of every possibility. And mebbe it's just all got too much for him and he's on the road feeling as down and desperate as I do sometimes. I need to know, Mr Dalziel, so I can work out what's best to do. Will you help?'

Dalziel considered. Scratching his corrugated neck he said, 'Chief Inspector Pascoe spoke with you the other day. Why'd you not ask him?'

She half-smiled and said, 'He were more interested in what I was reading. I read to get away from things. You look to me more interested in the things I'm getting away from.'

Dalziel smiled back.

'I shouldn't underestimate Mr Pascoe,' he said. But he felt flattered all the same.

'All right,' he said. 'You're on. No promises but it shouldn't be difficult. I may need to ask your dad about his trip down there in case he can help.'

He saw her expression and laughed. 'Doesn't much like the lad, does he? Not to worry. I won't let on about our arrangement. I'll say it's a social security inquiry or some such thing. Now, what can you tell me?'

'You ask the questions, I'll answer,' she said.

'Fair enough. How do you reckon Mr and Mrs Swain got on?'

She considered then said, 'All right. At first anyway.'

'At first?'

'When I first came to work here after Mr Swain had come in with Dad. I don't think it had dawned on her then how serious he was about running his own business, I mean.'

'And when it did?'

'She got more and more irritated. They had rows, mainly about going to America and money. I could hear them yelling in the house. She thought the business was useless. He said his roots were here, there was no way he was going to give up Moscow Farm to work for a gang of crooks like Delgado.'

'And she didn't show any sympathy?'

'No. She said the way he was going he'd have to give it up anyway when he went bankrupt. She said her family weren't crooks, just good efficient businessmen. She asked him where he got off criticizing her family when all that his had ever been good for was losing money and blowing their brains out.'

'And what did Mr Swain say to that?'

'He said, very quiet, that they'd always been able to get the farm back at no matter what cost. Well, he'd got it back and he wasn't going to let it go.'

'Tell me, lass,' said Dalziel in his friendliest tone. 'If he said this very quiet and they were in the house and you were out here, how come you managed to hear?'

'The outside bog freezes up in winter so sometimes I've got to go inside,' she said, meeting his gaze steadily.

'Fair enough. Do you know a man called Waterson, luv?'

'I wouldn't say I know him. He was a customer.'

'What did you make of him?'

'Fancied himself.'

'Did you fancy him?'

'No way.'

222

'Why not?'

She considered. 'For a start I could tell he didn't fancy me.'

'That makes a difference?'

'Dealing with them that does is bad enough without chasing after them as don't,' she said grimly.

Dalziel grinned. He liked her more and more.

'What about Mrs Swain. Did he fancy her?'

'I told Mr Pascoe that,' she said. 'He tried it on, but I thought she gave him the brush-off.'

'Would it surprise you if she'd taken up with him later?'

'No. I didn't know her well enough to be surprised.'

This was reasonable but not very helpful. Dalziel picked up another line and asked, 'How did Mr Swain get on with Mr Waterson?'

'Not very well.'

He waited for her to expand, but after a few moments she returned her gaze to her book. It was unnerving. She'd made a bargain to answer his questions, but they had to be asked first.

'How do you know?' he asked.

'I saw them quarrelling in the yard.'

'Could you hear what they were saying?' he asked, looking out of the window.

'No. Anyway, after a bit they went into the house.'

He hesitated, baffled. Every end a blank. What were Swain and Waterson rowing about? Had Swain begun to suspect something earlier than he claimed? And what different light could it throw on the events at Hambleton Road if he had?

He must have somehow contrived to look pathetic, for she took pity on him and said in an exasperated tone, 'Do you not want to know what it was about?'

'You said you couldn't hear.'

'I didn't need to. It was about Mr Waterson's account.

It hadn't been settled despite me sending reminders. The last one threatened the court.'

'Was it for much?'

'Enough. Mr Swain were having trouble with his overdraft and needed every penny he could get.'

'So how did it end up?'

'They went into the house and Mr Waterson gave Mr Swain a cheque.'

'How do you know?'

'Because Mr Swain came out to me later and handed over the cheque and told me to pay it into the business account.'

There it was. Not a jealous confrontation but a business squabble. All he had to do was ask.

He said, 'So Mr Swain were really strapped for cash till he got this cheque?'

She laughed, full-throated, musical, a sound to draw a man's eyes back after they'd registered and dismissed the square features, the lifeless hair.

'He were still strapped,' she said. 'It came back a week later. Returned to drawer. No funds.'

'It bounced? What happened then?'

She said, 'I gave it to Mr Swain. He said he'd see to it.'

'And did he?'

'Not that I know of. There was nowt in our last statement.'

It could mean a lot, it could mean nowt. Dalziel stored it away and glanced at his watch. He'd been here too long. If Swain caught him now he might get suspicious of this lovely lass and that'd be a shame. Who knows what other answers she might be able to give if Dalziel could only work out the questions?

He said, 'I'll be off now, luv, but I'll be in touch.'

He meant with more questions but when she replied, 'How long?' he saw she didn't. A bargain was a bargain.

He thought and said, 'Week at the outside. If you're sure. Sometimes no news is good news.'

'You reckon?' she said, picking up her book once more. This time he glimpsed its title. *Anna Karenina*. Dalziel's reading was not extensive. Fiction-wise, it was restricted almost entirely to Bulwer Lytton's *Last Days of Pompeii* which he'd stolen from his honeymoon hotel and read circularly as if it were *Finnegans Wake*. But *Anna Karenina* he knew because of the Garbo movie. He'd been more concerned with copping a feel from the buxom lass by his side than watching the elegant shadow on the screen, but he did remember it hadn't been a bundle of laughs.

He said, 'Careful you don't read your brain into train oil, like my old mam always used to say.'

She didn't look up but said, 'Mine says I'll read my life away. I say, why not?'

'There's no answer to that,' said Dalziel as he left.

Chapter 8

The station seemed full of solicitors on Dalziel's return, all crying police brutality. A headcount revealed that in fact there were only two, but they had enough sound and fury for a Labour Party Conference. Having ascertained that he was not the object of their wrath and that they had no connection with Messrs Thackeray, etc., Dalziel let himself be filled in by Sergeant Broomfield.

Upstairs in CID he found Pascoe eagerly awaiting his return.

'What's going on, Peter?' the fat man demanded. 'Here's me desperate to establish good community relations and you can't even take a witness statement without assault and battery.'

Pascoe didn't even bother to smile but said impatiently, 'I've just had the lab report on the veterinary samples I recovered from Harry Park. Four of the flea powder cartons contained heroin. That's two thousand grams.'

'What? Why didn't you say, lad? Let's go and kick shit out of the bugger!'

'Talking of shit, we searched Govan's shop and guess what we found down among the lentils?'

'Better and better. What have you done?'

'Everything, I think. Photos, prints, etc. are being faxed everywhere. Drug Squad, Customs have all been put in the picture. Everyone's moving at a hundred miles an hour trying to get as far back along Park's trail as possible before news spreads that we've picked him up.'

'And Park himself?'

'Quiet as the grave. He's scared. And not of us.'

'We'll see about that,' said Dalziel, reaching for the phone.

'Sir,' said Pascoe warningly. 'I really think this one's out of our hands. We've just been asked to keep him on ice till the Drug Squad decides how to play it.'

'He's in our cell, isn't he?' said Dalziel. 'All I want to ask him about is our friend, Waterson. Case in hand, possible unlawful killing, no one can complain about that. And you can fill me in while they're bringing him up.'

Pascoe gave a succinct account of everything that had happened that day and ten minutes later they were sitting opposite Harold Park in an interview room.

Pascoe was expecting Dalziel to attempt to be more frightening than the masters Park so clearly feared, and he wondered uneasily how far the fat man would go. But Dalziel, not for the first time, surprised him.

'Harold Park, isn't it?' he said, smiling. 'How are they treating you, Harry? Have you had something to eat? Coffee? Tea? Smoke?'

'Thanks,' said Park, accepting a cigarette.

'Only tobacco, I'm afraid,' said Dalziel as he lit it.

'That's all I take.'

'Oh, you don't practise what you push, then?' laughed Dalziel. 'Wise man. But you do have a problem, though, I can see that. Drugs are big money and big money has long arms and if you start grassing, one of them long arms can reach right inside the nick and tear your balls off, right? I'm sympathetic. That's why I'm not going to ask you to say anything at all about your set-up. There's others coming as'll do that, but not me. All I want from you is one little minnow, and it's nowt to do with drugs. Just tell me all about Gregory Waterson.'

'Waterson? Why's everyone interested in that wanker?' said Park with what sounded like genuine curiosity. Then sudden suspicion darkened his face. 'Was it him who put you on to me?'

'Don't be stupid,' sighed Dalziel. 'I could lie and say yes so that you'd get mad and spill all you know about him, but that's not the way I play, Harry. Mr Pascoe here was genuine when he came round to ask you about Waterson. It was just bad luck the way things worked out. If Mr Govan had kept his van in better nick . . .'

'That Scotch idiot! I'll see he gets his.'

'Your privilege, Harry. Meanwhile: Mr Waterson . . .?'

'And what do I get out of it?'

'My gratitude, Harry. That's worth a million to anyone in your shoes. It'll be me who'll be there in court when you're asking for bail, remember that, Harry,' Dalziel lied easily.

'Bail? They'd never give me bail,' said Park. But there was a glimmer of hope in his eyes.

'They might, if the police weren't all that convincing in opposing it,' said Dalziel, tapping the side of his nose significantly.

Pascoe groaned inwardly at this combination of shaky morality and awful acting. Park considered, shrugged and said, 'All right. I'll tell you what I know. But only you.' He cast an unfriendly eye on Pascoe. 'I'm not making any admissions, you understand that? This has all been a complete misunderstanding.'

'Of course it has,' said Dalziel unctuously. 'Mr Pascoe, why not take a little walk, see if you can rustle up some tea for me and Mr Park. With doughnuts. I like a doughnut and Mr Park I'm sure has a lot in common with me.'

Pascoe left, not without relief. Ten minutes later he returned, bearing a tray with two cups of tea and a plateful of doughnuts. Dalziel took one and bit massively. Sugar glistened on his lips and raspberry jam trickled down his chin.

'Lovely,' he said. 'I sometimes think I'd as lief have a doughnut as a woman. One bang's like any other, but every time you sink your teeth into a doughnut's like the very first time. Now I hope you feel the same, Harry, 'cos where you're going, there's not much choice, and you only get doughnuts every second Sunday.'

Downing a cup of scalding tea, he led the way out.

'Well?' said Pascoe as they walked along the corridor.

'It's like we thought,' said Dalziel. 'Park's a middleman between the big-time dealers and the small-time pushers. It was Govan that Waterson dealt with, very small time to start with, a few ounces of grass now and then, but eventually getting a bit harder, and when he started asking for more than he needed to feed a personal habit, Govan mentioned him to Park. They met and had a chat in the Sally. Park says he was impressed with Waterson at first. Very laid back, and he gave the impression he had lots of well-heeled contacts. Me, I've just seen Waterson as a snivelling wreck but from what everyone else says, when he's on top of things, he can be very impressive. It took our Harry a wee while to suss out that he was just another wanker who liked to talk big in front of his mates and fancy women. He began to get suspicious when Waterson just seemed to want to go on buying little nibbles, to sample the merchandise, he said. When Park told him to put up some real money or back off, Waterson became all indignant and sure enough he came up with an order worth several thou. What's more, he actually produced the money on time and took delivery at the end of January. No wonder the stupid sod couldn't pay Swain's bill!'

'But what about the profit on pushing the stuff? It should have been five times his investment, minimum.'

'Park knows nowt about that. All he knows is when he next saw Waterson only a week later he was ready to treat him as a serious customer till he realized he was back to buying a few fixes at a time. He was in such a state that at first Park reckoned they must be for himself. But it came out they were for some bird. He wanted to pay the wholesale price rather than the street price and he tried to lean on Park a bit by hinting that if his girl didn't get fixed up, she might start talking. Park wasn't explicit but he seems to have made it clear that if this bird started singing, it'd be Greg who got his neck pulled! After that he didn't see him again till last night, and that was by chance, at least on Park's part. He was in the Sally, having a social drink, he says – and I'm to be Queen of the May, I said – when Waterson came wandering over, all smiles, very much man-of-the-world. He'd had a couple of drinks and was talking expansively of doing some real big business with Park. Harry got out of the place as quickly as possible with his chums, before, as he put it, Waterson's gob could drop him in the shite.'

Pascoe frowned and said, 'I'd have thought he'd have

wanted to give Waterson a stiff warning, perhaps even a lesson.'

Dalziel smiled and said, 'And so he did, my boy. But not there in front of witnesses, and not straight after, when he and Waterson had been seen leaving the pub together. No, the lesson was planned for this morning, a couple of Park's mates, mebbe the big lads you saw last night, going round to talk to him while Harry was safely chatting to a vet somewhere in Halifax.'

'Then he got Waterson's address?'

'Of course he got his bloody address. Where the hell do you think we're going?'

He led the way to his car parked on a double yellow just outside the car park. The gatehouse was finished and now the final area of concrete was being laid across the entrance with Arnie Stringer supervising the work.

'Nearly done, are you?' bellowed Dalziel.

'Aye. Tomorrow we'll clear up and that's it.'

'Not before time. More tea-breaks than the Queen Mother, you lot. I'd like a word about your son-in-law, Tony Appleyard, some time.'

Stringer looked as if the Angel Gabriel had just announced his pregnancy over a tannoy. He came as close as he could without treading wet concrete.

'What about him?' he grated.

'Don't take on. Social Security inquiry, uniformed's job really, but as I was out at Moscow today I said I'd ask your girl, and she said she'd no idea where he was, but you'd gone south in January to look for him.'

'Did she now? Then likely she told you I didn't find him.'

'That's right. I just wondered if you got any clue where he might have gone?'

'Do you not think I'd have gone after him if I had?' demanded Stringer.

'Come on, Arnie. It sticks out a mile you didn't much like the lad,' said Dalziel insinuatingly. 'Can't blame you, getting your lass into trouble like that, then buggering off south. In your shoes, even if I did find him, I might be tempted to squeeze his goolies and tell him to stay down there among the yuppies. You can tell me, man. It'll go no further.'

Pascoe could see what the fat man was doing. There was little chance that Stringer was going to accept a genuine invitation to confide, so Dalziel was couching his pseudo-invitation in terms calculated to get under the other's skin. It certainly worked.

'No wonder the country's falling apart with things like you in charge of the law,' sneered Stringer. 'Seems like none of you have owt better to do than stand around here sticking your noses into other people's private business. There's drug-pushers out there, and muggers, and football hooligans, and child-molesters, and all the hordes of Gideon, and what are you two doing about it?'

'Well, thanks for the warning,' said Dalziel gravely. 'Watch your back for prowling Sodomites!'

He walked away with Pascoe at his heel.

'What was all that about?' he asked as he put on his seat-belt.

'Private business,' said Dalziel. 'Talking of football hooligans, I've not heard of many arrests. Throwing buggers off trains in Cambridgeshire's one thing. Duffing up landlords on my patch is getting serious!'

'Come on,' said Pascoe indignantly. 'I've had the lads doing what they can but that's not much. The only way you get anywhere with something like this is getting an undercover team into the gangs. That's a big operation, and the way things have gone in court recently, it's damned hard to get a result.'

'I only asked, lad. No need to get touchy,' said Dalziel.

'I've noticed you've been very sensitive since you got back. Still taking the tablets, are you?'

Pascoe did not rise to the provocation but asked brightly, 'Am I allowed to know where we're going, sir?'

'Messing about on a boat, lad. Hope you don't get seasick.'

'Not the *Bluebell*?' said Pascoe in disappointment. 'I told you I went down to Bulmer's Wharf and it wasn't there. Didn't you listen?'

'Aye. Thing is, you didn't ask hard enough or look far enough. Get that map out of the glove compartment. Now follow the cut out of town about half a mile north. It goes under an unclassified road near a place called Badger Farm, right? That's where we'll find the *Bluebell*, Chief Inspector. And once aboard the lugger, Mr Gregory fucking Waterson is mine!'

Dalziel was half right. After no more than two misdirections they found the bridge, humped high to give maximum clearance to the canal traffic beneath. Evening was drawing on fast, the last rays of a cold-eyed sun turning the water into a mockery of a yellow-brick road and the black furrows of the huge field bordering the canal into a desolate seascape. The tow-path was puddled and muddy here, the bank crumbling and overgrown. The only sign of habitation was Badger Farm a couple of furlongs away, black against the skyline with a narrow skein of smoke rising from a lanky chimney stack as though its owner were burning one stick at a time.

It was not a place of obvious attraction to the pleasure craft which were the canal's main users these days, but moored almost under the bridge was a dilapidated boat on whose bow it was just possible to discern the word *Bluebell*.

But there Dalziel's rightness ended. Even to the landsman's eye the boat had the look of a deserted and vandalized house, and when Pascoe scrambled awkwardly on board, he realized quickly he had been right in both particulars.

'Jesus Christ,' said Dalziel, who had followed him with shame-making nimbleness.

Everything in the tiny cabin that could be broken had been broken. Smashed crockery lay among torn clothes and splintered wood from the destroyed bunk. A pair of waist-length waders, gashed with a knife, had been laid like a corpse across the debris and the contents of a chemical lavatory emptied over the lot.

'Harry Park's lesson?' wondered Pascoe.

'Aye. But where are Waterson and this Beverley King, that's the question?'

Pascoe looked over the side into the black water. The canal ran straight and dark and deep here.

'I don't think so,' said Dalziel at his side.

'No,' said Pascoe. 'On the other hand . . .'

'We'll have to look.' Dalziel sighed and leaned his head back to scratch beneath his chin. High above, a trio of unidentifiable birds beat silently across the darkening sky. He shuddered gelatinously.

'Cold, sir?' asked Pascoe.

'No, lad. It's just that I prefer my ceilings no more than four feet over my head and preferably nicely browned with nicotine. Come on. Let's get back to civilization before the vampire bats come out to play!'

Chapter 9

Seal-like, the police frogmen disported themselves in the canal's murky waters by the corpse light of a grey dawn. A broken wheelbarrow they brought up, a tractor tyre and half a scythe, plus sundry tins, jars, bottles, boxes, all suggestive of a systematic dumping of household detritus from the bridge. But the nearest they came to bodies was a fertilizer bag containing six drowned kittens.

The tenant of Badger Farm turned out to be as stingy with words as he was with fuel till Dalziel's threat of RSPCA and Environmental Health inspectors touched a lingual nerve. Then he recalled noting *Bluebell*'s arrival some four weeks earlier. He kept a close eye on it for a while, suspicious that it should remain so long in such an unattractive mooring. But once assured that its sole occupants were a man and a woman with no kids, no dogs, and no desire to trespass on his land and bother him for milk, eggs or fresh water, he'd lost interest. He was a man of no curiosity and less sympathy. He remarked that he'd spotted the man wading around in the canal a couple of times with what he assumed was a fishing rod . . . 'though what the stupid sod was looking to catch, God alone knows. There's been no fish in that cut since the First War.'

'You likely pointed this out?' said Dalziel.

'Nay! Let folk find out their own errors, that's my way.'

It seemed a not unattractive philosophy, so Dalziel did not tell the farmer that he'd set the RSPCA and Environmental Health people on to him anyway.

Harry Park, given another sniff at the carrot of possible bail, came up with the address of an associate who might possibly have called on Waterson the morning after the meeting in the Sally. This man denied everything till Dalziel made him an offer he couldn't refuse, which Pascoe, who had come to recognize the signs, only just managed not to hear. Then he admitted he and his mate, Park's companions in the Sally, had called on Waterson with a view to persuading him that his sole hope of a happy future was total amnesia and he'd better not forget it. Finding the boat deserted, they had left a message to this effect.

'It's pretty clear what happened,' said Pascoe. 'Waterson must have spotted Wieldy that night, headed back to the boat, rousted out Beverley King and made off into the wild blue yonder.'

'You reckon?' said Dalziel. 'Likely you're right. Check out her parents' house in Monksley. Waterson doesn't sound the type to saddle himself with a woman once she'd stopped being useful and mebbe the lass has headed for home by herself.'

She hadn't. Her parents who applied the epithet *godfearing* to themselves five times in as many minutes, said they hadn't seen their daughter since the second Sunday in February when they'd had what sounded like the usual quarrel about money and lifestyle. The Kings showed some natural concern, though not a lot, and expressed the opinion that her sojourn in London had left her irremediably tainted. Recalling what Peter Coombes had said to him about her return north, Pascoe caused inquiry to be made at Chester Belcourt. The reply came very promptly, mainly because within thirty minutes of the Met ringing the firm to ask if someone could give them any information about Miss King, a middle-aged director with a wife and three children in Sevenoaks was round at the local station offering to cooperate fully in return for the utmost discretion. That he had been screwing Beverley King on a regular basis he did not seem to find at all reprehensible.

Moral revulsion only appeared in his tone when he described his shock at finding her shooting up in a hotel bathroom prior to one of their sessions. Ultimately he had come to believe that it was in the best interests of both the girl and the company if she returned to the bosom of her family in the North. The sincerity of this belief was underlined by the large personal severance payment he made her and by his carefully worded letter of recommendation for future employment in Mid-Yorkshire.

'So. Another druggie,' said Pascoe. 'Waterson seems to collect them.'

'If you bed down with foxes you'll end up with fleas,' declared Dalziel, managing to make it sound like an old country saw, though Pascoe had his doubts. 'But it don't take us much further forward.'

'It's another piece in the puzzle, sir,' said Pascoe with a noble attempt at optimism.

Wield provided one more piece on his return the following day. Despite Dalziel's slanderous allegations, he looked terrible and Pascoe tried to urge him back to bed. They settled on a compromise which kept the sergeant safely seated at his desk, catching up with routine paperwork. There was no keeping his mind at rest, however, and half way through the morning he came into Pascoe's room.

'I got to thinking,' he said. 'Waterson's file, I studied it pretty closely, seeing it was me that lost him in the first place. I've been looking at the update and something struck me. That time he got done for taking off when the patrol car flashed him to stop, that was January thirtieth. Park doesn't give an exact date for that big deal he did with him, but he says it was the end of January. Suppose it was the same day?'

'Explain,' said Pascoe.

'He's driving home with a parcel full of dope. We flash

him. He panics – that sounds in character. They pick him up half an hour later. He's all apologetic. He's also here.'

He pointed at a location to the north of the city on Pascoe's wall map.

'And he was flashed here, about two miles away. Now the car lads reported he took off along the bypass, so let's suppose he cut off here, took this fork, see where it'd take him?'

'Past Badger Farm,' said Pascoe.

'Right. He stops on the bridge. He's really on the boil. No lights in sight, but he doesn't know the moment when they'll appear, and they've probably got his number anyway. So what does a man who loses control like Waterson do now?'

'Tosses his parcel over the parapet into the canal, you mean? Why not just hide it in a ditch?'

'That'd be the sensible thing to do, but he's not got much talent for doing sensible things, has he?' said Wield. 'And a couple of days later *Bluebell* moves from Bulmer's Wharf to the bridge near Badger Farm.'

'And Waterson spends a lot of time wading around with a pole! Wieldy, you could be a genius. Let's see if we can find out!'

He picked up the phone and dialled.

'Joe, it's Peter Pascoe. All that rubbish your lads trawled up yesterday, what happened to it?'

He listened, replaced the receiver.

'We're in luck. They wanted to dump it back in the cut but Joe's got an environmental conscience and he made them stick it in rubbish bags and leave it at the farm for the bin man to collect.'

'We'd best get a move on, then,' said Wield, rising.

'I thought we'd agreed you were staying indoors today?'

'Not if I'm going to be a genius,' said Wield. 'You know what *he* thinks of geniuses.'

Pascoe laughed.

'All right. But don't blame me if you catch typhoid.'

Half an hour later, watched by the puzzled and suspicious tenant of Badger Farm, they began emptying the plastic rubbish bags. What precisely they were looking for Pascoe didn't know, but he saw it almost at once. A cardboard cylinder on whose water-stained and faded label he could just make out the words *Romany Rye Veterinary Products*.

He opened it. Inside was a sealed plastic lining protecting about 500 grams of white powder. He pulled it open and tasted it gingerly.

'No wonder fleas hop so high,' he said.

They found three other containers and the frogmen were re-summoned to check for more. Wield wore his genius status modestly till Dalziel appeared to remind him modesty was no defence.

'So now we know why he got the lass to move the boat down here,' he growled. 'So what? It still doesn't move us much further forward.'

'It gives us a lot more clout in getting resources allocated to finding them,' protested Pascoe.

Dalziel shook his head more in sorrow than in anger. Had he taught this boy nothing? You didn't leave some faceless twat to decide what was important. You made up your own mind, and resources were then allocated not on the basis of argued priorities but by gentle vibrations sent out across a web of owed favours, or if that failed, by a not so gentle rattling of cupboarded skeletons. Appleyard, for instance, wouldn't even register on a scale of official priorities. But there was a Chief Superintendent in the Met who'd never have made it past constable if Dalziel hadn't lied him out of a gross indecency charge after a rugby team booze-up a couple of decades before. And there was a Mid-Yorks DHSS chief whose wife had tried to carve her own exit out of the car park after Ladies Night at the Gents. He did not doubt he would be able to deliver the errant husband to Shirley Appleyard within the promised week.

As for Waterson, no need to call in favours here and even less to throw up road blocks and alert airports! Flushed out of his lair, short of cash, and with a deprived druggy in tow, how could a man with his track record avoid drawing attention to himself? A week was too long for him. Dalziel gave him three days, four at the most.

Eight days later both his certainties were beginning to feel slightly worn, and when Dan Trimble summoned him, he knew he was like a batsman walking out, unhelmeted and boxless, to face the West Indian attack.

It started with a head-high bouncer.

'Tell me, Andy,' said the Chief Constable. 'Is there any reason I should keep on being showered with shit because I won't close the Swain case?'

'Once I get hold of Waterson . . .'

'Waterson! You're no nearer finding him, are you? And even if you do and he sticks to his statement, he's going to be no use whatsoever to you, is he? Well, *is he*!'

The best answer Dalziel could manage was a neutral grunt. He'd played the drug connection for all it was worth to keep the Swain case open, suggesting that Swain could have used it to blackmail Waterson into a conspiracy. No one was convinced. Even Swain's laughter when Dalziel put the thesis to him had rung genuine and Thackeray had made yet another sonorous complaint of harassment to the Chief Constable.

'So we're where we were at the beginning,' said Trimble heavily. 'All right, Andy, I'll spell it out. I'm informing the coroner that the Swain inquest can be reopened. I do not doubt what the verdict will be. And that will be the end of it, Andy. No more harassment of Mr Swain. Do you understand me? And in the meantime you will do and say nothing which Eden Thackeray can interpret as even hinting a suspicion that Philip Swain might have been responsible for his wife's death.'

Dalziel said, 'I'm not sure what – ' but Trimble cut right across him.

'Andy, you'd better hear this and hear it well. In matters recreational, you may choose to ignore my advice and go ahead and make a fool of yourself. I don't like it, but I'm not going to match your foolishness by making a public spectacle of myself in openly trying to forbid you.'

He paused to draw in breath. For a small man he was pretty impressive, admitted Dalziel.

He resumed. 'But I'm not giving you advice here. As your superior I'm giving you a direct order. And I assure you, failure to obey my direct orders will result in instant suspension. Is that understood?'

'Yes, sir. Suspension, sir. By what, sir?'

Trimble smiled sadly.

'By the book, Andy. Which, though you may not believe it, can be a lot more painful than by the balls. That will be all for now.'

So. Dismissed from the presence without a sniff of the Caledonian nectar.

'Right, sir. Thank you,' said Dalziel, rising. 'Going to the ball, sir?'

It was the night of the Mayor's Hospice Appeal Ball.

'Indeed I am,' said Trimble. 'A man in my position can hardly afford to miss what I gather is the county's premier social occasion. And you?'

'Oh aye. They let the lower orders in too,' said Dalziel. 'I'll save you a dance mebbe.'

'How kind,' murmured Trimble. 'I'm sure that you'll do a lovely Dashing White Sergeant. Especially if you don't take care.'

240

It was the ultimate degradation. Yorked by a Cornishman! No point in even bothering to look at the umpire. Slowly, sadly, Dalziel walked away.

Chapter 10

Trimble was right. Despite the competing claims of the Liberal Club's Barndance, the Rugby Club's Barbecue, and the Federation of Working Men's Clubs' Festival of Brass, the Mayor's Hospice Appeal Ball was Mid-Yorkshire's most scintillating social occasion.

Nobody with pretensions to rank, power, charitable works, social concern or high fashion could afford to be absent.

True, to underline its democratic appeal, the tickets stated *Dress Optional*; and Peter Pascoe, unable to resist his wife's anti-élitist arguments, had come along in his charcoal grey flannel suit, only to be dazzled on all sides by frothy shirt fronts, bow ties like butterflies, and cummerbunds of every colour in the TV test-card. Nor were his drab feathers smoothed by his awareness that Ellie's egalitarian principles had not prevented her from investing in an off-the-shoulder and just-on-the-bosom blue silk gown in a style which Princess Di had made fashionable only a week before.

But even Ellie was upstaged by Dalziel's entrance. Immaculate in a d.j. of the latest cut, with heliographic shoes, and diamond studs glinting like ice in his snow-white shirt, he was a fitting foil for his companion. Though in truth she needed no foil. It was Chung, the Occident in her birth suppressed and the Orient given full sway. She wore a cheong-sam in green and yellow silk around which a bejewelled dragon caressed her sinuous body. The split up the side started at her ankle and seemed as if it went on for ever. At every stride, strong men gasped, and strong women ground their teeth in blasé smiles.

'Down, boy,' Ellie murmured in Pascoe's ear.

He grinned, divided in admiration between Chung's beauty and Dalziel's aplomb as he blew a kiss to the Lady Mayor and called out cheerfully, 'What fettle, Joe?' to the Lord Bishop, before settling himself and his partner at a table shared with Trimble and Eden Thackeray among others.

'Now that's what I call an odd couple,' said one of Ellie's politico-academic chums who made up the eight-place table, Ellie having pre-conditioned an evening free from constabulary conversation. 'Beauty and the Beast aren't in it!'

'Not odd at all,' corrected someone else. 'After all, where there's pork, you generally find crackling.'

There was a noise like the thud of a toe against a shin and the speaker let out a cry of pain. The age of diplomacy was not dead, thought Pascoe. Then he caught Ellie's eye and saw her lid droop in a conspiratorial wink and knew that the kick had after all been punitive not cautionary. He smiled back but he could fight his own battles. Turning to the kicked man whose Ph.D. thesis on medieval crop rotation he knew had just been referred for the second time, he said, 'Those gardening notes you've been working on, got anyone interested yet?'

Academics are naturally cannibalistic and this taste of their own blood put the rest of the table in the best of humours and the evening thereafter went with a bang. Everything was as it should be on such a splendid public occasion. The drink prices were exorbitant, the band played like a committee, and the buffet was as glorious to the sight as it was tasteless to the palate.

Midway through the evening, there was a charity auction of items donated by various 'personalities'. Bidding was particularly brisk for a Yorkshire cap presented by the county's greatest post-war cricketer, but silence fell after a voice jumped the offer from £550 to a thousand.

'No advance?' inquired the auctioneer. 'Then sold to Mr Philip Swain!'

Pascoe followed his gesture and for the first time saw Swain. Whatever Dalziel's threats and Picardy's hopes, locally his credit must once more be good. He looked relaxed and at his ease as he accepted the congratulations of those at his table. Pascoe could put names to most of them except one young woman, good-looking in a heavy-featured way, who looked familiar but defied identification till he spotted Arnie Stringer beside her. It was Shirley Appleyard. She didn't look as if she were enjoying herself very much. As he watched, she rose and moved across the ballroom till she reached Dalziel's table. She caught Dalziel's attention, he got up and moved aside with her a little way, they talked, then both went back to their seats.

'Very interesting,' Pascoe said half to himself.

'What?' said Ellie.

'What some people will pay for a second-hand hat,' he answered vaguely.

'Second-head, you mean, surely,' said a would-be wit.

'Which would you prefer, a second head or a second cock?' interposed another.

'Depends if you're buying or selling.'

They could spin skeins of this pedantic waggery. Pascoe excused himself and went to the loo. As he came out, he walked into a very English low-voiced, high-keyed scene. A woman, whom he recognized as Mrs Horncastle, must have just emerged from the Ladies to find her husband waiting to intercept her.

'But it's so early,' she was protesting. 'And you agreed yourself it was a good cause.'

'I'm not sure if the end altogether justifies the means,' said the Canon. 'In any case, I feel we have done our duty. Our presence will have been noted.'

'So will our departure,' she replied. 'I can't possibly leave without saying goodbye to the people on our table.'

'I have made the farewells for both of us,' said the Canon.

At this point he became aware of Pascoe's presence and glared at him indignantly. Pascoe smiled back and said, 'Good evening, Canon, Mrs Horncastle. It's going rather well, I think. Perhaps we can have a dance later, Mrs Horncastle.'

She smiled pallidly and he left them to their synod.

Back in the ballroom the dancing had started again and the first thing he saw was Dalziel doing a nifty quickstep with Chung. The second was Ellie in the close clutches of the mediaeval vegetable man. Before he could analyse what he felt about either of these conjunctions, a bleeper went off. It said much for the atonality of the band that at first no one noticed. Then all eyes focused on a stationary couple, one of whom was fishing angrily through his pockets. It was Dr Ellison Marwood, and his partner was Pamela Waterson. The bleeper was found and switched off. He spoke apologetically to the woman. Pascoe walked over to them and said, 'Duty calling, Dr Marwood? I know the feeling. Don't worry about Mrs Waterson. I'll take over while you find a phone.'

'You're too kind,' said Marwood satirically. 'I'll get back soon as I can, Pam. Sorry.'

She came into his arms and danced lifelessly till the quickstep ended. A ripple of applause was enough to send the band off into a tango.

'Do you?' said Pascoe.

'Not if I can help it. You haven't found him, then?'

'No. You haven't heard anything, I suppose?'

'No. I don't think I will. I think he's dead.'

'Good lord, no need to talk like that,' said Pascoe, genuinely shocked. 'He'll turn up just now, believe me.'

'I don't think so,' she said. She spoke without emotion but, as last time he spoke to her, he got that sense of black despair not far beneath the surface.

Could it be the kind of despair which would make her write letters to a stranger? He hadn't forgotten the letter-writer's hints that she would be here tonight, but it had hardly seemed worth exercising his mind on. There were getting on for two hundred women here, all wearing their most public faces. What hope of penetrating to the pain beneath that cosmetic finery?

Now here was someone who didn't, or couldn't, keep it hidden. Would a direct question surprise an honest answer? And how would he know? To ask would be to warn. Better to watch and ward.

He escorted her back to her table which seemed mainly medical. When he returned to his own, he found Ellie had just abandoned the fray, limping heavily. The vegetable man was most apologetic, but there was a glint in his eye which made Pascoe wonder if after all he had identified the toe which cracked his shin.

On the dance floor Dalziel and Chung swept from side to side in what should have been a parody of a Valentino tango but somehow wasn't. As if inspired by their togeth-erness the band was playing almost in tune.

'It's like the last night of the *Titanic*,' someone opined above the swelling music.

'Or the Waterloo ball,' suggested another.

They could be right, thought Pascoe. Except that the silent icebergs and the blazing cannon were not external but had probably been brought right into the middle of

245

this merry rout in the minds and the hearts of some of the revellers. Oh Christ. Two glasses of anti-freeze and his mind was turning purple!

He felt Ellie's gaze on him.

'Penny for them?' she said.

'I was just wondering if you'd ever play football again,' he said.

The tango ended and the band stuttered into an old-fashioned waltz.

'Try me,' said Ellie, rising.

They did a couple of circuits without talking. Then Pascoe felt a tap on his shoulder.

'Excuse me,' said Dalziel, a gigolo grin scimitaring his face. 'Man with a wooden leg can't be satisfying a lovely mover like this.'

'Fuck off,' said Pascoe amiably.

They waltzed away. Ellie's arms were round his neck pulling him close.

'That's the nicest thing I've heard tonight,' she said. 'I love you.'

'Me too.'

'So why don't we practise what you preach?'

'Eh?'

'I mean fuck off.'

They stole away without fuss. How simple life could be sometimes, thought Pascoe. All you had to do was walk away from the *Titanic*.

As long as you were aware, of course, that you might be stumbling into the Battle of Waterloo.

Part Five

LUCIFER: Me needs not of noy for to neven,
   All wealth in my wield have I wielding;
   Above yet shall I be bielding,
   On height in the highest of heaven.

   There shall I set myself full seemly to sight,
   To receive my reverence through right of
    renown;
   I shall be like unto him that is highest on height.
   Oh, what I am dearworth and deft – oh deuce!
    all goes down!

       The York Cycle: 'The Fall of the Angels'

Dear Mr Dalziel,

It's been a long time, more than a month. Did you think I'd given up the idea? Or perhaps simply gone off quietly and done it? I don't suppose you'd much care which as long as I was out of your hair! Don't think I'm complaining. It was your likely indifference I chose you for in the first place, remember? The last thing I want is for the Great Detective to actually set about tracking me down! Of course, even though I'm beneath your notice, you might fob me off on to one of your underlings. That bothers me a bit. I shouldn't like to think that someone who actually cares might end up picking up the pieces, particularly if I opted for something messy like jumping under a train. Now what put that idea into my head? Perhaps because it's St Pancras' day? Wrong St Pancras, I think, so no need to send your minions rushing off to the station!

I'm rambling. Sorry. Just because it's a ramshackle meaningless world we live in doesn't mean we should give up control of our own thoughts. What I'm saying is I don't want to add to all the misery on offer, so keep me clear of the sensitive plants if you can.

It was good to see you enjoying yourself at the ball last month, by the way, even though you didn't ask me to dance! The Hospice Fund must have done well. I felt so unselfish, knowing I couldn't personally benefit from it. And at the same time I felt like standing up and saying, no need to waste your money, I can teach you how to die! But that would have been a dead giveaway, wouldn't it? And I

249

mustn't make life easy for you. Though come to think of it, it might be nice if I could. I owe you something for laying all my troubles on you like this. It would really please me if I could compensate for dropping one insoluble problem in your lap by helping you out with another. The coroner wasn't very kind to you the other day, was he? And by all accounts you weren't very happy with him. Naturally I can hardly hope to succeed where the Great Detective has failed, but I promise I'll keep my ears open.

It will give me something useful to do during the countdown.

Chapter 1

It had been a mistake to play God.

Especially when you'd solved the old paradox: if God created everything, who created God?

The answer was Chung. And Chung the creator was very different from Chung the malt whisky drinker, or Chung the last tangoist.

Rehearsals at ground level had been demanding enough both of time and energy. But it was his first sight of a pageant wagon that brought matters to a head.

'I'm not going up that,' proclaimed Dalziel. 'Not even if you fit me with crampons.'

That was a narrow ladder up the back of a triple decker stage mounted on a flat-car. The lower deck represented hell, the middle earth, and the upper heaven. And over the upper deck, perched amid polystyrene clouds, was a tiny platform for the maker unmade, the mover unmoved, God Almighty, Andrew Dalziel.

'Come on, Andy,' said Chung. 'The frame's really secure. And there's a safety harness.'

'Aye, but is there a bloody parachute?' asked Dalziel.

'A couple of times and you'll be running up there like a mountain goat,' she said persuasively. 'Look.'

She was more like a mountain lion, lithe and tawny, as she scaled the ladder with no apparent effort. Dalziel looked up at her, erect and magnificent, on the tiny platform. She beckoned to him, smiling encouragingly.

'Care for a bunk up, Superintendent?'

He turned and looked at Philip Swain. This was another of the troubles with playing God. As Chung had rightly judged, Swain's presence in the cast had been a positive incentive to someone of Dalziel's character. But Trimble's warning about harassment had inhibited him more than he cared to admit, and now, to add injury to inhibition, the jury at the re-convened inquest on Gail Swain had brought in a verdict of death by misadventure. Swain had left the court with words of sympathy ringing in his ears, while Dalziel's had been filled with the flea-like buzz of pained reproof.

He had brought much of it on himself by refusing to desist from his efforts to blow clouds of suspicion Swain's way, thus obliging Eden Thackeray to waft them aside with reluctant ease.

'You had been *where* that night, Superintendent?' he had asked, smiling.

It turned out that Thackeray knew exactly where he'd been, how much he'd supped, and, their friendship notwithstanding, would bring witnesses to prove it if necessary. When the old solicitor somehow contrived to get him to admit he was being sick into a bucket when he first noticed Gail Swain at the window, his credibility was completely ruined and the coroner's summing up had come close to a recommendation that his conduct of the case be investigated by his superiors.

'Shouldn't you be in California?' he said to Swain now.

'I'm flying out with the coffin at the weekend.'

'Well, I hope it all goes off all right.'

'Thank you,' said Swain, surprised. 'Yes, it's going to be an extremely fraught experience. Not helped, of course, by the delay.'

'What? Oh aye. You're talking about the funeral. I meant the really important thing, your talks with them

Delgado lawyers. I reckon they'd have made me mayor of LA if I'd pinned a murder charge on you!'

Swain came close to anger, then opted for amusement.

'That's better, Superintendent,' he said. 'I thought for a moment you were going soft. But thanks for your good wishes all the same. If they're sincere.'

'They're sincere enough,' said Dalziel. 'I want you back here in my reach as soon as possible.'

'How touching. And why is that?'

Dalziel smiled like a polar bear.

'Because of the Mysteries, of course,' he said. 'Because your understudy's crap, and Chung reckons you're the very best Devil she's ever directed.'

He was telling the truth. Swain was excellent in his part and Chung had been very annoyed to learn he was likely to be away for as long as a week.

'I'm flattered,' he said, smiling. 'And I do hope you've managed to reach your heaven by the time I return.'

'I'll get there in the end,' said Dalziel. 'I usually do. Don't forget your lines while you're away. I'll be listening carefully.'

'Andy, are you going to get your ass up here or not?' yelled Chung.

'All right, I'm coming,' said Dalziel. And began the long ascent.

Back at the station later, he parked his car in the refurbished car park which was like a constant mocking reminder of his failure. In his office he rummaged through his mail and groaned as he came across another letter from what Pascoe called the Dark Lady. As if conjured by his thought, Pascoe came into the room.

'Stopped knocking, have we?'

'Sorry, sir. Thought you were still at your theatricals. I was going to drop this on your desk.'

'Tell me about it. I'm pig sick of reading words just now.'

'I just had a call from Leeds Central. As you know, they've had real trouble with their football yobs. But because they're highly organized over there, that's meant they're vulnerable to infiltration and the Leeds undercover operation's had one or two excellent results.'

'Send the buggers a medal, then. What's this got to do with us?'

'The word is that during the last couple of seasons some of our City supporters, short of any real action over here, got themselves into the Leeds gang for their jollies. But now they're dividing themselves between the two because they've got big ambitions to make a name for themselves as the City mob. Just first names so far, which isn't much help, but as soon as they can get some real detail, they'll let us know. Promising, eh?

'Yes, must be nice to get other buggers to do your work for you,' said Dalziel sourly. 'I wish I could manage it. I seem to recollect asking some idle sod to get this joker sorted.'

He tossed the latest letter across to Pascoe who read it with a troubled look on his face.

'Doesn't sound like a joker to me,' he said.

'No? Then get her off my back! Christ, you've had long enough!'

This from a man who found the Dark Lady's plight an irritation too trivial to waste his own precious time on was too unjust for argument. Pascoe rang Pottle and got invited to have a drink in the University Staff Club. The psychiatrist read the letter twice.

'She's very confused,' he said.

Pascoe, with a guest's sensitivity, suppressed the mock amazement which rose to his lips by taking a long pull at his spritzer. Pottle regarded him with a slight smile which suggested he had noted the suppression.

'That may seem obvious,' he went on. 'But what I detect is a confusion beyond the basic mental and spiritual turmoil which has brought her to the point of suicide. It's all to do with this understanding of her own motives which hovers between the conscious and the subconscious. Despite her disclaimer, she began to suspect her use of Dalziel as a sounding-board was also an appeal for discovery, so she ended the correspondence after letter two. Then her need to "talk" grew so strong she had to start again to protect herself from discovery! After another two letters, the pattern repeats itself, and she resolves to stop once more, though this time without announcing it.'

Pascoe interrupted, 'Not out of fear of being tracked down so much as fear that that's what she really wanted?'

'More or less,' said Pottle. 'Several weeks pass. And finally an awareness that she is rapidly approaching the point of no return brings with it a desire to be prevented so strong that she has re-opened the correspondence. Such fascinating ambiguities! She claims to be distressed lest Dalziel had passed the case to a more feeling subordinate. An inspired guess or actual knowledge? Subconsciously, of course, she is probably simply miffed that the great detective as she calls him isn't taking her seriously. Happily, you are.'

He regarded the detective sympathetically and poured another inch of Muscadet into his glass, not hiding his disapproval as Pascoe topped it up with soda.

'I'm driving,' said Pascoe. In fact he quite liked the combination and didn't think anyway that the Staff Club's Muscadet was worth getting religious over.

'Last time you said she was probably as likely to give clues for policemen as psychiatrists,' he went on. 'Does it still look that way?'

'I believe so. But they may not be all that obvious.'

'Policemen aren't allowed to ignore the obvious,' said Pascoe. 'I've already asked Mr Dalziel for a list of his partners at the ball. That should eliminate half a dozen.'

'So many? I should have thought one veleta would have sent him reeling to the bar,' said Pottle, who had suffered much abuse from Dalziel over the years. 'Yes, that was certainly a very obvious clue, reducing your suspects by about fifty thousand at a stroke. And she's started talking about methods at last. *Jumping under a train.* Possibly just a tease. Never take what she says too literally. But clues there are, and there'll be more before the end.'

'She'll write again.'

'Oh yes. No doubt about it. The closer she gets, the more nods and winks she'll give. But you'll need to be sharp. Don't expect a name and address!'

'It'd make life a lot easier,' said Pascoe.

'That's what we'd all like,' said Pottle gently. 'Including your Dark Lady.'

As Pascoe drove back to Headquarters, he brooded on what Pottle had said. He recognized in himself the growth of an obsession, but he did not know or perhaps did not want to know how to combat it. It was all right for Pottle to tell him to be a detective, but he didn't feel like a detective, more like a medium striving to make contact with a lost soul and having to work through some not totally sympathetic spirit guide! These intermediaries often figured as Red Indians, or Chinamen. He'd got Dalziel.

He picked up his car radio mike and intoned, 'Is there anybody there?'

'Say again, over,' crackled the radio.

Hastily he replaced the mike. A chief inspector was too senior to be wild, too junior to be eccentric. It was the sober middle age of a police career. But even the middle-aged were allowed their obsessions and if you had one, there was only one thing to do – ride it till either you fell off or it dropped from under you.

Outside his room, he bumped into Dalziel and said rather aggressively, 'You won't forget that list of your dancing partners, will you, sir?'

Dalziel didn't reply but opened the door and ushered Pascoe inside, then overtook him and sat at his desk.

'This is your in-tray, lad,' he said kindly. 'And this sheet of paper here is the list I promised. And these sheets here are the complete guest list. So if you take this list from this one, you'll find you've got close on two hundred names, one of which might belong to this daft tart who's wasting so much of your highly expensive time.'

'At least it's a life I'm trying to save, not just my self-esteem,' retorted Pascoe, allowing himself to be stung.

'Meaning?' said Dalziel.

Pascoe was already regretting his outburst but he knew better than to back down.

'Meaning we still seem to be spending a lot of time and energy chasing around after Gregory Waterson so you can try to re-open the Swain case.'

'I'm not denying it,' said Dalziel equably. 'But he is a criminal suspect, isn't he?'

'All right. But Tony Appleyard's not a criminal, is he?' said Pascoe obstinately. 'And we seem to have got half the police in north London and all the DHSS looking for him.'

'It's about time them buggers had something useful to do,' said Dalziel. 'Anyroad, I made a promise, lad.'

'To Shirley Appleyard, you mean? But you've said yourself she's not pressurizing you.'

'That's right. I wasn't sure from the start why she really wanted to see him. Stick a knife in him, mebbe. Anyroad, yes, she seems to have lost interest. Last time I told her I'd heard nowt, she just shrugged and said, *I shouldn't bother any more. It's not worth it. Likely he's dead.*'

'And why are you still bothering?' asked Pascoe, rancour erased by genuine interest.

'Because it's worth it to me,' grunted Dalziel. 'One, I'll break my own promises, not wait till someone gives me permission. And two, I want to know. He might be a useless specimen but he's from off my patch, and he went south to work, not to die, if that's what's happened to him. I wouldn't put it past them cockneys. *Here's a dead 'un, not one of ours, another bloody northerner, when's the next load of rubbish going out to the tip?* It's time they knew they've got me to answer to!'

This was the nearest thing to a radical political statement Pascoe had ever heard from the Superintendent. It wasn't going to usher in the Socialist Millennium, but shouted loud enough, it might cause a little unease in Thatcherland.

'Look, sir,' he said. 'I'm sorry if I sounded off a bit . . .'

'Never apologize, never explain,' said Dalziel, rising. 'Just do your job, and never forget the golden rule.'

'Which is?'

'When in doubt, it's your shout. Come on, lad, the Bull's been open for nigh on ten minutes!'

Chapter 2

Eustace Horncastle was no connoisseur of revenge. Hot or cold, it was a dish his cloth forbade him, and he felt this no great deprivation, believing with that fervour reserved for the more militant tenets of his faith that the Lord would repay.

Unhappily, his knowledge of what the Lord would do was not matched by an equal degree of self-awareness. Vengeance, plainly served at whatever temperature, would have been pushed aside with genuine moral revulsion; but Mrs Horncastle could testify that, reconstituted, it had been a staple of his diet for many years.

The way it worked was this. At the conscious level, wrongs were forgiven, slights forgotten, provocations met with forbearance and pain with fortitude. But somehow, somewhere, some time, something would emerge, justifiable in terms of logic, Christian teaching, and the greatest good of the greatest number, which without bearing much resemblance to most known forms of vengeance, yet had its sweet and sour aftertaste.

April 21st

Dear Miss Chung,

You will recall when I promised my support in obtaining for you permission to use the area around the ruins of St Bega's Abbey as the fixed site for your production of the Mysteries I pointed out that any decision on this would require the ratification of the Cathedral Chapter. For various reasons it did not prove possible to lay the proposal before a full Chapter till yesterday and I regret to inform you that the feeling of the meeting was strongly against the idea. The environs of St Bega's have a very special ambience and it was felt that it would be inappropriate for such a peaceful and holy spot to be used for what is essentially a secular and commercial entertainment.

I do not doubt that the City Council will renew its offer of Charter Park, however, and I assure you of my continued personal support for your endeavours.

Yours very sincerely,
Eustace Horncastle

'Oh you bastard,' said Eileen Chung.

She picked up the phone on her desk at the Kemble and dialled. A woman's voice answered.

'Dorothy, is that you? Hi. Chung here. Is your lovely husband in?'

'I'm afraid not. Can I help?'

'I don't think so. It's not important. I'll catch up with him later,' said Chung with Erinnic certainty. 'How're you doing?'

'I'm fine.'

'That's good. It's time you dropped by for a coffee. I know you're up to your halo with good works and all that, but we can always put you to work if you feel guilty. How about this afternoon?'

The two women had met several times since their encounter over the Pliny tomb. Their exchanges had been light and social but undershot on both sides by a strong current of memory.

'I might do that. Ought I to get Eustace to ring you back?'

It was a strange turn of phrase.

She knows what this is about, thought Chung. And she's hinting a doubt at my strategy.

'No need,' she said easily. 'I'd prefer to see him. Perhaps we can plot an ambush when you come round.'

She replaced the phone. Dorothy Horncastle had been right. She would get nowhere talking to the Canon on the phone. Even face to face her charms were uncertain now that he'd cried Lamia. But without St Bega's, her production felt flat and dull, as flat and dull as Charter Park. She should have taken more care of this. She stood up and walked restlessly around the room. The walls were papered with the Mysteries – storyboard, scripts, routes, costume and pageant designs – it was all there, in every sense. This was what had attracted her in the first place. The only other way to get such a comprehensive statement of life was to do all of Shakespeare from *Hung be the heavens with black, yield day to night!* to *And my ending is despair*, a journey not to be concentrated into a holiday week!

'What's up with you, lass? You look like you bit an apple and swallowed a worm.'

It was Dalziel. Sometimes you knew backstage when he was in the foyer; others, he came up behind you like a scouting Indian.

'Worm's about it,' she said handing him the letter.

He read it and said, 'Makes a difference using Charter Park, does it?'

'Like playing at Barnsley instead of Wembley,' she said.

'I'm a rugby man meself,' he said, 'and clart's clart whatever the scenery. What's the plan, then?'

She shrugged hopelessly. Dalziel watched and thought that Chung shrugging should have a government health warning. No mere shoulder movement this but an undulation running down her long lithe body like a Mexican wave.

He grinned and said, 'Right. Let the dog see the rabbit.'

'What are you doing?' she asked as he dialled a number on her phone.

'Can't compete with you at shaking titties, luv,' he said. 'But I'm a dab hand at shaking other things, like fists, faith and front row forwards. Hello! Bishop in? He can't be busy, it's not Sunday. Tell him it's Andy Dalziel and there may be a problem about his ticket for the Welsh game next season. What? No, I don't want him to ring back, I want him now. If the monkey's around, the organ-grinder can't be far away.'

He smiled sweetly at Chung, who hissed, 'Who are you talking to, for God's sake?'

'Bishop's chaplain. Nice lad, but he plays lacrosse. Lacrosse! No wonder there's no respect for religion. Hello, Joe. About time. No, the lad got it wrong, of course there's no problem about your international tickets.

261

Have I ever let you down? I'd fix you up with a helmet and let you walk the line if that was the only way to get you in. That's me, reliable. Like you, Joe. You can trust me like I trust you. Right, I'll come to the point, I know you're a busy man. Friend of mine's got a problem . . .'

Ten minutes later he put the phone down and said, 'There you are. All fixed.'

'My God, Andy. And I mean that literally! But what about the Chapter? And I thought the Bish was shit-scared of Eustace?'

'It seems at this Chapter meeting the use of St Bega's wasn't really on the agenda. It had all been fixed ages back. It was old Horny-cassock himself who brought it up and naturally there were a couple of sniping speeches at him because he gets up a lot of noses, and suddenly he says, right, I think I've got the feeling of the meeting and they're into any other business, no vote taken. As for Joe being scared of Horncastle – ' Dalziel smiled ursinely – 'who'd you be more scared of, luv? A wanked-out cleric or me?'

'No competition,' said Chung. 'But how do you know him, the Bishop, I mean . . .'

'Didn't anyone tell you I was a failed priest?' said Dalziel so seriously that she let her astounded half-belief show till his huge frame started to shake with convulsions of laughter which were Krakatoa to her Mexican wave.

'Oh, you bastard,' she said joining in.

'I told you,' he said between guffaws. 'He were one of the front row forwards I was good at shaking. Bugger tried to bite me ear off once. I had three stitches. He told me after it were a kind of reverse transubstantiation, my blood tasted like Sam Smith's beer. Now, I'm no bishop, I really am busy, so what about this rehearsal? Lucifer still on his travels, is he?'

'Philip? Yes, it's a damn nuisance. He said a week and its been more than two.'

'Don't worry, luv,' said Dalziel. 'He'll be back, word of God. Now I've got this grand idea for when I'm talking to Noah . . .'

There had to be easier ways of earning a crust than rehearsing Andrew Dalziel, thought Chung. But, once she got it into his head that though in matters criminal and even episcopal he might reign supreme, in matters theatrical she was boss, he could be sensational as God.

She explained this to Dorothy Horncastle that afternoon. The Canon's wife smiled as if the idea pleased her. Chung, whose curiosity about masks and motives was the mainspring of her professional life, said, 'You like the idea of a big fat copper as God, don't you? What's the appeal? Rude sign at the Church? Put-down for the Canon? Or what?'

It was a step into an intimacy which had yet to be proved, but Chung hadn't got where she was by pussyfooting around.

For a few moments the woman froze, her features setting into just the kind of umbraged mask a lady of her class and condition ought to wear in face of such intrusive familiarity. Then a slow thaw set in, another smile struggled through like a weak spring sun, and she said ruefully, 'Sorry, I'm still getting used to your . . .'

'My big mouth. Say it, hon,' laughed Chung. 'It's my best feature.'

'Your directness,' corrected Dorothy. 'Your honesty.'

'Come on! You're so honest, it drips out of you!'

'No. I obey rules, I follow the law. That's not the same. I only approach real honesty in fantasy.'

'Me too,' said Chung. 'It's my job. But don't think honesty means you've got to put up with crap. It can also mean telling the people who dish it out to go screw themselves.'

'Go screw . . .' Dorothy tested the words. 'I'm not quite sure if I'm ready for that. Don't misunderstand me. All I mean is that profanity should come as naturally as the leaves to a tree or it should not come at all.'

'You work at it, hon. Meanwhile, you can just tell me to mind my own business.'

'You know, I don't think I will. Why do I like the idea of Mr Dalziel making a hit as God? Certainly not because of any sense of rude gesture, or put down. On the contrary, I think he is perfect for the part! After all, isn't the image most people have of God precisely that of a big fat copper who will put everything right?'

'Is it? I suppose so. But there's more to Andy than that. He can make a lot of noise when he wants but he can also manage to be so quiet he's practically invisible. And he ought to be a straight up and down establishment figure, but he doesn't really fit in anywhere. Usually when people say someone's their own man, they mean they haven't sussed out who owns him. But with Andy, I reckon it might actually be true. Hell, am I making any kind of sense?'

'Of course you are,' said Dorothy Horncastle, who had been listening intensely. 'You're saying Mr Dalziel is ubiquitous, omniscient and immortal. My dear, clearly you didn't cast him as God. He *is* God!'

She spoke very seriously and for the second time that day Chung found herself inhibited from taking as joke what had to be a joke.

Then the Canon's wife began to smile and soon the two women were laughing together, or at least they were laughing at the same time.

Chapter 3

Philip Swain landed at Manchester Airport at 7.30 on the morning of one of those days of early May which can make a Yorkshireman feel good to be alive even in Lancashire. His trip had taken three weeks rather than the one he had anticipated, but he had gone out tourist and come back first and there was no sign of flight fatigue on his face as he collected his luggage from the carousel.

He strode confidently through the green channel and out into the main arrivals hall, heading for the exit like a pit pony eager for the sky. Footsteps accelerated behind him and a hand clamped heavily on to his shoulder. He halted, spun round, then smiled broadly.

'Arnie,' he said. 'You needn't have come all this way. I'd have got a taxi.'

'Cost you a fortune,' said Arnie Stringer lugubriously.

'Arnie, I've got a fortune,' said Swain.

'All settled, is it?'

'I said so when I rang, didn't I? It took a bit longer than I thought, but once it dawned it was cash I wanted, not Delgado voting shares, we did a deal.'

'Aye, I don't doubt them Yankee lawyers are as tricky as us own. Thackeray rang to check when you'd be back. Says he'll be out to see you. Money's toasted cheese to them rattons.'

'We need a good lawyer now,' said Swain reprovingly. 'Come on, Arnie. Where's the car? I can't wait to get back to Moscow. Christ, how I'm sick of air-conditioning and muzak!'

The two men said little more till they were out of Manchester and on the motorway, climbing high up into the Pennines. Swain wound down the window and breathed in deep as he gazed out over the bleak moorland stretching away on either side.

'That's good,' he said.

'Good? It's ninety per cent diesel,' said Stringer. 'You'll get fresher air in a multi-storey car park.'

Swain regarded his partner speculatively. There was a streak of sardonic humour in the man which sometimes made Swain believe the stories of their common ancestry. But his Nonconformist conscience was pure Stringer.

'What's up, Arnie?' he asked. 'You've been a real misery, even by your low standards.'

'Nowt's up. I'd have told you else, wouldn't I?'

'I know you would. But there's something . . .'

They were at the top now. Behind them, Lancashire. Ahead, Yorkshire. The morning sun was bright in their eyes. Stringer had pulled down the visor to keep it out, but Swain was happy to relax with its warmth on his face.

'It's our Shirley,' said Stringer abruptly.

'What? She's not still on about that husband of hers, is she?'

'Not so much now, but she were. We had a big row about it. I told her again I'd tried looking for him, but there was no finding them as don't want found. We got a bit heated. She seems to have settled down since, but she let on it was her as set that fat bastard looking for him. Social Security inquiry! God, he's cunning.'

'I never doubted that. But what's in it for him?' wondered Swain. 'He dishes out favours like Nero on a bad day. He's probably only going through the motions. So stop worrying.'

'It's Shirley I worry about.'

'Yes, I know that, Arnie. But you said she seemed more settled now.'

'Settled? Aye, but sometimes it's more than settled.

266

Resigned, maybe. Or just plain given up. I think maybe it's not knowing where she's at.'

'Well, Arnie, I can see you're upset, but there's nothing you can do about it. Absolutely nothing. You mustn't risk hurting Shirley. Or that lovely grandson of yours. God gave *you* the strength to bear things, but he didn't give everyone that strength. It'll all come out all right in the end. Divine providence. That will take care of things, won't it?'

Swain spoke earnestly, his eyes fixed on the driver's silhouetted face.

'Yes,' said Stringer. 'I suppose it will.'

'Right, then. Let's get home,' said Philip Swain.

As they dropped down into Yorkshire, Swain grew more and more relaxed and Stringer increasingly morose. When they climbed out of the car in the yard at Moscow Farm, it could have been the driver who'd made the long trip from the States and the passenger who had spent the night in his own bed.

Eden Thackeray who had been sitting in his Saab listening to a tape of *The Yeomen of the Guard* clearly thought so.

'You're looking well, Philip,' he said as they shook hands. 'So well, I assume your trip was successful, financially speaking?'

'Oh yes,' said Swain. 'I think even you will have to agree that Swain and Stringer are at last on a sound footing. But why are you sitting out here? Shirley's got a key.'

He glanced at the office window.

'Shirley, Mrs Appleyard, did offer to let me into the house, but I demurred. I don't think our musical tastes coincide.'

Swain frowned slightly at the excuse, then said, 'Well, come in now. Thanks, Arnie. We'll talk later.'

Stringer accepted his dismissal blankly and made for the office.

Swain led the lawyer into the house, his face glowing with visible delight in being home once more.

'What'll you drink?' he said.

'It's a little early. A glass of Perrier perhaps to toast your safe return.'

Swain pulled a face but he poured himself the same.

'So what's new here?' he asked.

'Not much. The police still haven't traced Mr Waterson or Miss King.'

'What's that to do with me?' asked Swain in irritation. 'If and when they find Waterson, he'll just confirm what the inquest has already settled. I want to put all that behind me and start remembering Gail as she was, not the subject of a police investigation, or an estate for blood-sucking lawyers to haggle over. Sorry. I mean the Americans, of course. They make you lot look like a bunch of social workers.'

'Which is what we are at heart,' said Thackeray.

'You say so? And presumably you've come rushing out here simply to check up on my well-being?' smiled Swain. 'How very kind. But while you're here we might as well chat about the firm's future. I've got real plans. You know that development on Crimpers Knoll I talked about? Well, now . . .'

But he became aware that Thackeray was holding up his hand and shaking his head.

'What's up?' said Swain.

'Philip, you're quite right, it is the firm's future I wanted to see you about. I always knew that if you became a rich man, you would not be content to sit back; you would want to use your money to move your business on to a much more elevated plane, and what I've been wondering is whether my firm can offer you the kind of representation

268

you will now require. In short, it seems to me that now would be a good time to take stock and ask ourselves if the interests of a burgeoning company and of its clients and employees might not be better served by a more specialized law firm.'

Swain was regarding him in astonishment and dismay.

He said, 'Look, if this is pique because I didn't consult you about my negotiations with Delgado . . .'

'No, no. How could you? I know nothing of American law. And that's precisely my point. For special circumstances you want specialists. I do not believe we can serve you in the future as we have served you in the past. And since I do not wish that any mistaken loyalty on your part should postpone the parting till it assumes the dimension of a dismissal, I think it behoves me to make the first move. I have prepared a list of commercially orientated firms I can personally recommend.'

He put his glass on the table, laid an envelope alongside it, rose and offered his hand.

Swain ignored it, saying, 'For God's sake, Thackeray, what's going on? You've been my lawyer for years . . .'

'But am so no longer. I'm sorry to seem so precipitate but you were away longer than expected and I'm off for a bit of a break in Sardinia in a couple of days. I wanted the decks to be cleared before I left, for your sake, I mean. Good luck, Philip. I know how hard you've worked to earn it.'

The lawyer dropped his unclaimed hand, smiled pleasantly, nodded and walked from the room.

Behind him, Swain stared unseeingly into his Perrier water. Then he shook his head as though to wake himself, emptied the glass into an ashtray, drew the top from his whisky decanter and poured himself a long measure.

Suddenly he looked indeed as a man might be expected to look who had just flown six thousand miles and lost eight hours in the process.

Part Six

SCRIBE: Alas the time that this betid!
         Right bitter care doth me embrace;
         All my sins be now unhid:
         Yon man before me them all doth trace.

The N. Town Cycle: 'The Woman Taken In Adultery'

Dear Mr Dalziel,

Another month without a letter! To tell the truth I seemed to have hit bottom as far as human life was concerned, i.e. I knew everyone who really mattered to me was dead and I stopped hoping to hear mystic voices from afar summoning me to a tearful reunion. And of course anyone who reads the papers had long ago given up on man as a species worth anything more than early extinction. But curiously this final death of hope in humanity seemed to open me up to nature and for a while I was almost able to lose myself in little lambs and daffodils and all the blossom of spring. Then last week a big wind blew and suddenly I was treading petals underfoot, and watching the rain beat down the flowers, and on the news they were still arguing about which areas of the country were producing lambs fit to eat post-Chernobyl.

So much for nature! So now I'm confirmed in my resolution. But I've not forgotten my promise to help if I could. It's harder than I thought. You really earn your money, don't you? But something I heard might interest you. Did you know that Eden Thackeray has stopped being Philip Swain's lawyer? Probably you did, and probably it doesn't mean anything anyway. But remember the widow's mite. When you've not got much to give, a little can be a lot!

I'll try to do better next time. If there's time for a next time. Meanwhile you could do worse than apply to John of Beverley whose day this is. A Yorkshire bobby and a

Yorkshire saint! What a combination. He was very good with the poor and the handicapped. Also he helped the English win at Agincourt. So either way you might find him useful!

Chapter 1

'Got the sack, did he? What? Oh, I see. Mind you, he would say that, wouldn't he? No need to get aereated. Tara.'

Dalziel put the phone down. Pascoe and Wield had come into the room while he was talking and he regarded them parsonically as he intoned, 'There be three things which are too wonderful for me, yea, four which I know not.'

'And what might they be, sir?' inquired Pascoe politely.

'You don't know? Jesus, what's religious bloody education coming to? Tell him, Wieldy.'

'Don't remember exactly,' said Wield. 'Isn't one of 'em something about the way of a man with a maid?'

'Oh aye. I might have guessed that'd be the one that stuck in your mind. That'd be a bit too wonderful for you right enough, wouldn't it?'

Pascoe, though suspecting he was the only one to feel embarrassed, said quickly, 'And what are the others, then?'

'Summat about ships and serpents, or is that the Walrus and the Carpenter? Anyroad, here's a fifth. Eden Thackeray's no longer representing Swain.'

He tossed Pascoe the Dark Lady's letter.

'I wonder how she knows?' said Pascoe.

'Oh, sod that,' said Dalziel impatiently. 'All that matters is, it's true.'

'So what's so wonderful about a man with new money wanting a new lawyer?'

'Nowt. Except that that's not the way it was. I just rang up the firm to check. old Eden's away in Sardinia till the weekend but I charmed his secretary into telling me the truth. It was Eden who sacked Swain, not the other way round. And a lawyer giving up money, *that's* a lot too wonderful for me!'

Pascoe still couldn't share the fat man's wonder. The Swain case was yesterday's news, the only loose end being the continued absence of Greg Waterson and his girl-friend, and they were more the Drug Squad's concern than Dalziel's. His lack of enthusiasm showed, for Dalziel snarled, 'All right. Doubting bloody Thomas, leave it to me. I'll sort old Eden out when he gets back. Meanwhile what have you got that needs a conference on a Monday morning? And it had better be something a lot more important than tracking down that dotty tart!'

This seemed grossly ungrateful in view of the signifi-cance the Superintendent seemed to have found in the Dark Lady's information, but only a fool tried to score debating points off Dalziel.

Pascoe said, 'It's this football gang. Leeds have come up with something positive.'

'Not afore time,' said Dalziel. 'Further West you get, more useless and idle the buggers become. Lancashire, Wales, Ireland, America. Must be something to do with the Gulf Stream. So, what have they got, lad?'

'Seems now that the season proper's over, these yob-boes are at a bit of a loose end. So our City breakaway group have issued an invitation to their Leeds mates to come across here and have a bit of a joust.'

'You're joking! You're not? When?' demanded Dalziel.

'Three weeks' time. Bank Holiday Monday, May thir-tieth. Day of your dramatic debut, sir. Perhaps that's the real attraction . . .'

The fat man's face told him he'd picked the wrong subject for humour and he quickly became serious. 'Leeds reckon their undercover team have got enough evidence for conspiracy to cause an affray. They've given us four names . . .'

'Four? Is that all they could manage?'

'They're the ringleaders. With another dozen being rounded up in Leeds, it should nip things in the bud and prevention's better than cure.'

'I suppose so. It'll just leave the steamers, the druggies, the yardies and the dips to sort out. What's the plan?'

'There's a few loose ends to tie up. Then next week, Tuesday morning, at the crack, we'll pick up our four, do a preliminary interrogation here, then ferry them over to Leeds to join their dozen.'

'What's up? Don't the miserable sods trust us?'

'They've done all the graft,' said Pascoe, 'so we've got to play their rules. But it'll give us a chance to see if we can tie any of our lot in with chucking that lad off the train or smashing up the Rose and Crown.'

'You'll be lucky,' said Dalziel pessimistically. 'Still, it's better than nowt. Let's make a really big splash out of this and mebbe it'll persuade some of the other villains to pick somewhere else for their holiday outing.'

He really doesn't want his debut spoiled! thought Pascoe.

He said, 'How's it all going, sir? The Mysteries, I mean.'

Dalziel eyed him assessingly, decided to take it this time as genuine interest, and said, 'It's bloody hard work, I'll tell you that for nowt. I sometimes wonder how I got conned into taking it on.'

'Chung's hard to resist,' smiled Pascoe complacently, sure now that his role as Judas-goat was undetectable.

'A lot of 'em are,' growled Dalziel. 'At first. Then you let 'em talk you into something daft, like marriage or play-acting. That's when you see the change. But I've said I'll do it and I'll not go back on my word. Someone round here's got to show a bit of community spirit. I'm surprised you've not got yourself involved, Peter, your missus being so thick with Chung. You must have boxed real clever to keep out.'

He was regarding Pascoe assessingly once more and Pascoe's sense of security evaporated like spit on a flat-iron.

That night he described the scene to Ellie and said casually, 'Chung *is* completely discreet, I suppose?'

'No, thank God, else I'd have a very dull article.'

Ellie was now deeply immersed in preparing a profile of Chung for the *Evening Post*'s Mysteries Souvenir Edition. She'd been flattered when Chung had insisted she should write it rather than one of the paper's regular reporters, who, she alleged, couldn't be trusted to get the facts straight about a flower show. Ellie's enjoyment of the task was marred only by the difficulty of getting Chung to sit still. Most of her interviews were given on the move, but it was all great copy and Ellie was increasingly optimistic that her piece would be the jewel in the crown of the Souvenir Edition.

'Any chance of a preview?' asked Pascoe.

'No way. You'll pay your money like everybody else,' said Ellie firmly.

There was nothing in her tone to hint reprisal for his own unwillingness to let her see the Dark Lady letters, but he felt it as such. Since that unacknowledged clash, he had made an effort to talk about this and other cases, but she had registered only a polite interest and slipped away from the subject as soon as possible. He felt, though did not feel ready to argue, that police evidence was a bit different from Chung's biography. Instead he managed a smile and said, he hoped not too tartly, 'Then I shall feel as entitled to be critical as anyone else. Incidentally, as you chase her around, have you come across Fat Andy in rehearsal?'

'I saw him distantly. He was curiously impressive.'

'Curiously?'

'I mean, he was just himself. No acting that you could notice, just Andy Dalziel on high, bellowing mediaeval verse. But it sounded like he was saying it, not reciting it, I mean actually saying it, his own words.'

'Do you think we've been wrong all these years and he really is God?'

'Have you noticed the state of the world lately?' asked Ellie. 'How could you ever doubt it?'

Chapter 2

''Evening, Mr Thackeray,' said the barman at the Gents. 'You look as if you enjoyed your holiday.'

'I think I did, John,' said the lawyer, a smile splitting his bronzed face. 'The usual, please.'

As the barman reached for the twelve-year-old Macallan, a finger like a Colt Python dug into Thackeray's spine.

'And another of the same, John,' he said without turning. 'Andrew, how are you?'

'Better than you, I'd say,' said Dalziel, hoisting one bovine buttock on to a stool. 'You've got a terrible colour, did you know that? You ought to try a holiday.'

'I'll think about it. I understand you rang the office while I was away.'

'That's right,' said Dalziel. 'Not very helpful, that lass of thine.'

'I'm sorry to hear that. Cheers.'

279

'Up yours,' said Dalziel threateningly. 'Never fear, I'll get to the bottom of it.'

'No one quicker,' said Thackeray, peering admiringly into Dalziel's empty glass.

'You know what I mean.'

'I haven't the faintest idea.' The lawyer placed his equally vacant glass next to Dalziel's and inquired politely, 'Are you thirsting for Oxfam this week, perhaps?'

'You'd not take a drink off a man who's about to call you a bloody liar, would you?'

'Certainly not. On the other hand, you'd not have taken a drink from a man you were just about to call a bloody liar, so there must be some misunderstanding.'

Dalziel considered this, nodded and said, 'All right. But you'll cough before we leave here tonight and that's a promise. John, are you a plant from the League of Temperance or what? There's empty glasses here. Monday's Toad-in-the-Hole night and we'll need a solid base for that.'

With the empty smile of one who wishes the cook were of his mind, John reached for the Macallan.

The old long-case clock in the vestibule of the Gents had struck two and John had fallen asleep at his post before Dalziel found the key to unlock Eden Thackeray's confidences.

Drink he had tried till the Toad was awash in its hole with Burgundy and Scotch. Bribery had followed, with promise of advance viewing of police evidence in any two cases of the lawyer's choice over the next year. Then blackmail in the form of marvelling references to the tolerant attitudes of Thackeray's older, richer clients to the eighteen-year-old 'niece' he had taken with him to Sardinia.

Apart from a raised eyebrow at Dalziel's familiarity

with his private life, the lawyer had treated all these gambits with equal indifference. Baffled, Dalziel rose and went for a regrouping pee. On his return he paused at the bar to order more malt.

'Mr Thackeray all right, is he?' said John with the thick accent of the newly awoken.

'Yes. Why?'

'Eleven's his usual limit. Midnight on Club Nights. I've never known him so late before.'

It was a brave attempt to get rid of his last two customers but it failed miserably. Dalziel's face lit up like dawn across the bay.

He said, 'You're right, lad. Make them doubles.'

'You've been drinking doubles these past four hours,' said John sourly.

'Then double doubles!' said Dalziel.

He put the glass down in front of Thackeray and said, 'Sup up. That's your last.'

'Is it?'

'Aye. It's long past your bedtime and I need to be up at the crack too. So no more pissing about. Cards on the table. What we both know is I want to find out why you jacked in representing Phil Swain. But what I've only just realized is you're as keen to tell me as I am to find out!'

'What on earth makes you think that?'

'You'd have buggered off hours ago else! You've just been hanging on hoping I'll come up with a reason good enough to let you blab without too much damage to your professional bloody conscience.'

Thackeray considered, smiled, said, 'That's terribly subtle, Andy. But having tried intoxication, corruption and threat, what remains? A good kicking?'

'Man's got to try what he knows,' said Dalziel unapologetically. 'No, I'm giving up on you. That's why first thing tomorrow, I mean today, I'm going to start shoving Swain around till he cries harassment. Then I'll keep on shoving till he gets another brief to stop me. Then I'll keep on shoving till I get hauled up before Desperate Dan or mebbe even the courts. Then I'll keep on shoving till . . . you get the picture?'

'You'll be in deep trouble?'

'Aye.'

'And it will all be my fault?'

'Aye.'

'I don't know if my conscience can permit that,' said Thackeray gravely. 'Particularly when what I know is so little. The needs of a present friend are more pressing than those of a former client, *sub specie aeternatis*, wouldn't you say?'

'Likely I would if I could pronounce it,' agreed Dalziel.

'Then listen carefully, for I am about to talk to myself. While Swain was in America, I received a phone call from a man called Crawford who works for a company called Muncaster Securities. Basically all that Crawford seemed to want was assurance that Swain really was in America, tying up the details of his wife's estate. When I started to inquire as to the exact nature of Muncaster Securities' connection with my client, he cut our conversation short very politely and rang off. My curiosity was naturally roused. So I made some discreet inquiries . . .'

'Oh aye?' laughed Dalziel. 'You mean you didn't rest till you'd pulled every string you could lay your hands on!'

'I have fairly extensive connections in the finance world,' admitted Thackeray. 'To cut things short, what I discovered was that Swain's financial position was far more perilous than I knew. Moscow Farm was mortgaged up to the hilt and in as bad a state financially as when Tom Swain shot himself. In theory the date had already passed on which Muncaster Securities were entitled to call in the debt and possess the farm. In practice, of course, they would rather have their money with additional penalty interest, and the imminence of Swain's inheritance had made them hold their horses. Crawford was simply double-checking.'

He stopped talking, raised his glass and drank carefully, observing Dalziel over the rim.

'And?' said the fat man.

'And what?'

'You're not telling me you threw over a potentially stinking rich client because you took the huff he'd not told you all his business, are you?' sneered Dalziel. 'So what's the rest? You might as well spill it. Be less painful for your influential mates. I've got strings I can pull too, only most of 'em are tied round influential bollocks!'

'Oh dear,' sighed Thackeray. 'I knew there'd come a moment when I wondered if this were such a good idea. All right, there were a couple of other things to give me pause. One was that between February 7th when Gail left allegedly en route for America and February 15th when she was shot, three cheques were issued on her account to pay off Swain's most immediate debts.'

Dalziel digested this with the peptic assistance of his double double.

'Farewell present?' he suggested.

'Perhaps.'

'Or are you thinking that mebbe he gave himself the present of one of her cheque-books and reckoned with her out of the country, she wasn't likely to be paying much attention to her UK account for a while?'

'It's possible. Doubtless by examination of the signature on those cheques, it would be provable. Though of course as the money is now his . . .'

'It wasn't then,' said Dalziel. 'So you began to wonder if your client was a forger? Well, well. Hold on. Once he'd started down that path, why not pay off Muncaster the same way?'

'This was a current account. All right for a couple of thousand, but wholly inadequate for the Moscow Farm mortgage.'

'Stole the wrong cheque-book, did he? Not much use, these Swains, when it comes to money, are they? Incidentally, what happened to the cash he borrowed? I know his business was staggering along, but he can't have lost that much in a tuppenny-ha'penny set-up like that.'

'Every Swain finds his own South Sea Bubble. Swain found his very close to home. You remember I told you that when Delgado were preparing to pull the rug from under Atlas Tayler, they threw up a smokescreen to fool the Unions by letting rumours develop about a possible expansion in the UK via a small components firm in Milton Keynes?'

'But you said Swain knew nowt about that and got all indignant with the Yanks when they suddenly threw everyone out of work.'

'And I told you true,' said Thackeray. 'It was merely the cause of the indignation I mistook.'

Dalziel digested this, then began to grin. 'You mean that's where the money went . . .?'

'Yes. They didn't trust him enough to make him privy to their schemes, but he was close enough to get the first whisper of their interest in the Milton Keynes firm. Perhaps they were even ruthless enough to use him as an unwitting disseminator of their smoke. But what actually happened was Swain suddenly saw a chance to get rich and independent. He borrowed every penny he could, mortgaging Moscow up to the hilt, and started buying shares in the components firm. Once the rumours got out – and they'd be fuelled by Swain's purchases – the shares started rising, but he kept on buying.'

'Hey, I know nowt about City law, but that's criminal, isn't it?' said Dalziel, suddenly alert to a new possibility of getting something he could stick on Swain.

'Swain certainly thought so,' said Thackeray grimly. 'That's why he covered his tracks so well. But settle down, Andrew. It's only criminal if you make a profit. Delgado weren't interested in a takeover, so insider trading doesn't come into it. You can hardly prosecute a man for making a foolish investment and suffering a substantial loss.'

'I suppose not. No wonder he told Delgado's to stuff their bloody job!' Dalziel began to smile, almost admiringly. 'But it wasn't all loss, was it? He managed to get himself elected as the workers' friend by taking a moral stand against the big bad capitalists. Christ, you've got to give it to the sod. If he lost an arm, he'd sell it for sausagemeat!'

'It was unforgivable hypocrisy,' said Thackeray, with distaste.

'Well, that's not a crime either,' said Dalziel. 'So now you're wondering if when he saw he couldn't hold off these Muncaster people any longer, he mightn't have started wondering how it would be if his missus snuffed it.'

'No, Andrew. The facts are so plain that I cannot see how even your prejudice can maintain you in your belief that Swain is culpable in his wife's death. Hypocritical, self-centred and immoral he may be, but that doesn't make him a killer.'

'Doesn't make him unfit to be your client either,' said Dalziel shrewdly. 'I mean, that description must fit half the buggers on your books! There has to be something else.'

'Perhaps you have merely lost touch with the workings of a sensitive conscience, Andrew,' said Thackeray, rising.

At the bar, John yawned a heartfelt prayer of thanksgiving.

Dalziel shook his head thoughtfully and said, 'Money. It's something to do with money. In the bank's where you sods keep your conscience, isn't it?'

Then a broad smile spread over his face.

'Here! It wasn't . . . it couldn't . . . I bet it was! One of them pressing debts that got paid off out of Mrs Swain's account, was it a lawyer's bill? Did the cheeky bugger pay off your account with a forged cheque? By God, I've not been much taken with Swain so far, I admit it. But there's good in everyone if you look close enough. Paying off his lawyer with a forged cheque! I'd drink to the cheeky bugger if I had a drink! What a good idea! Sit yourself down, Eden, and stop looking so longfaced. John, set 'em up again. Double double doubles!'

Chapter 3

Not long after Dalziel finally answered John's increasingly blasphemous prayers by leaving the Gents, Sergeant Wield was on his way to work. This was the day of the soccer hooligan dawn raid. Let's make a big splash with this one, Dalziel had said. But as usual, Wield thought as he shook the drizzle out of his raincoat, it was the poor bloody infantry that got wet.

At least he had the consolation of being inside. Pascoe was in the great outdoors, coordinating the uniformed teams making the arrests. He would move behind them from house to house, getting what he could from parents and family, and making sure his searchers picked up any scraps of supportive evidence from the youths' rooms.

Wield's task meanwhile was to welcome the arrested

men and take down initial statements, hoping to squeeze some nice gobbets of self-incrimination from them while sleep was still hot in their eyes and dawn-knock fear still sour in their guts.

The first three were, in varying proportions, surly, defiant, indignant and afraid, but that was all they seemed to have in common. What was it that united in violence a nineteen-year old car mechanic, a twenty-one-year-old who'd never worked, and a newly-wed twenty-three-year-old who'd just passed the second part of his exams to become a solicitor's clerk? He, oddly enough, was the only one who didn't start mewling for a lawyer. Perhaps already he was anticipating what this might do to his career and hoping for an anonymous exit route. Wield applied pressure and soon a steady trickle of names and information emerged, interrupted at intervals by protestations of personal innocence. Only when pressed about the train killing and the pub assault did the trickle dry completely. He had enough legal nous to know where grassing stopped and witnessing began.

The fourth and last was eighteen, unemployed, and the least distressed of those arrested, perhaps because he had had the longest time to recompose himself.

He was also the ringleader of the gang that had attacked Wield at the park gates the night he had followed Waterson.

There was no sign of recognition. Wield, accustomed to being unforgettable in his cragginess, felt strangely piqued.

'Medwin, Jason,' recited Wield. 'Seventy-six Jude's Lane. Unemployed.'

'That's me,' agreed the youth pleasantly.

'Ever been employed?'

'Apprentice fitter when I left school. Redundant. Then I was with the Parks Department for a few months.'

'Redundant again?'

'Nah. Jacked it in. Didn't suit me.'

'What do you reckon would suit you, son?' asked Wield.

'Don't know. Job like yours mebbe.' He grinned. 'Must be grand to be able to thump people with no comeback!'

Wield said gently, 'Like thumping people, do you?'

Medwin shrugged.

'Don't mind a bit of a mill,' he said.

'Is that right? Why *is* that?'

'Don't know. Gives me a buzz. Let's me know I'm alive.'

'Someone thumps you back hard enough, it might let you know you're dead,' suggested Wield.

Another shrug. He was a good-looking boy; blond hair cropped short up the sides, fashionably coiffured on top; nose slightly crooked (result of some old fight perhaps?); eyes deep blue; smile attractive; cheeks lightly downed; jaw edged with stubble to show he'd been too quickly roused for shaving . . . Wield pulled himself up. What had started as a professional description was turning into . . . what? He reminded himself that Medwin, Jason, went to football matches to cause mayhem, lay in wait for gays at park gates, was planning to disrupt the holiday pleasure of thousands of visitors to the city.

'So you don't mind if someone hurts you or kills you?' he said.

'Not much. No one else does.'

'No? I see. No friends, eh? Find it hard to get on with people?'

He touched a nerve. For a second he saw the eyes that had glared at him with a killing hatred the night of the attack. Then a blink, and the smiling boy with the crooked nose was back.

'I got friends,' he said. 'Lots of them.'

'Name six,' said Wield.

'What do you mean?' demanded Medwin, puzzled. 'You

288

don't think I'm going to give you lot my mates' names just like that!'

'Why not? They're not crooks, are they?'

'I'm not a crook and I'm here,' said Medwin.

'All right, I'll put it another way. Tell me what you were doing on these three nights and give me the names of any witnesses who'll support you.'

He scribbled three dates on a sheet of paper and pushed it across the table.

Medwin looked at them blankly. The first was February 6th, the night the young man had been thrown from the London train. The second was February 26th when the Rose and Crown had been wrecked and the landlord put into hospital. The third was March 1st, the night that Wield had been attacked.

'Well?' prompted the sergeant.

'You've got to be joking,' said Medwin. 'Takes me all my time to remember last night.'

'Let me jog your memory. Sixth of Feb, City lost four nil in the Smoke, and a young lad was pushed off a train near Peterborough.'

'Now hang about!' exclaimed Medwin. 'No way can you tie me in with that.'

He sounded genuinely indignant.

'You didn't go to the game, then?'

'Of course I did. Never miss. But I weren't on that train or any train. Went down by car with some of my mates.'

'Names. Addresses,' said Wield tossing a pencil over the table, adding as Medwin didn't pick it up, 'Come on, son. They'll be witnessing they couldn't have been on the train either, won't they?'

Reluctantly he admitted the logic and began scrawling on the paper.

When he'd finished Wield looked at the list.

'Crowded car,' he observed. 'Here, this one's got no address.'

'Don't know where he's living now. He moved away south. We bumped into each other at the game and had a few bevvies after and he said he was thinking of coming back up on a visit so I said would he like a lift and he said yeah. He's likely gone south again by now. I might try it myself. I mean, there's nowt to keep anyone up here, is there?'

'You'd be surprised,' said Wield menacingly. 'Right, now try City's home game against the Reds. Nil-nil draw.'

He let the youth work this one out for himself, saw realization dawn, but there was no indignant protestation of innocence this time, just a veiling of the eyes and a shaking of the head.

'Got me there,' he said. 'Don't remember that one.'

'I thought you never missed a match?' said Wield.

'Almost never. But when you see such a lot, you can't recall 'em all, can you?'

Wield nodded friendly agreement and made a note that this was one for the injured landlord to see.

'So what about the other date?' he asked.

'March first?' said the youth shaking his head once more. 'Means nowt.'

'It means you know that the Reds game was on Friday February twenty-sixth for a start,' observed Wield drily. 'Now there wasn't a game this night, you're right. Not a game of football anyway.'

'So what did happen? Give us a clue, won't you?' the youth said, grinning.

He really has no idea, Wield assessed. Queer-bashing probably wasn't worth remembering, a mere training session for the real fights at the weekend. Now was the moment to jump on him, to watch his expression as he realized he'd assaulted a cop, to listen to his lies and to squeeze from him a list of names to support some extempore alibi. One of them would break, kids always did. And a cop's word would be enough for most magistrates to pour shit on him from a great height.

But Wield found himself hesitating. He could sense danger here. A bright lawyer could offer the defence that Medwin had genuinely believed he was being propositioned in the hope that a normally prejudiced jury would accept this as provocation to violence. Suppose he went further and tried to find something in Wield's words or manner which might have justified such a mistake? Suppose he sensed a hesitation and asked Wield direct if he were gay? Philosophically, ever since his life crisis some eighteen months earlier, Wield had been 'out'. In practical terms, and certainly in terms of his professional image this had meant very little so far, but he had derived peace and strength from the certainty that he would never again prevaricate if faced by the question direct.

But to risk inviting this question in open court with some twinkle-toed brief tap-dancing all over him was no part of his bargain. It could bring the Force into ridicule, possibly get the charge dismissed, certainly set the right wing press sniffing around, scenting blood, offering deals, hinting protection. It could mean his career gone.

But perhaps, in fact probably, it would never come to this or anywhere near it. Simple evidence of what he was doing at the time, a police officer on duty viciously assaulted by a gang of young thugs, dealt with by a nice fascist magistrate with some bored legal aid brief somnambulating through the cross-questioning. . .

He had to do it, whatever. Big risk, little risk, no risk at all. Duty, faith, call it what you will; that personal imperative which, expanded to a general principle, makes religions; corrupted, makes fanatics; but ignored, makes existence meaningless; this was the only arbiter.

He said, 'On Tuesday March the first, you waylaid a man at the entrance to Kipling Gardens, and with the assistance of others as yet unknown, you assaulted him.'

'You what? Who says?' demanded Medwin, unable to hide his consternation.

'I say,' said Wield. 'You should try to pick on people your own size, son. Like dwarves.'

'You're saying it was you?' He stared at Wield in dawning recognition first of the face, then of the trap he'd fallen into.

'That's right,' said Wield. 'You really are in trouble, aren't you?'

There was a tap at the door and Seymour stuck his head in.

'Super's here and wondering how you're getting on,' he said.

'I'll have a word,' said Wield. 'Mr Medwin here turns out to be the young gent who assaulted me in March. He's just going to write a statement. Give him a hand, will you?'

He went out glancing at his watch. Not yet seven. I bet the fat sod's feeling all virtuous about getting up early, he thought.

He was being unjust though he couldn't have guessed it, for there was nothing in Dalziel's appearance to show he hadn't been to bed at all. On his return home from the Gents, he had soaked in a piping hot bath for more than an hour. Then, feeling himself more famished than fatigued, he had breakfasted on a black pudding boiled up in a panful of oxtail soup, sitting naked at his kitchen table, staring out through the soft focus of mucky glass and a damp May morning towards the window where he'd had his only living glimpse of Gail Swain.

Her face he couldn't remember, and next time he saw it, it mostly wasn't there. But the tits . . . in his mind's eye he saw the tits again. His libido seemed to be having an Indian summer, or perhaps it was a Malayan summer, for it was since his close contact with Chung that he'd noticed his imagination running hot. Which reminded him, he was due at rehearsal at ten, so instead of sitting here exciting himself, he'd be better off getting a couple of early hours in.

'Not done yet?' he now greeted his sergeant. 'You're just supposed to be processing these lads, not getting their life stories.'

'This one turned out to be a bit more complicated. Seems to be clear on the train job, says he travelled by car that day, gave me these names as back-up,' said Wield, passing over the list. 'I reckon he's worth looking at for the pub riot, though. He went very amnesiac on that one. And something else came up. I recognized him as the leader of that gang that beat me up.'

'Oh yes,' said Dalziel with a lack of interest almost hurtful in the light of Wield's recent soul-searching. 'Wieldy, this name here, the one without an address . . .'

'Oh, him. Medwin says he was an old mate he bumped into at the match and gave a lift to. Living down south and just fancied coming back here on impulse. Sounds like he was pleased. Why the interest, sir?'

'The name, lad. The *name*. Tony Appleyard! I'm surprised you didn't spot it. Too early in the morning for you, is it?'

Even now it didn't register immediately. One man's obsession is another man's yawn. Then he remembered. Arnie Stringer's vanished son-in-law, whose continued absence Dalziel seemed to take as a personal affront! If he'd made the connection himself and gone running, he might have picked up a house point. Now his only reward for getting up so early was Dalziel's reproof.

He said, 'Needn't be the same, sir. Lots of Appleyards in Yorkshire.'

Dalziel looked heavenward and said, 'O ye of little faith! Let's go and find out, shall we?'

Though Dalziel's interview with Jason Medwin breached no human rights agreement, it was nevertheless an act of terror.

The fat man oozed avuncular charm, but as he smiled encouragement and nodded approval, his hands were doing terrible things to a sheet of paper, a plastic cup, and finally a lead pencil which he snapped into four pieces each of which he crumbled to splinters between finger and thumb.

Medwin had started with cheek – 'Fucking hell, you're really bringing in the heavy mob, aren't you?' – then laughed uproariously.

Dalziel joined in and for a few seconds the two laughed in unison. But Medwin's amusement slowly diminuendoed through a nervous chuckle to a fearful silence, while Dalziel's guffaws went on and on, putting Wield in mind of the Laughing Policeman on the front at Blackpool which as a child he'd always found more frightening than funny. At last Dalziel too modulated to a smile, but by now it was clear that as far as Medwin was concerned, Dalziel's smile held more threat than Wield's grim features set at maximum grue.

It was quickly established that the youth's friend was indeed the Super's own Appleyard.

'Got some slag in the club, and her dad made him marry her. I'd have told him to sod off but Tone never had much bottle.'

'Can't all be heroes,' agreed Dalziel amicably. 'So he ran off south?'

The youth considered. None of this was self-incriminatory, so there was no point in misleading this fat bastard and (eyeing those restless hands) mebbe a lot of point cooperating with him.

'Nah, I reckon he went looking for work to start off, then just sort of got lost.'

'And it was just chance you met him?'

'Yeah. He were always a supporter, mind, and with them being down there, it was natural he'd go to the game.'

'But you didn't know he was in that bit of London?'

'Nah. Look, we weren't that friendly, just saw each other around the games, know what I mean? It was him came after me at the match. I thought I must owe him money or something, the way he grabbed hold of me.'

'So he was glad to see you.'

Medwin nodded. 'Yeah, he was. He looked a bit rough and I asked him if he was working and he said he'd been doing a bit on the lump, nothing regular, and he'd not felt up to much recently anyway. He kept on asking questions about back here, about his wife and things. Well, I didn't know her from shit and in the end when we'd had a few bevvies, I said why don't you come back up and see for yourself? It's only a quick belt up the mo'way. He said, why not? dead casual like, but underneath he were right keen. I'll tell you what, old Tone were no advert for heading south to make your fortune!'

'If he was in such a bad way, why'd he not come back earlier?' said Dalziel. It sounded more like a question to himself than to the youth but Medwin wasn't taking chances.

'Would have done if the tart's old man hadn't warned him off.'

'What's that? Appleyard said he'd been warned off by his father-in-law? When? How?'

The intensity of Dalziel's interest hit the youth like a fist.

'I don't know, do I? I'm just saying what Tone said. I said he'd be OK back here with the Security plus whatever he could bum off his wife's family. And he said, the only brass I'll get from her fucking preaching father is coffin handles. Then he went on – But sod him, I don't care what he says, I'll come back if I like, and see what he can do! I said you should stick one on the old wanker, Tone, and he said yeah, but I reckoned it were the drink talking.'

Who needed hypnotism to trigger total recall? Wield asked himself admiringly. Fat Andy could induce it wide awaking, and probably plant as many conditioned responses as he liked too.

'And when you got here, what did you do?'

'It were close on midnight and we dropped him near the pea-canning factory on the ring road.'

'Because that's where he wanted to be?'

'Not exactly. To tell the truth he were a bit of a pain. We'd had to stop a few times so he could honk, and when he had to get out again on the edge of town we thought, fuck it! and drove off. I mean, you try to help some people but they just won't help themselves, will they?'

He looked at Dalziel with wide-eyed appeal.

The Fat Man smiled once more.

'You're right, Jason. But you've helped me, haven't you? And I think that deserves a reward. Tell you what I'm going to do. Can't drop all the charges against you, but I'm going to give you a break on one of them. Let's see, what've we got? Oh aye. You were in the Rose and Crown when the landlord got duffed up. Don't try to play innocent, lad. This isn't an audition for the Mysteries. We've got witnesses. What else? You've got an alibi for the train job, if it checks out. And you were boss of the gang that beat up my sergeant here, right? That's the one to scrub, I reckon. You could get a couple of years for assault on a police officer and I shouldn't like to think of a good-looking boy like you in an over-crowded cell.'

He smacked his leathery lips together in an obscene kissing noise. Medwin was looking dazed. Dalziel went on, 'Don't worry so much, son. Full cooperation on the pub job, lots of names, and we'll go easy, never fear. Youthful high jinks in a bar, we've all done it, even magistrates. Bound over, a fine mebbe. And we'll keep stumm about the other, eh? Constable Seymour here will steer you straight. And I'm always handy if you need any assistance!'

With a genial wave, Dalziel led the way out.

As soon as the door closed behind them, Wield said indignantly, 'What's going off, sir? You'd got what you wanted, you didn't need any deal, and that bastard beat the shit out of me and God knows how many more besides . . .'

'Hold on to your hat, Sergeant,' said Dalziel. 'Do you really want to sit in court and hear that clever little sod tell the beak that you offered him a fiver for a quick wank? That's what he'd likely say; and what do you do if some clever brief comes sniffing round your private life?'

This was such a precise re-run of his own fears that Wield could find no words of protest that wouldn't ring hypocritically.

Dalziel continued, 'And don't worry about Jason. I heard yesterday afternoon that that landlord's had a relapse, long-term kidney damage, so anyone tied up with that rumpus isn't going to walk. Also there's the little matter of conspiracy to cause an affray charge which is why he's been picked up in the first place. That'll come as a nice little surprise when we ferry him across to Leeds in an hour or so. Meanwhile you and me have got work to do. Come on.'

'Yes, sir. Where to, sir?' said Wield, trying not so much to conceal as not to feel the great wave of relief washing over him.

'Where to? Do you not listen when I'm interrogating?' He glanced at his watch. 'Builders start bright and early, don't they? I reckon our best bet for having a little chat with Arnie Stringer will be at Moscow Farm! Let's get a move on. I've got a rehearsal at ten and God can't be late, can he?'

Chapter 4

It had stopped raining and the sky was beginning to clear with promise of a fine summer day. The yard at Moscow Farm was full of noise and activity. Shirley Appleyard was climbing up the outside stair to her office. Her father was loading a surveyor's level on to a shiny new pick-up, and Philip Swain was backing a gleaming yellow JCB out of the barn door.

But when Dalziel's car drove into the yard, they all paused. And when Swain switched off the JCB's engine, the pause turned into a stillness against which the drift of clouds across the pale blue sky seemed like frenzy.

Slowly Dalziel raised his hand, in greeting presumably, but it seemed to Wield as if the puppet-master had twitched the strings, for the three figures before him instantly returned to life.

'Superintendent, what can I do for you?' said Swain, jumping down.

'You?' Dalziel considered long enough to telepath several grossly offensive suggestions. 'You could tell me who your new lawyer is.'

Swain raised his eyebrows, specially plucked by Chung to look more diabolic.

'So I could,' he said pleasantly. 'But why should you want to know?'

'Just so I'll know who to expect next time we have you down at the station,' said Dalziel.

'In that case, it's hardly worth telling you as I might have changed him several times by then.'

Dalziel laughed, untroubled by Swain's show of assurance. The man was bright enough to have looked behind Thackeray's upfront reasons for breaking the connection, and it wouldn't be comfortable for him to find Dalziel's great grey head peering behind the screen too. But it was early days to decide what, if anything, might be made of the lawyer's doubts.

He said, 'Man knows his own business best. It's Mr Stringer I've come to see today, if you can spare him.'

'We're very busy . . .'

'So I see. Must be grand to be able to afford decent equipment at last. Take a lass out in one of these things and she'd not be able to complain you didn't make the earth move for her!' He patted the JCB admiringly. 'Big job, is it? Someone's drive? Or more garages?'

It only became a gibe if you let it. Swain said, 'We're clearing a bit of land on the farm estate. Crimper's Knoll. Do you know it? Not much use for anything but grazing a few sheep, but it will make a lovely setting for a few quality homes.'

'Is that right? You'll have got planning permission?'

Swain smiled a smile compounded of new money and old blood.

'It's in train,' he said. 'So if you could let me have my partner back as quickly as possible. Do you want to talk inside?'

'Out here will do fine,' replied Dalziel.

He put his arm around the foreman's shoulders and led him away. Wield said, 'Use your phone?' and without waiting for an answer went up the stairway to the office.

Shirley Appleyard said as he passed her on the stair, 'What's he want?'

'There's divided opinion on that, luv,' said Wield.

Inside the office he closed the door firmly behind him and dialled the station number asking for Pascoe, who did not sound happy when he came on.

'Where the hell are you?' he demanded. 'I've just got in and the place is like a morgue.'

Rapidly Wield explained what had happened, then went on, 'Seymour should be in the interview room with Medwin still. There's something I should have asked the boy and he'll likely be en route for Leeds by the time I get back. It's about the night he attacked me.'

'I thought you said Il Duce had promised him immunity on that? He must be going soft in the head.'

This was no time to explain Dalziel's motives. Wield said, 'This is just information. It's simply that when Medwin and his gang were beating me up, a vehicle went by. It slowed down, might even have stopped, then it took off again.'

'Like the driver thought of helping, then decided not to get involved?'

'Or like he mebbe picked up Waterson,' said Wield. 'Just a thought. It could be worth asking.'

'You're not getting as dotty about Waterson as the old man is about Appleyard, are you, Wieldy? Good job someone's here doing the real work, isn't it?'

'Anything you want me to tell the Super?' said Wield innocently.

'With his hearing, likely he's heard me already! Cheers.'

Wield left the office and joined Shirley Appleyard at the head of the stair.

She said, 'What're they talking about? Is it about Tony? Have you heard something?'

'Like what?'

'Like . . . like he's dead maybe.'

'Why should he be dead?' wondered Wield.

'I don't know. I wake up in the night sometimes and I'm sure he's dead. Then I tell myself in the morning it was just one of them daft turns you get in the night. But recently it's not mattered whether it's been black dark or broad day, I've still felt the same. So is that why he's come?'

'No,' said Wield, moved by the pain he could see on the girl's face. 'The Super would be up here talking to you if he'd brought bad news, wouldn't he?'

'Would he?' she scoffed. 'You men! We even get our tragedies as drippings from your pot!'

She turned away abruptly and went into the office. Wield, no stranger to pain himself, felt her loneliness and abandonment crying out to him.

He turned and glared down angrily towards the two big men rapt in each other's company.

'So you lied,' Dalziel was saying.

'I said so, didn't I? I lied to me own daughter, you don't think I was going to be bothered lying to the sodding police!'

'That sounds reasonable,' said Dalziel with complete sincerity. 'So now you say that when you went looking for your son-in-law, he'd left the lodging-house you had as his address, but one of the other lodgers said he thought Tony might be staying with a friend in what-was-it Street?'

'Webster Street. Have you got cloth ears or what?' said Stringer angrily.

'Good tale stands twice telling,' reproved Dalziel. 'So you went round . . .'

'. . . and I sat in my car, not knowing which house it

might be. It were a long street, tall terraces, mainly flats or bedsits, there was no way I could try 'em all. So all I could do was sit and hope . . .'

'What did you hope, Mr Stringer?' asked Dalziel gently. 'That you'd see Tony and persuade him to come home with you? Or that you'd warn him off forever?'

'I just wanted to talk,' said Stringer. 'I'm a reasonable man. I didn't blame him for going off looking for work. Better than sitting on your backside up here, drinking your dole like some I know.'

'You could have given him a job yourself, couldn't you?'

'Do you think I didn't offer?' exclaimed Stringer indignantly. 'He didn't want to work for me, told me flat. Said it were bad enough living with me. I said he could soon put that right if he had a mind to.'

'And he took off south. Right. So now you're sitting in Webster Street and suddenly you see your son-in-law walking along the pavement and he's with this lass . . .'

'This tart!' said Stringer fiercely. 'I know a whore when I see one.'

'That's a great talent,' said Dalziel admiringly. 'Saves you a lot of bother in a nunnery. So you follow them into this house and have a row . . .'

'I didn't want a row. I just wanted to know what the useless article were playing at.'

'So there wasn't a row?'

'It weren't all that quiet,' admitted Stringer. 'Upshot were that this tart started yelling she'd had enough, this were her pad, she were going out and when she came back she didn't want to find either of us here.'

'And after she'd gone, you got down to some really serious discussion?'

Stringer said grimly, 'I told him straight I didn't want him coming back up here and being around my lass and my grandson, not after he'd been rolling around with that slag and picking up everything she'd got!'

'Oh aye? And how did you make sure he got the message? Nut him and knee him, the old Liverpool reminder?'

'I never laid a hand on him,' said Stringer. 'Didn't need to. He were passing bricks just listening to me.'

'And you left him well persuaded he'd best not show up here again?'

'I reckon I did,' said Stringer.

'It'll mebbe come as a shock, Mr Stringer, but you were a lot less persuasive than you think,' said Dalziel. 'But mebbe you know that already.'

'What are you on about?'

'I mean your son-in-law, Tony Appleyard, did come back, Mr Stringer. Reappeared and vanished again, like a magician's mate.'

Stringer regarded him blankly.

He said, 'Come back, you say? He'd not come near me, would he? Not after what I'd said to him.'

'It wouldn't be you he wanted to see, would it?' said Dalziel.

He turned and looked up at the stair leading to the office. It was empty now. Wield had descended and was talking to Swain. But a shadowy figure could be seen behind the grimy window.

'And he didn't come near Shirley, if that's what you're thinking. What's all this about anyway?'

'I should've thought that were obvious. Lad goes missing, it's our job to find him.'

'Come off it! You showed no interest before. And you lot don't waste time chasing after folk unless you think you've got good reason.'

'We chase when we're asked sometimes, Mr Stringer.'

'Is that right? And who asked you?'

Dalziel shrugged massively. It was Stringer's turn to raise his eyes to the office window.

'Why's she so concerned about him?' he asked in genuine bewilderment. 'Useless idle lout that's brought her nowt but tribulation.'

'And a child,' said Dalziel. 'You'd not be without your grandson, would you? At least you owe him that.'

'I owe him nowt,' said Stringer fiercely. 'Nowt! Look, will you have to tell her that I saw him in London?'

'That would bother you?'

Stringer thought for a moment. He looked old and defeated. He said, 'No, you're right. Why should something like that . . . something so trivial . . . Do you believe in God, Mr Dalziel?'

'As a last resort,' said Dalziel.

'What? Oh aye. Well, I've believed in Him as a first and last and only resort. I've tried to run my life proper. I always reckoned if you did that, then nowt could happen that wasn't meant to happen. I don't mean it'd all be plain sailing, I'm not an idiot, but that it'd all have a meaning and God's will would show through everything!'

'And?'

'Well, that's all right till things start going to pieces, one thing after another, and all the time you're saying, Thy will, not mine, and sometimes you're excusing God, and sometimes you're excusing yourself . . . Do you understand what I mean? No! Why the hell should you?'

He looked at Dalziel with a terrible contempt but the fat man did not feel it was all directed at him, nor would he have much cared if it had been.

He said, 'Mebbe I understand how your lass feels playing second fiddle to a pile of red bricks. Excuse me.'

He walked away and ran lightly up the stairway to the office.

Shirley Appleyard said, 'What's up?'

'Nowt,' said Dalziel. 'We heard a rumour that your husband came back up here early in February. I were just asking your dad if he'd heard owt about it.'

'And what's he say?'

'That he hadn't. I don't suppose you knew owt about it either, else you'd have told me when you asked me to find him, wouldn't you?'

She didn't meet his gaze for a moment but when she did, hers was as unblinking as his.

'That's what they say about you,' she said. 'Doesn't matter what's in front of you, you'll keep walking straight forward till you tread on the truth, even if it means bringing it back broken.'

'So you did know he'd been back?'

'I heard a rumour, that was all. A lad said another lad said . . .'

'But you didn't make more inquiries?'

'I've got some pride,' she flashed. 'If he'd come back to see me, he knew where I was. I didn't want people to think I was crawling after him.'

'So you kept quiet till you saw the chance to get someone else doing the crawling for you?'

'No!' she said. 'You're not built for crawling, are you?'

It was, he decided, mainly a compliment.

'So shall I keep on looking?' he asked. Her answer wasn't going to influence him in the slightest, but he wanted to hear what it was.

'Please yourself,' she said.

'What's up, lass? Lost interest? Or hope?'

'What's it matter? In the long run, what's any of it matter?'

'The truth matters,' he said. 'Tread on it hard as you like, you'll not break it. It's only lies that crack easily.'

He trotted down the stairs thinking that Pascoe would

have been proud to hear him coming over so philosophical.

Stringer was in the pick-up, Swain in the JCB. Both had their engines running.

'All done, Superintendent?' Swain shouted above the noise.

'Just about,' bellowed Dalziel. 'Your brother shot himself in there, didn't he?'

He pointed into the barn. The pride of the Diplomatic Corps, thought Wield.

'That's right.'

'Must have asked yourself a thousand times why he did it?'

Only Dalziel could contrive to have an intimate tête-à-tête fortissimo.

'No. Only once,' shouted Swain, clearly determined not to back away.

'You mean you got the right answer straight off?'

'I mean he obviously shot himself because there was no way he could see to save the farm.'

'At the inquest you said no *other* way.'

'Did I? I may have done. Makes no difference, does it?'

'Didn't he try to borrow money from you to pay off his debts?'

'Naturally. But I didn't have enough to lend.'

'What about your wife? Didn't he ask her?'

'Possibly. But she would not have been inclined to put money into a bankrupt farm. Nor am I inclined to listen to your offensive questions any more, Dalziel. I thought you'd been officially warned about harassing me over Gail's death.'

'It's not your wife's death I'm talking about, sir, it's your brother's,' yelled Dalziel. 'But I gather Mrs Swain coughed up quick enough once you'd inherited Moscow?'

'It was our home then. A good investment.'

'So if you did say no *other* way, you'd have been right? I mean, your brother must have known that once you inherited, there'd be a much better chance of Mrs Swain sorting things out?'

'I doubt if Tom was in the right state of mind for such abstruse calculations, Superintendent,' said Swain, his effort at control now clearly visible along the jaw line.

'But it was a pretty clear message he left,' objected Dalziel.

'He left no message, as you well know!' snarled Swain.

'Using your wife's Python to blow his head off sounds to me like he was trying to say something,' said Dalziel genially. 'But I mustn't keep you back. You're rehearsing this afternoon, aren't you? She's got me at it later this morning. Real slave-driver, that Chung, isn't she?'

'I begin to feel she has committed a monstrous blasphemy in casting something as gross as you to play the Godhead, Dalziel!' shouted Swain, pale-faced. His hands worked at the gear levers, Dalziel stepped smartly aside and the huge machine roared out of the yard narrowly missing the policeman's car.

'What's up with him, do you think?' wondered Dalziel.

'I suppose having to shout like the town crier about your dead brother and your dead wife might upset some folk, sir,' suggested Wield.

'Mebbe so,' said Dalziel. 'But it were interesting how long it took to get him upset. Christ, look at the time. Nowt done, half the morning gone, and that Chung gets right nasty if you're late for rehearsals. You'd think she'd have more respect for Superior Beings, but not her. Comes of mixing the blood, I reckon. Like chemicals. You've got to be careful or you end up with a hell of a bang.' Then, smacking his lips grossly, he added, 'And that's what she'd be, I dare say. A hell of a bang!'

Was it all in the mind or did he really have immoral longings in him? wondered an intrigued Wield.

'Fancy your chances there, do you, sir?' he prodded.

'Go and wash your mind out, Sergeant,' ordered Dalziel sternly. 'Professional and platonic, that's me and Chung. Never forget, a virtuous woman's price is far above rubies.'

Then, pushing a near fatal finger into Wield's ribs, he added, 'And I'm not sure these days if I could even afford Ruby!'

And shaking with mirth at his own high wit, he headed for the car.

Chapter 5

Crimper's Knoll was a pleasant place to be on a fine summer morning. It was a pleasure Philip Swain planned to share with perhaps half a dozen householders at about two hundred thousand pounds apiece. But there was more than money involved here. This would be his showcase. After this people would start thinking of Swain and Stringer as creators as well as constructors. Such was his excitement at the project that though detailed plans were still to be drawn up and he had not yet obtained even outline planning permission, he couldn't wait to set his mark on the ground. 'We'll need an access road,' he told his partner. 'A man doesn't need planning permission to give himself access to his own land. I've got all my life to shape my behind to an office chair. This is one job I'm going to start myself!'

But the JCB had rested like a sleeping mastodon in the lee of the Knoll ever since its arrival more than an hour earlier, and the two men sat almost as still on a grey rock, looking westward over the sun-flooded central Yorkshire plain.

Stringer broke the long silence.

'You've been a good mate to me, Phil,' he said. 'And I'll not say owt to harm you, rest assured.'

'You'll lie, you mean?' said Swain. 'I thought the whole point was to stop lying.'

'Another little 'un in a good cause won't harm me. But the big one . . .'

'That was in a good cause too. A better cause,' insisted Swain. 'For your own daughter, your grandson . . .'

'Mebbe it were for them, part of it. But mostly it were for me. I see that now.'

'And what's opened your eyes? That fat policeman? A strange instrument of virtue if ever I saw one!'

'Aye, he's a mad bad bugger, right enough,' agreed Stringer. 'But God's not choosy. It's the Devil who sends his agents in fancy wrapping. And no matter who sent him, one thing's certain, he'll get there in the end. So I'm not being brave or virtuous. I just want to be the one who tells our Shirley.'

'Arnie, you're wrong,' insisted Swain. 'Sit it out. Keep quiet and there's no way Dalziel can . . .'

'Nay, my mind's made up,' said Stringer, rising. 'I know you're only thinking of me, but believe me, Phil, this will be the best for me too. I'll mebbe be able to sleep quiet in my bed again.'

Swain rose too.

'If that's the way you want it, Arnie,' he said.

'It is.'

'Then I'll see you get the best help money can buy. Meanwhile you're still a partner in this business, so let's get some work done, shall we?'

* * *

It was getting on for noon and in the less than pastoral surroundings of the police canteen before Wield caught up with Pascoe.

'It's been hell,' said Pascoe. 'We were just going to ship them off to Leeds when Medwin's doting parents turned up with a very nasty solicitor. Seems young Jason didn't turn eighteen till March the twentieth, and the brief got very stroppy about his rights as a minor if he was questioned about offences committed before that date. He had a point.'

'Shit,' said Wield, angry with himself. 'I should have spotted that. It was recognizing him that threw me.'

'Not to worry. I got it sorted,' said Pascoe.

'Thanks. And did you have time to . . .?'

'Ask your supplementary? What else are chief inspectors for but to clean up after sergeants? Now let me see.' He produced a notebook and thumbed through it. 'You wanted to know if he noticed a vehicle slowing down as he was enjoying himself beating you up. Yes, he did. And it might have been a car or it could have been a van or maybe even a pick-up. And it might have been black or blue or brown or burgundy, and it may have stopped and someone could have got into it, but by this time he was being so cooperative, I reckon he'd have said it was a snow-white stretch limo with Father Christmas in the back if I'd pressed him. Odd. I'd not have put him down as the cooperative type.'

'Mr Dalziel had a heart to heart with him,' said Wield.

Pascoe grimaced understandingly, and grimaced again as he sipped his coffee which occupied the grey area between emetic and enuretic.

'So what you're positing,' he said, 'is maybe someone else was following Waterson too? And you fancy Swain. Any reason other than the fact that the Super would like to fit him up for everything since the Princes in the Tower?'

'Not really. But he did know the meeting was arranged. Mrs Waterson told him.'

'But not where.'

'He could have followed her to start with.'

'Why not just go into the Sally then and speak to Waterson?'

'Because he wanted somewhere more private. Or perhaps he wanted to find out where Waterson was hiding out. Or it could even be he spotted me tailing Waterson and held back. Then when I got attacked, he saw his chance to get to him before I did, drove up and told him to hop in if he didn't want to have his collar felt.'

'And then?'

'Paid him off mebbe. Gave him enough for him and the girl to make themselves scarce.'

'Must've been a hell of a pay-off for them to afford to vanish so completely,' said Pascoe. 'And a pay-off for what? And if Swain owed him money, why not approach him direct to get paid instead of hiding out till he's so broke he's got to touch his wife for a few bob? And why . . .'

Wield was saved from further catechismal punishment by the intervention of Sergeant Broomfield.

'Thought I'd find CID busy down here,' he said. 'Look, I just got this report of an accident. Normally I'd send one of my lads to sort out details but when I saw it was on Philip Swain's land . . .'

Pascoe took the sheet of paper.

'Good God,' he said. 'This sounds nasty.'

'They say it's critical,' said Broomfield grimly.

'What's up? Has Swain been hurt?' asked Wield.

'Not Swain. Arnie Stringer. The JCB went over on him. Thanks, I'll take care of this.'

311

He passed the paper to Wield.

'Not very lucky, the Swains, are they?' said the sergeant.

'Luckier than the Stringers by all accounts,' said Pascoe. 'Mr Dalziel needs to be told. He's rehearsing, you say?'

'That's right.'

A slow smile split Pascoe's face.

'Tell you what, Wieldy. You get yourself down to the Infirmary and see what's going off there. While I personally will assault the battlements of heaven!'

The cathedral precincts were thronged with small groups of people whom Pascoe at first took for sightseers on a guided tour. But soon he realized that the focal figure in each group was not a travel courier but one of Chung's company busily rehearsing a section of a crowd. He recalled Chung saying, 'You've no idea how much work it takes to get people to look and act like themselves!'

He also spotted Canon Horncastle standing in the dark shadow cast by the Great Tower, his black cloth blending in so closely with the shade that his thin white face looked like some marble gargoyle peering out with malicious disapproval at the activity around. Pascoe waved, but the Canon either did not see or did not care to acknowledge him, and he pressed on to the ruins of the abbey.

Here he found the Greatest Story Ever Told had stopped for a tea-break. Dorothy Horncastle was dispensing mugs of the stuff from a large copper urn, and close by in the midst of a crowd of acolytes stood Chung. She was talking with her usual total animation but when she saw Pascoe approaching, she fell silent and watched him as if he were the person in the world she most wanted to see, making everyone else watch him too.

'I feel like I should be carrying a message from Marathon,' he said, rather embarrassed as she drew him aside.

'And you're not?'

'Not for you,' he grinned, his embarrassment ebbing as he began to glow in the focal heat of her complete attention. 'And I'm not sure if we've won or lost.'

'Either way it's always good to see you, Pete. Was it Ellie you wanted? She was here, sticking her little mike in my face. I thought it was only a little background piece the *Post* wanted but she's going at it like it's the full biography! I hate to think what shock-horror revelations she's going to make. Maybe I should appoint you as my editorial representative in the Pascoe household?'

'No, thanks. I'd rather run a marathon. Is my other boss around?'

'What? Oh, Andy. Yeah. Behold.'

She pointed. It was such a gracefully sensuous gesture that Pascoe had to force his attention from its execution to its direction.

There sitting on a broken pillar a little removed from all the activity was Dalziel. He had his spectacles on and he was busy conning his part, his heavy lips moving as he read the lines.

'I didn't know God was short-sighted,' said Pascoe.

'Shit, I thought everybody knew *that*!' said Chung. 'Watch how you go with him. His mind's not on the job this morning and I've had to give him a kick or two. He's about ready to start chucking thunderbolts.'

The picture of Chung kicking Dalziel was so delightful that Pascoe laughed as he reluctantly moved away. Meeting Chung always made him feel good.

Meeting Dalziel on the other hand wasn't so invariably pleasant.

'I'm sorry to interrupt,' he said.

'I doubt it,' snarled Dalziel, not looking up. 'But it can likely be arranged. What do you want? Forgotten how to wipe your nose?'

If not a thunderbolt, it was certainly a very torrid blast.

'Things going well, I hope, sir?' said Pascoe with unctuous solicitude.

Now Dalziel looked up.

'No,' he said. 'They're not, as mebbe yon Chung's told you already. You two look very matey. I hope you're behaving yourself, lad. Man with a wife and kiddie should look for his naughties with a discreet widow in another town.'

The old sod's jealous, thought Pascoe with a shame-making pang of triumphal delight.

'I'm sorry you're having trouble,' he said. 'Is it the lines?'

'No, it's not just the lines. I can make up the lines. It's the whole bloody daft business! How the hell I got myself into it in the first place I'll never know.'

Pascoe made his face a blank and said, 'It'll be all right on the night, I'm sure. But there was something I thought you would like to know about Swain . . .'

'Swain! That bugger. It's him that's been on my mind all morning. Here's me playing God and I can't even nail one miserable bloody sinner. What's he done now?'

'Nothing that I know of, but there has been an accident.'

He gave what details he could. Dalziel rose, stuffing his script into his pocket.

'There's altogether too many accidents happen around that sod,' he said, his eyes gleaming. 'It's time I arranged a few of my own.'

'I know you want to keep him in the frame for his wife's death . . .'

'The frame I want to keep him in's got bars on it and a sign on the door saying "not wanted on voyage".'

'Andy, where are you going? We're ready to start again.'

It was Chung blocking their path. Now this is true elemental drama, thought Pascoe. The irresistible force and the immovable object.

'Sorry, luv. This is urgent. Deathbed deposition, likely. And as it's not Lazarus, I'd best get a move on.'

'For Christ sake, Andy! Can't Pete here handle it? You've got any number of highly qualified staff but I've got only one God!'

She was gorgeously angry, and using a joke to keep it under control.

'Some things are too important to be left to the help,' said Dalziel portentously. 'Anyroad, God is everywhere, isn't that what the Bible says? So really I'm not going at all, am I?'

It was all rather disappointing. Suddenly the immovable object stepped aside and the irresistible force swept on.

'Sorry,' said Pascoe with a ruefully apologetic smile.

'For what? He was no use to us today anyway. Perhaps I should have gone for you after all, Pete,' said Chung.

It was, he hoped, another controlling joke, but he didn't stay to find out.

Wield was waiting for them at the main entrance to the Infirmary.

'They're still working on him,' he said. 'I've spoken to Swain. He's so cut up it's hard to make sense of him, but what seems to have happened is, he was working the JCB on the steepest bit of Crimper's Knoll when it began to slide. Stringer was down the slope a ways. When he realized what was happening he tried to get out of the way but the ground was still slippery from the overnight rain, and he lost his footing and the JCB went over him. Mrs Stringer and the daughter are up in the waiting-room on the surgery ward.'

'How're they?' asked Pascoe.

'Holding on,' said Wield. 'It's Swain who looks like he's falling apart.'

315

'That's how I like 'em,' said Dalziel, rubbing his hands. 'Wieldy, you've got somewhere I can talk to him?'

'Sister lent me an office. He's still in there.'

'Right. Show me. Peter, you've got a nice sympathetic smile. You go and keep the Stringers company.'

'I doubt if sympathetic smiles are what they want right now,' said Pascoe.

'Jesus,' said Dalziel. 'I'm not asking you to pay a social call. Go and talk to them and see if they know anything!'

'What about?'

'If I knew that, I wouldn't have to go down on my hands and knees to get you to find out, would I?'

Both men looked at Wield. Both shook their heads sadly inviting support. Wield arranged the Alpine rugosities of his face into what he hoped was a Swiss neutrality and quickly turned away.

Swain did indeed look to be deeply distressed. Dalziel, who considered he had a fair nose for bullshit, was surprised to detect the scent of genuine emotion, but he comforted himself with the thought that even a cold cunt like Swain might be expected to be temporarily taken aback after running a JCB over his mate.

'Any news?' demanded Swain as the Superintendent entered the office.

'About what?' asked Dalziel. 'Oh, you mean about Stringer. No, I think they're still trying to reassemble the pieces. You brought everything back, did you? Marvellous what they can stitch back on if they get it while it's still hot.'

The builder's emotional turmoil coalesced for a moment into a glance of pure hatred as he demanded, 'What the hell do you want here, Dalziel?'

'Accident. Culpable negligence maybe. That's police business, wouldn't you say? But we know that's not the whole of it, or even the half, don't we, Mr Swain? We both know what I'm really after is nailing you for topping your missus. Nay, lad. You sit still. No need to get excited. This is just a friendly chat between chums. Yes, we are chums in a way. It's shared intimacies that bind friendships, and there's nowt much more intimate than watching a man blow his wife's head off, is there? All right, screwing her, maybe, but I've never been keen on watching that sort of thing. It either turns you on or it turns you off, and either way's not much help to a busy milkman. So come on, Phil! Between mates, why'd you run your digger over poor old Arnie? I mean, it couldn't be to save Moscow Farm again! You'll have paid off Muncaster Securities by now, I expect. And anyroad, poor old Arnie won't be leaving you a wagonload of dollars, will he? Or had you been forging his signature too perhaps? But what to, for God's sake? By the look of him, if you stuffed every penny he'd got into the poor box, it'd still rattle. Nay, this is all too deep for me. This'll take some plumbing and you know what it's like getting a plumber these days. So I'll need your help, Phil. Tell you what. Why don't we sneak off somewhere and have a pint and you can get it all off your chest, then I'll put you down and you can rest peaceful in your bed till slopping-out time? What do you say?'

It was an avalanche of a speech, meant to sweep Swain off his feet while he was still emotionally off balance. But Eden Thackeray had been right about Swain's temperament. However flawed his long-term judgements, when it came to here and now, he was a downhill racer.

Shaking his head in disbelief, he said, 'You really are mad, Dalziel, it's not just an act. You're right off your trolley.'

'No need to talk like that, lad,' said Dalziel. 'What's up? Can't you take a joke? Is this all the thanks I get for trying to cheer you up while you wait to see if you've killed your mate or not?'

At last he got through, for suddenly Swain was on his feet. But whether his rage had impetus enough to carry through a physical attack was not to be proved for at the moment of truth the door opened and Wield appeared.

He looked at the scene disinterestedly and said, 'Sorry to butt in, sir, but they've brought Mr Stringer back from the theatre.'

'Let's hope he enjoyed the show. How is he?'

'They wrap it up, sir, but as far as I can make out, it's touch and go whether he wakes up before he snuffs it.'

'Bad as that? Hardly seems worth the bother. On the other hand, a man's last words should always be listened to with respect, wouldn't you agree, Mr Swain?'

Swain did not reply but pushed past the two policemen and disappeared down the corridor.

'Any luck there, sir?'

'Hard to say. No visible damage but if you keep pounding away at the ribs, you're bound to sap a bit of their strength. Couple of hours somewhere with no windows and a thick wall and I reckon he'd cave in. But I dare say Mr Pascoe's missus would be sticking Amnesiacs International on to us before I could get a result. Peter, what the hell are you doing here?'

'Didn't Wieldy tell you?' said Pascoe, who was standing peering out of a window into the green and pleasant Infirmary gardens. 'Stringer's in the recovery room and they've let his wife and daughter sit by his bed.'

'And that's where you should be too, lad. Front row stalls! I bet Swain's trying to book his ticket.'

'I saw him a moment ago. He looks terrible, really upset.'

'Aye. I believe he really is,' said Dalziel. 'Wouldn't you be?'

'If I thought I'd killed a friend? Yes, of course I would.'

'Oh aye? Well, that's one way of looking at it.'

'I can't think of any other,' said Pascoe.

'You can't?' said Dalziel. 'How about if you thought you'd killed an enemy and found out maybe you'd done a botched job? How would you feel then, Detective Chief Inspector?'

Chapter 6

Arnie Stringer opened his eyes for the last time at three o'clock in the afternoon. Though he lay in a sunlit room, for a few moments everything seemed grey and fuzzy. Then like a holiday slide coming into focus, he saw things sharp and clear, his wife and his daughter, dark-eyed and pale; his friend and partner, dry-lipped with worry; and a half-familiar youngish man, his eyes screwed up in mute apology.

It occurred to Stringer that if this were a holiday slide it had been a lousy holiday. His jokes were rare enough for him to want to share this one, but he was aware that he had life-force enough left for only a very few words. His mind seemed to be compensating for his bodily weakness by working at the speed of light and he had already rehearsed a dozen sage and serious family valedictions when it came to him who the stranger was.

Staring straight at Pascoe, he said slowly and distinctly, 'Phil not to blame. God's will. Only helping a friend. Good friend to me.'

And that was it. Time for one last look of . . . affection? exhortation? regret? . . . at his wife and daughter, then he let himself slip to his reward, the exact nature of which had always been something of a puzzle to him. He did not doubt it would contain an opportunity for chapel folk to say a big I-told-you-so to the church folk across the way, but the rest was . . . the rest was . . . mystery . . .

A nurse, needing to confirm what needed no confirmation, summoned a doctor. It was Marwood. He made to draw the sheet over the dead man's face but Mrs Stringer said, 'No, he couldn't thole being covered up.'

Marwood nodded and moved away. Pascoe said, 'Mrs Stringer, Shirley, I'm sorry. He was a good man.' Mrs Stringer said tearfully, 'Thank you, he were,' but Shirley only returned his gaze blankly. He went after Marwood and found him outside the door.

'All roads lead you lot to the Infirmary, it seems,' said the doctor.

'Too many of them,' said Pascoe. 'How's Mrs Waterson by the way?'

'Looking like she ought to be one of her own patients,' said Marwood. 'You making any progress, or is that too much to ask?'

'No.'

'No, it's not? Or no progress?'

'Both, I fear,' said Pascoe.

'At least you're honest.'

'A good quality in a policeman and in a doctor too, wouldn't you say?'

'Depends on the patient. And on the suspect, I'd guess. Be healthy.'

Pascoe watched him walk away. He had sensed an ambiguity in the man's inquiry into progress in the hunt for Waterson. It figured that a man in love with a woman whose husband was missing might have mixed feelings about his reappearance. Yet earlier Marwood had been keen to the point of snouting to see the police get their hands on Waterson.

Suddenly Pascoe thought of Wield and the car which

had slowed down as he was being beaten up by Jason Medwin. He had been very sceptical of the sergeant's attempts to implicate Swain, but now it occurred to him that there had been someone else who knew of the Sally rendezvous that evening.

Marwood.

He had rung Wield with the tip-off. What if then he had gone along himself to see the fun? And instead of the expected arrest, he had seen Wield diverted and Waterson on the point of getting away, so he had acted himself and offered Waterson a lift and . . .

And what? Here the hypothesis petered out. Marwood had come on duty by the time Wield got taken to the Infirmary, so that left very little time for . . . anything.

But how much time did it take for . . . anything? Especially for a doctor?

And here was a classic explanation of that ambiguity he had sensed.

A man, a woman, and a body. Only if the body is found will the woman feel free to give herself to the man. But if the body is found and something in the manner of death points at the man, then he loses both the woman and his liberty.

'Mr Pascoe!'

It was Swain, obviously addressing him for the second or third time.

'I'm sorry. I was miles away.'

'So I gathered. I would like some information. What is the procedure for laying a complaint against a member of the police force?'

Pascoe was jerked back to full alertness. Swain, he observed, seemed to have made a rapid recovery from the trauma of Stringer's death and looked quite his old self again.

'Depends what you have in mind, sir,' said Pascoe.

321

'What I have in mind is to do whatever is necessary to prevent that creature Dalziel from harassing and maligning me.'

'I'm sure the Superintendent has no intention of causing you offence,' lied Pascoe. 'I know he can be a little heavy-handed at times. It's really just a matter of style . . .'

'Telling me I murdered my wife and deliberately turned the JCB over on Stringer, that's style? You heard what Arnie said? I hope you made a note of it. It was an accident, a tragic accident. But what's the use of talking to you? Another five stone and fifteen years and you'll just be the same as Dalziel. I'll leave it to my lawyer. Once he gets to work, you won't be able to close ranks tight enough to hide that fat bastard!'

He turned and strode away. For the first time Pascoe noticed that Shirley Appleyard had come out into the corridor and was standing a few feet away.

'Is it right what he said, that Mr Dalziel reckons he might have deliberately killed Dad?' she said.

'I don't honestly think so,' said Pascoe. 'Mr Dalziel sometimes likes to stir things up, that's all. Besides, what your father said at the end seems to make it clear it was an accident.'

'I suppose so. Pity he couldn't have managed a few words for his family, though,' she said with a surface irony that didn't altogether conceal real pain.

'How's your mother?' asked Pascoe.

'She wants to sit there a bit longer. But I've got to shoot off now and see to my boy. A neighbour's looking after him. At least I'll see a bit more of him now.'

'Why? I mean, your job . . .'

'I'll not stay. I only took it in the first place 'cos Dad fixed it up and I couldn't bear for him to go on about me being a layabout like he did when Tony told him to stuff his job. But I've never liked Mr Swain much, and anyroad with Dad gone and all that money in the bank, he's going to be wanting something a bit more cut-glass than me answering the phone, isn't he?'

'I don't know,' said Pascoe. 'Only a fool bothers with cut-glass when he's got immortal diamond.'

It was a line which could have sounded emptily corny, but the grave pleasure with which Shirley Appleyard accepted it made the risk worthwhile.

'Thanks,' she said. 'I'll mebbe see you.'

He watched her walking away. Life had tested her hard during her nineteen brief years. He hoped it wasn't a test to destruction.

'Make a complaint?' said Dalziel. 'But why'd he ask *you*?'

'Because I was there, I suppose,' said Pascoe.

'He knows you're on my team and he knows the first thing you're going to do is warn me,' said Dalziel reflectively. 'And he could have said all that to my face, couldn't he, and achieved the same effect? So it must have been you in particular he wanted to talk to. But why?'

'I think you're reading too much into it, sir. He was just very angry. Incidentally, was what he said true? *Did* you accuse him of those things?'

'In a manner of speaking,' said Dalziel with the long-suffering expression of one used to misinterpretation.

'In what manner of speaking do you tell a man he's murdered not only his wife but his business partner?' wondered Pascoe.

'In a bloody uncompromising manner,' growled Dalziel.

'But how can you be so sure, sir?' demanded Pascoe. 'Until we can talk to Waterson and Beverley King, we're stuck with Waterson's statement, and as for Stringer, there's no motive or evidence to suggest anything but an accident, and Stringer's last words confirm this.'

323

'Mebbe. Bit odd he felt he had to confirm it. Wouldn't you say?'

'He opened his eyes, saw me and Swain side by side, put two and two together and wanted to get things straight. Human nature, when you're dying.'

'You reckon?' said Dalziel, shaking his head. 'Funny view of human nature they sold you at that college, Peter. If I were you, I'd write and ask for a refund. What was it he said again?'

'He said it wasn't Swain's fault, how many times do I have to tell you,' said Pascoe, driven to petulance.

'No, the exact words. First rule of detective work, lad. Always be precise.'

Pascoe took a deep breath, closed his eyes and recited, 'Phil not to blame. God's will. Only helping a friend. Good friend to me.'

'That's it? You're sure?'

'Yes, I'm sure.'

'Then why did you say all he said was that it wasn't Swain's fault?'

'Because that's what he did say!' exclaimed Pascoe indignantly. 'That was the gist.'

'The gist.' Dalziel chewed on the word. 'Aye, the gist. Mebbe that's what Swain wanted you to remember, just the gist! Mebbe that's why he grabbed you and made all that commotion about getting my wrist slapped so you'd come back here full of his pathetic threats and with no better bloody recollection of what Stringer actually said than the sodding bloody gist!'

Dalziel struck his desktop so hard that his telephone jumped inches in the air with a little squeak of alarm and a pile of papers fluttered out of his in-tray on to Pascoe's lap.

'But what else did he say besides it wasn't Swain's fault?' asked Pascoe, clutching the errant mail. A familiar typeface caught his eye and he tried to shuffle it to the top.

'He said, helping a friend, right? How was running a JCB over Stringer helping a friend?'

'He was referring to the job . . .'

'They were business partners! If Marks went out with Spencer to stock shelves, you'd not call that helping a friend, would you?'

'Probably not,' said Pascoe. 'Sir, have you looked at your mail yet?'

'No! When have I had time to look at mail, doing every other bugger's job?' said Dalziel irritably. 'Like yours. You're supposed to be the clever sod with words, aren't you? Well, you've not been so clever here, lad. *Helping a friend* . . . I'll tell you what it means to me, shall I? I think it means there was something Swain did to help Stringer out, and it was a bit dodgy, and when Arnie realized he were popping his clogs, he wanted to be sure his mate didn't get lumbered . . . Are you listening to me, Chief Inspector?'

'Yes, sir. Sorry. It's just that there's a letter here from the Dark Lady.'

'Not another! It's barely a week since the last. I wish she'd put up or shut up!'

'She was helpful last time, sir,' reminded Pascoe.

'I'd have heard about Thackeray soon enough,' said Dalziel ungraciously. 'What's she say this time? Knows who Jack the Ripper was, does she?'

'Nothing so dramatic,' said Pascoe, troubled. 'But you said Tony Appleyard came back up here in February, and you were wondering how it might be that Swain helped a friend . . .'

He held out the letter. Impatiently Dalziel snatched it, scanned it quickly then read it again more slowly.

'Christ, it's a bit cryptic, isn't it?'

'Yes. Rings a bell though . . . *beneath these pavements* . . .'

'I don't mean the fancy bloody words! I mean, which bloody pavements?'

Pascoe rose and went to the window and looked down. He heard himself saying, 'If Marks went out with Spencer to plant potatoes, he might call *that* helping a friend.'

Instantly he regretted what might later be classified as persuasion, but to his relief, Dalziel was still shaking his head.

'No! I'd need to be dafter than that mad lass of thine! I'd need a lot more to persuade me, let alone Dan Trimble . . .'

The telephone rang. He picked it up and grunted, 'Yes?' and listened.

Putting his hand over the mouthpiece, he said to Pascoe, 'It's George Broomfield. He says Swain's just turned up. Wants to see Trimble but he's out feeding his face at one of them civic lunches that don't finish till tea-time. Swain doesn't seem bothered, though. Says he'll wait.'

'Come to complain?' speculated Pascoe.

'Or to check up,' said Dalziel. With sudden decision he spoke into the phone. 'George, where is he? Right, I want you to do something for me. Ring the Council Works Department and ask if we can borrow a couple of pneumatic drills straightaway. And George, use the phone on the desk and speak up loud and clear like it's a bad line. That's the idea.'

He replaced the receiver.

'What . . .?' began Pascoe but Dalziel laid his forefinger to his lips.

'Silent prayer,' he said. 'Mebbe God'll send us a sign.'

He folded his arms on the bow-front of his belly.

A minute passed. The phone rang again.

'Yes,' rapped Dalziel.

A slow smile oozed over his lips as he listened, then he said, 'Of course. It's open house up here. Fetch him right up.'

He relapsed once more into a Buddha-like repose.

Two minutes passed. There was a tap at the door.

'Come in,' he said gently.

The door was opened by Sergeant Broomfield who said, 'Mr Swain to see you, sir.'

He stood aside and Swain stepped in. He was elegantly dressed in grey slacks and a royal blue blazer, but his hair was ruffled and his face was pale.

'Superintendent. Mr Pascoe,' he said.

'Mr Swain,' said Dalziel genially. 'Didn't expect to see you again so soon. What can we do for you?'

Swain took another step forward, waited till Broomfield had pulled the door shut behind him, then said in a voice almost too low to be heard, 'I couldn't keep away. I've come here to confess.'

Part Seven

ANGEL: Ilka creature, both old and young;
Believe I bid you that you rise;
Body and soul with you ye bring,
And come before the high justice.
For I am sent from heaven king
To call you to this great assize.

The York Cycle: 'The Last Judgment'

Dear Mr Dalziel,

It's St Brendan's day. Funny that Ireland which produces so much of the mindless violence which has helped me to despair also produced so many saints. The Navigator they call him, because he travelled around so much. Thinking of him reminded me of another watery story I once read, about a poet, Shelley I think, who went out in a rowing-boat with a friend and her young children. Suddenly his eyes lit up and he said, 'Now let us together solve the great mystery!' Seeing that he was very close to tipping the boat over, the poor terrified woman managed to say sharply, 'No, thank you, not now. I should like my dinner first and so should the children.' And Shelley rowed them back to the shore instead.

Me, I've run out of smart answers, and when there's nothing left inside to cope with the greater nothingness outside, I reckon that's the time to start rocking the boat!

I don't know if what I told you last time was any use. Probably not. It would have been nice to help you solve your little mystery before I solved my Great One. But I don't suppose it matters much to you. Win some, lose some, there's always another one round the corner. Anyway, here's a farewell thought so obvious, you've probably got it painted on your office wall. If I was looking for someone with no talent for hiding, and he couldn't be found in the places he was likely to hide, I'd start looking in the places he was likely to have been hidden. In times of stress we all turn to what we know. A sailor would turn to the sea, a farmer to the earth; and a builder . . . well, we're only lightly covered in buttoned cloth and beneath these pavements are shells, bones and silence.

Good luck with your searching. And you're right not to waste time on me. I'm not hidden, only lost.

Chapter 1

They took Philip Swain down to the car park. He led the way into the very first garage to have its foundations dug early in February. Here in one corner he drew an oblong on the concrete floor with a piece of chalk.

'You're very precise,' said Pascoe.

'It's not something a man's likely to forget,' said Swain.

As they came out of the garage a council truck pulled into the car park.

'The drills,' said Dalziel with satisfaction. 'They've been quick for a change. Let's get them to work.'

'Sir, mightn't it be best to wait for Mr Trimble?' suggested Pascoe, back in his role of moderating influence.

'What for?' demanded Dalziel, whose euphoria when Swain first appeared had been replaced by a kind of irritated watchfulness as the nature of the man's 'confession' became clear. 'Wieldy's a tidy sort of fellow. He'll keep the mess down, won't you, lad? Come on, sir. Let's get back inside and put a bit of fat on this tale of thine.'

By the time they reached the interview room, they could hear the drills at work.

'Now, sir, in your own time,' said Dalziel. 'You've been cautioned, remember, and Constable Seymour here will be taking notes. So go ahead.'

'I want to start by apologizing,' said Swain quietly. 'I know I've acted very stupidly. All I can say in my defence is I did it for my friend, but even then I wouldn't have become involved if I'd thought that a serious crime had been committed. Arnie told me it was an accident, and he was a man I trusted beyond reserve.'

'The facts, sir,' urged Dalziel.

'Of course. Arnie came to me that Saturday night or early Sunday morning. It was the first weekend in February, I can't recall the exact date. I've never seen a man so distressed. What had happened was he'd heard a noise outside his cottage and went down to find his son-in-law trying to force a window. Obviously he wanted to get in and make contact with Shirley without disturbing her parents. Arnie said he was in a disgusting condition, stinking of drink and vomit. Not only that, he looked so wasted and unwell that Arnie feared it was more than just drink. I'm afraid that Arnie's attitude to things like AIDS was rather fundamentalist. He regarded it as a judgment of God and he did not doubt his son-in-law deserved to be heavily judged.'

'To the point of death, you mean?' said Dalziel.

'If God willed. But not at Arnie's hand, you must believe that. Appleyard took off when he saw Arnie. He made for the farm and Arnie caught up with him by the old barn. He pushed him inside and told him to get away from Yorkshire and never show his face here again. And when he thought he'd made his point, he turned away to go back to the cottage. Now I'm not saying he wouldn't have given the lad a good shaking while this was going on, but nothing more. Only, when he turned away, the boy who must have been almost demented flung himself on Arnie and tried to strangle him from behind. Arnie staggered round trying to shake him off, and finally he got rid of him by throwing him over his head. Unfortunately the boy fell on to an old spike harrow that had been lying around with a lot of other junk for years. One of the spikes went clean through his throat, and when Arnie dragged him clear he was dead. I'm sure a post-mortem will confirm all this.'

'It would have confirmed it then,' grunted Dalziel. 'Why'd he not call the police, this pillar of the chapel? Why didn't you call the police for that matter?'

'It wasn't that he didn't recognize his duty, it was just that he couldn't face the thought of what Shirley would think and say.'

'And you?'

'He was my partner and my friend. I believed him absolutely when he said it was an accident. So when he suggested hiding the body, I went along with it.'

'He suggested hiding the body here?'

'No,' admitted Swain. 'He wanted to dig a hole in one of my fields and bury it. I told him that was stupid. It was almost certain to be found. We'd just started work on your garages and even though it went against his grain, I'd persuaded Arnie to work Sundays to catch the mild weather. It'd just be the two of us, we couldn't afford to be paying our labourers overtime, so it was an ideal opportunity for hiding the body. And that's what we did. Next day we excavated the foundations a couple of feet deeper in that corner than we needed. Then Arnie kept watch while I got the body out of the pick-up and covered it with concrete.'

'You did the dirty work, then?' said Pascoe.

'Arnie couldn't face it,' said Swain. 'You cannot begin to believe the turmoil the poor chap was in. As time went by, it got a little better because I persuaded him that if God really disapproved of what he'd done, then He'd find a way of bringing it out. I did what I could to help by having the old barn cleared out, but there was nothing I could do about the most poignant reminders – Shirley and his little grandson.'

'But he still kept quiet,' said Dalziel. 'Waiting for God to do his confessing for him, was that it?'

'Indeed. And odd though it may seem, I think he'd begun to regard you as the Almighty's instrument, Superintendent. When you spoke to him this morning about the boy coming back here, he was really shaken up. I think he came close to making a clean breast of it.'

'And how would you have felt about that, Mr Swain?'

'Like I said just now, glad that it was out. I've had troubles of my own. Now I seem to be getting them behind me and it will be grand to clear the decks absolutely. But I'd give anything for it not to have happened like this. The memory of the digger sliding towards poor Arnie will never leave me. The only thing that eases the burden slightly is something I couldn't say before. In those last few moments I could see his face, and I'm not certain how much of an effort he was really making to get out of the way.'

He said this with the utmost seriousness. How else, indeed, would he say it? But Pascoe waited for the incredulous guffaw from Dalziel. Instead the fat man murmured softly, 'Well, well, another suicide, eh?'

'Not conscious, of course,' said Swain. 'That would have been impossible for a man of Arnie's beliefs. But a slackening of the will to live. That's what a secret like this can do to a man, Superintendent. That's why I decided I owed it to myself as well as Arnie's memory to bring this whole business out into the open.'

At some point after his arrival the initiative seemed to have been firmly claimed by Swain. And at some point while he had been talking the drills had stopped.

The door opened and Wield looked in.

'Sir,' he said, 'I think we're there.'

Dalziel said, 'Constable Seymour here will start knocking your statement into shape, sir. Excuse me.'

On the way downstairs he said fiercely, 'For fuck's sake, Peter, give me a hand in there! We're losing the slippery sod and you just sit there smiling like a curate at a christening.'

In the garage he stooped over the hole. Swain's chalk marks had been very precise. It always surprised Dalziel to see what a small space the human body could fit into, especially when folded into a foetal position. He frowned severely at the young man as though willing him to speak.

Then he said, 'All right. Everyone out. Photos first, then Forensic.'

'All informed, sir,' said Wield.

'Someone will have to tell the girl,' said Pascoe, as they went into the welcome sunshine.

'What? Oh aye. For identification. Look who's here. Man his size should use a moped.'

The Chief Constable was climbing out of a big Rover. He was resplendent in full fig, and the ratepayers' generosity was still written in his face. But the message changed like a teletext screen as he took in Dalziel, and the Roads Department truck, and the two men coming out of the garage with pneumatic drills.

Dalziel approached and Trimble said, 'Andrew, am I sure I want to hear this?'

'Nowt to worry about,' said Dalziel. 'Just an unexpected visitor.'

Quickly he filled Trimble in on the course of events. The Chief Constable groaned gently when he heard about the body but otherwise he listened in silence, asked a couple of pertinent questions when Dalziel had finished, then said, 'Let's hope he's telling the truth and Forensic confirm it. A manslaughter victim in our own backyard's marginally preferable to a murder victim.'

Pascoe said to Dalziel, 'Sir, did you want me to inform Mrs Appleyard?'

He intended only a gentle reminder that people were more important than public relations, but somehow it came out like an ex cathedra rebuke. Dalziel didn't respond. He seemed to have drifted off into some unimaginable inner world. But Trimble took the point well.

'Of course. The young wife. And she's lost her father today. This will be very hard for her. Whoever tells her, I want an experienced WPC present, and the counselling services alerted. But we mustn't jump the gun. Andrew!'

Dalziel rejoined them with a start.

'Sir?'

'I was just saying we should keep the wraps on this till we're absolutely sure what we've got here. And that's for the relatives' sake as well as our own.'

This was for Pascoe's benefit. Reassured by the Chief's reaction to his earlier intervention, he could now admit a smidgeon of sympathy for Trimble's distaste for the anticipated newspaper mockery. It wasn't all that long ago that a dead Italian had been found in a car in this same park, and Pascoe could still recall the yards of wearisome waggery churned out by everyone from the yellow press to the red satirists.*

'Aye, you're right,' said Dalziel vaguely.

There was something on his mind, something he was not altogether confident of bringing into the open. Pascoe didn't like this. Dalziel might not always be right, but he was rarely uncertain.

Trimble had sensed it too and he said gently, 'Andrew, I once had toothache and broke my favourite toy engine on my birthday. Since then I've been disaster-proof. What else is on your mind?'

Dalziel said, 'Greg Waterson, sir.'

'Meaning?'

* *Child's Play*

'It's two months almost since he was last seen. We've looked everywhere. Not just us. The Drug Squad. And they *really* look.'

'So?'

'So think about it, sir. If you're looking for someone with no talent for hiding, and he can't be found in the places he seems likely to hide, doesn't it make sense to start looking in the places someone else is likely to have hidden him?'

Pascoe had to admire the way he used the Dark Lady's phrases as though struck fresh in his personal mint. And he had to admire even more the way in which Trimble digested the implications of his CID chief's remarks without spewing forth rage.

'You're sure you want to do this, Andrew?' was all he said mildly.

'Aye. I'm sure.'

Trimble sighed. He's as worried about Dalziel's obsession with Swain as I am, thought Pascoe. But he's got to let him prove himself right or wrong.

'And which part of my lovely car park do you propose destroying now?'

Dalziel pointed towards the gatehouse.

'That's the last bit done,' he said. 'The bit they were working at when Waterson did his vanishing trick.'

'Right,' said Trimble with sudden decision. 'Go ahead. But I'm not having us on public display. I want that section of the street shut off. Put out some story about a gas leak, anything. And, Andrew, try to look a little happier. The sight of anything less than utter certainty on that face of yours gives me acid indigestion.'

He strode smartly into the building.

'He's all right for a dwarf,' said Dalziel. 'Right, lad. You heard what the man said. I'll leave you to get that sorted. Wieldy, you come with me. Let's see if we can give young Seymour a hand with Mr Swain's statement.'

He glanced at his watch.

'And I want the work to commence in exactly thirty minutes, right?'

'Why so precise?' inquired Pascoe.

'Because I want to make sure I'm looking straight into Mr Philip bloody Swain's eyes when he hears the drills start up again!'

Chapter 2

It was not often that Andrew Dalziel admitted a tactical error, but as he sat in the interview room and listened to Sergeant Wield reading out the statement prior to Swain's signing it, it occurred to him that a clever dog didn't do the same trick twice.

He'd provoked a response from Swain by letting him overhear his request for the pneumatic drills. This time, might it not have been cleverer to get the slippery sod out of earshot rather than alerting him too soon to the continued search?

Wield's voice droned on. '. . . and I realize I was both committing and compounding a felony by aiding Arnie Stringer to conceal his son-in-law's body . . .'

Dalziel glanced at his watch. A minute to go. He'd left it too late. Swain was watching him. Perhaps he'd already alerted that sharp mind. He let his gaze lock with Swain's. There was no resistance, no effort to break free. The moment seemed timeless. But time had not stopped. Three storeys below in the car park, the drills suddenly chattered into life, and there was an exchange along their

340

eye beams as telergetic as any ever experienced by enraptured lovers.

'. . . and I am prepared to accept the full legal consequences of my error of judgement,' concluded Wield. 'That's it, sir. Would you care to sign?'

Swain broke the eye contact and bowed his head as though in prayer.

'No,' he said softly. 'Not yet. I'm sorry, but the slate has got to be wiped completely clean, hasn't it? I know, *de mortuis*, and all that. But it's the living I have to think of. That poor woman. I hope to God I may be wrong, but I've no way of checking this thing out for myself. Only you can do that, Mr Dalziel.'

'Do what?' growled Dalziel. He knew now he'd been wrong. Don't play people at their own games. Clever buggers didn't play clever buggers with other clever buggers. Now he was speaking lines Swain had cued from him, but he didn't know how not to respond.

'Look for firm evidence of what I only suspect and fear.'

'Which is?'

'That Arnie Stringer might have killed Greg Waterson!'

'What?' Dalziel had been expecting nifty footwork but this took his breath away. Tactics forgotten, he spoke from the heart.

'You'd be better off flogging condoms to cardinals than trying to sell that one, Swain!'

Philip Swain nodded earnestly and said, 'Yes, I can see how hard it must be for you to grasp such an idea, Superintendent, but listen to what I've got to say before you pass final judgement. Arnie Stringer was always very loyal to me, and after I helped him with his son-in-law, he clearly felt deeply in my debt, emotionally I mean. When this tragic business of Gail's death occurred, he was desperate to do anything he could to console me. He blamed Greg Waterson entirely and made no secret of

341

what he reckoned a man like that deserved. I found myself in the odd position of actually defending the man who'd seduced my wife and created the situation which led to her tragic death. But Arnie was a black-and-white man, and though he shut up, I should have realized he hadn't changed his mind when I asked him to follow Mrs Waterson that night.'

'Which night was this?' inquired Dalziel, yawning unconvincingly.

'The night she was meeting Greg. She told me he'd rung, you probably know that, and I was very keen to talk to him . . .'

'Why was that, then?' interrupted Dalziel.

'To get him to come forward, of course,' said Swain. 'I didn't know then that you already had a statement from Greg completely exonerating me. I know you have a difficult job to do, Superintendent, but I still feel that letting me suffer so long was an unnecessary cruelty.'

Dalziel closed his eyes for a moment in prayer, or perhaps pain.

'So you asked Arnie to follow Mrs Waterson?' he said. 'Why not go yourself?'

'She knew me by sight, and of course Greg knew me too. Being the kind of person he was, if he spotted me, I suspected he'd have taken off as fast as he could. I just wanted to find out where he was living so I could approach him privately and have a talk. So I asked Arnie if he could find out by following Mrs Waterson and he agreed.'

'What kind of vehicle did he use?' interposed Wield, ignoring Dalziel's malevolent glance.

'I don't know. The pick-up, I expect. Anyway I didn't see him that same evening. I had an appointment up near Darlington and as things worked out, I didn't get back till late.'

He paused and took a drink from the cup of cold coffee before him. Wield waited for Dalziel to demand details of this Darlington appointment, but the fat man stayed quiet till Swain resumed.

'Next morning when I got down here – that job was getting pretty near the end then, you'll remember – I found Arnie had made a really early start. I asked him what had happened the previous night. He said he'd followed Mrs Waterson to a pub, the Pilgrim's Salvation. He'd waited outside and seen her come out by herself. Then he'd hung around till closing time, watching for Waterson, but he must have missed him.'

'He didn't go in the pub?' said Dalziel.

'He said not. He wasn't a man who approved of public houses,' said Swain. 'So it made sense. Only, well, even for Arnie he was rather brusque and off-hand about the whole business.'

'And that made you suspect he wasn't telling you the truth,' sneered Dalziel.

'It wasn't as clear-cut as that,' said Swain. 'But I remember just before I went off to America, I said to Arnie that I wasn't looking forward to it and he said it'd be all right, I'd be back in no time with everything sorted out, and I said no, nothing could be finally sorted out till Greg Waterson turned up, and he said if that was all I was worrying about, I should rest easy as he doubted if I'd be bothered by that bastard again. His words came back to me on the plane and I started wondering . . . all kinds of things. But I soon forgot about them in California, there was far too much else to occupy my mind and I hardly gave the business another thought. Till this morning. God! Was it only this morning? It seems an age ago.'

'That's because you go all round the houses telling a tale,' growled Dalziel.

'I'm sorry,' said Swain, unruffled. 'This morning, as I've told you, Arnie's mind was much occupied by his son-in-law. We sat and talked about it. Then we did some work but I could see he wasn't concentrating. And I said to him from the cab, "For heaven's sake, Arnie. Stop moping. All right, make a clean breast if you must and let the law take its course. But don't take more on yourself than you deserve. All you've done is conceal a terrible accident. That's all it was. An accident!" And he replied more to himself than me, "Aye, that's what that one was. But not that other fornicator!" Then before I could ask him what he meant, he went back to working, and I did too, and not long after . . . oh God, perhaps neither of us had our minds fully on what we should have been doing. I'll never forgive myself!'

His voice had broken momentarily.

Dalziel belched and said, 'I still don't see what put Waterson in your mind.'

'Don't you see? It was what he said before he died. "Not Phil's fault. God's will. Helping a friend. Good friend to me." I thought at first he was referring to the accident. Then later I thought it must be referring to Appleyard. But how could anyone imagine that was my fault? And finally it struck me. What if poor Arnie, feeling himself deeply indebted to me, and hating Waterson not just because of what he'd done to me, but because he was involved in filth like drugs and casual sex, had felt himself to be doing the will of God by putting him out of the way?'

He looked at the two policemen urgently, as though begging them to contradict his dreadful suspicion.

Dalziel said, 'Oh aye? And what do you think he might have done with the body?'

'I've no idea,' said Swain. 'But you have to look for it,

Superintendent. I beg that you will spare no effort in looking for it.'

And outside the sound of the pneumatic drills ceased.

It was Waterson without a doubt, almost perfectly preserved. He had been buried beneath the concrete behind the gatehouse. Unfortunately for the appearance of the car park, the drillers had started at the other side and worked round, so there was a trench some twelve feet in length.

Dan Trimble regarded this defacing scar sadly.

'I suppose it could have been worse,' he said.

'It will be,' said Dalziel laconically.

'What?'

'We've not found the girl yet. Beverley King.'

'You think she's in here too?'

'Where else? She were on that boat with Waterson and she's not been seen for God knows how long. He'd not leave her alive when he killed this poor sod, would he?'

'Stringer? Andrew, are you sure? From what you say, he might well think he was the instrument of God in dealing with Waterson, but he'd have to be stark staring mad to include the girl.'

'Stringer? Who's talking about Stringer?' demanded Dalziel. 'You don't think I swallowed that load of crap, do you? No, it's that bastard up there I'm after. Oh God, he thinks he's so clever. Correction, he is clever. Credit where it's due. He thinks fast, like a rat in a corner. He heard the drills start up again and he guessed what I was after. So quick as a flash, before he's faced with this poor sod's body and asked for an explanation, he gives one!'

Trimble was unimpressed.

'That's one way of looking at it,' he said. 'The other is

that he's telling the truth. I want both possibilities thoroughly investigated. I gather Swain says he went up to Darlington on business the night Waterson was seen at the Sally. Have you checked this?'

'What's the rush when I know what we'll find?' retorted Dalziel. 'It'll be a good story. But there won't be any good witnesses.'

'Mr Pascoe, I wonder if you'd care to check the Superintendent's prognosis?' murmured Trimble. 'But even if it's accurate, it still proves nothing.'

'Bev King's body'll prove something,' asserted Dalziel. 'And it shouldn't take us long to find. They must've been put in close together.'

'You'd better be right, Andy,' said Trimble, trying to lighten the tone. 'It's my heart those drills are digging into, you realize that?'

'Then they'll need to be right sharp,' replied Dalziel.

By the time Pascoe reached the interview room, the drills were back at their work but Swain showed no sign of reaction to the new outburst of noise.

The next ten minutes saw a lot of points being marked up to Dalziel. Swain's story was that he had driven north to look at an old house shortly to be demolished, with a view to buying the bricks and some fixtures. The contractor hadn't turned up and on phoning him at home, Swain had discovered one of them had got the wrong date. The man had been unable to join Swain that night, so he had taken a look around by himself, then had a drink and a sandwich at a pub in Darlington called the Crown or something royal. When he came out, he found he had a flat tyre. He had changed it with some difficulty and finally got home after midnight.

'So apart perhaps from a barmaid in a possibly regal

pub, you've got no one who can support your story,' said Pascoe.

'The demolition contractor can confirm my phone call,' said Swain. 'And I dare say someone saw me changing my wheel in the car park. But why all this interest in my whereabouts, Mr Pascoe?'

'Routine, sir.'

'Come on! I'm not an idiot.' He regarded Pascoe reflectively, then suspicion rounded his eyes and his mouth as he exclaimed, 'Oh my God! Those bloody drills . . . have you found . . . not Waterson? Oh Arnie, Arnie. Once he got an idea in his mind . . . And you think I helped him again? Come on, Chief Inspector! I've admitted my part in helping him hide one body, but I assure you I didn't make a habit of it! I am right, aren't I? You have found Waterson?'

Pascoe nodded, never taking his eyes off the man's face.

'Damn, damn, damn! I told you that was what I feared, but I still hoped I'd been wrong about Arnie. Couldn't he see it was in my interest for Waterson to turn up alive and well so he could clear up Gail's death absolutely, once and for all?'

He spoke with a passionate earnestness Pascoe could not fault.

He stood up abruptly and went to tell Dalziel he'd earned ten out of ten for his prognosis.

But in the car park he found the fat man's credit as a clairvoyant was fast running out. A Somme of new trenches serpentined away from Waterson's grave and it was clear that the area which might reasonably have been concreted at the same time was almost exhausted. Trimble's face had smoothed to an emotionless mask more revealing than tic or grimace, and the drillers, sensitive to vibrations stronger than those of their machines, paused and looked inquiringly at Dalziel.

'Keep going,' he said harshly. 'She's here. Peter, how'd you get on?'

Pascoe retailed what Swain had said, loyally stressing the accuracy of Dalziel's prediction. Trimble was not impressed.

'There's still nothing to link Swain with Waterson's death,' he said. 'Not even a good motive. Why on earth *should* he want to murder a man whose testimony cleared him of any suspicion of complicity in his wife's death?'

'Man who trains fleas needs a big thumb,' said Dalziel.

'I'm sorry?'

'Mr Waterson was a very volatile character,' said Pascoe, feeling that Dalziel's gnomic utterance required some slight exegesis. 'I think the Super means that, like a photographic negative, he needed to be fixed at a very precise point to preserve the desired result.'

Trimble said, 'I think I'll go inside before I'm tempted to ask any more questions.'

As they watched him walk away, Dalziel said, 'What the fuck were you on about!'

'Same as you, I think.'

'In that case, book me in to see Pottle!'

By six o'clock Pascoe was beginning to wonder if a trip to the psychiatrist mightn't be such a bad idea for Dalziel.

'Sir,' he said diffidently. 'I'm sure you appreciate you're well back into the area that was completed in February?'

'So what?'

'Well, Waterson was last seen on March the first, wasn't he?'

'I know that.'

'So if your theory is the girl was killed at the same time, then wherever she is she can't be . . . there.'

He gestured to where the last bit of concrete was being ripped up in front of the new garages.

'Who said she was killed at the same time?' said Dalziel.

'Well, I just assumed . . .'

'Leave assumption to the Virgin Mary,' snapped Dalziel. 'When's the last sight there was of this lass?'

'She moved from Bulmer's Wharf on February the third. She last visited her parents on February the fourteenth. The farmer at Badger Farm reckons there was someone round the boat for most of February . . .'

'That peasant! Bugger's too tight to buy a calendar let alone a pair of specs!' interrupted Dalziel.

'Nevertheless. Look, if she is buried here, she must have been killed by either Swain or Stringer. And as you've got back beyond the March level already, she must have been killed in the second half of February. Why, for God's sake? Why?'

'I don't know why,' grated Dalziel. 'All I know is that sod killed his missus, and in my book he's guilty of everything else that happened round here till some cleverer sod than me proves him innocent!'

He was close to running amok, thought Pascoe. He looked desperately for some brake he could apply.

'Then logically you intend digging up everything that was concreted over since Valentine's Day?'

'If that's what it takes,' said Dalziel.

'Even if it means going inside some of the new inspection garages? Mr Trimble's not going to like it.'

'You leave Desperate Dan to me,' said Dalziel. 'He may do the Floral Dance, but it's me who plays the fiddle.'

But at eight o'clock the music came to an abrupt end.

An hour earlier, Swain, who had been remarkably laid back about the whole protracted business, finally summoned his lawyer. Trimble conferred with the man for a while, then came down to talk to his head of CID. He didn't talk long. The drills had gouged random inspection holes in a good sixty per cent of the garage floors. When Dalziel reluctantly admitted they were into concrete laid at least a week before the last reported sighting of Beverley King, Trimble said, 'That's it, Andy.'

'But . . .'

'No buts. Work stops now. If I hear those drills again, you're suspended. You'd better believe me.'

He strode away. Five minutes later he reappeared in the silent car park with Swain and his solicitor, a bat-faced man with a switched-on memo-cassette in his hand. Trimble was at his most man-of-the-world conciliatory, but Swain didn't look as if he needed his feathers smoothed.

'Please,' he said. 'Don't forget, I'm here because I've committed an offence and I know I shall have to answer for it. I can well understand Mr Dalziel's keenness to make sure there were no more unpleasant surprises in store. No, no need of a lift. I came in my own car. Fortunately I didn't leave it in here.'

He looked around the devastated car park and smiled in Dalziel's direction. Pascoe felt the fat man's tension. Please don't say anything actionable, he prayed, not with Trimble and this mechanized scion of Dodson and Fogg in earshot.

Trimble must have felt the danger too. He said sharply, 'Mr Dalziel, I'd like to see you in my office in ten minutes, please.'

'Sir!' barked Dalziel, then turned on his heel like a dismissed soldier and marched away. Pascoe smiled a conciliatory smile at Swain and followed. He caught up with his boss in the first garage, staring gloomily into the hole from which Tony Appleyard had been lifted.

'I had him, Peter,' he said. 'I had him by the short and curlies! What went wrong? Three bloody corpses, and still the bastard's walking away with a million quid in the bank and Desperate Dan dusting off his jacket like an Eyetie barber! What in the name of God went wrong?'

This appeal to the heavens touched Pascoe beyond mere rhetoric. This was *Götterdämmerung*, this was old Saturn in his branch-charmed forest acknowledging that the time of the Titans was past.

He said, 'Perhaps nothing went wrong, sir. Perhaps Swain's been telling the truth all along, in which case everything's gone right, hasn't it?'

It was, he acknowledged later, an attempt at comfort on a par with assuring Mrs Lincoln she'd have hated the rest of the show. Dalziel's face glowed like a nuclear pile and a hand like a mechanical shovel seized Pascoe's arm. Perhaps foolishly, he opted for rational argument rather than kneeing the fat man in the crotch. Urgently he said, 'Swain's cooperated all down the line, you've got to admit that. All right, he changed his statement a bit, but Waterson's backed him up. And he volunteered all that info about Appleyard's death, and he brought us straight to the spot . . .'

The nuclear glow faded and the grip on his arm relaxed enough for his arteries to resume a limited service.

'Aye, he did too. And he even drew us a diagram, didn't he? Whose chalk did he use, Peter?'

'Sorry?'

'The chalk he marked the spot with! Were you the clever little boy scout who came all prepared?'

'No, sir. All I recall is Swain drawing the outline and saying we should drill here.'

'And he was spot on, wasn't he? And if it weren't your chalk, and it weren't my chalk, then it must've been *his* chalk, mustn't it?'

'I suppose so. Perhaps builders carry chalk around with them,' suggested Pascoe, uncertain why Dalziel was labouring the point. 'Tool of the trade.'

'Mebbe. In his overalls. In his working gear. But Swain had got changed since we saw him at the hospital. He was in one of them fancy blazers with the bullet proof badges. Not the kind of thing a man of taste wants a cloud of chalk dust billowing out of every time he blows his nose!'

'Sir, I don't see that it matters. Main thing is that he did show us exactly where Appleyard was buried. Think of the mess we could have made of Mr Trimble's car park if Swain had been vague!'

It was less provocative than his earlier attempt at comfort but not much more effective.

'Mebbe I should write a thank-you note,' growled Dalziel.

Pascoe was saved from having to answer by the appearance of Sergeant Broomfield in the doorway.

'Mr Swain gone, has he?' he asked.

'If you hurry, you might still catch the Chief kissing his arse across the road in the public car park,' said Dalziel.

Broomfield turned away, but Dalziel called him back.

'What's up? Why do you want him?' he demanded.

'Nowt really. He left his pen, that's all. Looks a bit pricey and I didn't want him thinking it'd got lifted while he were here.'

'Careless bugger. Hold on, George, don't rush off. Peter, you're a clever sod, what's it the head bangers say about leaving things?'

'What? Oh, you mean that you don't leave things by accident really, but because you want to come back to the place you leave them? Of course, that's only a simplified version of – '

'It'll do for a simplified copper,' said Dalziel. 'Now why should Swain want an excuse to come back here?'

'I don't think that anyone says that every act of forgetfulness fulfils some subconscious purpose – '

'Who's talking subconscious?' snarled Dalziel. 'That

352

bastard'd be wide awake sleepwalking. An excuse to come back tonight. Why? Only one thing. To make certain we'd not started drilling again! George, those drillers, are they still here?'

'In the canteen, I think.'

'Get down there. I want them back out here in two minutes flat.'

'But Mr Swain's pen –'

'Give it here,' said Dalziel. 'I'll see he gets it. He'll need it to sign his next bloody statement! Now get a move on!'

Shaking his head, the sergeant left.

Pascoe said, 'Sir! are you sure you really want to do this? Remember, we've got it worked out that this garage was completed by the eighth of February. There's no sign the floor was touched till we started digging today. Beverley King was alive and well on the thirteenth, we know that for certain. It doesn't make any kind of sense . . .'

'You reckon? What doesn't make sense to me, lad, is that yon bugger hates my guts, yet he comes along here all cooperative. He doesn't just say, "It's in there somewhere," he brings us right inside and sketches out the exact spot with a stick of chalk he just happens to have about his person. He sits upstairs all day with hardly a murmur. And when he goes off, he leaves summat behind so he can come back later and put his mind at rest that he's got away with it.'

'Got away with *what*?' exploded Pascoe.

'Fuck knows! But he hasn't!' snarled Dalziel. 'Where's them drills?'

He stepped out of the door and stepped back inside immediately. Over his shoulder, Pascoe saw Trimble picking his way across the devastated yard.

He vanished inside. It must have been a close-cut thing, for a couple of minutes later Broomfield emerged with the puzzled drillers.

'Mr Trimble didn't see you?' confirmed Dalziel.

'No. Doesn't he know . . .?'

'Mind your own business,' snarled Dalziel. 'Right, lads, sorry to keep you so late, but here's what I want you to do. Start drilling here and work across the floor. And do me a favour, keep it quiet as you can.'

The drillers exchanged glances.

'Sorry,' one of them said. 'There's only two levels with these things. That's *off* and *bloody noisy*.'

'All right,' growled Dalziel. 'If you can't be quiet, at least be quick.'

And once again the drills rattled into life.

'I give him two minutes,' shouted Pascoe.

'Three,' said Dalziel. 'He'll take a minute to believe it. I'll try to cut him off. You keep these buggers hard at it.'

He strode towards the entrance to the station but he had underestimated Trimble's reaction time and he met the man on the threshold. The incredulity was certainly there, however.

'Andy, what's going on? What's that noise?'

'What noise, sir?' said Dalziel cupping his ear.

'That noise! It's the drills, isn't it?' shouted Trimble in anger, and also perhaps slightly in fear that the sound existed solely in his mind.

'Oh, *that* noise,' said Dalziel dismissively.

And as though his words were a command, the drills fell instantly still.

Dalziel smiled benevolently at the Chief Constable. It could be a simultaneous technical hitch but the odds must be heavily against that? The silence stretched on and on till Trimble said impatiently, 'Well?'

'You mean the drills, sir?' said Dalziel with a hint of reproach. 'That's what I was coming to tell you about. Come and take a look.'

At what? he wondered as he strode confidently across

the car park, hands deep in his jacket pockets to hide the tightly crossed fingers.

Pascoe appeared at the garage door. He gave a slight confirmatory nod, but it was the bewildered expression on his face which Dalziel found most reassuring, and he let his fingers disentangle as he waved Trimble into the garage ahead of him.

Now there was a second, smaller hole in the concrete floor. It had been dead reckoning with Swain. Only eighteen inches away from his boundary chalk mark, and there gleaming in the harsh light of a bare bulb was a sinuous tress of bright blonde hair.

'It's not possible,' said Trimble.

'Isn't it, sir? What?' said Dalziel.

'It can't be Beverley King. Can it?'

'No, sir,' said Dalziel with the pleasant condescension of re-established authority. 'I think this time you may be right.'

'Then who?'

There was a noise behind them. They turned. Standing in the doorway was Philip Swain.

'Hello, sir,' said Dalziel. 'Come to pick up your pen, have you?'

The man looked at him blankly, then said in a faraway voice, 'I had to come back . . . one last secret, then it's all over . . . life can begin again . . .'

'Gosh,' said Dalziel. 'Not something else to tell us? Not another uncoerced and purely voluntary statement? I'm thinking of publishing a collected edition!'

But Swain was not to be thrown from his part, if part it were. Slowly he advanced till he could see into the hole. When he could make out the blonde tress, he let out a little cry of shock or of pain.

Then he dropped to his knees, flung back his head, and shrieked, 'Gail! Gail! Gail!'

Chapter 3

It should have been Dalziel's greatest triumph, and for a little while that's how it came over, marred only by the need of explaining to Chung that he'd jumped the gun by consigning her Lucifer to the nether regions a fortnight before the Mysteries opened.

'Bail?' he said in answer to her question. 'I'd love to help, luv, but there's no way a magistrate would wear bail, not in a serious case like this.'

When he said this, he was at least half sincere, but within a very short space of time it became apparent to all concerned that it was mainly the sheer bulk of Dalziel's objections that stood between Swain and a limited freedom. Challenged by Chung, he growled, 'Makes no odds. You don't think I could act with that bugger now, do you? If he was back in the cast, I'd be out. I'm saving you a problem, keeping him inside.'

'Don't do me any favours, Andy,' said Chung steadily. 'I've made harder choices than that.'

Abashment was a new experience for Andrew Dalziel, but he felt it now.

But abashment was no part of his reaction when Dan Trimble brought up the case.

'Andrew, I'm a little worried. You've given the magistrates' court the impression that the charges against Swain will be so serious that turning him loose would be like sending Jack the Ripper back into Whitechapel. I presume this means you're confident you can overturn his statement . . .'

'Statement!' exclaimed Dalziel. 'That thing ought to be short-listed for the Booker!'

'You think so? Then perhaps you can separate the fact from fiction for me, with supportive evidence, of course. I have a copy here. Let's go through it, shall we?'

He began reading, pausing now and then for Dalziel to intervene. But during the early part of the statement which consisted of a description of the arrival of Arnie Stringer with news of his son-in-law's death, the fat man listened in silence. Only when Swain laid claim to motives of loyalty and friendship for agreeing to help did he let out a derisive snort.

'You dispute his motives?' said Trimble.

'Aye, do I! This loyalty and friendship didn't stop him running a JCB over the bugger to shut him up, did it?'

'You have proof of that allegation? Eye-witnesses? Forensic evidence?'

'No! But it stands to reason . . .'

'No, it doesn't, Andrew. To continue. "My wife, Gail, had gone to bed early as she was leaving on her trip to see her sick mother in the States the following morning. I should say now that though I admit we had had our differences about the future, there was the very real possibility of a compromise, and I certainly believed her visit to the States was going to be temporary. Arnie's arrival had woken her and after I'd calmed Arnie down and sent him home, she came into the room and told me she'd heard most of what we'd said. She couldn't believe that I was really going to help conceal Appleyard's death. If she'd talked purely in terms of right and wrong, I might have listened, but it soon became clear that this tragic accident seemed to her to provide the perfect excuse for me to break my partnership agreement with Arnie, whom she had never liked. I tried to explain my feelings, but she just grew progressively angrier, ending up almost hysterically demanding that I should leave with her the following day and fly to California, ready to take up the Delgado job offer. I said that though I'd by no means finally made my decision about the job, her proposal was manifestly impossible, but by now she was past reason and into hysteria. I slapped her face to try to get her to recover control but it just made her worse. She rushed at me, I stepped aside, I didn't mean to trip her, but she stumbled over my foot, and next thing she was lying across the hearth quite still. The side of her head had struck the old stone hearth. There was scarcely any blood, but she was quite clearly dead. I remember her once saying that in her childhood, her American doctor had warned her mother she had an abnormally thin skull and needed to be kept clear of the rough and tumble of the playground. I know I should have rung 999 but I wasn't thinking straight . . ." Yes, Andy?'

'That story's so old it's got grey hairs,' exclaimed Dalziel. 'If I had a penny for every time I've heard some punter tell me his missus slipped accidentally and banged her head on the hearth, I'd be better off than you!'

Trimble drew another paper from the pile on his desk.

'The post-mortem report states that Mrs Swain died from a blow to the side of her head not incompatible with the claim that she struck it against the corner of an upraised hearth. There was no sign of any other violence. And it was confirmed that she did have a very thin skull which might have been a contributory factor. Contra-evidence, please?'

'Forensic's checked out the hearth, found nowt,' said Dalziel.

'There is a cleaning woman who confirms she washed and polished the hearth at least twice a week,' said Trimble. 'Anything else? No? Then let's go on. ". . . thinking straight. All I could think was that if I summoned an ambulance and the police, Arnie was bound to hear the sirens, and in his state, he'd be certain I'd betrayed him,

and that might tip him right over the edge. I sat in that room and I thought and thought, and in my confusion there seemed no other way out of my predicament but to do with Gail what I had undertaken to do with Appleyard. And that is what I did. It was stupid, it had tragic consequences, and I regret it with all my heart. But when someone you love dearly has died in a tragic accident, and when at the same time a man of the quality of Arnie Stringer has put his whole life and happiness in your hands, it is hard to think straight. So in the end, I wrapped Gail up in a blanket and hid her body in the pick-up, and next day on the site, I dug the hole while Arnie mixed the concrete. We were working on the section behind the coroner's offices which were empty on a Sunday, and no one from the Police HQ showed any interest in us. Nevertheless I told Arnie to stand watch while I buried Appleyard and naturally I used the opportunity to bury Gail too. I nearly stopped then and told Arnie I couldn't go on, but Gail was dead and perhaps mistakenly I felt my higher duty was to the living, to the needs of my old friend. So I said a simple prayer and laid her to rest."
Andrew, you're making strange noises again. Surely whatever else you think of Swain, you have to give him some credit for wanting to help a friend in need?'

Dalziel exploded, 'Jesus, sir! Have you not twigged yet? Slippery sod like Swain only ever tells the truth when it happens to support his lies! My guess is his missus was long dead when Arnie turned up, mebbe for as much as a couple of days, though if he'd just done her in that night, he must have come close to shitting himself when Stringer started banging on his door! You don't really think he was going to let her take off to the States, do you? And get a quick divorce and dump him out of her will? No, she were dead, and he were still wondering how best to proceed

359

when Arnie turns up with just the same problem. Solving that helps him solve his own!'

Trimble said, 'Let me be quite clear. Are you alleging that Swain had all the subsequent business with Waterson and Beverley King worked out before he killed his wife?'

'No way!' said Dalziel dismissively. 'Swain couldn't plan a school picnic. He just reacts fast to events, that's the trick of him. Thing that puzzles most people about him is how he could settle to being a small-time builder. But ask yourself, what are small-time builders like? They come round, scratch their heads, size up a job, scribble on the back of an envelope, give you a price. They turn up late 'cos some other bugger has asked them to fix a roof or put in a window. They're always coming across unexpected snags because they can never see more than a couple of moves ahead. But they're bloody ingenious at sorting out the snags when they arise, because that's their talent, that's how they survive. They're never going to build you the Taj Mahal, but they can offer a price on a new set of garages that'll get a mean bloody finance committee's mouth watering. Take away Swain's fancy blazers and posh accent and what have you got? A dodgy small-time builder, smart enough to stay one step ahead of the game, but too short-sighted to make the jump into the bigtime.'

'Swain's come close to making it,' objected Trimble.

'No, sir. Topping your missus doesn't rate as business acumen,' said Dalziel in a kindly tone. 'Anyroad, with his family's track record, he'd likely have got through his wife's money in a twelvemonth, so I reckon we're doing him a favour by putting him away.'

'Andy, you haven't yet said anything which fills me with confidence that we *are* going to put him away, not for long anyway. No, don't say anything. I realize the most serious part of this odd affair is still to come. Where was I? Oh yes. "In the days immediately following, I was surprised to find I was able to continue with no apparent after-effects. I have since been advised by medical experts that this process of going through the motions of a normal working life is quite usual in cases of severe shock. It took another shock to show me how unbalanced my mental state really was, and unfortunately that revelation, instead of leading me to seek professional aid, merely pushed me into yet another monstrous misjudgement.

'"It began three or four days later when I called on Greg Waterson to ask what he intended to do about his unpaid bill. The business had serious cash-flow problems. Gail had signed some cheques to pay our more pressing bills . . ."'

'Forgeries!'

'Proof?'

There was none. Naturally none of the payees (including Thackeray) was interested in making a complaint, the account had been wound up and the funds transferred to Swain, and the bank claimed it would be almost impossible to produce the cancelled cheques even if a genuine plaintiff were found.

'I'll get proof,' said Dalziel.

'Perhaps,' said Trimble, frowning. 'Let's press on. ". . . bills, but we still needed every penny that was owed us. Waterson reluctantly invited me in, but as I entered the living-room, all thought of money was driven out of my mind. A woman was standing in front of the fireplace with her back to me. She was tall and slim with long blonde hair, and for a second I was sure it was Gail! Then she turned and facially there was no resemblance at all. But the damage had been done. Curiously she didn't seem to register my shock and left the room almost immediately, pushing by me with a brusqueness which in other circumstances I might have thought rude. But Waterson noticed. He asked if I was all right. In reaction I immediately

361

became untypically aggressive in my demands for instant payment of the five thousand pounds he owed the firm. He went into a rigmarole of evasion, but finally under pressure he admitted he didn't have the money. It was as if the floodgates had opened, for with no further prompting from me, he went on to tell me that he was being blackmailed by the woman I had seen. He said they were having an affair and he'd been foolish enough to supply her with some drugs. Subsequently she had pestered him to get her more and he'd obliged, but eventually he had drawn the line, as it was both expensive and dangerous. Then she had turned nasty, demanding he supplied either the drugs or the money to buy them, on threat that if he didn't she would turn for help to the authorities and expose him as a major supplier. There was some story too of a large consignment which had been lost. I told him he wasn't the only one with money troubles, he made some remark about my rich American wife, and I reacted at first by being very angry, but gradually my anger turned to grief, and suddenly, with no conscious decision, I found myself telling this comparative stranger everything! The trigger, I am sure, had been the sight of the woman I mistook for Gail, but my mental and emotional state must have been like a volcano, which was bound to burst out eventually. Greg Waterson, whatever his other faults, had a most charming and sympathetic manner. I was in desperate need of someone to talk to, and he made the perfect listener. When I explained how I'd felt when I saw the woman I now know to have been Beverley King, he said yes, he'd noticed my reaction and wondered about it. I think it was now that the mad idea began to form in his mind.

'"We had a drink and I began to recover a little. I began to talk about going to the police and making a clean breast of everything. In fact it seemed to me as I grew a little more rational that in telling the story to a stranger, I had taken an irreversible step in that direction. But Waterson urged me to think hard about it. He painted a dark picture of the likely official reaction, of a long and nasty investigation, of the high probability of a murder charge. This made me hesitate, but the greatest impediment to confession was my knowledge that I couldn't tell the police my story without implicating poor Arnie.

'"And now Waterson, seeing that I was lukewarm in my resolve, began to explore what other explanation I might give for Gail's disappearance. The police would certainly soon discover she'd never got back to America, and immediately they would focus all their interest on me. Also, he pointed out, even if I did convince them I knew nothing of her whereabouts, it could be years before a court would presume her dead, by which time my business could have failed and I might even have been forced to give up Moscow Farm. What I really needed, he said, was some way of getting her death recognized immediately, without implicating myself in it to the extent of possibly invalidating her will.

'"And it was now he came out quite baldly with this incredible proposition; that we should contrive to kill Beverley King in such a way that I could get away with identifying her body as Gail's! This way he would be free of her blackmailing threats, she would become a missing person with no prospect of the police ever finding her, and I would be officially a widower with access to my wife's estate." What was that, Andy?'

'I just said, *oh, the clever bugger*,' repeated Dalziel with reluctant admiration.

'Waterson?'

'No! Swain. Swapping it all round like that.'

'You believe it was his idea?'

'Of course it was his bloody idea!' exclaimed Dalziel. 'It

had dawned on him he might have been a bit hasty in concreting his missus under our garages. True, he could forge a few cheques, but without her official death, the big spondulicks were well out of his reach. Then he sees this long-legged blonde, hears Waterson's hard-luck I'm-being-blackmailed story, and bingo! He sees his way through.'

'But would he put so much reliance on a man he hardly knew, a man who by all accounts rates as a Grade A twit?'

'Aye, but not on the surface,' said Dalziel. 'Waterson liked to come across as really cool, to talk big. That's what got him into bother all the time. It was only when the shit hit the fan that he started falling to pieces. And then it was too late for Swain to back away. He just had to adjust to circumstances as best he could.'

Trimble frowned doubtfully and said, 'Evidence? I asked for evidence.'

'Evidence? It stands to reason it was Swain's plan. It was Swain who had most to gain, wasn't it? Swain who could lay his hands on a Colt Python and Swain who knew what a mess it made of a face from seeing what it had done to his brother. It was Swain who had the clothes and jewellery and bits and pieces to back up their tale. It was Swain who would be identifying the body. It all stinks of Philip bloody Swain!'

'Olfactory evidence is rarely admissible,' murmured Trimble with a smile that Dalziel did not return. 'Let's move on to his account of the actual shooting. Here we are. They go up to the bedroom together. Waterson has the gun. The girl is on the bed, very drunk. The plan is for Waterson to shoot her at close quarters. "As I saw Waterson lift the gun I knew I couldn't go through with it. It was as if I'd been living in a sort of unreal cinematic world created by the shock and pain of Gail's death, a world in which normal reactions and behaviour didn't apply. Now all at once the mists cleared, the distortions straightened out, and I saw what a monstrous thing it was that Waterson had planned. I rushed at him to divert his aim but he was surprisingly strong and pushed me away. I stumbled, almost fell. Then the gun went off. I dived forward and this time managed to wrestle the gun free from his hand, but it was too late. The poor girl was slumped over the bed with blood and bone everywhere. And I was plunged even deeper into that nether world of shock, so deep indeed that I can remember hardly anything of the next few hours, and not much of the next few days. When I started to surface a little, I realized that some basic impulse for self-protection had made me stick to the story that this was Gail, though I took upon myself far more of the guilt for her death than was actually mine. When I heard that Waterson had disappeared, I understood why. He must have been convinced I was going to reveal the whole truth, and that in fact was my intention. But I felt I owed it to him to talk with him first. Perhaps he wouldn't have pulled the trigger if I hadn't tried to interfere. I knew from my own dreadful experience how accidents can look and feel like acts of murder, and I could not condemn without a hearing. I only wish I could have got to the poor chap before Arnie Stringer so tragically repaid his debt of friendship!

'"My only desire now is to do all I can to clear up this whole ghastly business and put it behind me. After I left the Station earlier today, I realized I could never rest easy again until the whole truth was known, which was why I returned voluntarily to show where Gail was buried. My life is in ruins. I can only pray that eventually I shall find the strength to start rebuilding it." End of statement.'

'Can't be, sir,' said Dalziel. 'You've missed out the swelling music! Jesus wept, it's worse than *Gone with the Wind*!'

'All right, Andrew,' said Trimble patiently. 'What do *you* think happened?'

'What I bloody well saw!' snarled the fat man. 'At least, most on it. What I reckon they agreed was that Waterson should pull the trigger. Swain had done his bit of murder and he wasn't about to go into partnership with someone who wouldn't put himself on an equal footing. Waterson'd agree to anything in advance. Full of bullshit, that one, and Swain still hadn't sussed him out. Then comes the moment and Waterson bottles out. Swain's gone too far to turn back now and he says he'll do it himself. Waterson grabs at the gun, Swain pushes him away, sticks the gun under that poor spaced-out lass's chin, and blows her face away. And that's it for Waterson. He goes catatonic and that's how I find 'em when I come steaming to the rescue.'

'And how do you explain Swain's first statement?'

'He had to think quick. No way as far as he could see that Waterson was going to stick to their original story. In fact it seems likely the little shit is going to cough the lot, so he gives a modified version, with himself involved in a struggle in which the gun might have gone off accidentally, as a fail-safe in case we start talking murder. At the same time he's still hoping he can get to Waterson before he coughs and try to minimize the damage. He underestimated Greg's powers of recovery! Goes to bed a quivering wreck, has a good night's sleep, and he's superstud again. So he sets out to repair matters by more or less writing the statement he'd agreed to give in the first place. A bit longer, and he might have changed his mind. But first his wife comes in to see him and he can't resist making himself the star in a big drama in her eyes. Then Sergeant Wield turns up and he hands over his statement, all blasé man of the world again. Which lasts till Wield is daft enough to leave him by himself.'

'Why did he take off then?'

'Because he got to thinking that not only was he in for a nasty grilling from us, but Swain would be none too pleased with him either. Also there was the drugs business. Ordinary trouble Waterson seems to have met by screaming and shouting. Real trouble, and he runs like buggery. So off he goes and hides on the lass's boat, best place he could have chosen as it turned out, but I doubt if he were that clever. It was just that there was nowhere else! But his luck ran out the day he rang his wife. Swain followed her to the Sally and was hanging around outside waiting for him when he realized that Sergeant Wield was there too. But Wield got mixed up with that gang of yobboes and Swain took his chance and picked up Greg. It'd be all sweetness and light till he established exactly what Greg had told us, then bang! Another one for his favourite boneyard. Now Waterson couldn't change his story, which left only Arnie Stringer, and once *he* started getting twinges of conscience 'cause I was sniffing around, that was him for the chop too. End of story.'

'And a very good story it is,' said Trimble. 'And sitting here listening to it, I'm inclined to go along with you, Andy. The trouble is that Philip Swain tells a good story too. And he's going to have psychiatrists and doctors and lawyers and character witnesses to support it. What are we going to have to support yours, Andy?'

'You've got what I tell you! You've got whatever those useless sods in Forensic can dig up! You've got the evidence of your own common bloody sense! You've got my own witness statement!'

Trimble shook his head sadly.

'If it were my decision,' he said, 'there'd be no question. But we merely feed what we have into the judiciary. That's as it should be. It must be left to the legal mind to decide what charges can confidently be brought. You don't disagree with that, do you?'

Dalziel was sitting very still.

'What are you trying to say?' he asked. 'Come on. Spit it out!'

Trimble said, 'Please. I'm not a suspect, Andy.'

'You're making me bloody suspicious, I tell you that for nowt,' said Dalziel. 'What's going off here?'

'I think you've guessed. Swain is at present remanded in custody until Thursday, June the second, Corpus Christi day, I believe. You must have been concerned that your Thespian pursuits might have had to be interrupted by an appearance in court, but you can rest easy. You shan't be required. Unless something even more dramatic than your appearance in a nightshirt on a trolley happens before then, we shall be withdrawing our objections to bail.'

'In a murder case? We can't!'

'Not in a murder case,' agreed Trimble. 'Only, there doesn't seem to be a case for murder here, Andy. At least that's the opinion of the Prosecutor's office. Swain is willing to cooperate on a whole range of lesser charges. The feeling is they'd rather get him on something definite than be made ridiculous by having a murder case thrown out on grounds of insufficient evidence. Andy, I'm sorry. Look, sit down, let's talk it through, over a drink . . .'

But Dalziel was gone beyond even the conjurative powers, hitherto infallible, of a full bottle of Glen Morangie.

Chapter 4

It is a curious facet of human nature that while success often inspires resentment, failure can rekindle faith.

Up till now, even after the excavation of the car park, Pascoe had been unable to share his boss's certainty in Swain's total guilt. But immediately Dalziel stormed into his office with news of what he perhaps unfairly categorized as Trimble's treachery, Pascoe found himself overwhelmed by an equal and unqualified indignation.

'I'd back him against a bunch of dried-up lawyers any day,' he told Wield later.

'You're not overcompensating a bit, are you?' wondered Wield.

'Because I had some reservations before?'

'Because you thought he were off his chump!' said Wield.

'Surely you can't still think Swain's not guilty?' said Pascoe, defensively aggressive.

'He's guilty of something, that's clear.'

'But not murder?'

'Look, you've got one arrangement of the known facts, that's the boss's. You've got another, that's Swain's. What's to choose between them? Benefit of the doubt, that's what it all comes down to.'

'Perhaps. But I'd like to help the Super, that's all.'

'So what are you going to do?'

It was a good question. It was not easy to give it a good answer.

'Well,' said Pascoe slowly, 'at least I can do what I've been moaning he's not been bothered to do with this Dark

Lady business. I can take what he says seriously for a change.'

He started that evening by gathering copies of all the statements, and various reports on the Swain affair together and taking them home. Ellie was at a meeting of her Bat Group so he was able to spread himself across the dining-room table in an attempt at spotting an unnoticed dimension via visual cross-referencing. But after a couple of hours all he had was a feeling, obviously shared by the Prosecutor, that if Swain put on a good show in court (and even Dalziel admitted his nimbleness as a counter-puncher) there was no way of getting him for murder. Perhaps all that that meant was he was indeed innocent of murder . . . Pascoe pushed away the negative thought. He'd promised himself he would use Dalziel's certainty as his guiding light here. But it was beginning to feel like a candle in a blizzard.

When Ellie came home, he was still staring blankly at the papers. She expressed no curiosity about them and he offered no explanation. Their polite neutrality about each other's work was beginning to harden into a trade barrier.

'Good meeting?' he asked.

'Yes, it was. We're updating our survey of types and locations in the district. You might keep your ears open at work. I wouldn't be surprised to hear Fat Andy's got a few vampires in his cellar.'

'Come to think of it,' he said, his memory stirred by his recent reading, 'there were some bats hibernating in this old barn out at Moscow Farm, Philip Swain's place. Pipistrelles, someone said.'

'What? You never mentioned them. Don't you know you're required by law to notify the authorities?'

'Am I? Sorry. Anyway this was back in February, so they've probably taken off by now.'

The revelation that his acquaintance with these disturbing creatures went back for months merely added to Ellie's irritation. Fortunately a noise from Rose's room diverted her before Pascoe could excuse himself into more trouble. Alone again, his attention returned to the Swain papers. In his physical arrangement, those relating to the killing of Beverley King in Hambleton Road were placed at the centre, while those to do with the death of Tony Appleyard were pushed to the edge.

But now the bat connection brought the barn where the boy had died into the forefront of his thoughts. It occurred to him that everybody accepted the Swain version of the youth's death, or rather the Swain version of the Stringer version. And why not? It fitted with both projections of Swain – as a loyal friend or as a quick-thinking bastard. That was the trouble with almost everything they had. It was as consistent with Swain's story as with Dalziel's theory.

But had the consistency test itself been applied consistently?

Only one way to find out.

He rearranged the papers in as strict a chronological order as possible, said to himself, 'Swain is a loving husband and a loyal friend,' and began reading.

After a while Ellie looked in, then withdrew, and he heard the television come on in the lounge.

Half an hour later she looked in again.

'Not finished yet?' she asked.

'I've finished being a loving husband,' he said. 'Now I'm going to be a right bastard.'

'Oh, sorry, I blinked. There, I missed it,' she said. 'I'm off to bed.'

'I'll be up in half an hour or so.'

'Which one of you? 'Night.'

He smiled after her, then returned to his papers.

Forty minutes later he read through his notes.

And there it was. Not much; in fact almost totally insignificant. Except that when it was all you had, it had to signify.

He glanced at his watch. Too late to disturb anyone. Except a wife. Wives were not *anyone*.

She opened one eye as he entered the room, then closed it again. He squeezed her shoulder gently till she reopened it.

'Do I have to guess which one it is?' she asked sleepily.

'Neither. It's a benighted male in search of female illumination. Wake up, my sweet, and tell me all about our little friends, the bats.'

The following morning he was up early. By eight o'clock he was passing through a creaking doorway beneath a vandalized legend which read JOE SWINDLES – CRAP MERCHANT. In a miasmic office a stout white-haired man was smoking a small cheroot, eating a fried egg sandwich and reading the *Sun*. He looked up with the ill-tempered expression of one who does not care to have his matutinal pleasures interrupted, then smiled yolkily as he recognized his visitor.

'Mr Pascoe. This is a nice surprise. Haven't seen you in ages. I've been feeling right neglected. What can it mean, I ask myself? Have I given offence? Or has he simply left me for another?'

'I expect it means, Joe, that either you've got honester or I've got slower,' said Pascoe.

'Well, you might have got slower, Mr Pascoe. Happens to the best of us. But if I got any honester, they'd have had to pick me for God in these Mysteries instead of that lovely Mr Dalziel. How is the dear old chap, by the way? Must be getting close to retirement now?'

Pascoe smiled. It was Joe Swindles's alcoholic ambition

to get Dalziel into his crusher before he died to repay him for what he considered to be various injustices perpetrated over the years.

'I'll pass on your regards,' he said. 'Now, Joe, I want a favour.'

Swindles listened as Pascoe explained, then he scratched his venerable pate and said, 'In February, you say? Now that's asking a lot, Mr Pascoe. That could take a lot of looking for, and then it'd most likely have gone in the crusher.'

Pascoe was not impressed. One thing he had learned about Joe Swindles was that he had an almost supernaturally accurate knowledge of the contents of his scrapyard. All he was doing now was negotiating.

'I know your time's valuable, Joe,' said Pascoe. 'So I'll give you a fiver a minute. That's a fiver for every minute less than five it takes to find them.'

It cost him twenty pounds. He looked at the rusting heap of agricultural machinery and tools removed from the barn at Moscow Farm and wondered if he was doing a wise thing.

'Why'd you hang on to them, Joe?' he asked.

'Agricultural archaeology,' Swindles replied promptly. 'There's money in it already. This stuff's not old enough yet, but a few more years and one of these country museums'll be paying a pretty penny for this junk.'

'Is that what you call a spike harrow?' said Pascoe pointing.

'Either that, or a hell of a hairbrush,' said Swindles.

Pascoe examined the implement in silence for a few minutes. Then he said, 'I'll need to borrow it, Joe.'

'Just the harrow?'

'No. Best take the lot. You'll get it back.'

'Bloody right I will!' Swindles thought for a moment

then said, 'You'll need someone to lift it wherever you want it taken.'

'Are you volunteering?'

'I'd have to charge my usual rates. Discount for cash.'

Pascoe laughed.

'Joe, he said, 'if Mrs Thatcher knew about you, she'd make you a lord.'

He was still chuckling as Swindles unloaded the scrap on to the paved area in front of the police laboratories.

Gentry, the Head of the Forensic Examination Unit, did not share his amusement. He extended a skeletal finger towards the heap of rusting rubbish and said harshly, 'What is *that*?'

Pascoe, knowing from experience that there was no way to charm him into cooperation, replied crisply, 'Evidence in the case of Anthony Appleyard. Here's a copy of the path. report. You'll see it says he died as a result of his windpipe being pierced by a metal spike. Here's a copy of the relevant section of a witness statement which claims the metal spike was one of those on that harrow. Would you check it out?'

'But this was three months ago and this thing has obviously been standing out in the open.'

'Yes. You've already done an examination of Appleyard's clothing. Also of the clothing of Gail Swain. I'd like some further work done on both of these.'

'Are you saying there are inaccuracies?' demanded Gentry.

'I'm inviting you to be more precise than your first brief required,' said Pascoe. 'Particularly in the area of staining on the outer garments.'

'You have authorization for this?' interrupted Gentry harshly.

'I can get Mr Trimble's signature in the hour if that's what it takes to make you do your job,' said Pascoe.

'I don't think that is called for!'

Unsure whether the man was referring to the signature or the slur, Pascoe said, 'Then I'll expect to hear from you,' and left. Such brusqueness did not come naturally to him, but it was the only way to deal with Dr Death.

Not that there weren't other sharper stings to be wary of.

'Where the hell have you been?' demanded Dalziel as he entered his office. 'Mooning around after yon dotty tart, I'll be bound.'

'If you mean the disturbed woman who has made the mistake of looking to you for help, no, I haven't,' snapped Pascoe.

'Bloody hell,' said Dalziel. 'What's up with you? Time of the month, is it, lad? Try to leave your hang-ups at home, eh? It's not fair on them you work with.'

These reasoned reproaches coming from a man who since his last talk with Trimble had been ready to boil babies was almost too much.

'Looking for something, are you, sir?' said Pascoe banging shut the drawers and cupboards which the fat man had clearly been going through.

'Bit of a tension headache. Thought you might have an aspirin. But it doesn't matter,' said Dalziel long-sufferingly. 'It's all this acting business on top of running this madhouse. I must have been doolally to get involved.'

'How's it going with your new Lucifer?' asked Pascoe, deciding that conciliation was the better part of valour.

'He's all right. You know something? I miss Swain in the part! It made it all realler somehow. Now it's nowt but pantomime. Desperate Dan was right. I should never have got involved.'

'Not to worry, sir. It'll all be over soon.'

'Christ, lad, you sound like a nun in a hospice,' said

Dalziel. 'I need cheering up. I'll let you buy me a pint later to make up for being so rude to me.'

'I thought you had a headache,' objected Pascoe.

'That's what I tell all the girls,' said Dalziel.

Alone, Pascoe realized that he really did have a headache. In fact, on and off, he'd had one for some time now. It sometimes felt as if there was too much in there trying to get out. Or too much outside trying to get in.

Some time he was going to have to sit down quietly and spread his life out over a table as he'd spread the Swain case last night. But not yet. He couldn't approach his own actions in two rôles and find only one inconsistency. No, the rôles were as myriad as minutes in a day and the inconsistencies . . . well, how many pins could you stick in the bum of an angel?

He tried to smile at his own joke, failed, stood up, winced as his bad leg had a relapse, closed his eyes, saw the dark mine in which he'd suffered his injury, felt the rotten ceiling sagging low towards him, saw it was crawling with millions of squeaking slithering bats . . .

'Are you all right?'

It was Wield, his craggy face anxious.

'Yes. Fine. Really, I'm fine. Could do with a bit more sleep, that's all. I was burrowing away at the Swain case last night.'

'Oh aye? Any amazing revelations?'

'You never know, Wieldy,' said Pascoe, managing a smile. 'Let me tell you about it.'

The sergeant listened in silence and when Pascoe was done all he said was, 'Well, best of luck. But I wouldn't draw my savings from the building society to invest in it!'

'Thanks a lot,' said Pascoe, disappointed. 'Let's just wait and see, shall we?'

* * *

Twenty-four hours later he was still waiting. He was resolved not to ring Gentry and give him the chance to be acid about CID's notorious impatience. Also, whatever else he felt about the man, he trusted his professionalism implicitly.

Finally a message came. Would he care to step round to the laboratories? He went. He looked. He listened.

When Gentry had finished, Pascoe said with sincere feeling, 'I can't thank you enough. You've done wonders.'

'We've done our job,' said Gentry. 'We can only work on what we're given, what we're told.'

But there was something which might have been a flush of pleasure beneath the parchment skin.

Dalziel was out rehearsing and Pascoe had to wait till that afternoon before he could see him. He was sitting behind the Superintendent's desk when the fat man walked into his room. He stopped short in the doorway when he saw his Chief Inspector smiling at him from his own chair with a broken-shafted pitchfork in his hand.

'Bloody hell, you've finally flipped,' said Dalziel. 'Think you're Britannia, do you?'

'No, sir. I've just come to wish you happy birthday.'

'It's not my birthday.'

'You'll think it is by the time I'm finished,' said Pascoe.

He talked. Dalziel listened. There was no doubt about the intensity of his listening, but no other emotion showed on his face.

'And what started you on this tack?' Dalziel asked sombrely when the story was finished.

'Like I said, Swain's either a right bastard or a loyal friend. A right bastard wouldn't have helped Stringer in the first place unless circumstances forced him. And if he was a right bastard when he helped Arnie, that meant it wasn't Arnie he was covering up for when he had the barn cleared out. Simple, really, when you think about it.'

377

'If it's that simple, I won't be grateful,' growled Dalziel. 'But what I meant was, what decided you to turn your massive intellect to proving me right when for months you've been going around behind my back telling any bugger that would listen that I was wrong?'

Blow, blow, thou winter wind! thought Pascoe.

He said, 'Because I wanted you to be right. Who needs a fallible God?'

Dalziel advanced; a great threatening hand thrust forward. Pascoe half rose in trepidation, then his own hand was enclosed and shaken till it lost all sensible contact with his wrist, and Dalziel intoned, *'This day's work is done ilka deal, And all this work likes me right well, And bainly I give it my blessing.'*

'Sorry?' said Pascoe.

'Sorry? Being God means never having to say you're sorry! *All that I ever said should be, Is now fulfilled through prophecy, Therefore now is it time to me To make an ending of man's folly!* Play it through for me again, lad. Play it again!'

Part Eight

DEVIL: For it is written, as well is kenned,
How God shall angels to thee send,
And they shall keep thee in their hend
Whereso thou goes,
That thou shall on no stones descend
To hurt thy toes.

And since thou may without wothe
Fall and do thyself no scathe,
Tumble down to ease us both
Here to my feet;
And but thou do I will be wroth,
That I thee hete.

The York Cycle: 'The Temptation'

Dear Andy,

I've thought of you as Andy for a long time, only I was brought up to respect authority and it seemed better to keep this particular correspondence on a formal footing. But this is the last, so I think I can safely drop all that formal respect stuff, don't you?

So tomorrow's your big day, the day you finally get to play God. It's been in all the papers and I'm looking forward to reading all about you in the Post's *souvenir edition tomorrow morning. Through the town you'll go, riding high, looking down on the ordinary folk and seeing everything. I've never doubted that God does see everything, but that just makes it worse, doesn't it? For seeing's not the same as caring, and priests and terrorists both favour black.*

I'm sorry. I mustn't ramble. It's just that I'm rather nervous. You see, I've decided tomorrow's my big day too. Don't worry. I'll hang around long enough to look out as you ride by in triumph. I wouldn't miss that, not for all the world, tower and town, forest and field! Then I'll slip quietly away and leave you in peace.

I'm not sure if you'll be reading this before or after the event. No post today, or tomorrow either, being a holiday, so I'll drop it in by hand. Are you the conscientious kind, I wonder, who'll look in to check things over, even on a Bank Holiday when you're on leave? I doubt it somehow! Not that it makes any difference as I'm not about to sign myself. That's for you to guess, though by this time tomorrow, you should have a clue even you can't miss!

I gather you did manage to clear up that other little puzzle. Did my pathetic suggestions help at all? Probably not. Probably, as usual, you did it all by yourself, you and your sidekicks, the pretty inspector and the ugly sergeant. The Holy Trinity! Three in One, and that One's you! And this is your day, isn't it? Trinity Sunday. Well, praise where it's due. But what about that other trinity, the ones you dug out of the concrete in your car park? Shouldn't we remember them today also? In fact, when we set your little triumph alongside the pain, the grief, the emptiness, the loss, that their discovery has caused, shouldn't we forget your triumph altogether and think of nothing else? What kind of world is it where things like this . . . but I'm sorry, we both know what kind of world it is, only you feel it's controllable, and I know it's out of control, and that's why I'm going to leave it while you ride by in triumphal majesty.

Goodbye, Andy Dalziel. Will you remember me? I doubt it. But try to remember in your triumph that you're not really a god.

Thanks for everything you've done.

Which is to say, thanks for doing nothing.

Except making it easy.

Chapter 1

Andrew Dalziel got out of his car, stretched, yawned, scratched, and critically examined the blue sky, the golden sun, the russet-bricked walls edged with a neatly tended border of green grass broken at regular intervals by quincunxes of orange marigolds. And he saw that it was good.

There was something about an old prison, even when declined into a mere remand centre, that brought comfort to the weariest soul, a sense of tried and tested purpose, a feeling of solidarity in a shifting world. Hither men had come to pay for their crimes, and paid, and hence returned to the society that had judged them, and thence more often than not returned again to this same spot in a cycle of crime and punishment, wrong and retribution, as endless and unremitting as all those other cycles of day and night, birth and death, Left and Right, Romantic and Classical, promotion and relegation, marriage and divorce, ingestion and defecation, permissiveness and puritanism, itching and scratching, whose centrifugal forces hold the timeless, limitless, meaningless universe together.

Some there were, of course, who had come to this place and never left it, but that was in other harsher days, though these too might yet return. Dalziel was no opponent of capital punishment, but he had little faith in those who administered justice. There was nowt wrong with hanging, he'd say, so long as judges too got hanged for their mistakes. But in case this should be regarded as a sort of crypto-liberalism, he also advocated that those responsible for putting crooks back on the streets should personally indemnify society against all their future depredations.

Tucked away at the back of the prison grounds was an area, entered through a wicket gate, which might have been mistaken for an old walled garden except that the walls were too high to admit any procreant sunlight and the earth too sour to nourish any but the hardiest weeds. Deep down here, dissolved in lime lest their rotting flesh should spread a moral corruption, the bodies of those executed in the good old days had been hidden away. Dalziel had been known to stroll at length within these walls, like a laird walking his policies, so deeply rapt that those glimpsing him got an impression that he was listening to some sage and serious conversation. And the truth was that he knew the names and histories of nearly every soul who rested here, and knew also that in his judgement a good proportion of them were almost certainly innocent of the crimes laid on them, hence his cynicism about the efficacy of the courts.

But this was not his destination this fine Monday morning. Nor was it his concern with the condemnation of innocence that brought him here.

Whatever his reasons, the prison authorities at all levels clearly felt it odd that a man couldn't find something better to do on a fine Bank Holiday Monday.

'Thought you were in this procession, Mr Dalziel,' said the officer who conducted him to the interview room. 'Mysteries or something, isn't it?'

'Aye, lad, you're right,' said Dalziel amiably. 'But we don't kick off till midday, so I thought I'd just pay a few calls first.'

'If you like it so much here, you can do my shift and I'll take your part,' laughed the officer.

'You're better off here, son,' advised Dalziel. 'Kick him up, will you?'

'Only if he wants,' said the officer primly. 'He doesn't have to come.'

'Don't worry. When you mention my name, he'll not be able to stay away.'

A few minutes later the door opened and Philip Swain came into the room. His short time in custody had already faded the healthy glow he had brought back with him from California, but it hadn't yet touched his old easy manner.

'Hello, Superintendent,' he said. 'What's up? Stage fright?'

'Hello, Mr Swain. How are they treating you?'

'All right. But I won't hide that I'll be glad to be out and back at Moscow.'

Dalziel smiled. Mockery, bravado, or genuine confidence, it was all one to him.

'Looking for bail, are you?' he said.

'Once you've completed your inquiries, you'll hardly oppose it again, surely?'

'Why not? Don't want you doing a bunk, do we?'

Swain smiled and said, 'Come on! If I wouldn't go to live abroad on a handsome salary, I'm scarcely going to slum it as a penniless fugitive.'

'So you *had* made your mind up not to take the Delgado job?' said Dalziel. 'Thought you were going to claim you and your missus were still debating? You'll need to remember your lines, lad. Not easy when you're up there with all eyes on you. I know.'

'What the hell do you want, Dalziel? I only agreed to see you to break the boredom, but I begin to suspect it would be less tedious in my cell.'

'Liar,' said Dalziel amicably. 'You came to hear what I

385

had to say 'cos despite what you think you think, and despite what you think your brief thinks, you won't really believe you're not going to be charged with murder till you hear it from me.'

Swain tried not quite successfully to look unconcerned.

'Look,' he said. 'I've confessed freely to what I've done wrong, and I'll take my punishment. But I'm not a murderer, and you know there's no evidence I'm a murderer, and I can't believe that British justice can make that sort of mistake.'

'Oh aye? There's a patch of ground not much more than a hundred yards from where we're sitting might make you change your tune,' said Dalziel. 'But let me put your mind at rest. That's why I'm here, you see. Bank Holiday Monday, sun shining, everyone out enjoying themselves, and I got to thinking about you, banged up in here, miserable, worried, not even able to ring your brief – he flew off yesterday to Barbados, I suppose you know that? Not short of a bob or two, them vultures. So here I am, errand of mercy, come to remove all doubt. Though that's a bit of a laugh really, isn't it? I mean doubt's what you want, isn't it? Doubt's your best friend.'

'What do you mean?' asked Swain long-sufferingly.

'Doubt, benefit of the, that's what I mean. To be given to accused prisoners by jaded juries. And you've got a lot to benefit from, Phil. Take your missus. You say it were an accident, and there's no evidence it wasn't. So, a doubt. Or Bev King. You say it were Waterson's idea and he carried it through after you changed your mind and tried to stop him. *Doubt*. Or Waterson himself. You say it must have been Arnie who killed him, out of gratitude to you and revulsion at the kind of man Waterson was. *Doubt*. And lastly, poor old Arnie. Got in the way of the JCB. Mebbe he didn't try hard enough to get out of the way because of all his guilt feelings. Anyroad, *doubt*. See what

I mean, Phil? Doubt's flavour of the month for you. And it's odd the way it works. Some might say that there's just too many deaths, that it goes way beyond coincidence, that benefit of doubt has got to stop somewhere. But juries don't think like that. It's addictive, doubt. Accept the Crown's got it wrong once, and next time it's that much easier; twice, and after that they're ready to think a trout in the milk got there by jumping out of the galley of a passing Concorde. So I reckon you've made it, Phil. I reckon the prosecution'll write off your wife and Arnie as accidents, accept you had nowt to do with Waterson's death, and slap your wrist for getting mixed up in the plot to kill King. Congratulations! I mean, they'll probably still send you down for a spell, but from what I've seen of you, I'm sure you can eat your porridge and come out smiling, specially when it's only Baby Bear's plate you've got to get through.'

He finished speaking and Swain studied his beaming face like a sailor still fearful of reefs between him and the sheltered harbour.

'Is this official, Superintendent?' he asked.

'It's better than official,' laughed Dalziel. 'It's what I think.'

Swain nodded and began to smile.

'Then that's good enough for me,' he said. 'I thank you for coming. It was an unexpected kindness.'

He stood up and extended his hand. Dalziel examined it for a moment, then grasped it firmly. For a few seconds the two men stood smile to smile, then Dalziel said, 'Only . . .'

'Only . . .?'

'Only it's a pity,' began Dalziel then broke off, shaking his head as though in regret. The smile left Swain's face. He tried to withdraw his hand but Dalziel's grip was not to be broken and slowly, without any obvious force exerted by the fat man, Swain found himself pressed back down into his chair.

'What are you talking about?' he gasped.

'It's a pity about the other body,' said Dalziel. 'I mean, you must have thought, like the Yanks say, if it's not broke, don't fix it. If there's no risk, why take precautions? If you've got certainty, who needs doubt? You can let go of my hand now, if you like, Phil. Don't want the screws talking, do we?'

'What the hell are you on about? What other body?' demanded Swain, nursing his bloodless hand.

'Young Tony Appleyard's, of course. I can see why you didn't bother much there, Phil. I mean, everything pointed so clearly to Arnie. Motive, opportunity, behaviour. And he even believed himself he'd done it!'

'He did do it! You bastard, what are you trying to pin on me? I don't need to listen to this. I want to talk to my solicitor!'

'Like I said, Phil, that'd either mean him coming back from Barbados, which he wouldn't like, or you going out there, which isn't convenient just at present. But of course you're free to terminate this interview any time you like. Just say the word. I can't stay much longer anyway. Got my public to think of. What's it to be?'

Swain made an effort to get control of himself and said, 'I think you're a bad loser, Dalziel, and this is just a little bit of compensatory sadism. But the telly's always lousy on a Bank Holiday, so I might as well let you entertain me for a while.'

Dalziel nodded approval.

'You know, Phil,' he said genially. 'I didn't like you at all when we first met, but recently you've grown on me. Like a polyp. I'll be almost sorry to cut you off. Right now, here's the case as I see it. Arnie came to you right enough, thinking he'd killed Appleyard. But all that

388

business of you agreeing to help, and your missus rowing with you because she overheard, was so much crap. No, what really made you sit up and take notice was when Arnie told you he'd been fighting with his son-in-law in your barn! Because that's where you'd dumped your missus when you killed her, probably the night before. So now you say you'll check up on the lad and you get out there pretty damn quick, and it's just as well you do, because young Appleyard was only stunned and he's just woken up in the corner where he fell and he's just realized he's not alone!'

Dalziel paused, shaking his head as though made speechless by his mental picture of the scene. Swain said thickly, 'This is pure fantasy.'

'Aye, it's fantastic all right,' said Dalziel. 'That's what the jury will have to understand, that two creatures as fantastic as you and Greg Waterson could exist. Between you, you'd just about have made a normal human being. But it was all you to start with. There you were with a witness to your wife's death, and back there in the house was a poor sod who thought he'd killed that witness. You must have thought the logic was inescapable, Phil. You picked up the nearest weapon, which happened to be an old broken-handled pitchfork, and you stuck it through that lad's throat. Good luck or good aim? Who knows? Down he went and back into the house you go to tell poor old Arnie, yes he was right, his son-in-law was dead.

'After that, well, we know the way it really was, Phil, and we know the way you say it was. Could be you'll still get away with it. Could be they'll even believe your missus died accidental, so you'll be able to keep the money. But it won't do you any good because you'll be serving a long, long time for the one killing you thought you need never worry about, the one you thought could never show up on your doorstep.'

389

'You're lying, Dalziel,' said Swain with some of his composure recovered. 'You haven't got the face for a bluff.'

'You think so? Oh, I see what you're getting at. You reckon because you took the precaution of having that barn cleared out, there can't be any physical evidence. Now that would be all right if only Joe Swindles had stuffed everything into his crusher. But he didn't, did he? I mean, he couldn't have, else how would I know about the pitchfork?'

He let Swain digest this for a moment, then added softly, 'And if you think that lying around Joe Swindles's yard all these weeks would mean there were no traces on the spike, think again. There's blood there right enough and it's the right group, you can take my word for it.'

As he spoke he gently caressed a large sticking plaster on the ball of his thumb.

Swain said, 'Why have you come here, Dalziel? Why are you telling me all this?'

Dalziel smiled and thought of all the things he wasn't telling Swain. He wasn't telling him that bats did not sleep consistently through their winter hibernation but woke up from time to time, because they were disturbed, or because of changes in temperature, or simply because they needed to get rid of the excess water created by the metabolizing of their fatty food reserves. Clever Pascoe to set Dr Death hunting for traces of bat piss! And clever Dr Death to find significantly larger traces on the woman's clothing than the youth's, suggesting that she'd been there first and longer. Gentry had also proved conclusively that Appleyard's neck wound could not have been made by any of the spikes on that harrow, not without some skin penetration by other spikes. But best of all had been the discovery during the search for the urine stains of a minute spot of Appleyard's blood on the woman's clothing, as if on waking he had first put his hand to his wounded head, then stretched it out to push himself upright and found himself touching a corpse.

He said with a broad smile, 'Don't expect I'll be seeing much of you alone after this, Phil. Don't you think I deserve a bit of a gloat? See you on Thursday. We've fixed the hearing bright and early so it won't interfere with my play-acting. We all miss you, by the way. Your stand-in's OK, but not a patch on you. Doesn't have the same feeling for the part!'

As he walked away in the golden summer sunlight, Dalziel continued smiling. He had no objection to a good gloat but he wouldn't have wasted such a lovely morning on that alone. He'd been delighted with the new case that Pascoe had dumped in his lap, but by now he'd come to have a very healthy respect for Swain's ability to twist and turn and bob and weave as new evidence came hurtling at him. He could imagine the man's mind back there wheeling round like a bat in an attic, sending out spirals of sound in its desperate effort to find an exit hole.

Yes, he'd wanted to gloat, but he'd also wanted to confuse. Carefully he peeled off the plaster to reveal the ball of his thumb unsullied by cut or scar. There had been a trace of blood on the point of the pitchfork, and it was the same group as Tony Appleyard's. But that was not the same group as Dalziel's. When you're dealing with clever buggers don't play them at their own game was a lesson he'd learned the hard way. But there was no harm in giving them something to be clever about!

Now it was all in the hands of the lawyers.

And of God too, of course.

He glanced at his watch. Chung would be getting impatient.

He took a deep breath of the good air and went to begin the Creation.

391

Chapter 2

The letter lay unnoticed in the centre of Dalziel's for once uncluttered desk till the middle of the morning when Pascoe walked into the room.

So far it had been a relatively quiet day but the town was filling up rapidly. Already the central car parks were turning away disgruntled motorists and soon the pubs would be open. No doubt five hundred years ago the authorities were faced with similar problems of public merriment fomenting public disorder and holiday crowds inviting holiday crime, but Pascoe for once found no comfort in a sense of historical continuity. If the Mysteries had stayed in the Middle Ages where they belonged, and all these trippers had stopped at home to watch Bank Holiday sport on the telly, life for Mid-Yorkshire's finest would have been so much easier.

Or am I merely bottling out at the thought of being in charge of the shop? he asked himself. It was funny; he had been absolutely certain Dalziel would not be able to resist popping in to check that all was well, and he'd been ready to greet him with a nice line in sarcastic exasperation. But now with the procession due off at midday, it didn't seem likely the fat man would show, and Pascoe found he was experiencing a reaction distressingly like disappointment.

Perhaps, he thought as he opened the door of the Super's office, perhaps I have not really come up here in search of the file I suspect Fat Andy has abstracted from my cabinet, but to inhale his aura. The thought was so disgusting he almost turned on his heel. Then he noticed the letter.

Even upside down he recognized the typing. He didn't

touch it but walked slowly round the desk till he could see it the right way up. It was addressed to Detective-Superintendent Andrew Dalziel, Head of CID, Mid-Yorkshire Constabulary. In the top left hand corner was typed the word PERSONAL. It bore no stamp.

He picked up the phone and buzzed the desk.

'There's a letter on Mr Dalziel's desk,' he said. 'When did it come?'

There was a pause for consultation, then Sergeant Broomfield came on.

'Came through the box first thing,' he said. 'About half seven. No one saw anyone posting it. Said "Personal", so I stuck it in the Super's room. Thought he'd have looked in this morning some time. Usually does when he's on leave, unless he's at least a hundred miles away.'

'Yes, I know,' said Pascoe. 'Thanks, George.'

He replaced the receiver and sat down. After a moment he picked up the letter and opened it.

He read it twice then reached for the phone again.

'Central Hospital.'

He gave Pottle's extension but the voice that answered was not Pottle's.

'I'm afraid the doctor's not here today.'

'Can I get him at home? It's urgent.'

'No, I'm sorry. He's at a conference in Strasbourg. Can I help?'

'No,' said Pascoe. He put the phone down and read the letter again. There was no time to fill anyone else in, but another mind would have been so good to interpret these words – and to share the burden he felt they placed upon him. He wished now he'd shown the letters to Ellie. He wished Dalziel was here to take his share of responsibility. Which was large. Huge, in fact. For that was what the letter was about, wasn't it? Telling Dalziel he'd failed.

He recalled now what Pottle had said about the suicide

as gamester, offering life as a stake. The psychiatrist had suggested that the reasons alleged for the choice of Dalziel as correspondent might be fallacious. It wasn't his reputation of being too hard to be upset by the letters that had made him the candidate, but his fame as a detective, a man who walked through brick walls as he headed for the truth.

Here in this last letter the Dark Lady had let the veil fall, not from her identity but from her feelings. It was a bitter letter, full of implied reproach. Gone was the tone of grateful respect, to be replaced by a more accusatory almost sneering note. And he was lumped in it with Dalziel. The pretty inspector and the ugly sergeant making up a Holy Trinity, sharing in the same triumphs, the same failures . . . That was unfair, she hadn't chosen to write to him, it wasn't his . . . Angrily he pushed aside these time-wasting justifications. He was the one with the letter before him, a letter which stated that the Dark Lady was going to kill herself that very day. No one else could stop her, that was certain. It was down to him. But how? He recalled something else that Pottle had said. Any clues she offered were likely to be such clues as a policeman might interpret. It was time to ignore distress, guilt, anger; time to be a cop.

He read through the letter one more time.

He felt he knew this woman. He could infer acquaintance from the letter, though of course it would be possible for her to know him but not vice versa. In that case there was no hope. So start from the premise that he knew her. She mentioned Wield also. The ugly sergeant. And she referred to a specific case. The Swain case. There were two women involved there, both with considerable cause to feel disenchanted with life. He reviewed them clinically in his mind. Shirley Appleyard was the younger, but he'd always felt a mature strength there. And she had a child to hang on to.

Pam Waterson was strong too. But her personal tragedy would be compounded by hard work and long hours in an environment full of death, decay, disease . . .

He reached for the phone and dialled the number of the Infirmary.

Mrs Waterson was not on duty, he was told. Next he dialled the nurses' annexe. After some time, a woman's voice answered the communal phone. Yes, she thought Pam was in. She'd give her a knock. A couple of minutes later she came back on. Sorry, she must have been mistaken. There was no reply.

And she rang off before Pascoe could make up his mind whether his fears were strong enough to demand that she immediately raised the alarm.

But he couldn't spend any more time in abstract speculation. Picking up the letter, he set off back to his own room where he grabbed the complete Dark Lady file. As he made for the door, Wield came in, his face contorted in a smile.

'Have you seen this?' he said, waving the *Post*'s souvenir edition in Pascoe's face. 'It's got a photo of the Super in it. Makes him look like Old Mother Riley!'

Pascoe ignored the paper and bore the sergeant with him along the corridor, down the stairway and out into the car park which still bore its scars like a British heavyweight. In the car, the puzzled Wield read the letter as Pascoe explained where they were going. He'd heard Pascoe refer to the case but this was the first time he'd actually seen one of the letters and he was clearly puzzled by the Chief Inspector's agitation.

'Is there something in the rest of this lot which makes you think it could be her?' he said.

'Yes. I don't know. Maybe. I can't take the risk, you see that?'

'I see you'd want to stop her. Yes, obviously. I mean,

its obvious you'd want to stop her, though not necessarily obvious you should . . .'

Pascoe turned angry eyes on Wield and said, 'Don't give me any crap about free choice! Read those letters. There's no free choice there. She's been driven . . .'

'Yes, all right,' said the sergeant soothingly. 'I wasn't meaning to debate morality. Only to say, well, I can't see why you're taking it so personal. It's not even like it's you she's been writing to . . .'

'She wants to be found, she wants to be stopped, I know she does!' interrupted Pascoe. 'All right, she made the wrong choice with Dalziel, but she got a second chance with me, and what have I done?'

'A damn sight more than anyone else would have, from the sound of it. You've nowt to reproach yourself with.'

'Haven't I? All right, I've gone through the motions, but what's it amounted to? Nothing. A façade. At least Andy was open. Chuck them aside. They're an irrelevance. It's the Samaritans she should be writing to. If she wants police time, let her go out and commit an indictable offence! So on he boldly goes, passing by on the other side. While me, I pussyfoot down the middle of the road, a bit closer to the action maybe, but not getting close enough to actually do any good.

They had reached the Infirmary grounds. He ignored all signs diverting him to car parks, and drove straight up to the nurses' annexe. Leaving the car door wide open behind him, he rushed inside and bounded up the stairs, two at a time. Despite his efforts to keep pace, Wield was left behind. He had never seen Pascoe so agitated before. By thought association he recalled his recent comment that he had never seen Dalziel so obsessed before. One with punishment, the other with protection. The twin poles of policing. Pascoe, Dalziel, as far apart as you could get, but with a world in precarious balance between them . . .

what the hell was he doing with a head full of philosophical waffle when he should be concentrating on (a) stopping Pascoe from making a fool of himself and (b) stopping himself from inducing a heart attack?

Breathless, he reached the second landing. Already he could hear Pascoe hammering on a door, calling, 'Mrs Waterson! Pamela! Are you in there?' Other doors had opened and heads were peering out. Pascoe seemed unaware of them. As Wield joined him, he said, 'We'll have to break it down. I know she's in there. I just know!'

And Wield, observing over Pascoe's shoulder the door handle beginning to turn, said, 'Yes, I believe you're right.'

The door was flung open. Pam Waterson stood there with a dressing-gown held tight around her body. Her eyes were bright with anger.

'What the hell's going on?' she demanded.

Pascoe turned and looked at her with an amazement too strong to be as yet compounded with relief. Indeed, to find his certainty proved so unarguably delusive amounted almost to a disappointment.

He said, 'Are you all right? I thought . . .'

'Yes, of course I'm all right.' She glanced along the corridor at the line of curious heads protruding from each doorway like a colonnade of caryatids. 'Come in and see for yourself if you must.'

This invitation puzzled Wield until he stepped into the flat and a man's voice said, 'Pam, what's going on?'

It was Ellison Marwood experiencing the difficulty of the newly awoken in pulling on a pair of trousers. Pam Waterson had obviously decided that inviting them in was the lesser of two perils when the other was the risk of Marwood displaying himself thus to that gauntlet of eyes.

'I'm sorry. It's nothing. I thought . . .'

Pascoe was doing a bad job, and Wield, who knew the

value of presenting a stolid official face on occasions, said, 'We had reason to suspect that a woman as yet unknown to us might be at risk, and we wished to eliminate Mrs Waterson from our inquiries.'

This stiff formula calmed things down for a second while they prised some meaning from it.

'At risk from me?' demanded Marwood.

'Don't be daft,' said the woman. 'You mean she's going to harm herself, don't you?'

'Yes, I'm sorry,' said Pascoe, still floundering.

'You haven't written any letters to the police, have you, Mrs Waterson?' said Wield, still playing it official.

'No, I haven't.'

'Hey, this is outrageous, you know that?' intervened Marwood, putting on indignation with his clothes. 'What are you suggesting? What right do you think you've got, bursting in here and telling Pam she's some sort of nut case . . .'

'Be quiet, Ellison,' she said. 'They didn't burst in. And there have been times recently when I thought . . . well, never mind what I thought. But I haven't written any letters. And I'm going to be OK, believe me. Greg almost ruined my life when he was alive. I promise you, he's not going to finish the job now he's dead.'

She lit a cigarette and drew on it long and deep.

Marwood said, 'You said you'd give those things up.'

'No. That's what you said,' stated Pam Waterson. 'Which is not, and is never going to be, the same thing.'

It was time to go and let this little skirmish either explode into war or implode into bed.

'Come on, sir,' said Wield to Pascoe. 'Didn't you say you wanted to check Mrs Appleyard?'

'What? Oh yes.'

'Appleyard?' said Marwood, glad of a diversion which without dishonour might allow him to back off from the tobacco war. 'Shirley Appleyard, the Stringer girl? Is she on your list too? Well, tough tittie again, boys. Her mother was admitted late last night and last I saw, young Shirley was sitting by her bedside in Ward seventeen.'

They left. Pascoe needed to check, of course, but this time Wield had no difficulty in convincing him to take a less precipitate approach.

The ward sister told them that Mrs Stringer had been admitted for observation after collapsing the previous evening. So far no specific medical condition had been diagnosed beyond that covered by the vague term nervous exhaustion. Her daughter had brought her in, stayed till satisfied there was no immediate danger, gone home to look after her child, and returned that morning.

As they spoke the girl herself appeared. Her eyes took in Pascoe and Wield but she made no sign of recognition as she said to the nurse, 'She's sleeping again. I'll head home now. I've got a neighbour looking after Antony and I don't like to impose. But I'll be back later.'

'Fine,' said the nurse. 'Don't worry. She's in good hands.'

Shirley Appleyard nodded and walked away. The two policemen, taken by surprise, had to hurry to catch up with her.

'Mrs Appleyard, could we have a word?' said Pascoe.

'I thought we were done with you lot, till the trial anyway,' said the woman, still walking.

'Yes, I'm sorry. And I'm sorry about your mother too. I'm glad it doesn't sound too serious.'

'No? If she'd lost a leg, would that sound serious?'

'Yes, of course, but . . .'

'Well, she's lost something that's left a far bigger gap!'

She halted and swung round to confront Pascoe. For a moment she looked ready to explode in anger, then she took a deep breath and resumed control.

'I'm sorry,' she said. 'I shouldn't take it out on you. I'd no idea either. I was stupid and thought that once she got over the first shock, she'd really be able to relax and start enjoying life now Dad had gone. I thought I'd have the much bigger gap because Tony and me were young and I still had some daft romantic notions hidden away. Shows what I know, doesn't it? I tried to feel properly upset when I found out Tony were dead, but a sort of relief kept on breaking in; not relief that he was dead, I didn't want that, but relief that I didn't need to wonder what was going on any more. Mam, though, well, she'd had to put up with Dad for over twenty years, at least that's how I saw it. But it wasn't just putting up, there was a lot more to it than that. I never realized, and there I was telling her to buck up and enjoy life, like she'd just won first dividend on the pools, and all the time . . .'

She shook her head in self-rebuke.

'That's the way anyone would have seen it, believe me,' said Pascoe earnestly.

'It'd be nice to think so,' said the girl. 'But it's not true. I was moaning on about her yesterday to this old girl I met at the Kemble. That Chung asked me to do some poster-work, did you know that? And then I got on helping with other things like painting backcloths and so on. There were lots of other people there, she's really marvellous at getting people to help, and I mean, normally I'd not have done more than say hello to someone like this Mrs Horncastle, she's a Canon's wife and talks dead posh, but that doesn't matter when you're around Chung, and I found myself moaning on about Mam not being able to jolly herself up. She didn't say a lot but she must have had a word with Chung, 'cos next thing she's working alongside me and talking about Mam, and suddenly I was seeing things in a completely different way. Funny, isn't it? She only met her the once and she seemed to know more about her than I did! When I got home last night, I started talking to Mam, really talking *to* her, not at her, and suddenly she started talking back like I'd never heard before, on and on and on, just one great flood. Something like that's supposed to make you better, I always thought, getting it out of the system, that sort of thing. Only it wasn't like that. She went through the whole of their life together, good and bad, and it left her exhausted, more than exhausted, collapsed. I thought she'd had an attack and I rang the doctor and he got her in here. They say there's nowt specific, it's just that she's been hanging on, using all her strength just to hang on, and I never saw it, I never saw . . .'

There were tears in her eyes. Pascoe took her arm and squeezed it, helplessly. His distress seemed to act homeopathically on hers, for she recovered her composure almost instantly and said, 'Anyroad, what are you two after now?'

Pascoe glanced at Wield then said, 'Nothing. Really, there was just a medical query to clear up, that's all, then someone told us about your mother . . .'

'Is that it? Then I'll be off. I don't want to get stuck in the crowds. I'd have thought you two would have been out cheering your boss.'

Pascoe grinned and said, 'Oh, we do that all the time. Aren't you going to watch, especially now you're involved?'

She shook her head and said, 'Later perhaps, but not today. Though I could have had a ringside seat. This Mrs Horncastle invited me to go along and sit in her bedroom window overlooking the Close. The wagons will pass right outside, she said, and we would have been just on a level with Mr Dalziel. Not every day you get to be on a level with God, is it? I might have gone, but not with Mam coming in here. Look, I'll have to rush. See you.'

401

She hurried away, a young woman vital and strong, with a capacity to love and bear, and a will to survive the most devastating wreck of her hopes.

'You didn't ask about the letters,' said Wield.

'I think I did,' said Pascoe. 'But listen, did you hear what she said about Mrs Horncastle?'

'The Canon's wife? Aye, she said she offered her a seat in her bedroom. I never thought of the Super being so high he could peer into folks' bedroom windows. I bet he gives some poor sods a nasty shock!'

Pascoe didn't smile. He said, 'In that last letter it said something about looking out at Dalziel as he passed, didn't it?'

'Yes, I think it did,' said Wield. 'But it was just a manner of speaking, wasn't it? And even if it wasn't, we can't really check on everyone who's got a house overlooking the procession route, can we?'

'We can check on Mrs Horncastle.'

Wield looked at Pascoe as though he thought he had finally gone mad.

'Look,' he said. 'I can see this is bothering you, but we can't just go around bursting in on folk to see if they're about to top themselves. All right, these two, there was mebbe some real cause for concern, but this Canon's wife . . . How well do you know her anyway?'

'I've only met her a couple of times,' admitted Pascoe. 'But it sticks out like a sore thumb that she's not a happy woman.'

'That covers a hell of a lot of people,' said Wield. 'And if she's so miserable she's going to top herself after the Super rides by, why'd she invite young Shirley up to share the view?'

'So she wouldn't be able to do it,' said Pascoe. 'It fits with what Pottle said, a sort of gamble. And she was at the ball and didn't get asked to dance. And she's in a position to know the religious calendar inside out and she laughed like a drain when I told her Dalziel was short-listed for God and there was that dream about her dog . . .'

They were almost at the trot again as they headed for the main exit from the Infirmary. Wield gasped, 'I don't understand half what you're on about . . .'

'If you bothered to read the file, perhaps you would,' barked Pascoe in a reprimand as unfair as any ever hurled by Dalziel at a shell-shocked subordinate.

Wield registered, assessed, forgave, and, once back in the car, he turned to the beginning of the file and began a slow analytical examination of the letters.

He was interrupted after only half a minute.

'That paper of yours, does it have a pageant timetable?'

'I think so. Yes, here it is. Let's see . . . the first wagon, that's Mr Dalziel's, should be leaving the market place now and heading towards the close, due there in about fifteen minutes.

'Right,' said Pascoe, and Wield returned to the Dark Lady.

They made good progress through quiet back streets, but as they neared the close, holiday crowds and traffic diverted from the pageant route began to clog their way. Finally they were halted by an irritated uniformed policeman who stooped to the window and said, 'Can't you bloody well read? It's all closed to traffic up ahead till the pageant's passed. You'll have to back up and . . .'

He finally became aware that what Pascoe was waving at him wasn't a driving licence.

'Sorry, sir,' he said. 'Didn't recognize you. Thing is, the road ahead's . . .'

'Just get us through!' grated Pascoe.

A few moments later by dislodging angry sightseers from hard won vantage-points, the constable got them through on to the actual pageant route. Away to his left

Pascoe glimpsed the head of the procession. Chung might have held back on the Nubian slaves, but otherwise she'd gone the whole hog in search of God's plenty. Dalziel's wagon must be a good ten minutes behind, which meant it wouldn't be passing between the cathedral and the Canon's house for almost half an hour. He relaxed a little.

Beside him Wield was deeply immersed in the letter file. There were things here that were bothering him and he was beginning to share something of Pascoe's sense of urgency, but he kept it under control. This was a time for cold analysis. Pointless two of them going off half-cocked.

As they passed through the gateless gateway of the close, they were greeted by ironic cheers from the pressing crowds who, expecting God on top of a machine, were amused to be offered a pair of mere mortals in a dusty Sierra. Once more an angry policeman intercepted them, but this one recognized them before he opened his mouth.

'Park this somewhere nice and safe, lad,' ordered Pascoe, climbing out. 'I'll be in Canon Horncastle's house. Come on, Wieldy.'

Clutching the file and his newspaper, Wield found himself once more in pursuit of Pascoe who was shouldering his way through the crowd like an All Black in sight of the line. He caught up with him at the forbidding entrance to a dark narrow house right opposite the Great Tower of the Cathedral.

'Peter,' he said. 'There's something . . .'

But the door was already opening in response to Pascoe's imperious knocking, and a dark clad figure confronted them with the amazed scorn of a Victorian butler finding trade on his front step.

'What on earth is the meaning of this din?' demanded Canon Horncastle.

'Police,' said Pascoe. 'May we come in?'

As his request was spoken over his shoulder, it seemed

to Wield a little redundant. The Canon thought so too, for his thin face flushed like pack ice during a seal hunt and he cried, 'How dare you force your way into my house like this!'

'I'd like to speak to your wife, sir,' said Pascoe.

'My wife!' exclaimed Horncastle as though Pascoe had made an indecent suggestion. 'I assure you of this, Inspector or whatever you are, you will not speak to my wife without a considerably more detailed account of your reasons than you have yet given me.'

'Thank you for being so protective, Eustace, but I think I'm of an age to make my own decisions.'

The voice came from the head of a brown varnished stairway rising out of the gloomy hall which despite the warmth of the day outside contrived to be damp and chilly. The woman was silhouetted against the light of a landing window and for all Wield could see, she might indeed have been clutching a poison bottle in one hand while with the other she pressed a dagger through her bloodstained nightgown into her ravaged heart. Such Gothic notions seemed entirely appropriate to this sepulchral house and its cadaverous master, but in the event as she descended she proved to be wearing a light grey twinset and a tweedy skirt and carrying nothing more sinister than a pair of spectacles.

Pascoe advanced to meet her. For the third time in the space of less than an hour he was faced with the delicate task of finding out if the woman he was speaking to was on the point of killing herself. With Pam Waterson, he had put the question more or less direct. With Shirley Appleyard he had let his own observations give him the answer. What would be his approach this time? Wield asked himself.

'Could we have a word alone, Mrs Horncastle?' he asked.

'No, you could not.' It was the Canon, his voice thin and dangerous. 'Anything you have to say to my wife will be said in front of me.'

Pascoe scratched his ear and looked interrogatively at the woman. He had no doubt that the Canon opposed the ordination of women and probably didn't much care to see them hatless in church, but this attempt at domestic domination was straight out of Trollope! Surely Victorian values stopped somewhere short of this?

But the woman surprised him.

'Eustace is of course right, Mr Pascoe,' she said quietly. 'There is nothing which can be said to me nor anything which I might say in reply that I would wish to keep from his ears.'

This was either total submission or . . . could it be total war? He looked into her calm features, but found no clue there. Suddenly, however, he was ninety per cent certain she was not his Dark Lady, but he couldn't back off without the missing tenth.

He said, 'Mrs Horncastle, have you ever written any letters to Chief Superintendent Dalziel?'

'No,' she said. 'I have not.'

Her voice carried conviction. But she would say that, wouldn't she? He had to press on.

'These letters were unsigned,' he said.

She saw his drift immediately and half smiled. 'I see you think my association with the Church might have turned me Jesuitical. But no, when I say I have never written to Mr Dalziel, I mean I have never written to him using my own name, or anyone else's name or no name at all. Does that satisfy you?'

Before Pascoe could reply, the Canon's fragile patience snapped.

'This is truly beyond belief,' he cried. 'The Chief Constable shall be apprised of this outrage. How dare you force your way into my house and accuse my wife of writing abusive anonymous letters?'

'I'm sorry, sir, but I've accused your wife of nothing. And why should you think the letters were abusive?'

'Because I have no doubt that that gross man invites his fair share of abuse!' snapped Horncastle. 'If not abusive, then what?'

· 'That's a good question, Eustace,' said his wife approvingly. 'I should be interested to know what I might be thought capable of, Mr Pascoe. So tell me. Is the correspondence threatening? Inflammatory? Obscene?'

The Canon looked ready to explode again but Pascoe got in quickly, 'In a way, threatening,' he said. 'But not against the Super. Against the writer herself.'

'You mean a threat of suicide?' said Mrs Horncastle. 'The poor woman. I hope with all my heart you find her.'

'You've come here to accuse my wife of threatening suicide?' exclaimed the Canon, attaining a new level of incredulous indignation which his wife obviously felt required explaining.

'There is a special opprobrium attached to suicide in the Church's scale of sins,' she said, in a pedagogic tone. 'My husband would, I think, have preferred obscenity.'

'Dorothy, what has got into you?' said Horncastle in genuine as well as rhetorical amazement. 'I think it best if you go through into the drawing-room while I remove these people from the premises.'

'No, thank you, Eustace,' she said. 'I shall see Mr Pascoe and his friend out. Then I shall return to my room to watch the procession pass. I wouldn't miss it for worlds. I've been helping Chung, you know, Mr Pascoe. I met your wife on several occasions and I enjoyed her company very much.'

'I'm glad,' smiled Pascoe.

'Dorothy! Did you hear what I said? The drawing-room. At once. I have a great deal I want to say to you.'

The Canon looked more animated than Pascoe had ever seen him.

His wife said thoughtfully, 'And I have something I want to say to you, dear. Chung said the time would come and I didn't really believe her. But she was right, I think. She's truly marvellous, isn't she, Mr Pascoe? Without her, I might indeed have been writing letters, if not to Mr Dalziel, certainly on the same subject as that poor woman.'

'Dorothy, do you hear me? I forbid you to go on talking to this man!'

It was the last desperate cry of a shaman who begins to suspect his magic staff has got dry rot.

Dorothy Horncastle wrinkled her nostrils like an animal testing the wind for danger. Then she smiled joyously.

'I hear you, Eustace,' she said. 'But I'm afraid I can no longer obey. Let me see; what was it that Chung said? Oh yes . . . I remember. Eustace, why don't you go and screw yourself?'

It was a magic moment but it was flawed for Pascoe by being the moment also when any last scintilla of doubt vanished. Dorothy Horncastle was not the Dark Lady. Which meant if the threat of that last letter were serious that he had failed.

He wasn't even permitted to watch the final collapse of the Canon whose self-image was fracturing like a cartoon cat running into a brick wall. Wield was pulling at his arm and saying urgently, 'I think there's something you ought to take a look at. I dare say it's nowt as you must've seen it already, only after reading them letters, well, it fits so well . . .'

He was thrusting the *Evening Post* souvenir edition into Pascoe's hands.

Pascoe read, impatiently at first, and then incredulously; and for a while the disbelief on his face brought relief to Wield's.

Then he seized the Dark Lady file from Wield's hands and began to riffle through it.

'No, it can't be,' he said. 'It can't.'

He took out the last letter and scanned it despairingly.

'Mrs Horncastle,' he said. 'These words, *not for all the world, tower and town, forest and field*, do they mean anything to you?'

'They sound familiar,' said the woman. 'Let me see. Yes, I'm pretty sure they are from one of the Mystery plays. That's right. The Temptation. The Devil takes Christ up to the top of the Temple and first of all tells him to prove his godhead by jumping. Then he claims to have all the world to wield, that is to rule, tower and town, forest and field, and offers this to Christ in return for his homage.'

'The top of the Temple, you say? Oh God,' cried Pascoe. 'Oh God.'

Chapter 3

Once more they were running, forcing their way through the dense-packed crowds and across the narrow street up which a roar came funnelling like a tidal bore to signal the passage of the procession through the old gateway into the close.

The cathedral steps were crowded and the great oak doors with their double frieze of intricate carving in which the sacred was embraced by the profane, were firmly shut. Wield split off to the left, Pascoe to the right, and for once the symbols proved correct for within a few seconds of leaving the crowds behind as he explored behind the view-defying buttresses along the side of the building, he found a small low door which yielded to his touch.

Inside, it was dark and still, with an impression of something waiting and listening, as though the great old church was straining to catch the sound of the approaching procession which it had not heard for over a hundred years.

No time for fanciful reflection, none for respect either. He sprinted with sacrilegious haste down a side aisle through a disapproving forest of columns till he reached the doorway to the Great Tower. This too was open, and from vast space filled with vibrations of infinity, he moved into the stifling confines of a spiral stair filled only with the heat and harsh rasp of his own breathing.

It was a totally enclosed stairway with no lucent points of reference, and after a couple of moments Pascoe felt as if he were running on a treadmill, ever aspiring, ever low. But his mind was fuelled with fragments of thought which kept his legs pumping away.

. . . her father was a Scot who went to Malaya as a young padre during the troubles of the post-war era . . . for a serving officer to marry a Chinese girl at this time, perhaps at any time, was an act of social self-destruction. . .

Self-destruction. He knew all about self-destruction! Why hadn't he shown more interest in Ellie's article? Why hadn't he encouraged her to talk about it?

. . . the family moved to the UK after Malaya achieved independence . . . the Reverend Graham obtained a sprawling parish in west Birmingham . . . what his parishioners thought when they first met their new vicar's wife and young daughter is not recorded . . .

Suddenly there was light. The spiral broke on a narrow landing at the furthermost point of which was a small lancet window, scarcely more than a loophole really, but

410

it admitted the blessed gold of the sun. He staggered to it, sucking at the fresh air. It was too narrow and the wall too thick to let him look down, but he could see straight out over the roofs of the town and so gauge how disappointingly low he still was. He turned his back on the light and plunged again into the timeless spaceless hopeless helix.

. . . at boarding-school she started acting . . . her greatest joy was in the holidays when she went on camping trips with her parents in the Border country which had been her father's birthplace . . .

It was he decided a nightmare. He was not really here, he was safe in bed at home, and one last thrust of his aching legs would drive him through the surface of this awful dream into the familiar world of the warm duvet, the white curtains with the blue flowers silhouetted by the first rays of dawn, and by his side, Ellie, soft-breathing, as neat and orderly in sleep as she was loose-limbed and sprawling awake, as though all her natural rebelliousness vanished when she closed her eyes and some deep-seated longing for order and conformity took over. Ellie, whose souvenir article he should have been the first to read, who had been picked to write it so that he would be the first!

. . . she was eighteen and just about to start drama school when her mother died. It was her father's suggestion that she should take her mother's name. 'Eileen Chung,' he told her, 'will be able to get away with things that Eileen Graham never could!' But, Chung adds, they both knew it wasn't just a showbiz decision. It was a way of extending the dead woman's existence for both of them . . .

Light again! The surface of the dream or the surface of reality was close. This light seeped down from above and grew stronger with every muscle-straining step. Up there somewhere was an open door. But open on to what?

. . . at twenty-six she was devastated when her father

411

died, and she threw herself into her work with that unre-mitting energy which is the hallmark of everything she does . . . How old is Chung? I'm afraid that I cannot tell you, for in the only bit of coyness I encountered in this refresh-ingly frank and open woman, she refused to say! And why would she? For everyone who knows her is agreed that, like the great dramas she produces, time is meaningless in the case of someone as complete, as talented, as unique as Eileen Chung. We in Mid-Yorkshire are very lucky to have her. We should take care that we treasure her according to her worth, and when, as they surely will, pressures come upon her to leave us for new challenges elsewhere, we owe it to ourselves to make it very hard for her to go . . .

He burst through the doorway into the dazzle of the midday sun and reeled with the heat and the light and the joy of it. He caught at the door frame to steady himself and closed his eyes. When he opened them again, he was still and no longer dazzled. And he was looking at Chung.

She was leaning backwards against the shallow parapet, looking towards him with a welcoming smile, beautiful beyond the scope of brush or pen.

She called, 'Hello, Pete, baby. I was beginning to think no one would make it.'

'Chung. Hi.'

He began to move towards her. She shook her head slightly. He stopped.

'Chung,' he said. 'There's no need for this.'

'Need for what? I'm just enjoying the best view in town. Will you listen to those cheers? They're just loving it, aren't they? And why not? It's just another show, a change from the telly. Let's go out and have a laugh at the God on wheels! Perhaps he'll give a wave as he passes! Do you think he'll give us a wave, Peter? Probably not. God doesn't need to look up, does he? What's the point when everything's below?'

Beneath the lightness, he sensed desperation. He said urgently, 'He did his best!'

'You're very loyal, Pete. I knew you wouldn't be right for Lucifer. Treachery's not your style. But no, he didn't do his best. You know it, I know it. But I'm not saying he deceived me. I managed that all by myself. I said I picked him because he wouldn't give a damn, so I can hardly complain about being right!'

Pascoe examined this and thought he saw a glimmer of hope.

'Chung, if you know it's a game, I mean, not a game, I realize it's deadly serious, but a gamble, a life and death gamble, if you know that . . .'

'Why does a bright girl like me carry on with it?' She laughed and then turned serious. 'Pete, the *me* that thinks it's in control never meant to lay this thing on Andy. That *me* was telling the truth in those letters. But there's another *me* . . . look, it's like when you're acting sometimes, something takes over, you become the part you're playing even though you know you're out there on a stage. What I mean is, if you're in my game, there's no problem to being two or three contradictory things at the same time!'

He tried another small step forward. She didn't seem to notice, but there was still twenty feet between them. He could hear the sound of shawms and timbrels in the wind, and he thought he could trace Dalziel's approach in the swell of applause.

He said, 'OK, it's not simply a game, but that doesn't entitle you to cheat.'

'What do you mean?'

'You said Andy never asked you to dance at the ball. Hell, your tango nearly stopped the show!'

'Not guilty!' she replied. 'It was *me* who asked *him*, the first time anyway. After that he just grabbed me. So it was

413

subtle misdirection, not cheating. No point in making things too easy for the great detective, was there? Not that I need have bothered, for all the interest he took.'

It was time for a change of direction. By talking about the game, he was merely playing the game. She was peering over the parapet and he moved slowly forward, saying, 'OK, so he had a lot of other things on his mind. But he did pass the case on to me, you know that. It's my responsibility now. Please don't make it my guilt.'

She turned to look at him, catching him in mid-step. He froze for a moment, like a child playing statues, then under her quizzical gaze smiled sheepishly and lowered his foot to the ground.

She said, 'I like you, Pete. Always have done. If Ellie hadn't been such a good friend, who knows? But fucking's easy, and friends are hard to find. You should bear that in mind. Sometimes being nice and reasonable can make a person just as self-absorbed as being a real selfish bastard. Take a day off, Pete, and let it all hang out! Let Ellie know if she gets right up your nose or if some little scrubber in the pub with her skirt round her bum gets you horny. She'll probably break your jaw but at least you'll know why you're hurting. There's no profit in partial openness. If it's not wide open, it might as well be locked. Was that in a play or did I say it? It gets hard to tell sometimes.'

'I don't know,' said Pascoe, trying for a matching lightness. 'But it didn't sound like Shakespeare.'

'No? Think you know your Shakespeare, huh?'

'Better than I know my Mysteries.'

'Well, this week's your chance to learn! Though I'm not sure if it's worth it.'

She was no longer looking at him, but even as he tensed his muscles for an explosive sprint, she leaned far out over the parapet in her effort to follow the progress of the

414

pageant wagon which sounded to be passing right in front of the cathedral. In that position, he didn't even dare essay another small step.

'Surely any learning experience is worth it?' he said.

She pulled herself back to the vertical and his pulse returned to a mere fifty per cent above normal.

'Depends what you learn in the end,' she said. 'It's a funny thing about plays, Pete. They're all about pain, did you know that? Even the comedies; *especially* the comedies. *They* end in union, tragedy in separation, because that's the only answer we've found. I know about separation. Mummy died when I was eighteen, Daddy when I was twenty-six. This surprises you, don't it, Pete? Big girl like me missing her mummy and daddy? But I was nothing and nowhere without them. And I never found anyone else, because I seemed to get too busy with other people finding me. The world's full of shit, Peter. Read the papers, watch the box, it's coming thick and fast from all sides and it's getting worse. You stick to Ellie, hon. Two people clinging together get to ward off some of the crap for a while at least. That's all that comedy is, a tragedy postponed!'

He could see her cracking up before him with pain and despair showing through. It was more than he could bear, yet within his own pain he felt an admixture of resentment. Chung shouldn't be like this, not Chung who had come among them like a goddess, asking nothing but worship for her healing touch.

He took another step and said urgently, 'Isn't it possible to make sense of it? Isn't that what all these plays and books and works of art are about?'

'You reckon?' she said. 'So what's to do when you realize that all that Shakespeare can offer us in the end is resignation? And all that the Mysteries can offer is . . . mystery.'

'Chung, for God's sake, I mean, for my sake, for our sakes. Whatever you feel, we love you, we need you.'

'Love,' she said. 'Need.' As if they were foreign words.

Far below, the noise of the crowd reached a climax as Dalziel arrived. Then suddenly Chung smiled and in an instant was herself again, beautiful, and strong.

'Jesus, Pete, you look terrible! Look, it's OK, baby. No need to come rushing over here to make a grab at me! You don't really think I'd let someone I like as much as you watch me jump, do you? Come on! God's passing by, the show's nearly over. Time to start planning the next one, huh? I'm really glad you're here, though. Would you mind leading the way down those nasty stairs? They really give me the creeps. You'll never believe this, but I'm terrified of falling!'

She moved away from the parapet, laughing joyously, and Pascoe, his limbs trembling with relief, laughed too as he turned towards the doorway.

But even as he laughed and turned and lost sight of her, he knew he was in error.

He spun round and his mind kept spinning as his eyes sought desperately for some sign, some trace. But he had known before he turned that he was at last completely alone on the tower.

And now to the half admiring, half mocking cheers of the crowd as the God, Dalziel, passed in all his glory, was added a new wailing, shrieking noise, haled out of horror and dismay. It rose up the sides of the great cathedral, spiralling towards the sun like the thin piping of a bird, and was absorbed as though it had never been into the vast empty sky.

Raging, Pascoe looked upwards and cried, 'Damn you! Damn you! Damn you!'

And did not know if he was addressing Chung, or God, or Dalziel, or merely himself.